SHADOWS
OF THE LOVING HEARTS

SHADOWS
OF THE LOVING HEARTS

HARSHINI KUMAR

Chief Editor
Mr K. Adishesha, B.Com.

PARTRIDGE
A Penguin Random House Company

Print information available on the last page.

To order additional copies of this book, contact
Partridge India
000 800 10062 62
orders.india@partridgepublishing.com

www.partridgepublishing.com/india

Contents

DEDICATION

To my brother **Naveen**, who is no more in this world . . . well, not really, because he is very much alive in my memories

And

My father, **K. Adishesha**, who provided every brick to this novel; he's the one who made me understand the world, each and every glory of my smile, and success shall reach him.

My father has provided the platform to the main characters and has enriched them. In fact, chapters like 'Anu's birth' and 'What happened next?' are solely his creation. He has given a new dimension to the novel, writing about the topic of life after death.

Harshini Kumar

FOREWORD

With eight years of its long journey, *Shadows of the Loving Hearts*, a novel written by Mrs Harshini Kumar, who is my daughter, finally saw its completion in the format of a book. It was in the year 2006 she told me that she had woven a beautiful story in her mind. Then she started writing after my persuasion to bring that story in writing. During her writing, I asked her once about the subject of the novel but she refused to reveal it to me, probably having a fear of my counterargument about it. After three years, she handed over to me the copy of the novel, which contained nearly five hundred pages. The task of finding the editor to edit her novel was on my shoulders since I promised her earlier to take up that one.

After reading few pages of the novel, it took me very little time to realize that the tough job of editing was ahead. The subject that she had chosen was about present-day youths' love adventures, their struggle and aspirations in the backdrop of the present scenario of our society as a whole. Her age and inexperience did not permit her to write maturely on such a complex subject but the creativity of events were quite amazing and the characterization was extremely good. After reading it completely, I concluded that no professional editor would come forward to edit.

Having no other option, I took up the job of editing though I was inexperienced. Unable to edit, I have decided to restructure the whole story. Keeping the storyline intact, considering each and every input of her story, I started the restructuring. In some way, it paved me an opportunity to add my creativeness as well into the novel and enabled me to include present-day youths' psychological turmoil and its repercussions very effectively. The spectrum of the novel was so huge, it came as a boon to include my imagination and I found no difficulty in adding antisocial and criminal activities which are happening in our society. Undoubtedly, the readers will self-realize and would not like to be the same after reading the novel. Whatever so far I told you about negative aspects of her work doesn't mean to sideline her work. Her story imagination and creativity of amazing events wouldn't come so easy and I would like to say that her imagination and creativity led me to create much more. Perfecting each and every weak link, I completed the restructuring work of the novel.

I am thankful to Mr Raghav Yamadagni, who runs a coaching centre and has associated with me to edit the novel further at the initial stages. Later on, the novel saw many self-re-editing processes until I found Mr Sayed Abdul Baari, a tutor to my daughter during her studies, who took an initiative to do the editing, and his literary knowledge has helped me to overcome the logical mistakes in the novel.

I am hopeful that the novel journeys through the reader's mind until the end of the novel and becomes relevant even to coming generations as well and a worthy gift to the society as a whole.

K. Adishesha

ABOUT THE AUTHOR

*M*rs Harshini Kumar, a Bengalurian, was born in the year 1988. She studied in Sri Aurobindo Memorial School until tenth standard.

During her school days, the school management arranged story-writing workshops, which she attended as part of her routine. Little did she know that destiny was actually transforming her into a story writer.

One day, her teacher asked her to write a composition, and just to fill the sheets, she wrote more elaborately of a small topic. After reading it, the teacher cursed her, 'You are fit to be a story writer.'

She started writing the story in the year 2006 and the novel would have been in the hands of the readers soon, but her parents got her married in the year 2007 and because of additional responsibilities, the novel did not see its completion phase until now. Probably destiny wanted her to gain more knowledge and practically experience different phases of life being a loving wife and a sweet-but-responsible mother.

According to her, youths in and around the age group of 15 to 25 years have a lot of fascinating and thrilling stuff in their lives. That is where they come across many crossroads, wondering which way to move forward. This may result in anxiety, depression, confusion, and disappointment, especially in emotional matters like love when they encounter failure.

This novel gives love a completely new perspective and attempts to make the reader feel that *although love is blind, it can see through inner vision!*

GLOSSARY

Amma, Maa, Ma – Mother
Anna – Elder brother
Didi – Elder sister
Grandpa – Grandfather
Palav – South Indian spicy rice with vegetables
Rasam – South Indian soup
Sambar – South Indian gravy
Yaar – Friend

THE JOURNEY TO THE PAST

*A*run, a twenty-eight-year-old person, tall and handsome, anxiously looking around, stood near an A/C minibus. His friends and relatives had already taken their seats, and the mood was upbeat since they were meeting each other after a very long time. The whole area was brimming with people and traffic; the surrounding buildings and shopping malls were illuminated with colourful lights as it was the last day of the year. The whole nation was waiting to greet the New Year but to Arun it made no difference. His past memories were still haunting him but he looked calm and he was waiting for his wife Monika, who had gone to get some snacks and water. A little later, he saw her coming carrying stuff and helped her with it. They were cheered loudly as they entered the bus. Monika was very excited as she saw a banner printed with 'Happy Married Life' and everyone wished them well. They settled down after keeping their luggage on the shelves.

Arun was at the window seat, to cool off his head as many thoughts were swirling in his mind. He pulled the knob of the seat in order to lean back comfortably and Monika did the same. The tour manager signalled as everyone settled on their seats and the driver started the bus. Every face but Arun's glittered with joy as the bus moved to leave Bengaluru town.

Arun felt guilty of himself and pity on Monika while looking at her smiling face. A little later, he glanced towards his close friend Sandhya and her husband Prashanth. In response, they simultaneously showed thumbs up with a smile but everything went blank around him as his past memories recurred in his mind. A little later, he slowly turned towards Monika and she was sleeping. Looking at his watch, he said in a low voice, 'Have gone to sleep so fast, you're lucky.' Hearing what he said, she looked at her watch and yawning, replied, 'It's ten thirty, goodnight.'

'What about twelve o'clock?' Arun asked.

'Let's see,' she replied.

After a few moments, someone tapped Arun's back. Turning backwards, he saw Sandhya and greeted her just by nodding his head. She looked at Monika to check whether she was really asleep or just pretending and meanwhile Prashanth was keenly watching Sandhya.

'Don't be overexcited in case if you see her . . .' Sandhya said in a low voice. Ignoring her words, he pretended to go asleep. To alert him, she pushed him towards Monika and immediately sat back next to Prashanth. Monika sprang up before Arun's eyes; he seriously pointed his finger at the laughing couple. They caught their ears and shook their head. He smiled at their funny looks.

The bus entered the forest zone. Except for the outline of the giant trees, Arun could see nothing, as he peeped out of the window. As everyone, except a woman who was busy snoring, started dancing with excitement, turning back, he saw them and returned quickly towards the window to look through. As the cheers and music were coming from the back, he turned to see their dance and clapping. The driver occasionally turned back to see their fun. Everyone in the bus said 'Oomph!' as the driver applied sudden brakes, except the snoring woman, who murmured something in her sleep.

As the time was nearing twelve o'clock, Prashanth got up from his seat, holding a soft drink can as mike and began to give a speech.

'Hello, everybody, open your eyes to welcome the New Year which is just a few minutes away. Don't hesitate to pull the hair of those sleeping!' Hearing this, everyone shouted, 'Hurray!' Monika woke up, rubbed her eyes, and looked around to see what was happening. She saw Arun standing with others to greet the New Year.

Sandhya began to decorate the bus with balloons at various points. Looking at his watch, Prashanth announced to get ready and started the countdown to greet the New Year: 'Ten, nine, eight, seven, six, five, four, three, two . . .' Instead of saying 'one', Sandhya said 'zero'. '*Happy New Year!*' everyone shouted and they wished each other well. After a pause, Prashanth took his can as fake mike to announce, 'It's the greatest New Year party we ever had,' and everyone shouted 'Hooo!'

The tour manager gave an unwilling smile at Prashanth's announcement and moved inside the driver's cabin. He took a small whisky bottle and two glasses. Looking at the driver, he said, 'Sorry, you're driving,' and poured water into one and whisky in another glass. He gave the glass filled with water to the driver and gulped the whisky at once. Grudgingly looking at him, the driver threw the glass outside.

After a while, the bus halted near a restaurant. The tour manager told everyone to come back in thirty minutes after being refreshed. Arun got down from the bus and stretched a helping hand to Monika. Holding his hand, she got down with a smile and turning back called her cousin Swapna to get down. 'I will be there in a few minutes,' she replied.

Arun and Monika walked towards the restaurant. Swapna, through the window, saw her husband was waiting along with their daughter near the restaurant. She quickly went to the seat at the back to wake the snoring woman but she ignored Swapna by giving an angry grunt and continued to sleep. 'OK, all right,' Swapna said to herself and moved towards the exit door. She glanced at the NO SMOKING board, took red lipstick to add another line, 'DO NOT DRINK IN THE BUS', and seriously stared at the manager after she wrote. He gave a guilty look and she headed towards the restaurant. Swapna's daughter Namrutha, a small pretty girl sitting next to her father, was waiting for her mother. Swapna came, carried her daughter, and hugged her, saying sorry for coming late.

At the restaurant, after everyone came in, Arun signalled the waiter to bring food. After having their dinner, all of them moved out of the restaurant. As he came out, he raised his eyebrows while talking to his wife and suddenly he caught sight of some white object that moved far above the mountain range. Monika was restlessly talking to Arun and he again saw a lengthy glowing white cloth moving along with the wind. Initially he was not listening to Monika. 'Is there anything visible out there?' he asked her in a confused way to confirm and pointed out towards the top of the mountain, but before Monika could answer, Sandhya came forward and sarcastically said, 'Oh yeah, you are right; I surely can see something over there!' She then turned towards Monika and said, 'You know what? He's jobless; I'll see to it that he does not show you some illusions.' Looking at their serious talk, Monika moved to board the bus.

Sandhya saw Monika walking to board the bus and turned towards Arun.

'Are you crazy? How many times should I have to tell you not to be excited whenever you see her sign? Control yourself.'

'You know, I told you that she will come . . . I knew it,' Arun replied excitedly.

'What is that you both are talking about?' A voice came out of the window. Both turned back towards the direction of the voice and saw Monika's head was completely out of the window.

'It's, it's . . .' Sandhya stammered.

'It's all right, I don't mind if there are any secrets between you guys. After all, both of you have been close friends for the past ten years,' Monika said with a broad smile, sat back comfortably on her seat, and pulled some magazine to read.

The driver started the bus and everyone hurried to board it. Arun gave a final look towards the mountain and boarded the bus. 'Has everyone come?' the manager asked. 'Yesss,' Namrutha replied. The manager signalled the driver to move and Swapna glanced at the last seat as the bus moved and tensely asked, 'Oh, where is Lakshmi?' and shouted, 'Stop the bus.' The driver stopped the bus suddenly. Tapping her head, 'Oh, snoring aunty, I forgot,' Namrutha said in a high voice. Both got down, accompanying Sandhya to find Lakshmi and bringing her back.

'Where's she?' Swapna asked Namrutha while walking.

'She's still in the washroom,' replied Namrutha.

'Why?' asked Sandhya.

'Aunt Lakshmi asked me to accompany her to the washroom and I went with her. Since the door could not be latched from inside, she told me to lock from outside and also to see that no one opens it. But I came back,' she said. Hearing this, Swapna burst out laughing. Few moments later, Namrutha saw her mother coming out of the washroom along with Aunt Lakshmi and quickly ran towards Monika and using Monika's shawl, hid her face and curiously watched Aunt Lakshmi. All of them boarded the bus and the manager signalled the driver to move. Keeping her hand on her chest, Namrutha gave a deep sigh of relief and fell asleep on her seat within no time.

Monika took her mobile and began to play ringtones; on a particular one, she said, 'It's really romantic,' and continued to listen keenly. Meanwhile, Arun offered her some fruit juice, for which she replied, 'No thanks! I'm afraid that I may get an urge for loo.'

He then asked, 'Is this your favourite ringtone?'

'It's . . . it's . . .' She hesitated.

'OK, that's all right,' he said and turned towards the other side. 'It's my friend's favourite,' Monika said but Arun ignored her. She pulled his shirt and he irritably turned back.

She then asked, 'Do you have any past?' for which he replied, 'I am sorry, could you be a little more specific?'

Hesitatingly, raising her eyebrows, she in turn asked, 'OK . . . have you fallen in—'

He instantly replied, 'You mean love?' and taking her affirmative look as a question, replied, 'Oh, no, not at all.'

She did not believe him, and in the meantime, the manager started switching off the lights.

After a pause, Arun asked, 'What about you?'

Nervously and in a very low voice, she replied, 'No . . . never . . .' and continued, 'It's not love exactly, I just had a small crush on a boy, my neighbour, who stayed right opposite to our house . . .' She nervously looked at Arun to see if he was getting angry; he was not, and instead said, 'Oh, OK . . . That's interesting . . . Please continue.'

She continued, saying, 'I had crush on him for about six months . . . To tell you the truth, my crush would have turned into love, but . . .'

Curiously he asked 'But, what?'

She continued, saying, 'About three years back, he went away from his house and did not return even after three days. His mother was very much worried. When I met her, she told me that he informed neither that he was going somewhere, nor has he contacted since then. The next day, I had been to a tailor shop for collecting my dress. On my way back home, while crossing the road, I saw him standing near a car and screamed out his name. He couldn't hear me. I ran towards the car, as he looked at me, he said, "Hi, Monika . . ." I replied, "Hi . . ." I was then surprised to see a beautiful woman sitting in his car.

'He then introduced us both and, while doing so, said that she was Priya Agarwal. He quickly wrote a letter for his mother and handed it over to me to pass on. I had to do the postman's job.

'Taking the letter, I asked him, "Why don't you go back to your home?" He opened the door of the car and, forcibly smiling, said, "Monika, I cannot explain it now but I'm sure you will understand it soon, please pass on this letter to my mother." I could not resist and soon reached his house. As I opened the gate, his parents quickly came out, thinking that their son had returned but they were disappointed seeing me. I told them, "Sorry, aunty, I just came to give this letter, this is from your son . . ." They worriedly took it. They did not even call me inside and quickly opened the letter to read. I heard aunt's cry as she read and learnt that her son was in love with Priya for the past six years, although his father was against it. Learning about his love, I asked myself, "Where does six months' crush stand compared to six years of love?"' Not getting any response from Arun, Monika looked at him to read his reaction but he had already fallen asleep. She reminisced regarding her crush for some more time and later slept.

After a few hours, Arun woke up around 6 a.m. He saw clouds passing through the mountain range. He turned back to see whether all had woken up but most of them were still asleep. He stood up from the seat and he carefully moved out from his window seat, taking care so as to not disturb Monika's sleep. He managed and walked near the driver's cabin to admire nature's beauty. He saw a narrow road, and the surroundings were completely covered with fog. It looked as though it was a vanilla ice cream decorated with unusual greyish curved lines. After a while, Arun heard 'Wow . . .' as even Monika saw the road covered with fog.

Around 7 a.m., the driver stopped the bus to have some refreshments. Finally, the snoring woman woke up and glanced towards the window side. After yawning, she remembered and shouted, 'Happy New Year!' Hearing her voice, Namrutha slowly peeped from the seat to see her; she felt a bit sorry for what she had done last night.

The driver signalled everyone to board the bus. As everyone took their respective seats, the bus continued its onward journey. Everyone's eyes were almost fixed at the window to enjoy the view. After about ninety minutes, the bus came to a halt near a resort that belonged to Nirmala, whose brother was none other than Arun. Everyone started getting out of the bus, with their luggage. Monika carried her hat and a brochure printed with 'ROYAL WOOD RESORTS Pvt Ltd'; she was surprised as none of them had the brochure. The driver sounded the horn to alert the resort's staff of their arrival, and the staff quickly came towards the bus to welcome the guests and carry their luggage.

Each and every hilltop was covered with thick fog, seeing which Sandhya, in a bubbly voice, said, 'Wow, fantastic!' Everyone's eyes were delighted.

As everyone approached the resort, an arrow board with the message 'WELCOME TO ROYAL WOOD RESORT' greeted the guests and showed the direction as well. The road became narrower and they couldn't see anything because of thick fog. Monika ran fast towards the resort and shouted 'Woohoo' with excitement. All the others quickly joined her and saw a huge A-shaped building, mostly built out of wood. All of them were stunned looking at the resort's architectural marvel. Even the handle of the doors were in 'A' shape and it was gold plated. There was a nameplate at the main entrance, on which was carved 'KRUPA' with gold plating.

The sleepy aunt started murmuring to Namrutha and asked doubtfully whether the cots in the resort were comfortable. 'If you don't feel comfortable lying down on the cot, you might feel so on the grass,' Namrutha replied and ran towards her father. The sleepy aunt gave a grudging look at her.

The guard opened the door with a broad smile as everyone approached the entrance.

The Royal Wood Resort manager quickly came near the entrance to greet Arun and offered a handshake. 'Hello, sir, welcome to the resort, it's a great pleasure to see you. Madam called me a few minutes ago and informed me about your arrival. Once again, a warm welcome to all of you.' He bowed and called the resort staff to escort all of them to their allotted rooms. Some hurried to their rooms to freshen up and relax as they were worn out from the journey's fatigue.

At about 11 a.m., Arun woke up and saw that Monika was awake. Looking at her, he said in an uncomfortable voice, 'Monika, you know what, everything just happened so quickly, we didn't get adequate time to know each other. I believe your parents didn't get your opinion as well and even my decision was under various dilemmas. Please give a little space and time for things to settle, I am sorry if it hurts.' Hearing this, Monika looked at him and recalled Nirmala's suggestions. She took his hand in hers and said, 'Look, Arun, I'm your wife now and will trust you as much as I trust God, I have lots of patience and I believe that there are lots of years ahead for us to nurture and develop our relationship.' Arun seemed quite relaxed.

Arun rested her hand on the bed, got up, and sat on the sofa. Monika also got up and sat beside him. Monika asked, stammering, 'Arun, do you mind if I would like to know more about your sister? I mean her . . . personal life, I do respect her a lot . . .' He smiled and nodded his head in affirmation.

'I am just curious why she didn't find her . . . I mean, her life partner, any reason?'

'Probably I am the reason,' Arun replied and continued, 'She struggled a lot and sacrificed her happiness to reach this stage. My father never cared about us and left us alone when I was a kid. Nirmala told me that our mother worked very hard to bring us up. But after my father left her to settle permanently in Australia, she became very depressed in her life and passed away because of low blood pressure, which finally led to heart attack. After that, it was only my sister, even she struggled very hard to look after me and also did a part-time job to meet our education expenses. She's pinned lots of hope on me.'

Arun was interrupted by the knock at the door; it was a bearer. On Arun's permission, the bearer came into the room, holding a coffee tray and kept it on the table and asked, 'Anything else, sir?'

As Arun didn't respond to the bearer since his mind journeyed into the past, Monika replied, 'No, thanks.'

While preparing coffee, Monika asked, 'When did you meet your father?' Arun replied, 'He never came back to see us.' Monika gave him the coffee cup; Arun took the cup and continued, 'Long ago, he called Nirmala to visit him, although I disagreed, she had been to his place, because he told her that he wanted to discuss an important matter. When she had been there, he introduced a woman as his wife, Nirmala did not feel like staying there even for a moment and asked him the reason he called her. He handed over my mother's property documents to her. After that, Nirmala decided that she would never see his face again,' Arun gave a pause and gulped the coffee at once, as it had turned cold.

Monika was looking at his dull face; he then continued, 'When I saw those property documents, I fumed out, "Why did you take it from that devil?" I asked angrily and she convinced me, saying, "These properties belonged to our mother, she earned them working round the clock and it's her wish to develop these properties. Mother was a great architect, and she's my inspiration. Her guidance has inspired me to reach this position today. She was worried a lot about you and your future. I will make sure that you will be happy forever . . ."' After saying this, Arun told Monika, 'I think now you will understand her better,' and moved towards the washbasin.

Monika took Arun's cell phone and started taking snaps of Arun. She saw previously clicked pictures as well, in which Nirmala appeared with a wide smile, putting hands around Arun in one of the snaps. She saw Arun coming out, wiping his face, and kept the cell phone on the sofa.

Arun asked Monika, 'Where are you planning to go?'

Monika, combing her hair, replied, 'Yet to decide.'

Suddenly, Sandhya flung open the door and said, 'I know that both of you are cursing me . . . no problem.' She saw that Arun was still not dressed to go out and said, 'You idiot, you're not ready yet!' and tried hitting him with her purse. He leaned backwards to avoid and hit her back with a pillow. Sandhya blasted at him again, saying, 'You are a devil . . .'

Looking at their fight, Monika thought to herself that this was probably how they usually behaved.

Sandhya then asked, 'I called you twice, why didn't you receive my call? Were you both busy in . . . in . . .' Hearing this,

Arun rushed to give a tap on her head, and Monika quickly blocked his hand smilingly.

'Why?' asked Arun.

Sandhya shouted excitedly, 'Let's go shopping!'

'Sorry, I'm tired,' Arun sounded as though he was lying.

'Even I'm not coming,' Prashanth said as he entered along with Swapna.

'Great, so, it's only ladies who will shop . . . that will be fun,' Swapna intervened in their talk and everyone laughed.

'No problem, we will definitely have lots of fun without you guys, thanks a lot, my dear,' Sandhya said to Prashanth angrily and pulled Monika's hand to go.

All the women walked towards the car arranged by the resort's staff for their shopping. As it was pretty cold outside, the guide had wrapped a rug around himself and was smoking a cigarette. He dropped the cigarette and put it out with his foot as he saw them coming. Swapna called Namrutha to come along for shopping, but she preferred to stay back with her father. Sandhya saw Prashanth waving his hands. She closed the car's window angrily, looking at him. Monika slowly peeped out from the window, and Arun waved smilingly as she waved. The car moved.

'None of the guys have come with us, I think they have planned something to enjoy without us, let them do whatever they want,' Sandhya said angrily.

'Where's Lakshmi?' Monika asked.

Swapna replied, 'Obviously, sleeping tight, what else does she do except sleeping? But even then I told her to look after Namrutha.' Changing her tone to sound suspicious, Swapna asked, 'Do you all know why the guys didn't come with us?' and she herself replied, 'They would have definitely planned for drinks . . .'

'We must trust our husbands . . .' Monika and Sandhya said together.

In the resort, Namrutha's father, sitting beside Namrutha, was trying to make her sleep by tapping her back. A little later, he saw that her eyes were closed and tried getting up, and accidentally his hand hit a glass tumbler. 'Oops . . .' He gave a deep sigh and turned to see her; her eyes were still closed. He went to the cupboard, opened it, pulled a bag's zip, and took out a big whisky bottle. His mobile started ringing loudly as he approached the door to go out, and cursing himself, he disconnected the call and turned towards Namrutha. She opened her eyes, and he quickly rushed near her to make her sleep again.

'You can go and have fun with uncles, I won't tell Mom,' Namrutha whispered in his ear. He kissed her on her forehead and moved out, smiling at her. She locked the door, went back to her room, and fell asleep on the bed.

Sunil went to the next door and zoomed in, shouting, 'Hands up!' pointing the bottle like a gun. Suddenly a thunderclap was heard and frightened Sunil dropped the bottle, but fortunately, Prashanth caught it.

'Nice catch, you must have been a good cricketer,' Sunil said and continued to ask, 'By the way, where is it thundering?'

'*Mission: Impossible*, a great action movie,' Prashanth replied and warned him not to booze.

'No problem, I got permission from my lady boss to booze while I am on vacation,' Sunil said.

'Hmm, OK,' Prashanth said and, turning his attention towards Arun, said, 'Come on, let's all go for a walk, cheer up, man . . .'

'Cheers,' Sunil said and already lifted a glass filled with whisky to gulp and continued, 'What will you all do by going out in such a cold weather? It's nice and cosy here, to booze and to have fun. Don't you mind if I drink here,' he said and gulped.

Arun ignored him and asked Prashanth when the ladies would come back. He replied around 7.30 p.m.

'Yuck, I'm allergic to liquor odour,' Prashanth said. Arun lifted his eyebrows and stared at the bottle, giving a teasing smile.

'Don't drink the whole bottle!' Arun said without realizing that it was almost empty. He took the bottle to put inside the wardrobe and locked the shelf. He handed over the keys to Prashanth and left the place. A little later, Sunil fell unconscious.

'Uncle!' A swinging voice reached Arun's ears while getting down the stairs. Realizing that the voice source was over his head, he looked up to see who called and saw Namrutha was about to fall as she was peeping from the staircase of third floor. He asked her to come down slowly. However, like all notorious kids, she was running down the stairs to reach him quickly. Her eyes came across a wall on which there was a beautiful wall painting of a woman dressed in red, and unable to control the momentum of her speed, she was about to slip. To her good luck, a woman from behind saved her from slipping and falling down the stairs. Namrutha heaved herself up and turned back to see who helped her.

'Thanks, aunty!' Namrutha said and hurried to reach down the stairs.

'Why are you roaming alone? Why didn't you go with Mom?' Arun asked.

'Who would look after my dad if I had gone with her?' Namrutha replied and continued to ask, 'Where is my dad? I've been searching for him for a while.'

He patted her on the back. 'Don't worry, he's safe in my room, let's go outside,' he said and put his arm around her shoulders. Both reached the exit door.

'I'll show you something really nice,' he said and took her outside. She started shivering, as the weather was cold. They continued to walk down the lane along the edge of the compound. She peeped to try looking down the mountain but couldn't see anything other than thick bushes. She asked, 'What's there?' pointing downwards.

Ignoring her, Arun shouted, 'We're on top of the mountain!' and it echoed. Listening to the echo, Namrutha shouted, 'I love my daddy!' and it echoed. Widening her arms and moving around, she shouted, 'Give me ice cream!' and it echoed. Arun saw a waiter passing nearby and signalled to call him.

Coming near, the waiter asked with a smile, 'Any order, sir?'

Arun replied, 'Strawberry with vanilla ice cream . . .' The waiter took the order and left to get it. They started playing with a spring ball. After a while, the ball fell on a man's feet, and he picked up the ball, passing it to Namrutha.

'Thanks, uncle,' she said and took the ball. A little later, Arun stopped playing, as she was tired. 'Tomorrow, I'll take you to a wonderful place,' he said. She was not very much interested in his offer and was busy trying to find something.

'What's wrong?' he anxiously enquired. She hesitated and showed her little finger. Arun laughed and took her to a washroom.

Namrutha entered the washroom and immediately came out.

'What happened?' he asked and she replied, 'Nobody is inside. I'm frightened. Can you please come with me?'

'Oh no, I'm a gentleman.'

'Uncle, no one is there, please come.'

'No, no, I cannot come to the ladies' room . . . But wait, we can work something out . . . You are still a small kid . . . So I can take you to men's room if you want.' She refused to go with him; taking the hint, he asked, 'Why are you so scared to go alone inside the washroom?'

She replied, 'Devils,' opening her eyes wide, and he laughed loudly.

Controlling his laugh, he said, 'Well, if you happen to see the devil, just scream, and I'll come to help,' and finally convinced her to go to the washroom.

Namrutha entered the washroom and saw the same lady who saved her from falling down the stairs.

'Hello, aunty, thank God you're here!'

The lady gave a gentle smile and asked her name.

'Namrutha,' she replied and asked curiously, 'Do devils really exist?'

'Maybe or maybe not,' the lady replied casually and continued, 'In case you are getting scared, you can sing.'

'If we sing, will it run away?' Namrutha questioned.

'No, no, it will enjoy and instead of attacking it will start dancing,' the lady replied and Namrutha laughed at her idea.

'Bye, I'm going.'

'One minute, aunty, I will come to your room later, let me know your room number,' she asked; the lady had already moved towards the exit door.

'No, no . . . I don't have a room here. I just came here to meet my friend.'

'Oh, OK . . . But please wait, aunty, I'm scared.'

'Be brave, don't be scared.'

'OK . . . OK,' Namrutha said restlessly. The lady told her to start singing and went out.

Meanwhile, Arun was busy looking at a bulletin board and sensed someone was passing nearby, and he felt a chilled sensation within. He turned back to see, but he saw no one.

Nearly fifteen minutes had passed; worrying that Namrutha might have got frightened because of being alone in the washroom, Arun walked near the washroom to call Namrutha. He couldn't hear her reply to his call as she was singing loudly, not sounding so good though. A fat lady walked up near Arun and stared at him from behind, guessing why he was near the ladies' washroom. Arun with frustration leaned close to the door and kept his ear to hear her reply, but to the fat lady, it looked as though he was trying to peep.

'You stupid man, don't you have any manners?'

'No, madam, actually I was—' Before he could say anything further, she angrily entered the washroom and banged the door with force.

Namrutha came out of the washroom. 'Mountains are so wonderful, gardens are so beautiful; dance, dance, dance!' she was singing loudly and more often used the word 'dance', thinking that she would prefer to see ghosts dancing instead of trying to attack her. Her heartbeat became faster as she got frightened, and she came near Arun, chanting, 'Dance, dance, dance'.

'Why are you singing so loudly?' Arun curiously asked her.

'Uncle, I got saved just because of her.' She sounded happy.

'Who saved you?' Arun asked in a keen voice.

'A lady, she's very beautiful, in fact, more than me!' Namrutha said and told of the incident that happened in the washroom. He smiled, caught her hand, and he walked towards the resort's restaurant.

Arun glanced inside the restaurant to see if anyone had come back. Namrutha saw her mother and ran towards her to hug her. Arun felt relaxed, as everyone had come. Prashanth met his eyes but pretended to read the menu of the restaurant. Arun walked towards Monika and sat next to her.

'By the way, how was the outing?' he asked Monika.

'Quite good,' she replied tiredly.

'Come on, dude, why are you hiding yourself?' Arun asked and called Prashanth; he came immediately to sit beside him. Lakshmi was looking at the wall hangings along with Namrutha. The waiter served their favourite dishes. Suddenly he remembered Sunil and asked Prashanth about his condition softly.

'As he was drunk more than he could handle, he began puking as you left the room, and I took him to his room, I've ordered some light food for him,' Prashanth whispered in Arun's ear.

'Where's Daddy?' Namrutha asked anxiously.

'He's not feeling good and is taking rest in the room,' Arun replied.

Sandhya was looking constantly at Prashanth as though she was capable of reading his face. His expressions looked like he was pleading and trying to convince her.

'Bye,' Swapna said and took her ice cream. She quickly got up for going to her room.

'Mummy, don't worry, I'll look after Daddy,' Namrutha said and ran towards the staircase to go to her room. Swapna was not that worried about Sunil, so she sat back and was seriously discussing about the earrings that she had purchased by showing these admiringly to others. A little later, Namrutha came back panting and said, 'Mummy, Daddy finished having his dinner, he's sleeping now.'

'You should have come by lift,' Monika said and gave her a glass of water. Arun signalled Namrutha and offered a seat on his lap, and she obliged happily.

'How much do you love your daddy?' he asked, and in response, she opened her arms as wide as she could, closing her eyes tightly. Looking at her, Swapna smiled admiringly. A little later, Namrutha went to her mother to see the jewels that her mother bought for her. Arun got up from his chair as he had finished his dinner and went towards the washbasin.

Arun's mobile, which was on the dining table, rang. As he was not around to pick up the call, Monika received it and heard, 'Hello, good evening, doctor . . .' It was a familiar voice for Monika.

'Hello . . . May I know who is speaking?' Monika tensely replied with a question.

'I'm Rahul.' Monika's fingers were on her lips as she heard the name, and she went towards the restaurant's exit door to speak with him freely.

'Rahul, it's me, Monika . . . remember . . . your neighbour . . . I stayed opposite . . . gave your letter . . . you went away . . . got it?' She gave clues.

'Oh, hi, Monika, how are you? And how come you received this call?' Rahul asked surprisingly.

'I got married to Arun recently,' Monika replied softly.

'Oh, it's really great, you're so lucky to be his life partner,' Rahul said in an energetic voice.

'It's OK, how come you know him,' Monika asked curiously.

He replied, 'My wife Priya . . .' and gave a pause.

'Oh, yes, Priya . . . How's she?'

He replied, 'She was not well, but now she's completely all right and all this is just because of Arun . . .' Hearing this, Monika lifted her eyebrows with surprise.

He continued, saying, 'We had a boy baby, and because of a problem in his heart, he survived only for six months. Priya fell unconscious when she heard this news. She opened her eyes after emergency treatment but didn't move or speak for about three months. The doctors told me that she was in a severe shock and so was not responding but otherwise she was fine and they discharged her.'

After a pause, thinking that there was some interruption in the call, he said, 'Hello, Monika . . . Monika . . .'

'Yeah, I am here, sorry, you please carry on,' Monika replied in a dull voice.

'I couldn't see Priya in that condition. A known person told me about Nirmala's hospital and Dr Arun . . . I explained to Arun about the tragedy. Arun told me that he would try his level best. I admitted my wife in his nursing home with some hope. He started her treatment, and a few days later, he told me to bring my son's photo and I was confused. Looking at my reaction, he said, "If you want your wife to recover quickly, you must." I gave him the photo. Nearly three months later, I was tense, as Priya wasn't there in the hospital, and I immediately called Arun. He told me not to be bothered and gave me an address to meet him. I reached there, and it was a pleasant ashram with greenery. I saw Arun was waiting near the front gate, and he showed me Priya holding a baby.'

'Shh,' Monika said, showing her mobile as Sandhya kept on calling her from the exit door. After a pause, Rahul continued to speak.

'I walked towards Priya but Arun stopped me and he moved forward. I couldn't resist and followed them as both turned to move. I was very surprised while Arun was talking to Priya. "Your baby is so cute, how old is it?" he asked and she replied six months. She said my son's name when he asked the baby's name. He turned back and signalled me to come. It was very hard to believe what was happening there . . .' With a very happy tone, he said, 'Priya was actually speaking! She smiled at me as I approached her, and I glanced at the baby. I was so surprised that the baby almost looked like my son. "Why am I staying here?" she asked me seriously, and I nodded my head with disbelief. A little later, a lady called her, and she went inside the ashram to feed the baby. "Do you have any problem with adopting the baby?" Arun asked firmly, and I couldn't control my tears. "It may take nearly six months for things to settle, don't remind her about the past and shift your residence if possible, now she's perfectly all right," Arun advised me.' He then said, 'Monika, I'm really grateful to him.'

'Why did you call him now, any urgent matter?' Monika interrupted.

'No, I just wanted to know whether he will be at the nursing home tomorrow to meet and wish him well on his birthday. He celebrated his last birthday in the nursing home,' Rahul said.

'Oh, sorry, you can't, we are out of station . . .' Monika sounded as though she was stammering.

'Oh, very sorry to take your time, please convey my wishes to the doctor,' Rahul replied.

'Sure, I'll do that. Bye, Rahul,' Monika said.

Her face turned pale, as she didn't have a clue about Arun's birthday.

'Thank God his birthday is tomorrow, I can surprise him,' she said to herself and entered the restaurant.

Monika saw Arun chatting with Namrutha. He was trying to confuse her and even pretending to act like a child. She thought to herself that although at first she was not very impressed when Nirmala told her about Arun because she felt that it was quite natural for someone to say good things about his or her brother, after she heard from Rahul, her attitude towards Arun changed and she began respecting him more than she did before. 'He is so simple but does a great job of curing depressed hearts. I don't understand why he himself looks so depressed. I must try to make him feel happy and support him,' she said to herself and sat next to him, admiring him in her thoughts.

'Monika, where were you?' Arun asked casually. Not realizing Arun was saying something, she suddenly said, 'Arun, you're great,' and hugged him.

Sandhya excitedly shouted 'Woohoo!' and clapped, not realizing that she was holding an ice cream.

'Are you senseless? Look what you have done to my sari!' Lakshmi blasted at Sandhya, who was keenly watching Arun and Monika. Sandhya ignored Lakshmi, as though she didn't hear anything. Arun didn't react much to Monika's hug and curiously lifted his eyebrows.

After hugging him tight, she drew herself back, held his hand, and said, 'Today I learnt about your true nature, your patience, and your love towards humanity, it is just great! Oh

God, I'm so blessed to be your life partner.' This time everyone clapped loudly. Sandhya observed that Arun was not responding positively to Monika's comments. She went close to Arun, held his hand, and murmured, 'Arun, please stop thinking about the past and instead think about the future.'

He was in no mood to listen to her but pretended to smile.

Monika felt satisfied as she told her feelings about him openly and happily left to reach her room.

Slowly, one after the other, everyone but Arun left the restaurant after having their dinner. Arun was in no mood for going back to the room and instead chose to move around the resort garden, which looked like heaven. After some time, he got a call and it was from Monika.

'I'll come,' he replied and quickly disconnected the call. He slowly walked around the garden and sat under a big tree. Gradually the fog started to cover the area. He looked up towards the far mountains and saw the full moon as the fog started clearing. His thoughts and emotions had begun to drive him towards the past and felt as though the world did not belong to him. He suddenly jerked as his mobile rang and he glanced at it slowly. The time was 10.30 p.m. He saw that it was Sandhya's call; he received it and pressed the speaker button to hear. Sandhya said, 'Why didn't you go to your room? You are stupid! Don't you know that Monika is alone in there? I can see you through the window. You should look forward and you very well know that it's her wish too.' Hearing all this, Arun irritably replied, 'Please leave me alone,' and ended the call.

After some time, all the lights went off barring few dull lights at main points. The sky was much clearer than before. All of a sudden, a strong breeze started blowing all over along with big thunder and lightning. The swings fitted with wooden planks had begun to swing with force. The whole area became invisible because of thick fog except the Royal Wood and dim lights around it. It started drizzling. The drizzle had made Arun alert, as he was thinking deeply and he saw clouds passing through the Royal Wood. After some time, it stopped drizzling but the weather was still foggy. The droplets collected on leaves had begun to fall on the ground. Arun didn't feel like going to his room and watched the wooden swings swinging. He suddenly sensed something was approaching from behind, and his heart shivered as someone patted him on the back mildly. He murmured to himself, 'I know you're here,' and turned backwards but he saw no one. He then ran towards the swing to see if anyone was pushing it. After a pause, he slowly looked around and shouted, 'Please, I want to see you,' and walked towards the edge of the boundary. He peeped to look down the mountain and could see nothing. He looked up towards the sky to trace and shouted, 'I want you!' Later he came near the swing and stood there, looking around.

It was nearly midnight. There, Monika fell asleep after waiting for a long time, and here, Arun was tired and lay down on the ground.

Arun opened his eyes and saw white lights glowing high above, all around him. He was not fully conscious and slowly got up to see what was happening. It looked as though the lights were carrying flowers towards the sky. To his surprise, the different-coloured flowers had begun to take the desired shape in no time. His emotions burst with joy as soon as he saw the formation of the flowers, and he could not believe his eyes. 'HAPPY BIRTHDAY'—the words were hanging in the air, formed by different flowers. He wanted to cry out loud, out of happiness, but felt as though something was blocking his voice, and he looked all around. He saw a woman dressed in red, coming from the far edge of the mountain, holding a beautiful flower. Her face was glowing brightly as she came near. She greeted him with a flower and handshake. As she said, 'Happy birthday,' he heard an enthralling music never heard before. With tears filling his eyes, he said in a low voice, 'Finally you have come to see me.'

She replied, 'Please listen to me, you know very well how much I love him. You're the only person who could breathe life into him but you are not doing so. It looks like your interest is more centred on me, and my appearances near him have made you lose your focus on thinking of new ways to cure him.'

Arun listened keenly. The weather had become breezy. Her shade had fallen on his face and he felt as though his heart was flying in air. He closed his eyes, feeling closer to her.

'Look, I'm not going to stay any longer in this world, my time is running out. Please cure him,' she requested. Arun didn't respond and stood like a statue. He slowly opened his eyes and tears rolled from his eyes. She quickly stretched her glowing hand to collect them.

Showing his teardrop on her palm, she emotionally said, 'At least feel pity on him, as much as this drop.'

'I'll definitely treat him but please . . . don't go away,' he said. Hearing his reply, her face began to glow even more. They heard somebody's footsteps and both looked at the direction of the sound. She took a few steps back, looking at Arun, and the very next second, headed towards the dead end of the compound. Looking at him, she waved her hands and he helplessly ran to call her disappearing shadow.

Arun felt that somebody playing violin was approaching him and turned back to find out. The violinist said hello and offered a handshake, saying, 'I'm Spandan.'

'How come you are here?' Arun asked in surprise, staring at him, realizing that it was late night.

'I was just about to ask you the same question,' he said with a smile and continued, 'I couldn't sleep and a tune flashed into my mind. I felt it would be nice to play it in the open,' and he started setting the violin strings. Arun's feelings in his heart were flooding but his mind was controlling the emotions.

'Can you play me a nice tune?' Arun asked.

'Sure,' he said and began to play the violin.

'I have heard this tune before, how come you are playing this tune?'

Spandan didn't hear what Arun said and played the violin emotionally. Even nature responded to his music by blowing a cool breeze; as it passed over the plants, their branches began to swing and sounded as though these were creating background music.

Arun couldn't control his emotion and lay down on the grass. His mind was pulling him to the present but his heart had already begun its *journey to the past*. At last, Spandan's tune made him fall asleep.

ANU'S BIRTH—
BEGINNING OF THE PAST

Buddham Sharanam gachami
Dharmam Sharanam gachami
Sangham Sharanam gachami

Prayers were being chanted all over the country in pagodas, a holy place for Buddhists. Buddha was an ambassador of love and peace to mankind who preached non-violence. It was a full-moon day and also a Sunday. Until late night, people were enjoying the holiday, and later, everyone settled to take rest. The sky was as clear as crystal and no clouds were seen at Bengaluru City. Around 1 a.m., near the bull temple road, an auto rickshaw was moving very fast to reach South End Road, Jayanagar. There were three passengers in the auto, an elderly woman named Sarasamma and her two daughters Chandrika and Radhika.

Chandrika was pregnant; she was in agony due to labour pain, and the other two were anxiously looking at her, holding her tightly.

'Why didn't you take her early to hospital?' the young lady seriously asked her mother.

'I asked her in the evening if we should go to hospital, but she told me that it was a slight pain and the baby was just kicking, that's all,' Sarasamma angrily replied.

'Doctor told me to come only if I have severe pain, and in the evening, it was not severe . . . Ouch!' Chandrika said and yelled with pain. The auto came near the Lalbagh gate and suddenly stopped. The driver vigorously began ratcheting to start the engine but it didn't start. He quickly checked for petrol, cursing himself and found that it was used up. He glanced around to see whether the nearby petrol bunk was still open; luckily, it was and was just about fifty feet away. He requested Radhika to help him push the auto up to the petrol bunk. Both quickly pushed the auto to reach the petrol bunk. As they reached it, he ran to bang the bunk's office door and an elderly person who was half asleep raised his head to question them. The driver requested the elderly person to come quickly and signalled that he had a pregnant passenger, by moving his hand in an arc beginning at the top and ending at the bottom of his stomach. The elderly person came running and filled the petrol as quickly as he could. The driver quickly paid the price, started the auto, and drove to the Prakruthi Nursing Home.

Sarasamma, aged about sixty-five years, hailed from an orthodox family and had ten children. Three expired in their infancy and only seven survived. Chandrika was the sixth surviving daughter. Sarasamma began chanting hymns when the auto stopped near the Lalbagh road and suddenly she remembered that she had forgotten something very important. Tapping her head, she removed a moonstone-beads chain from her neck to put around her elder daughter's neck and she began muttering after putting it on her daughter, 'It was my mother's rare and priceless collectible that she had, it is my lucky charm that she gave to me very affectionately. The famous astrologer had advised her to wear this one because of Chandra dosha, the curse of the moon. Today is full-moon day and these beads will protect you and your baby from evil spirits. Don't remove it, you saw the power of the beads that we got the petrol even at this odd situation because you wore it in a crucial time.' She stopped talking as Chandrika interrupted.

'Mother, I'm suffering from severe pain and you began to tell your parent's family's mythology, you will never change while you exist,' she said, mixing her laugh with pain.

'Very powerful beads, Grandmother very quickly went to the moon within a year, as she wore it,' Radhika said, pointing her finger upwards and laughed.

'Both of you stop talking, otherwise I may have to deliver here itself,' Chandrika said and loudly cried, mixing with her laugh. The driver speeded up as he heard 'here itself', but Sarasamma, angrily looking at the young daughter, said, 'Stupid, surely you will deserve punishment if you speak lightly about gods. It's not your fault; your father pampered you that you're the youngest one of all.' Both sisters tapped their foreheads.

Near the Prakruthi Nursing Home, two gentlemen who anxiously stood came running to help the pregnant woman, as the auto rickshaw stopped. Chandrika's husband Shankar, aged about thirty-six years, put his arms around her shoulders and slowly lifted her to get her out from the auto. Mohan, another guy aged about twenty-six years, Radhika's husband, removed a hundred-rupee note to give it to the driver but he refused to take it. Patting the auto man on the back, he put the note into the auto man's pocket.

Ramappa, the security guard of Prakruthi Nursing Home, pressed the intercom buttons to call the nurses, as he looked at the pregnant woman. A little later, the nurses came along with a stretcher for carrying her on the ramp to reach the first floor, where the labour room was located. Everyone helped Chandrika to lie down on the stretcher and took her quickly to the first floor. A nurse pressed the intercom buttons to call the doctor and she gave details of the patient and her condition, as the reply came from the other end. The doctor giving some instructions to the nurse, and finally said, 'I'll be there in about fifteen minutes.'

The nurse called Sarasamma to help with putting the hospital gown on Chandrika and to remove the jewels as well that she wore. Radhika loudly laughed as Sarasamma entered the labour ward to help. 'What's the reason to laugh?' Mohan asked curiously. Again laughing loudly, she said, 'Definitely, we will see a war of words,' recalling herself about the moonstone-beads chain.

Inside the labour ward, the nurse helped Chandrika to put on the gown by taking Sarasamma's help and told her to take off the jewels worn by the patient. She removed all the jewels which were worn by Chandrika, except the moonstone-beads chain. The nurse saw the moonstone-beads chain around Chandrika's neck while giving her an injection and told Sarasamma to remove it but she didn't; instead she began to tell about its power. The nurse firmly told her that the chain would be removed for safe delivery. 'What do you know about its power? I won't remove it, I'm a mother of ten children and I wore as much as four chains around my neck during delivery of my children,' she said proudly.

'You wear this one when you deliver next,' the nurse impatiently replied and removed the moonstone-beads chain from the patient's neck. The nurse put the same around Sarasamma's neck and pushed her outside to close the door. Everyone saw her coming out, loudly scolding the nurse. All of them laughed loudly, as Radhika predicted before what would happen.

Dr Pramila, the head of the Prakruthi Nursing Home, had run it for the past fifteen years. Dr Pramila was the one who spoke earlier on the phone with the nurse and was a gynaecologist aged about forty-five years. The nursing home was located at the centre of the Jayanagar fourth block and was well known to everyone. It had about twenty-four beds and was comprised by a reception hall, a consultancy room, and a laboratory on the ground floor along with a corridor with enough space and a big open place at the front portion of the first floor for providing enough ventilation to rooms. She was treating her patients round the clock since her residence was adjoining to the nursing home.

The doctor arrived and straightaway went inside the labour ward to check the status of Chandrika. She glanced at the previous test reports, and the senior nurse explained about the treatment given to the patient after admission. The doctor began to test the patient while the nurse got busy preparing all the necessary surgical instruments to help Chandrika deliver the baby.

'It'll be a normal delivery, you will have your baby within thirty minutes, which baby are you expecting?' the doctor asked, gently caressing her cheek.

'Any baby, doctor, I only pray to God to give us a healthy baby without this pain.' She yelled with pain and the doctor injected some fluids to deliver the baby smoothly.

Suddenly, a loud sound was heard and the intensity of the sound was that of a bomb blast. The whole building felt tremors as though there was an earthquake. The lights began flickering. Four transformers near the nursing home burst with huge fire. A little later, the whole area became silent and completely dark.

Everyone panicked and kneeled on the ground, as the blasts occurred. The atmosphere was filled with silence except for Chandrika's outcry. A little later, everyone stood up. The nurse quickly went near the first-floor veranda and yelled at Ramappa to go to the generator room and turn it on. Holding a torch, Ramappa went inside the generator room and saw all the installation had burnt because of some short circuit and informed the nurse about it. Hearing it, the nurse quickly walked inside the labour room to inform the doctor, and she was checking the pregnant woman with the help of an emergency lamp. The nurse informed them about the short circuit in the generator room. A little later, the emergency lamp began to get dim in the labour room, and after few minutes, the light went off.

The doctor thought to herself, 'How do we facilitate Chandrika's delivery? It's completely dark inside!' and was tense. Wondering, the doctor looked at the veranda, as some light was falling, and soon realized that it was moonlight. Luckily, the moon was shining more brightly than on the normal full-moon days. With some relief, the doctor told the nurses to take Chandrika on a stretcher and shift her to the veranda. The nurses quickly shifted Chandrika to the veranda on a stretcher and put three screens, leaving the front side open to give enough space for the moonlight to fall directly. The doctor took necessary surgical instruments as precaution.

The doctor also felt a sigh of relief, since Chandrika was the only patient who was admitted for delivery on that day. Everyone were tensed and prayed that the delivery should be normal. Chandrika's mother came near the stretcher on the pretext of seeing her daughter, and before somebody could notice, she quickly put the moonstone-beads chain under the pillow and quickly moved towards the corridor. The senior nurse saw Sarasamma walking quickly towards the corridor and went near Chandrika to check her neck suspiciously while also helping the doctor.

After a few minutes, the baby was delivered and it started crying. It was a girl! The nurse put the baby on a tray and got busy in treating the mother. The moon's light was falling right on the baby's face, and the baby opened her eyes. She looked at the moon, shaking hands and legs with a little smile before seeing her mother. Ramappa hurriedly came towards the first floor, holding two Petromax lamps.

Everyone was relieved after hearing the baby's cry. A little later, everyone greeted the doctor with a happy note on their faces as she came out near the corridor. In response, the doctor nodded with a smile and went to other rooms to check what had happened there. Ramappa followed the doctor, holding Petromax lamps.

Chandrika's mother started muttering, 'I prayed to God and also kept the moonstone-beads chain under her pillow, because of which she delivered safely, you people still don't understand,' and went inside the labour room since the nurses had already shifted the mother and baby into the room. She took out the moonstone-beads chain from under the pillow and started muttering, 'Hey, naughty baby, you saw the moon before your mother could see you first, I took an oath when lights went off that if you would be born safely, then I will give offerings to my deity.'

Radhika entered the room to see her sister and the baby. 'Don't mutter here, otherwise get ready to have another push from the nurse!' she said, looking at her mother, and took the baby from her. Sarasamma became quiet and angrily looked at Radhika. All of them were very happy to see the cute baby.

Next day, newspapers published about the transformers burst and the TV channels aired the incident. It also aired the incident that happened at Prakruthi Nursing Home, and they interviewed the doctor and Chandrika as well. The news channels flashed the headlines, calling the newborn baby a moonlight baby and praised the doctor's effort. The next day, the MLA of the area, in an interview, gave assurance to find out the reason behind the transformers burst.

After five days, the doctor told Chandrika that both were fine and gave discharge instructions to the nursing home staff, after giving necessary prescriptions, and told Chandrika to bring the baby to the nursing home every fortnight for check-up. Shankar and Radhika's husband Mohan came to the nursing home, accompanying the mother and the baby to get them discharged. They paid the nursing home charges and got them discharged. She said bye to the doctor and the nurses.

At Shankar's house, Radhika was waiting near the main door, holding a plate containing water, turmeric, and vermilion powder to perform a ritual to take out the evil-eye effect from Chandrika and her baby. While holding the plate with both her hands, she moved her arms clockwise three times in front of the mother and the baby near the main door. After the mother and the baby entered the house, she poured the liquid outside the door. The naming ceremony of the baby was held after two months on an auspicious day, and she was named Anushika.

Here is a little brief about Anushika's father Shankar. After graduation, Shankar opened a textile showroom near Srinagar main road. His honesty and straightforwardness had earned him goodwill from his customers, resulting in good business. He was also getting his portion of rent from the ancestral property in Tumkur. Shankar and Chandrika had good understanding and followed family traditions and customs strictly. They visited temples and holy places as and when they got free time. They were generous to donate food and clothes for the orphanage as per their ability. Theirs was a happy middle-class family.

After one year, Anushika became everybody's favourite baby because of her cute looks. She was very fond of looking at the moon. Her mother had to take her out often, to show the moon to make her quiet whenever she cried during nights. She began to speak unclear words, pointing towards the moon, and always tried to reach out to it by stretching her hands. Her mother felt that she was trying to communicate with the moon.

Anushika had completed three years. Everyone affectionately called her Anu and she won the hearts of many neighbours, as she looked very charming.

Chandrika always took Anu to visit the nearby Lord Shiva temple twice or thrice a week regularly. Anu was trying to do what her mother did and sometimes she was getting mild punishment for that. Anu completed four years and Shankar admitted her to the nursery school near NR colony. The school was only a mile away from their home. In school, the teachers were also very fond of her, as she was very co-operative. Her voice was melodious and she was very keen to learn rhymes and devotional songs.

Anu's parents had decided to have another baby and Chandrika became pregnant again. 'Which baby do you prefer, a boy or a girl?' they asked Anu. 'I want girl baby, boys are very naughty,' she replied.

'Pray to God, I'm sure he will fulfil your wish. If you don't pray, then you will have a brother,' her father said, laughing.

A few days later, Chandrika gave birth to another girl baby and named her Shwetha.

Colour TVs and VCRs had begun to enter every household across the length and breadth of India. Everyone, especially homemakers, was always glued to their TV sets for watching various programmes, particularly movies, and Shankar's family was not different. Anu and her mother watched the movies, serials, etc. during leisure. Anu believed the characters shown in the TV were real and was thrilled whenever a hero hit a villain. She thought angels, witches, and devils were also real and quickly began understanding the love stories without her mother noticing it. The WWF TV event had become a craze for the boys, and the playing cards of WWF characters had flooded the market. The boys had begun to pretend themselves as WWF characters.

After her kindergarten, Anu was promoted to first standard. Once she was driving a tricycle during games period, and a small nursery girl student sat behind her. A fat boy posing as WWF's Undertaker came near Anu and stopped the tricycle. He asked her to get down from the tricycle and shouted like Undertaker. Anu refused to get down from the tricycle and he hit her hard. Anu's head banged against the sharp edge of a door and started bleeding. The small girl who sat behind the tricycle fell on the ground. A boy who watched all these rushed towards the fat boy. He punched the fat boy's face and kicked hard on his stomach. The fat boy fell down and his mouth started bleeding.

The teacher came rushing to stop the fight and they stopped fighting as they saw the teacher. She quickly dressed Anu's head, applied ointment on the fat boy's wounds, and asked for the reason that led to that fight.

'He pushed her and hit me,' the fat guy lied to the teacher. The teacher ignored Anu's explanation since her voice was very low and badly hurt. The teacher did not know the name of the other boy who hit the fat boy, as he was newly admitted, and she asked his name. Even Anu did not know his name and looked at him admiringly.

'Vishaal,' the boy replied boldly.

'You're just six years old, who taught you to fight like this?' the teacher said, angrily looking at him.

'He pushed her,' Vishaal replied.

'I don't need any explanation from you both, inform your parents to come tomorrow around 3 p.m.,' she replied before he could explain to her. Later, the school van came to escort the children to their homes.

Anu reached home and her mother saw her head was dressed. 'What happened?' she asked, shocked. 'A fat boy hit me . . .' Anu replied with action. As she said Vishaal's name, her face blushed and he became her real hero. Anu's mother decided to visit the school to meet the principal to complain and to give a warning to the boy who hit Anu. She took Anu to a nearby clinic for getting further treatment.

The fat boy reached home; his mother saw her wounded son and the blood marks on his shirt. 'Who has done it?' she asked furiously and the boy repeated what he had told to the teacher. 'The teacher told me to bring parents tomorrow,' he said feverishly.

'I'll see that the boy gets punished by his parents in front of you, don't worry, your dad is a policeman,' she said, hugging him.

After reaching home, Vishaal hesitatingly told his mother about the incident that had happened in the school and she curiously listened to him. 'Why did you hit him? You could have instead complained against him to the teacher,' she said in a high tone.

To defend himself, Vishaal said, 'He's so fat; he hit that girl very hard and pushed badly. That is why I reacted. He has learnt a lesson and he will not hit others again.'

'Oh yeah, you are a great hero, which is why you had to defend her. Now because of your heroic act, I have to now convince your teachers. The next time something like this happens, you better complain to the teacher.'

'OK . . . But please, Mummy, don't miss coming to the school tomorrow, as asked by the teacher,' he pleaded.

Next day, Anu looked better and her mother told her to stay in the house.

'No, Mummy, I'm OK now, I'll go to school. The fat boy is very bad and I must tell the teacher about what happened yesterday,' Anu said. Her mother thought that it was difficult to convince her to stay at home and said, 'Be careful,' as Anu left to go to school.

Anu, Vishaal, and the fat boy reached their school. Anu greeted Vishaal admiringly. She moved very close to him and caught his arms. He felt a little hesitant and gently pushed her hands. During lunchtime, Anu saw Vishaal was sitting alone to have his lunch. She came near him and offered her food. The food looked very spicy; his mouth started watering, as he smelled its flavour and tasted it. 'It's very tasty, haven't eaten this dish before,' he said smilingly and took another bite. Anu handed him the lunch box, and in return, he said, 'You take mine,' opening his lunch box, and it was bread, butter, and chocolates. Anu gladly took it. The fat boy looked at them angrily.

Vishaal's mother Mamatha, aged around thirty-three years, had two sons, Sushanth and Vishaal. Her elder son was with his grandparents at Mysore. She worked as an executive in a reputed private firm. Her office was located near Basavanagudi area and her husband Venkatesh, a central government employee worked as an officer. They stayed in a rented house at Banashankari second stage.

Vishaal's mother reached his school and, after seeking permission from the office, went inside to see Vishaal. She watched him playing with the girl and felt bad as she saw Anu's head. They both looked very happy as they were playing together. A little later, Anu's mother also came. Both went running to reach them, as they saw their mothers. 'Be careful!' Anu's mother told her as she came running. Anu took her mother to introduce him.

'I know he has done wrong but you don't fight with anybody, it's bad,' she said, gently patting him on the back, and turned to Vishaal's mother to wish her well. Both began to speak and their frequencies matched each other. 'He's alone and doesn't have anyone near our house to play with. We reach our house at evening, he will be there waiting in the owner's house,' Vishaal's mother said dully.

The fat boy's parents came and entered the school but they greeted neither Anu's mother nor Vishaal's. They saw their son sitting and he got up as he saw his parents coming. They entered the principal's room and looked very angry.

The principal asked them to sit, and the fat boy's father introduced himself, 'I'm the sub-inspector of this area. Where is the boy who hit my son so badly?' he asked in a loud voice. Meantime, the security guard entered the principal's room to inform them that they had come.

Anu, Vishaal, and their mothers entered the principal's room and took their seats. Vishaal's mother opened her mouth to greet them and to say sorry but the fat boy's mother looked angrily at her before she could talk. 'See what your son has done to my boy. Is this the way you raise your son? See how badly he has hit my son. Would you keep quiet if others hit your son; he should be punished by you in front of us!' she said angrily. Anu immediately caught Vishaal's hands, as she was feeling as though his mother was going to punish him. Vishaal left her hand and caught his mother's hand.

The principal tried to calm them down but the inspector warned them, looking at Vishaal's mother, 'Let me remind you, I'm the sub-inspector of this area,' he said in a warning tone. Vishaal and Anu opened their mouths to reply but Vishaal's mother signalled them to be quiet and said, 'I agree that what my son has done is wrong. I'm not defending him. But both of you see what your son has done to her,' and pointed at Anu's head.

Before Vishaal's mother could continue, the inspector shouted, 'No, your son has hit her; the teacher has asked her already!'

Anu's mother intervened to say, 'No, your son caused this hurt by pushing her badly and the teacher didn't hear her words clearly. Your son has lied to the teacher and to you as well.'

The fat boy's face started sweating and the inspector turned towards Anu to ask her. She pointed her finger towards the fat boy.

The fat boy's father said, 'He would have pushed her by mistake. Why did he hit my son? He should have told the teacher. Now he must be punished, otherwise he will hit others also.'

Vishaal's mother got up and signalled the principal that she would be back in a few minutes.

Vishaal's mother went outside to make a phone call. She entered the room and sat quietly after making the phone call. The fat boy's mother angrily stared at her. A little later, the principal received a call and the caller told him to give the receiver to the sub-inspector. The sub-inspector stood up suddenly, and started saying, 'Yes, sir . . . yes, sir . . .' five to six times. He began to sweat as he heard 'Why you are making such a mess, look at the girl, do you want any action from me?' Everyone looked at him with a confused look except Vishaal's mother, who was smiling because the caller was none other than her brother who was serving as DIG. To his wife's surprise, the sub-inspector suddenly began to change his track: 'My son has lied to us and pushed her badly.' Now shifting his attention towards his son, he said, 'Don't do it again . . .' He then turned back to speak with Vishaal's mother, but they already moved towards the exit after wishing goodbye to the principal.

As days went on, Vishaal and Anu's friendship grew. Anu's mother was good at cooking, and Anu asked her mother to pack a little extra food into her tiffin box for sharing it with Vishaal. Anu invited Vishaal to come to her house. Anu's mother also invited Vishaal's mother to visit her house and she accepted. Anu was very happy since Vishaal was coming to her house with his mother.

A few days later, Vishaal and his mother visited Anu's house. Anu's mother welcomed them and, after initial talks of asking if everyone and everything was good at their house, served snacks. Anu held Vishaal's hand and pulled him to show her room, dolls, and other toys. They began to play as their mothers got busy talking to each other. After some time, not being able to see or hear Anu and Vishaal, Anu's mother shouted, 'Anu.' When she did not get any response, she looked outside and saw that both were playing with other children. Vishaal's mother also came out to see them and saw Vishaal happily playing with other children.

Seeing this, Vishaal's mother said to Anu's mother, 'Anu has got good company to play with, whereas Vishaal has to be alone waiting for us to come. Tomorrow our building owner's family is going out of station for about a week to attend the wedding ceremony of their relatives. They usually took care of Vishaal while we were out and now because they will not be around, Vishaal has to stay alone.'

Hearing this, Anu's mother replied, 'Don't worry, you can pick up Vishaal from here. Let him come to our house with Anu after the classes.' Hearing this, Vishaal's mother felt relieved, and to express her gratitude, she invited Anu's mother to her house and left after a while.

From the next day onwards, Anu brought Vishaal home after her classes, and she spent her time happily with Vishaal. They played with puppet dolls, which had characters like husband and wife.

One night she was alone looking at the moon on a full-moon day. It looked very bright and attractive to her. Seeing this, she said to herself, 'You look so beautiful, even my Vishaal you know. He also looks very handsome, I love him!'

Whether or not the thesis written by Sigmund Freud about dreams was proven correct, the thesis written by him about opposite-sex attraction was.

The next day, Anu's grandparents came to her house to leave her sister Shwetha, as they were taking care of her over a period. Her time passed quite happily for a week with Vishaal and her sister.

In Vishaal's house, Vishaal's parents told him that they would be taking him to their native place Mysore for spending his holidays. Anu was very upset and requested him to cancel his holiday trip. He convinced her that he would come back soon, although he felt a little dull while departing.

Anu got frustrated as Vishaal left for Mysore and began to watch the moon every night.

'Please, moon, please help me bring my Vishaal back, I want to play with him.' As she was conversing with the moon, her mother called, 'Anu . . . see who's on the line, come quickly, it's Vishaal. He wants to speak with you . . .' Hearing this, Anu ran towards the phone, and impulsively spoke to him in a tense manner. Vishaal could not hear anything and ended the call.

A little later, she ran towards the veranda to glance at the moon and happily said, 'Thank you, moon, I know that it is you who helped me speak with Vishaal . . . You are my best friend.' After standing there for a while and thanking her moon, she played with her sister for a while, and after the dinner, she fell asleep.

The next day was a Sunday. At 6 p.m., everyone sat eagerly near the TV to watch a blockbuster movie of the love-story genre. Everyone, including Anu, was in tears while looking at a scene in which the heroine's parents had locked her in a room and she started writing 'I love you, Balu' all over the room without leaving an inch of space. Anu watched the complete movie. The next evening, inside her room, she began writing 'I love VISHAL' on the walls, and her father curiously watched from behind.

Looking at her writing, Anu's father said, 'First correct the spelling of his name, and later love him.' Anu smiled, nodding her head, and went out to play.

The final exam results were announced, and Vishaal topped his class. He was promoted to class four. During the next academic year, students of their school began talking about Anu and Vishaal's close friendship in their absence. His friends even started calling him Anu's boyfriend. Likewise, Anu's friends called her Vishaal's girlfriend, but she ignored them with a smile. Vishaal was irritated when his friends started associating his name with Anu's. One day, Anu came running towards Vishaal, holding a flower, and gave it to him. Looking around and confirming that no one was around, she suddenly said, 'I love you' and wished him a happy birthday.

Vishaal became irritated and said, 'This is too much . . . We are not small kids anymore to imitate blindly like elders that we did in the past while playing. Do you know that everyone has started teasing us, associating our names together as girlfriend–boyfriend? This is enough, please, from now onwards, don't even come close to me.'

Hearing this, Anu firmly replied, 'We are close friends, are we not loving each other, let them say whatever they like. Why should you care?'

Vishaal angrily replied, 'Have you gone crazy? We both are just friends . . . I don't love you at all . . . I love only my parents. You are imitating everything you learn by watching love-story movies. That is only for adults, you understand?'

From then on, Vishaal started avoiding her, and at times, he played with boys alone. Once, Anu went to share her food with

Vishaal, but he left the place and instead chose to sit with other boys to have his lunch. When she saw this behaviour, tears rolled down from Anu's eyes.

Day by day, Anu became dull because Vishaal was avoiding her. She wanted to get busy in order to avoid his thoughts and began to show interest towards her studies, but her heart was filled with love. She thought Vishaal was for her and believed that one day or the other, he would come back to her. One night, she sat in the veranda looking at the moon; with tears filling her eyes, she said to herself 'Vishaal, when will I meet you?' and then started talking to the moon and said, 'Please, moon, bring him here.'

Next day at evening, to her great surprise, Anu saw Vishaal and his mother coming to her house. She ran quickly into the kitchen, calling her mother to receive them. Anu's mother invited them in and offered for them to be seated. A little later, Vishaal signalled at Anu to follow him and got up from his seat. Anu followed him and both stood outside in the veranda. He enquired about her studies and said, 'Let us both be like good friends and please remove other thoughts from your mind.' Hearing this, Anu was not able to react. She was just happy because she was talking with Vishaal and nodded her head in affirmation. After a short conversation, both went inside. Vishaal's mother got up from her seat, giving an invitation card to Anu's mother, and invited them to her sister's marriage reception. Vishaal also invited Anu to attend the function. She felt quite relaxed after Vishaal spoke to her and didn't forget to thank the moon after Vishaal and his mother left.

As years passed, Anu and Vishaal were promoted to eighth standard, and the school reopened as usual. On first day of school, Anu did not find Vishaal and thought that probably he was still not back from his native place. A week passed by but still she couldn't see Vishaal, she then enquired about him by asking his friend. With a surprised look, Vishaal's friend replied, 'Didn't he tell you? His father got transferred to Mumbai, and all of them left for Mumbai about twenty days back.'

Hearing this, Anu was very sad; she suddenly shook her head with raised eyebrows as if somebody brought her back from a shock and curiously asked, 'Did he give you his new address or phone number?'

Vishaal's friend replied, 'No, Anu, even I didn't meet him. One day I had been to his house and saw a board on his door which read "To Let". I then asked the house owner about them. He did not answer properly and spoke very rudely. Vishaal's neighbours told me that they left, to Mumbai. I asked them if Vishaal's family left any contact number or address. The neighbours replied that they gave neither contact number nor address and also they had to vacate the house at very short notice. I then realized that probably because they vacated the house at very short notice, the house owner spoke rudely.' After hearing this, Anu left from school for her house. She sat in the veranda with a depressed look in her eyes; looking at the moon, she started weeping.

Anu began to think about others seriously. The reason was she observed that her mother was giving leftover food to the poor people near the temple. Many a time, she sent Anu herself to serve the food for the poor people since the temple was located at just a stone's throw away.

One day, Anu's uncle (her mother's brother) came to her house. Anu's mother had prepared special dishes since she was aware that he was coming. As Anu's mother was performing pooja, she called Anu and told her to carefully serve food for her uncle. Anu hesitatingly went inside the kitchen and came out holding a plate with plain rice, curds, and a pickle. His face fell, as Anu put the plate on the table. Looking at his sister, he asked,

'Haven't you prepared breakfast today?' Anu's mother, surprised, turned to look at the plate, abruptly completing her prayer. She called Anu loudly, as Anu was in her room, and hearing her mother's cry, Anu came running to see what had happened. Anu's mother immediately caught Anu's hands tightly and in an angry tone asked, 'Why did you serve the stale food to your uncle, why didn't you serve the palav? Have you gone mad?'

Anu's uncle interrupted and said 'It's OK, she's still a child, and it's your fault. Why did you tell her to serve?'

Anu's mother replied, 'Oh! Do you believe that she is still a child? If we leave her, she will teach us.'

Anu replied, 'Mummy, I'm sorry, I served the palav to the poor children and nothing is left,' and started crying. Hearing her reply, they exchanged their broad looks, and she continued to speak, sobbing, 'Those children eat stale food daily, Mummy, we give them only stale food. Hence, I thought that let's eat stale food today and give them—'

Hearing this, Anu's uncle could not control his laugh; he called Anu and asked her to sit beside him. Patting Anu on the back, looking at his sister, he said, 'You should be very proud of your daughter. You know, Chandrika, children are very kind and merciful, and they always think of doing good deeds. We should learn from them.' Hugging Anu, he continued, 'It's OK, Anu, I'll eat, it will be very tasty since you've served it, but don't do it again without Mummy's permission.' Anu innocently nodded her head in response, and even Chandrika cooled down and warned Anu, saying, 'Don't do it again,' and went inside the kitchen to prepare coffee.

Anu did not repeat the same thing, since her mother had begun to serve hot food to the poor once or twice a month, accompanying Anu, for which she was very happy. One day, Anu's mother was folding Anu's clothes after those were washed and dried. Anu possessed a variety of dresses since her father was a cloth merchant. Anu's mother did not have a count of the number of dresses Anu had. Anu's mother felt that some of Anu's clothes were missing, but she could not figure it out exactly and approximately took the counting. After a few weeks, Anu's mother did not find a costly dress that was gifted by her brother, so she counted Anu's dresses while folding them and figured out that approximately about ten to twelve clothes were missing. Anu's mother had not appointed anyone for housekeeping. She wondered how they were missing but did not confront Anu. She decided to find how it was missing.

One Sunday, Anu's mother saw a gunny bag behind her house; after checking it, she found Anu's clothes inside the bag. She was surprised, but kept it as it was before and went inside. She stood near the window, hiding impatiently. After a few minutes, her neighbour Ramu, aged nine years, came inside the veranda and he said deliberately, 'Hey, I found the ball! Getting it right away . . .' and slowly came near the bag. He took the bag, watching all around, making sure that nobody saw him, and went out. Anu's mother watched with surprise and managed to follow him. A little later, to her surprise, Anu also joined him, holding a gunny bag, and both arrived near the Kannan's slum entrance.

Anu's mother saw a small queue formed by the downtrodden ladies and children. Both Anu and Ramu began to distribute saris, shirts, frocks, pants, and tops by looking at the physical appearance of the poor in the queue, refusing some who have already taken something. Meanwhile, an elderly person saw them distributing the clothes, and he came smilingly near them and said, 'Both of you are so wonderful and generous, may I join you to help?' Looking at their smiling faces and taking it as an affirmative response, he continued, saying, 'Next Sunday, I'll come with some items to give them,' and patted them on their backs.

Anu's mother quickly reached her house before they could see. Anu's father saw Anu's mother quickly coming into the house and curiously asked, 'Why you are coming so fast? What happened? Where is Anu? I didn't see her . . .'

Anu's mother, breathing fast, replied, 'See for yourself what your daughter has done, she's giving clothes to the slum children without my knowledge, and now I have to go and check whether our clothes are there or she has donated them as well. She has donated some new dresses also. Let her come back, she will have it from me. It is because of you that she has become like this. You have pampered her a lot, and as a result, she does not listen to me . . .'

Anu's parents saw Anu coming inside. 'Where have you been, Anu?' her mother questioned innocently.

Anu replied, 'Mummy, I was playing with Ramu.'

Looking at their conversation, her father could not control his smile. Anu's mother looked angrily at Anu and said, 'How dare you give clothes to the slum children without my knowledge.'

Anu replied, 'Sorry, Mummy, I did not tell you, but I gave them only the undersized clothes and well-used ones only. See now I have grown tall, and I thought that it would be difficult for you to maintain those clothes and also that you would allow me to give those clothes, if I had asked you before.'

Anu's mother reacted and said, 'Very great, should have given them all the clothes that you have.'

Anu replied, 'I don't mind if you agree, Mummy, four or five simple dresses are enough for me. I'll wear your sari if I want to attend any function . . .'

Turning towards Anu's father, Anu's mother said, 'Look at her guts, she's eyeing my saris, if I'm lenient now, even I will have to stand in a queue for getting back my saris . . .' Everyone laughed, including Anu's mother. Anu's mother then continued, 'I agree that you are helping the needy, but you have to get our consent before you do anything like this.'

Patting Anu on the back, her father said, 'Don't do it secretly, dear. Ask us before you do something like this,' and in order to boost her morale, he said, 'I'll give some unsold clothes to give to them.' Anu was very happy and at times asked her parents and continued donating clothes to the needy.

After a year, Anu was promoted to ninth standard. As time passed, Anu attained puberty and her parents held a function on that occasion, in accordance with their family tradition. Anu looked beautiful, as she wore a pure-silk sari with gold thread woven in it. After the function, Anu's parents fell into thoughts about her future, and they took her horoscope to show it to the temple's head priest, who was known to be a famous astrologer. The priest took Anu's horoscope and made some serious calculations on a paper. Later, Anu's father looked at him enquiringly.

The priest responded, saying, 'It would be better if you don't show this horoscope to another astrologer. This horoscope is the first of its kind that I saw in my life; she will become a great personality at an early age. Even the gods will envy her and I can't tell you further,' and he handed over the horoscope. Anu's parents left the place after getting blessings from the priest.

After serving two years in Mumbai, Vishaal's father was transferred back to Bengaluru. They purchased a flat near Koramangala since it was very convenient for his elder son to attend his college. Vishaal was in tenth standard, and he joined the Rose Mary High School, which was located near his house. He was well built, and his stay in Mumbai had changed his attitude. He had almost forgotten the past memories of his childhood that he spent in Bengaluru, but Anu's mind was still haunted with memories of Vishaal. She was still hoping to find him and loved him as much as before.

Nirmala and Arun

It was late night and Nirmala was still awake thinking about an interview that she had to attend the next day. The interview was a very important one that could prove to be a turning point to her career. Although after completing her engineering, she had worked as an assistant architect in a small firm in Bengaluru, she was still nervous about her interview. She was then discussing about their future with her brother Arun, and after a long discussion, she told her brother 'Night night, sleep tight' and went to sleep.

Next morning, Nirmala got up a little earlier than usual and got ready after preparing breakfast. Both had their breakfast. After packing his lunch and handing it over to him, she told Arun to lock the door and hurried to go, as she had to reach the brigade road in Bengaluru, for the interview.

Nirmala reached the administrative office of Orbit Construction Company. It was a multinational construction company and had its operations in about fifteen countries. On enquiry about the interview, the receptionist of Orbit Construction Company showed Nirmala the way to the conference room where the interview would take place. There were already many job aspirants, seated in the waiting area, awaiting their turn.

The interview was for the post of a chief architect for the company. The executives of the company were doing the interview, including the CEO. Nirmala entered the conference room when her name was called for interview by the facilitator. As she entered the room and took the offered seat to face the interview, everyone smiled since she looked very young and inexperienced for that post. Nirmala handed over her file that had her résumé and other details to a person from the interview panel who asked her to produce it. The interviewers then asked her some questions to test her knowledge on architecture and her answers impressed them for real.

Everyone, including the CEO, felt that she was innovative and had constructive ideas. During the interview, the CEO was gazing at her and thought her face resembled some known person but was not able to figure it out. The interviewers' panel then asked her to present a project design, and when she began her presentation, everyone listened enthusiastically. Her presentation was worth listening to, as they got learn a lot from the so-called young and inexperienced girl. It took her about an hour to expound her presentation. After she completed her presentation, to her surprise, everyone remained silent. As she walked towards her seat, everyone applauded, gave a standing ovation, and then congratulated her. Later, the CEO told her to meet him tomorrow for further discussion.

Next day, the receptionist of Orbit Construction saw Nirmala coming and told her colleague receptionist to take Nirmala to the CEO's cabin immediately. The CEO greeted Nirmala as she entered the cabin and offered her a seat. He saw her resume; to his surprise, there was no mention of her father's name and instead he saw her mother's name written as Late Krupa. He rubbed his chin for a while trying to remember something and curiously looked at her. Suddenly, he said to himself, 'I got it,' and excitedly asked, 'Is your father Sudarshan?' Nirmala was shocked by hearing her father's name. She immediately stood to take her files and started to leave his cabin. She was already near the exit door before he could speak any further.

The CEO, Anand Sharma, stood up and loudly said, 'Hey, Nirmala . . . your mother was my best friend.' She suddenly stopped and turned back. He continued to say, 'It's hard to believe that she has left this materialistic world. Her guidance has enabled me to build this empire.' Curiously listening, she walked back. He offered her the seat again and she took it. Meanwhile, a staff member from housekeeping entered the cabin to serve coffee. He signalled the staff member to leave after she kept the coffee tray. A little later, he served coffee to Nirmala and continued, 'We both studied in RV engineering college. My father was a rich businessman, and as a result, I was very careless about my studies. My father had enough influence and money to get me a seat in a college, and thus even with a low percentage, I graduated after my second attempt. Your mother got distinction in all the semesters. She always helped me in my studies and project works. After graduation, my father sent me to the US for further studies, and by the way, he is one of the main promoters of this company. After completion of my studies in the US, I became the CEO of this company. I was visiting India very rarely and met your mother about three to four times during my visits. Once when I met her, she told me that she was marrying a person who was working in her office as an architect. I offered for her to join my company and told her that she could settle in the US after her marriage, along with her husband. However, she refused, because she had to look after her parents. I attended her marriage. After that, hmm, after about five years or so, I met your mother again and she told me that she was not very happy with your father. Three years later, I received a letter from your mother that she was divorced. I was too busy at that time and could not meet her immediately. Later, I wrote a letter and offered for her to join my company. I think that letter did not reach her. A few days later, I visited your mother's house but she had shifted her house, I could not find her new residence address either.'

After a pause, Sharma asked, 'What happened to her, is your father with you?'

Nirmala replied, 'No, sir, he's not with us. After her divorce, my mother went into depression which led to low BP and eventually heart attack caused her death.' And even though Sharma did not ask, she continued, telling him, 'The reason for her divorce, as far as I know, is that my father had inferiority complex, thereby he left his job to venture by himself but did not succeed. He also used my mother's earnings to clear the loans and sold his inherited property. When he asked my mother to give consent for selling the joint properties, she refused. This led to the first crack towards splitting their relationship. My mother had to work harder to clear the debts that he made. Sometimes she was coming home late because of heavy workload and he began to doubt her. His habit of drinking excessive liquor cost him his job. One day, with a proud smile he showed an appointment letter to my mother and told her that he got a very good job in Australia. He compelled my mother to come along but she refused since she had a nice job and had no confidence in him. This led to the second crack, which eventually led to a fight, and he went to Australia alone. Later, he divorced my mother,' Nirmala said sadly and looked at a picture that was hung on the wall opposite to her, with a few lines printed on it. The lines read, 'Life is a peak; strive hard to reach the top.' Sharma then tried to distract her by talking about some projects to perk up her mood and bring her back to normal.

A little later, Sharma took her to the various sections of his office and introduced her to the rest of the staff. Everyone was surprised to see such a young girl being offered such a respectable and authoritative post, and some seniors looked envious. She took about two hours' time to interact with the rest of the staff. Sharma looked at his watch and it was around 1 p.m. He invited her for lunch at his house.

Nirmala hesitatingly replied, 'Thank you, sir, but not today, maybe some other time.' At seeing her hesitation, he put his arm on her shoulder and said, 'Nirmala, my father always talks about your mother, she was like his daughter. He will feel very happy to see Krupa's daughter, do you want to disappoint him?' And Nirmala nodded her head to indicate her acceptance to visit his house for lunch. They walked towards the exit, and the driver, who was waiting for his boss, opened the car's door upon seeing him.

It took nearly thirty minutes to reach Sharma's residence. Everyone curiously looked at Nirmala, as she entered. As it was lunchtime, the family members were seated around the dining table. He straightaway took Nirmala near his father and asked him to guess who she was. Adjusting his spectacles, his father keenly looked at her, and after a pause, tears of happiness rolled from his eyes. He then said, 'Ha, you look like my Krupa, am I right? Aren't you her daughter?' She was surprised to see that he recognized her. Taking her surprised look as a positive answer, he continued to ask, 'How's your mother?' As soon as she heard this question, tears started rolling down her face and she replied, 'Mother passed away long ago, leaving me and my younger brother . . .' He hugged her to console her.

Sharma's family members were very happy after knowing that Nirmala is Krupa's daughter. After lunch, everyone gathered to speak with her. A little later, Sharma explained how he met her. Looking at his father, he said, 'Daddy, today she has been appointed as our company's chief architect. In the beginning, I was surprised to see how a young girl could have such experienced thoughts and ideas at this early age but later realized that she has inherited her mother's talent. She is as talented as her mother.' Everyone clapped as he handed over the appointment letter to Nirmala.

A little later, Sharma's father affectionately put his arm around Nirmala's shoulders and said, 'You and your brother are like my grandchildren; I want both of you to stay with us forever.' Nirmala thanked Sharma's father for showing concern and said, 'Grandpa, it is very kind of you for wanting us to stay here but my brother is only sixteen years old. I want him to work hard in life and learn to value things to attain a bright future. Your emotional support will be more than enough for us, I'll meet you often.' Looking at Nirmala, Sharma said, 'You can serve the company as long as you wish. Please do not hesitate to tell me if you want to start your own venture. I am always ready to support you at any time, my child.' Nirmala thanked him for his kind words and, after some time, got up to leave. She thanked everyone and invited them to visit her house. Sharma accompanied her to drop her at her house.

They reached Nirmala's house, and Nirmala invited Sharma inside her house. 'I'll come some other time with my family,' he said and wished her goodbye. Arun curiously came out to see who had come as he heard the sound of a car and saw his sister walking towards their house after talking to somebody in the car. Arun asked Nirmala with whom she was talking. Nirmala replied, 'He's my boss, I got appointed, Mother and he studied in the same college and both were good friends.' Both entered the house and he took her to his room to introduce his new friend and said, 'He's Vishaal, he recently joined our school since his father got transferred from Mumbai and he's come here to copy the old notes . . .' After Arun introduced Vishaal, Vishaal said hi to her.

Nirmala responded, saying, 'Very pleased to meet you, carry on,' and patted him on the back. She went to the kitchen to bring some snacks to offer them. And the day nearly came to an end to greet the next day.

Next day in Bengaluru, Koramangala layout, it was a cool early morning not completely bright yet. The birds had already started chirping and gone in search of food for their young ones. As the day progressed, the sun rose to spread its golden rays on the earth, and the earth was ready to welcome the day. The locality had beautifully constructed bungalows, and among those was a cream-coloured building with dark orange outline, and it had six large windows. All the windows were closed except the east-side front window adjoining a room. Through the open window, the sunrays fell on Deepthi's face and simultaneously the alarm bell rang. She moved the blanket off her face to wake up. She switched off the alarm and kissed her favourite teddy bear.

Deepthi went to the washroom to switch on the water heater but there was no power. Cursing the electricity board, she opened the door and started snooping at the window of the opposite house, losing time consciousness. Suddenly, a sound of some object falling inside the gate of her house distracted her, and she realized that the newspaper boy threw the newspaper inside the gate. 'Oops! Time's up,' she said, looking at the clock. She hurried to take a bath, and chilled water splashed on her as she turned on the shower. Because the water was very cold, she quickly finished taking a bath, shivering and singing to distract her mind so as not to realize that it was very cold. After taking a bath, she wore a white skirt and a white top that had the print of two small bears holding roses. She admired herself, looking at the mirror with a broad smile. She blew air on her palm to check if she smelled fresh and said, 'Yuck!' because she had bad breath. She then realized that she had forgotten to brush her teeth. She quickly went to the washroom to freshen up her mouth. Again, after looking at the mirror, she checked her breath and felt satisfied with the fragrance of fresh mint. With an energetic look, adjusting her skirt, she said to herself, 'OK, now I'm fit and fine.' She looked beautiful. A little later, grudgingly she looked at the heater's power indicator after hearing the sound of the heater turning on due to power coming back and climbed down the stairs from her bedroom to go outside.

Deepthi, peeping at her parent's room, checked whether it was open and heard her mother's voice: 'Wait, Deepthi.'

'Bye, it's late, I'll move,' she replied and kissed her dog Snoopy, as it jumped up to reach her hand.

'Snoopy, wish me all the best,' she said, stretching her hand for a handshake, and meantime, her mother came out from her room. Deepthi asked her mother to wish her good luck.

'For what?' the mother replied, yawning. Deepthi ignored to reason out since she was in a hurry and hardly kick-started her Scooty (a two-wheeler for girls). Before moving, she turned back at the window of the opposite house to have a look, and meanwhile, her mother called her name loudly.

'What?' she asked impatiently turning back to look at her mother, who was standing at the window, and her mother in a warning tone, said, 'Don't forget to bring the roses from the market!' Deepthi nodded her head in response. Again, she turned back before she could move, to have a final look towards the opposite house's window and, not seeing anybody there, finally moved. She rode very fast since the traffic was sparse. Later, she reached near a tall gate and parked her vehicle in front of a no-parking board. She went inside and saw that the security guard was sleeping on a chair. To wake him up, she took off the cap from his head and said, 'It's time to do your duty,' and quickly walked towards the yoga classroom. The yoga class had already started.

Deepthi peeped inside the yoga class, saw all of them were meditating by closing their eyes. With a sigh of relief, she walked slowly to join them. A little later, the yoga guru looked at Deepthi and saw that she was doing the asana yoga posture incorrectly. He called her pleasantly and asked her, 'Deepthi beta, is something wrong?' Touching his feet, she dully replied, 'Exam, guruji.'

'I thought exams are already over.'

'Yes, guruji, but exams in the tuition,' she said with a guilty feeling. Gently patting her on the back, he said, 'It's just a small test, why are you so tense? You have to face so many tough challenges in life, we practice yoga to be relieved from these tensions. Don't put other things in your mind, practice suryasana.' And everyone in the class listened keenly while doing the asana. Deepthi did it very fast, and the guru told her to go home after hearing from her that she had completed her session.

She replied, 'It's all right; I'll be here until the class ends.'

'You can go, I'm sure that you will do your test very well, may success stay with you always,' the guruji said.

Touching guruji's feet, Deepthi said, 'Thank you, guruji.'

Happily, Deepthi left the yoga class and felt as though she had wings to fly. She walked quickly towards her scooter and on the way gently touched the flowers that had grown right across the lawn. She started her Scooty and drove fast. A little later, as the traffic increased, she had to reduce the speed. While passing near a temple, she let go of the handlebars of the Scooty to join her hands for praying. 'God, please,' she whispered and suddenly caught the Scooty's handlebars as she was about to lose control over the vehicle. A man passing by in a car watched her losing control of her vehicle while praying and laughed as the car passed close to her. Both the vehicles stopped near a signal. Looking at her, the man in the car, said, 'Be careful while you drive, it's enough to pray to God from the heart while driving,' and Deepthi nodded her head. Wishing her well, he said, 'Let your wishes come true.'

'Thank you,' she replied but the car had already moved past her before he could hear.

Deepthi reached an open field; to her surprise, no one had turned up and she looked at her watch. She tapped on her own head and said to herself, 'Oh my God, they are supposed to come at nine but I thought eight o'clock.' She suddenly remembered about flowers and said, 'Oops! I forgot to buy roses,' and quickly rode her Scooty to buy them. She reached the market, bought a bunch of roses, and quickly started her vehicle to reach her house. Meanwhile, she got a call from her friend Shruthi while riding. 'I'm working on that only, call you later,' curtly she replied and ended the call. Moving fast, she reached her home; sitting on her vehicle, in a high voice she called, 'Mom, come fast!' and took out a beautiful rose from the bunch and held its stalk in her mouth tightly, freeing her hands to drive. Hurriedly, she gave the rest of the bunch of roses, as her mother came near her. Pointing at the rose that she held, her mother asked in surprise, 'What's this rose for, how come you're so busy today?'

Weaving lies quickly, Deepthi replied, 'Mom, today is my friend's great-grandmother's hundredth birthday, I'm going to wish her well and have her blessings,' and left already before her mother could enquire further. Her heart had begun to beat faster, as she reached the playground. The boys had already started playing cricket. Tensely watching them, she stood at the corner of the field.

After a few minutes, a cricket ball came rolling near her and hurriedly a boy asked, 'Please, can you pass that ball?' Looking at him, Deepthi's heart began to beat even faster because the boy was none other than Arun, whom she was loving very much. She took the ball to hand it over to him. Holding a rose in her left hand and the ball in the right, she quickly walked much closer, instead of throwing the ball. Dreamily looking at him, she stretched the hand in which she was holding the rose to give it instead of the ball. Puzzled by her act, he quickly asked, 'You are our neighbour, right? How come you're here?'

After realizing her act, she started trembling and replied, 'I came . . . came—' Before she could complete the sentence, another boy snatched the ball from her hand, passing it to the bowler, and called Arun to join back quickly for fielding.

'OK, I'll meet you later,' Arun said and ran back fast to continue fielding.

Tensely biting her nails, Deepthi sat restlessly on a step, resting her face on her palms and bitterly watched him play since she had expected that Arun would react in a much better way. Meanwhile, Deepthi got a call from her close friend Shruthi. Deepthi received the call and heard, 'Did you succeed?'

With an upset mood mixed with anger, she replied, 'No, he's yet to respond, you irritating cockr—' and disconnected the call.

As the time passed, looking at the sky, Deepthi said to herself, 'Oh God, I haven't expressed my love yet, please help me . . .' And later, the match ended. One boy who was playing, looking at Deepthi curiously, said to Arun, 'Hey, look at her . . .' Arun ignored the boy, took his sports bag, and continued to walk. As he started walking without even looking at Deepthi, she loudly called, 'Arun . . .' and ran towards him. The other boys started taunting him. Arun angrily said, 'Shut up, OK . . . I'll see you guys tomorrow, all right?' and turning towards Deepthi, irritatedly he asked, 'What's the matter with you?'

Feeling better, closing her eyes, she replied, 'Yah, Arun, please can you spare me a few minutes?' and he smiled, turning to the other side. Making herself strong and firm, she said, 'I love you . . .'

Arun became annoyed, and asked 'What?' He took the rose from her hand and continued, 'Sorry, I would prefer this flower rather than your love . . .' After saying this, he hurriedly left the place, riding his bicycle. Deepthi sat on the ground as her desire did not turn into reality and tears started rolling from her eyes. After some time, agonized, she went back to her house.

Arun reached home; curiously looking at the rose that he held, Nirmala asked, 'Why are you so late, Arun?' and Arun gave her the rose smilingly. Seeing him smile, Nirmala asked, 'Oh, you stood in a line to get this flower in the market?'

'Ha! Superb guess,' he replied smilingly.

'You!' she said, pulling his ears, and later with the intention of offering the rose to their beloved late mother, placed the rose on their mother's photo frame. They both prayed for each other's well-being. Suddenly the rose fell down from the frame. Looking at the rose falling, Nirmala said, 'My wish will come true,' and to play out fun, Arun said seriously, 'My wishes will turn out true,' and both argued deliberately. Finally, Nirmala said smilingly, 'OK . . . OK, our wishes will turn out true,' and went to the kitchen, preparing coffee. Later, she served coffee to Arun, and while drinking her coffee, she stared at Arun admiringly, remembering sweet memories. She said, 'I want to see Arun who was once a cute baby, not this Arun who is a teenager now . . .' and laughing,

Arun replied, 'No, no, still I'm a baby and I'll remain as a baby for you until one hundred years,' and she kissed on his forehead affectionately.

Deepthi also reached home in more or less the same time that Arun took to reach his home. She straightaway walked into her room and locked the door. Her eyes were red, with wet lashes; she threw herself on the bed and soon fell asleep since she had not had a proper sleep the previous night. After a few hours, she heard a knock at the door and opened her eyes slowly. Restlessly, she walked towards the door to open it. Looking at Deepthi's red eyes, her mother said tensely, 'What has happened to your eyes, did you cry, what's the matter? It's already five o'clock, quickly have your lunch. Your daddy had called up from Delhi to speak with you. I said that you have gone to meet your friend, if he gets to know that you were out for so long, you will have it from him.'

'Mummy, I'll just wash my face and come soon,' she replied, and her mother was waiting until she washed her face. She caught Deepthi's hands to bring her down the stairs and served her lunch. After having lunch, she went back to her room and watched Arun's house to get a glimpse of Arun but she couldn't since the window was ajar.

After having dinner, Arun went to his room and sat comfortably on his bed. He switched off all the lights except the bed lamp beside him. He felt quite relaxed because his exams of class ten, which were going on for about a month, were finally over. He pulled the nearby drawer to take out a photo album in which there were snaps of his school along with his friends. He felt a little sad after looking at it since he was now missing his friends. Nirmala came near him to serve hot almond milk. Looking at her, he said dully, 'I'll be missing my friends,' and kept the album close to his chest.

'Don't worry, I heard it's a good college, I'm sure you will find new friends there,' Nirmala said, consoling him. He drank the milk, recalling school memories in his mind.

Arun couldn't sleep, as his school memories were recurring in his mind. He got up from his bed and came near the balcony to inhale fresh air. At the same time, Deepthi was waiting impatiently behind the window of her house to see him. She felt a little relaxed as she saw him but Arun didn't see her and was looking at the sky. Snoopy's barking sound distracted Arun and he looked at Snoopy and her room as well. To his surprise, she was dreamily staring at him with tears rolling down her face. He signalled her to come onto her terrace.

Immediately, Arun went inside his room, took a notepad, and wrote a few lines quickly. He came back to the balcony and saw Deepthi was already waiting near the front portion of her terrace. He signalled her to catch the notepad. He threw it with force and the notepad fell on Deepthi's terrace. Immediately, she took the notepad and went inside her room to read. Curiously, she opened the notepad and her eyes quickly ran through the words: 'Deepthi, please understand me. I don't think I am the right person for you, falling in love with me will be fruitless. It's just an infatuation and for sure you will meet the right person in future who will express his love truly from his heart to you, goodbye.'

Next day early morning, Arun got up rubbing his eyes, as he heard the routine Gayatri mantras and quickly realized that it was the day to vacate their house. He saw his sister had already started carefully packing the photos that included family photos. The packers and movers company staff had already come to pick up their stuff, for shifting it into a new 2BHK flat near Jayanagar 9th block which was provided for them by Sharma's uncle since the company's construction works were in progress around JP Nagar, Bannerghatta Road and he felt it would be convenient for Nirmala.

Deepthi was in a deep sleep, as she slept very late thinking about Arun, and her mobile was ringing. To answer the call, she stretched her hand in half-sleep but the mobile stopped ringing. She got up, went to the washroom, and splashed water on her face. The mobile started ringing again and that call was from her friend Shruthi; receiving it, Deepthi said, 'Hello, sorry I was sleeping.'
'It's OK, what happened?'
'Oh, it flopped miserably.'
'You didn't listen to me, as always you were overconfident?'

And as there was some problem in the network, Deepthi said, 'Shruthi, just a second, I can't hear,' and moved near the terrace. She looked down curiously, as her mother was waving hands at Nirmala and Arun. They were seated in a car, and the household stuff was loaded in two Canters. Looking at the moving car, shocked, she dropped her mobile.

Exclaiming, Deepthi said, 'No, no . . .' and kneeled down. Her eyes were soaked in tears. Somehow reacting quickly, she managed to come down the stairs but they had left already. She felt that she had lost all her strength. She came to her mother and desperately asked, 'How come they have shifted their house suddenly?'

Her mother replied, 'No, they told me long back, she was waiting for his exams to complete, she's so nice, I will miss her a lot . . .'

'How will you contact her, do you have their mobile number?' Deepthi asked innocently.

Realizing that she didn't, her worried mother replied, 'Oops! I forgot to ask her . . . How could I do that? I was just speaking to her now and forgot to ask such an important thing . . .'

Arun and Nirmala reached their new house after about an hour. The packers and movers' staff started shifting the household stuff to their flat. Nirmala was directing them in placing the stuff to her satisfaction. It took nearly two hours to put them all into the right places. The flat looked very nice. Nirmala entered the new kitchen to prepare coffee, and later, she served it to the helping staff too. The time was about 1 p.m. Nirmala and Arun were feeling hungry. She didn't feel like cooking and told him to get ready to go out for lunch at a nearby restaurant. They both went to the restaurant to have their lunch.

The SSLC board had announced the date of tenth-standard results, and ten days were left for it. Sharma uncle invited Nirmala and Arun to come along with them for a vacation. They had planned to visit Ooty and to stay there for three days. Nirmala also wanted a change and agreed happily.

Next day, everyone reached Ooty and lodged at the Mahindra resort. Unusually, the weather there was chill and foggy. Arun was very enthusiastic and got up early to roam around the outskirts of Ooty on a rented bicycle. Nirmala became tense since he was going alone. He told her not to worry, as he was carrying a road map.

Riding the bicycle, Arun covered nearly fifteen kilometres from his resort and saw beautiful hill slopes with tea gardens all around. It was early morning covered with fog, and he stood near a tea garden to watch the beautiful view. He was hearing birds chirping. A little later, he heard the melodious voice of a girl singing a romantic song. Curiously, he looked around to see who was singing. He could not see anybody out there and the voice vanished gradually. A little later, he heard the same voice again. Curious, Arun parked his bicycle and followed the voice; he went inside the tea garden covering about two hundred metres' distance but he failed to trace the voice source. He frustratedly looked around and did not find anybody. A little later, he walked back outside the tea garden and went to the place where he had parked his bicycle. To his surprise, he didn't find the bicycle, and with frustration, he kicked the ground. He guessed that someone was trying to fool him; he said to himself, 'Let's wait, how long can they fool me?' and stood silently looking round.

Nearly thirty minutes had passed. Arun became anxious, thinking about the distance from that place to the resort. A little later, quite far from him, he saw a girl, riding a bicycle along with a small boy. To Arun, she looked very beautiful, and it looked as though an angel was coming out from the clouds with thick fog around her. She looked more charming with her long hair.

As she came riding the bicycle near him, his heart had begun to thump vigorously for the first time and he felt his heart and mind were attracted to her. The love bug had bitten him and he stood watching her like a statue, dreaming about her.

Arun woke up from his lovely dream as he heard, 'Hello, are you dreaming? Why are you roaming around like a Romeo?' Stammering, Arun replied, 'Yah . . . No . . .' and the girl giggled loudly. A little later, he looked at her bicycle and was surprised when he realized that it was actually his. She got down from the bicycle, and surprised Arun asked, 'Excuse me, this is my bicycle, why did—' And before he could finish, the girl replied with the speed of an express train, 'Oh! So this is your cycle. I am really sorry! I am Anu. Actually, what happened is that while we were passing by a tea garden, this boy fell down and hurt his leg badly. Since no one was around this cycle and since it was a bit urgent to take this boy to a doctor, I took him to a nearby clinic on your bicycle. I'm sure you won't mind if I borrow your cycle again to drop him at his house. It's not far . . .' Arun didn't get a chance to speak a word. He slowly realized that the small boy had hurt his leg and she had got it dressed with bandage. While Arun was realizing this, Anu swiftly took the boy on the cycle to drop him at his house, without waiting for Arun's reply.

Arun gave a dreamy smile looking towards Anu. Within a few minutes, zooming, she came back, riding his bicycle along with a girl, and hurriedly getting down from the bicycle, she said 'Thanks a lot, she's my sister Shwetha . . .' and paused as she was a bit tired. Arun was constantly smiling at Anu; he offered her a handshake and said, 'Hi, I'm Arun from Bengaluru,' and felt a thrill as she held his hand for a handshake. Anu replied, 'Oh! Even you are from Bengaluru . . .' and continued speaking.

A little later, all of them began to walk. Curiously, Anu asked the whereabouts of his stay in Ooty since she saw him wandering in this place.

Arun replied, 'Mahindra resort.' He suddenly realized that he was getting late and worriedly said, 'Oops! It's already late; my sister will be worrying about me . . .'

Realizing that Arun was tense, the helping-natured Anu said, 'Don't worry; my uncle's farmhouse is just about a kilometre from here. You can call her from there. Every day my uncle passes by your resort to go to the city in his jeep, he will drop you,' and she smiled. She then took him to the farmhouse.

In the farmhouse, Arun saw around twenty members including about ten children who were busy chatting. Some children came near Arun and greeted him as he entered. Anu introduced Arun to everyone. The children pulled his hand and invited him to play with them. Meanwhile, Anu explained to her uncle about what had happened and asked for his help. Anu's uncle asked for the name of Arun's sister, and Arun replied, 'Her name is Nirmala.' He then gave a call to Mahindra resort, asked the reception to connect to Nirmala's room, and passed his mobile to Arun so he could speak with his sister.

'I met my friend on the way and he took me to his uncle's farmhouse. Don't worry, I will be back soon,' Arun said with a lie, on hearing his sister's voice. Hearing his lie, everyone laughed because Anu had already told them about what had happened. Anu's uncle invited Arun to have breakfast.

'No, I already . . .' he replied hesitatingly.

Patting Arun on the back, he said, 'OK then, stay here until noon and we can have lunch together,' and all of them giggled, including Arun. He then had breakfast with them.

After having their breakfast, Anu and Arun spoke about their studies and their near ones. He enjoyed being in such a large family as Anu's. He thought to himself, 'How joyous she is; money can't buy happiness . . .' and before he could continue thinking, Anu's uncle told Arun to put his cycle in his jeep and he did. Arun wished them well and the jeep moved. He already began cherishing the moments that he spent with Anu. He looked very happy and energetic.

Arun got down from the jeep as he reached the resort and he thanked Anu's uncle after taking his bicycle from the jeep. Nirmala was waiting tensely. She was relieved as she saw him coming. He parked his cycle and came near her. Arun became a little hesitant when she asked about his friend whom he met and whose farmhouse he even visited, and Arun lied, saying, 'He was in the other section of my class, I just know him, that's all.' Meanwhile all got ready to visit the Coonur garden. After two days, the vacation ended and they returned to Bengaluru. Arun could not forget the time that he spent with Anu in Ooty. He often thought about her and remembered asking about her residence, to which she casually replied with the address of the area where she stayed.

After a few days, the results were announced and Arun secured above 92 per cent. Nirmala was happy and satisfied looking at his success, as he had missed two years of schooling, because of problems in their family that they had. Nirmala asked him to bring the application forms of various colleges. Riding his bicycle, Arun went to various colleges, collecting forms. By afternoon, he had collected two forms and finally went to the Presidency College, where there was already a big queue to buy the application forms. A girl in the queue was familiar. Arun moved closer towards the girl; his heart was thumping faster. It was not Anu but she resembled her from behind. He went back disappointedly to join the queue later. After collecting the form, he thought to himself, 'Anyway, I am near her area, why not roam around to find her? Who knows, I might just see her by chance,' and he roamed for about thirty minutes but he couldn't find her. He disappointedly returned home later.

All the colleges had announced the first list of candidates eligible for admission. Arun was in the first list of all the colleges that he applied to. Nirmala chose the Presidency College and got him admitted in the science branch. One day, Nirmala and Arun went to a shopping mall at Jayanagar. She was busy selecting the clothes for Arun and herself. He came out of the shop to look around, leaving his sister alone to select dresses. Suddenly, he heard a voice and it was a familiar one. 'Oh God,' he said and curiously looked around. A little later, Arun saw Anu along with her friends, leaving the front gate of the mall. Quickly, Arun came out of the mall and ran towards her but she had already boarded a bus. Arun also ran to board the bus she boarded and succeeded in getting inside. He sat behind Anu, covering his face using a kerchief and decided to follow her until her house. The bus stopped at the next stop and a fat lady entered the bus. She angrily told Arun to go to the back since he was sitting on a seat that was reserved for ladies. Turning back, Anu saw him going to the back and laughed. She knew that he was following her because he was still covering his face while going to the back. Quickly she got ready to get down at the next stop, stood near the front door, and quickly got down before he could see. Arun saw her crossing the road as the bus moved, and quickly tried to get down but failed since he was stranded between passengers. An aged person scolded Arun, because he was trying to get down from a moving bus.

Arun got down at the next stop and quickly hired an auto to reach home. Nirmala had already reached the house ten minutes earlier. Looking at Arun angrily, she asked, 'Where did you vanish?'

'Sorry, Didi, I met my friend and he called me to have coffee. As we were chatting, we lost our sense of time. When I returned, you weren't there.'

After hearing his reasoning, she said, 'OK, OK,' and entered the kitchen to cook.

Looking up, Arun murmured, 'To succeed in love, it's so difficult, I lied to my sister. Sorry, God,' and he thought that he would meet Anu sooner or later in future.

Though Anu was behaving naughtily, she had a big heart. She spent her summer holidays in a good and helping way, in that she gave tuition classes for the Kannan slum children in a study centre that was run by three senior citizens to help the slum children, and Anu volunteered to lend her services by giving classes during her school holidays. One of them provided a room adjoining the Kannan slum area and the others gave necessary stationery. Anu was encouraging the handicapped and the downtrodden children to come regularly at evenings to learn. The number of students gradually increased, as the children felt that the classes she gave were very entertaining and they were enthusiastic to learn the alphabet, numbers, etc. The strength of the class had risen to thirty children.

The dengue fever had spread around Bengaluru. Anu was insisting the children should come as neatly as possible. Anu's mother was tense, as she was spending her time with the slum children, but Anu didn't care. One day, she noticed many of them were absent and came to know from other children that they were suffering from fever. After discussion, Anu and the three senior citizens approached a nearby doctor, persuading him to test the slum children's health. He agreed to test them on the condition that they should come clean.

Next day, at the study centre, Anu informed all the slum children to come for the medical check-up and also told them to bring other children along. To her surprise, nearly fifty children had come for check-up and some came with their parents. The doctor began the check-up and gave the necessary medication. Anu and the retired persons had dressed the wounds of the children and they also met the medicine's expenses. Later, Anu called all the children to gather, and a senior citizen distributed a phenol bottle to each family. Anu told them to spray the phenol on the open sewage lines that were near their houses and on the floorings as well daily. All the children listened carefully and they assured her that they would do as she advised.

At home, Anu was busy adjusting flowers in a vase and she heard the landline ringing. Her sister Shwetha answered the call and loudly called, 'Anu Didi . . . Didi, Sandhya is on the line, come quickly!'

Anu came to take her call and spoke. 'Hello, Sandhya.'

'Hello, Anu! You know, tomorrow is the first day of our college,' Sandhya said enthusiastically.

'My God, can't believe days are running so fast,' Anu replied, restlessly looking at the calendar.

'Don't worry, just inauguration, we can have a nice time,' Sandhya said in an energetic voice.

'Oh God, from now onwards, I have to start getting up early. I have become lazy since holidays. What I will do is, tomorrow I will get up early so I can practice getting up early but I'll bunk off college tomorrow, because I can't get up early and also attend the college on the same day,' Anu replied frustratedly. Sandhya banged the phone angrily because Anu poured cold water on her enthusiasm for attending the first day of college.

Anu wanted to call back Sandhya to cool her down and anxiously looked towards the kitchen whether her mother was looking at her. Her mother stared, as Anu dialed the number. 'Please, Mom, just allow me to speak for a minute,' Anu pleaded.

'Shut up! You say one minute but you will speak an hour. Your father was angry at me when he saw the last month's bill.'

The reason Anu's mother was worried about the bill was that Anu's father wanted to minimize his household expenses by avoiding expenses that were not actually needed, because he had bought a house by taking loan from a bank, for which he was paying instalments. This necessitated that he restrict generously giving pocket money to his daughters and he himself was providing them with what was needed in the best possible way. He did not allow them to spend lavishly, as he always had their future in mind. Sometimes with no other option, Anu was reasoning with her father to extract small amounts from him to buy something when her wallet was dry and that too when there was an absolute need. Anu's father did not allow his wife and Anu to have a mobile phone either and restricted his daughter from giving the phone number to boys.

'Don't blame me for that inflated bill! That hefty bill is a result of you calling uncles and aunts for a lengthy chat,' Anu replied teasingly and ran out to escape from her mother. Her mother gave a fed-up smile because there was truth in Anu's statement and also it was very normal to get these kinds of answers from Anu. Anu's mother suddenly realized that she had left vegetables to fry and forgotten. She tapped her head herself and hurried to the kitchen. Quickly, she called Shwetha to call Anu. When Shwetha entered the kitchen, she overheard her mother murmuring, 'Nowadays she's giving a lot of back answers, I'll have to take action before the water rises beyond the head.' Shwetha thought that Anu was going to be punished by their mother and happily went to call her. Looking at Anu, Shwetha innocently lied, 'Didi, Didi, Mummy is calling you, she gave me some sweets, come quickly!' Ignoring her, Anu quickly ran towards her father, as she saw him entering the gate. She stretched her hand before he could enter the house and asked him for forty bucks to buy bangles for a function.

Shwetha saw Anu asking money from their father. She came near their father and said, 'Daddy, she—' Before she could complete the sentence, Anu quickly closed her mouth and whispered in her ear, 'If you don't keep quiet, I'll tell Daddy about the twenty rupees that you took from him.' Seeing that Shwetha was not fully convinced, Anu continued, 'Idiot, shut up, I'll buy you a chocolate.' Shwetha showed two fingers, indicating that she would take two chocolates to keep quiet. Their father thought that they were playing something and he went inside smilingly.

A little later, Anu went to a nearby telephone kiosk and asked the shop owner to give change by handing over a ten-rupee note. There were three to four customers and he irritatedly took two coins of five rupees each and gave these to Anu.

Looking at the coins, Anu said hurriedly, 'No, uncle, please give me one-rupee coins.' After receiving one-rupee coins, she gave a call to Sandhya and said, 'I am really sorry, yaar, please forgive me. Mother did not allow me to call you back, so I am calling from a booth, surely I'll come tomorrow. You're my sweet darling . . .' Anu was a little loud and spoke with her friend for about ten minutes. The shopkeeper overheard Anu's talk, and turning towards his other customer who stood near him, he angrily said, 'This generation is fast turning out to be the worst of its kind. Especially girls, other than speaking with their boyfriend they are left with no better work.' Anu heard him commenting; meanwhile, his son aged about twenty years was demanding for the shopkeeper to give money to pay the college fees. The shopkeeper told him to wait, as he had to attend to the customers, and she learned that he was the shopkeeper's son.

After putting down the receiver, Anu straightaway came near the shopkeeper's son, who sat on a shop's step, and deliberately asked, 'Hello, brother, please, can you give your pen?' and he gave her the pen; she took a sheet and pretended writing on it, again smilingly she asked, 'Brother, what's your name and which course are you studying?'

'Pradeep, sixth-semester commerce course.'

'Do you have a girlfriend?'

'No, sister, he's so stingy, it's difficult to manage myself, how can I?'

'Don't worry, brother, you're so handsome, surely you'll get a nice one,' she said, tapping his shoulders. She even winked her eyes and was also laughing loudly. The shopkeeper noticed that his son was speaking closely with Anu.

After all the customers left, the shopkeeper's son went near his father to collect money for the college fees and Anu followed him. As both went near the shopkeeper, Anu was whispering in the shopkeeper's ear, 'Uncle, personally I want to talk to you, that's why I came here, my dad is a lawyer, Pradeep and I have planned to stay together in future. Please forgive us, I'll convince my . . .' and his son was looking curiously at them, unable to hear her talk.

After hearing her, the shopkeeper exclaimed, 'How dare you!'

'Uncle, you know this generation better than anyone else,' she replied coolly, and his son could not understand their argument and was seriously looking at his father.

'Dad, give me money, I've been waiting for such a long time, you better continue to argue later,' he said and the shopkeeper's blood was almost boiling.

Looking at his son, the shopkeeper said in a high voice, 'Idiot, get out from here and I'll talk to you later!' Looking at his father's anger, he restlessly turned to leave that place. While going, he turned back to look at his father. His father grunted at him and he quickly went away. A little later, thinking of his son's future life, the shopkeeper realized and decided to settle the matter immediately with Anu.

'Please leave him. Don't separate us. Kindly let me know as to what's that you want from me to leave him, I'll try to fulfil that,' he said pleadingly.

Looking seriously at the shopkeeper, Anu pointed at a jar which contained chocolates. 'These chocolates are enough for me to leave your son,' Anu replied and quickly he took the jar containing chocolates and packed all of them to give to her. After giving them to her, he pleaded for her to leave the place.

Anu was laughing and said, 'Don't worry, uncle. I'll not come in your son's way.' Meanwhile, the shopkeeper's eighteen-year-old daughter came to serve him coffee. Curiously, Anu saw her and recalled that she had seen her several times before with a boy. Anu whispered in the shopkeeper's ear, 'Uncle, I was just speaking with my boyfriend and did not leave my parents for him. But who knows, one day, unnoticed, your daughter may just elope with her boyfriend,' and left the shop to reach her home, holding the packet containing chocolates. The shopkeeper was turning into flames, listening to Anu.

On the way back home, Anu saw few poor children playing on the road and gave them all the chocolates, keeping one for Shwetha. She was also satisfied that she succeeded in teaching a right lesson to the shopkeeper.

A little later, Anu reached home and Shwetha was waiting to collect the chocolates from her. Anu gave her a chocolate; looking at her angrily, Shwetha said, 'Instead of two, you're giving only one, I'll tell Dad about the forty bucks,' and Anu in a convincing manner, replied with a lie.

'I didn't buy it; uncle has given to me freely, as I showed him one hundred rupees that had fallen near the shop, believe me.'

'You liar, don't think that I'm a fool to believe your cock and bull story,' Shwetha said and she ran towards their father and insisted for him to enquire about the forty bucks that Anu collected from him.

'Where are the bangles?' their father asked.

Anu looked grudgingly at Shwetha and then turned towards their father, 'I didn't get the perfect matching bangles, he told me that tomorrow I'll get those so I bought two chocolates, one for myself and the other one for Shwetha, she does not have any other better work except for searching faults in me,' she replied and showed the thirty bucks. The father gave Shwetha a serious warning not to complain again for any reason.

'Stupid, you trapped me, next time I'll make sure that you will have nice blasting from Dad,' Shwetha said angrily, pointing fingers at Anu, and Anu laughed.

'Let's see,' she replied and quickly Shwetha hit her and ran towards their mother to escape, but Anu kept quiet.

At night, Anu couldn't sleep. She felt that she was very alone. Vishaal's memory made her feel so and dully she went to the terrace to watch the moon. Looking at the moon, bringing her elusive thoughts into her mind, she began emotionally sharing her feelings with the moon: 'Oh, moon, sounds great, tomorrow is Vishaal's first day in his college. I hope that he feels comfortable there. Oh, moon, can you tell me when will my destiny allow me to meet him? Did he forget me? Oh, moon, you are always lively, glowing with eternal spirits, you must help me, you must send my feeling to my Vishaal. Make me feel the cool breeze if it reaches him,' and she blew a flying kiss. At the same time, Vishaal was sleeping on the swing and he felt a sudden jerk with a chilled feeling within him. Thereafter, a cool breeze hit Anu's face. Tears started rolling from her eyes. Looking at the moon, she waved at it with a happy note on her face and got down from the terrace to go for a sleep.

Arun also couldn't sleep as he was thinking about the college and Anu. He saw a big book on the shelf, *The Mystery of Miracles in Life*, and he took the book out of curiosity to read. After reading some pages, he thought, 'Do miracles happen?' and fell asleep later.

It was early morning. Anu was riding her bicycle very fast with Shwetha sitting behind her. She looked at a milestone and had already covered twenty kilometres. Some distance away, she saw a boy waving his hands at her to stop the bicycle. She came near him, and as she applied the brakes suddenly, Shwetha was about to fall but managed to get down. Looking at him, Anu was excited that he was Vishaal and he was wearing a brown cap with cream T-shirt. Anu asked him to sit behind her bicycle and he sat. 'I'll show my place,' he said smilingly and Anu started pedalling her bicycle. 'Don't leave me alone and go!' Shwetha screamed and Anu, turning backwards, replied seriously, 'Shut up, I'm going with him, I won't miss this opportunity, you go back walking, later, I'll come back to pick you up.' Anu began pedalling faster. He told her to go straight and both reached a hilly region surrounded by vast grassland. He told her to stop the bicycle and both got down later. A vulture as big as a dinosaur flying came near Vishaal, picking him up, and disappeared in no time. Anu fell on the ground, crying for her loved one. 'Help him, Vishaal . . . Vishaal!' she shouted and got up suddenly from her bed. Later, she realized that it was a dream. She was sweating all over.

Everyone believes that a true prayer always reaches the god; similarly, true feelings always reach the person whom we love truly in our heart. Vishaal also felt some kind of sensation in his heart when Anu cried in her dream for Vishaal. He saw a girl who looked like an angel come near him, holding a bunch of flowers, and his body suddenly jerked. Opening his eyes, he saw his mother was tapping his cheeks. 'Get up, it's already seven,' she said in a high voice, and he got up, cursing himself as he missed seeing the girl's face in his dream. He got ready to attend the college.

Same day in the morning, Deepthi's mother knocked on the door to wake up Deepthi, and she came near the door. 'Wait, Mom,' she said impatiently and opened the door.

'Why didn't you get ready to attend the yoga classes?'

'No, I'm burdened with failures; doing yoga is not helping me either,' Deepthi replied. Looking suspiciously at her, her mother said, 'It's hard to believe that these days you look strange and rude as well,' and she continued, 'OK, tell me, what failures have you faced?'

'No, nothing like that, I'll go tomorrow,' Deepthi replied.

'It would become a missed memorable day in case you miss the first day of your college life,' her mother said, keeping her hands on Deepthi's shoulders, and Deepthi gave a forced smile. Quickly she got ready and wore a pink top with grey pants.

Same day morning, Anu woke up around six o'clock and got ready to reach her college. She wore a dull-grey salwar and thought that it would be thrilling if she saw Vishaal in her college. Shwetha was staring disapprovingly at Anu's oily head and her dress that she wore. 'Didi, looking at your dressing, no person on earth will believe that you're a college student,' she said in a high voice and their mother came running.

'What happened, why are you speaking so loudly?'

'Mom, look at her head, so oily. Is this the way to dress up to go to college, on the first day?' Shwetha asked, and her mother, with a fed-up look, left to go to the kitchen for cooking. After a pause, Shwetha continued, 'Didi, today is the first day of your college life, dress up well,' and showed her a nice dress to wear and insisted she take a head bath, pulling her hand. Instead, Anu angrily pushed her sister inside the bathroom and locked its door bolt. Anu ran to go out but their mother stopped her.

'I won't allow you to go until you dress up neatly!' she said angrily, and honking, Sandhya came in a Scooty. Their mother saw Sandhya neatly dressed up.

'Mom, go quickly, the milk is spurting,' Anu said, and their mother went hurriedly to switch off the stove; meantime, Anu quickly went and sat behind Sandhya on her Scooty. A little later, the mother came out to stop them going but they had already left. Shwetha was shouting, knocking on the door angrily. While driving, Sandhya said, 'I don't understand why you hesitate to dress up well.' And Anu was thinking about Vishaal.

'After meeting my Vishaal, you'll see a change in my dressing, others shouldn't have an eye on me except Vishaal, that's why I want to look simple, and I'm wondering how he might have dressed up,' Anu replied and was trying to imagine him.

'Hundred times better than you,' Sandhya said irritatingly.

Anu and Sandhya were very close friends since they both studied together from eighth standard. Anu had told her everything about Vishaal and her childhood incidents. Sandhya's father was a software engineer and worked in a reputed software company at Jayanagar.

ENTER THE COLLEGE

*A*run wondered why Nirmala had chosen the Presidency College to get him admitted, a little less preferred college when compared to other high-profile colleges. However, Nirmala had enquired well before and had thought that it was the right college for Arun. It was founded in the year 1950, after three years of India's independence, by a group of teachers, most of whom had participated in the freedom struggle. These teachers together decided to open a college for arts, science, and commerce. The state government had granted three acres of land at K. R. Road, near the Basavanagudi area, for the college and the locals also donated generously to build it. It took about two years of construction time and was constructed using blocks of stone. The college was inaugurated by none other than the president of India himself and hence was named the Presidency College of Arts, Science, and Commerce. At the beginning, the courses were up to pre-university level. After five years, arts and commerce courses were extended up to graduation level. They hadn't extended science courses since the PUC science students were leaving the college to join the engineering, medical, and other science-related courses.

The college building was rectangular in shape with large open space as much as twice the size of the whole constructed area in the centre of the building to provide natural light to each and every classroom. All the rooms were constructed adjoining to the corridor leading from the inner open space for entering, and the staircase was at each corner of the corridor. The college had three floors, and the ground floor was occupied by offices, the principal's room, the vice principal's room, room for each faculty member, library room, laboratory room, rooms to keep lab equipments, canteen, etc. The first and second floor had about thirty-six rooms altogether. There were separate staircases for each course. The security allowed the students to enter only after checking their ID cards, in order to know which course they were studying, and barred the other group students from entering the block of a building in which they did not study. There was no connection between the students studying different courses to mingle with each other at first and second floor except small gates in between the corridors, and the gates were locked. The students also did not venture to meet the other course students in the upstairs.

Mr Ramanath, aged about seventy years was the principal, and there were vice principals for arts, science, and commerce divisions, namely Mr Subhas Karuna, Mr Krishna Rao, and Mr Abdullah respectively. Mr Subhas Karuna, aged sixty-three years, was the most popular. His father was a freedom fighter who organized a demonstration at Sivapura near Maddur Taluk, Mandya district during the Quit India movement under British rule. He was one of the founder members of this college and passed away about five years back. His son Subhas Karuna was teaching in this college for the past twenty-four years and also ran the academy of self-defence and martial arts in the college as extracurricular activities. Many students had benefited from the academy and many were serving in the police and army department.

The college had nearly 2,000 students, about 750 students each in arts and commerce divisions and the rest were science students. Perhaps it was the only college in Bengaluru which had not conducted the students' election openly. The administration worked in tandem and addressed all the problems effectively. Only secret ballots were held to choose the student representatives of each section and no politics was entertained. The college also reserved some seats to the students who lived in rural areas. There wasn't any place for caste domination and all were treated equally. The students were emerging bright and intelligent after finishing their courses. Overall, the education imparted was good.

Sandhya had to convince Anu's parents to let Anu join in the Presidency College, as it was a co-education college. 'It's a very good college, she will even have my company,' Sandhya said and they agreed to let Anu join in that college.

Arun reached the college's front gate, riding his new bike, and looked around the college.

On the same day, Sandhya and Anu reached the college and came near the back gate since the road from their house led to the back gate of the college, and they entered from there. Remembering her mother's advice, Anu told Sandhya to put her right leg inside before entering and both entered the college.

Sandhya got a call from her father that her grandmother was critical and she had been admitted to a hospital. Hearing this, Sandhya jumped with joy, 'I'll come back in an hour. You know, my grandmother is an evil person. She had tortured my mom a lot. To tell you the truth, my mom died because of her torture. My bad luck, if I return within an hour. If I don't, you can assume that my grandmother got the ticket to go to the highest place,' she said, pointing towards the sky.

'Why are you speaking so harshly and that too about elders?' Anu replied but she ignored the harsh words. Anu decided to go along with her but Sandhya stopped her. 'No, stay here, I'll be back in an hour, cruel people won't die so easily,' Sandhya said and started her vehicle. Dully looking at her, Anu waved her hands.

In the college, Anu sat alone on a long bench which was near the staircase. The atmosphere became deserted, as Sandhya left. Anu started thinking about Vishaal. Everything around her was still. Suddenly, the swaying sound of trees' branches in the strong breeze alerted her. She turned towards the trees and caught sight of a heart shape etched on a tree's bark. She failed to read the names etched next to it as these were vague from weathering. 'Whoever they might be, let their love remain forever,' she thought, and somebody's throbbing footsteps jolted her. She turned towards the staircase and saw a person climbing up the stairs, and a paper sheet was flying in the air near his leg. She thought that the person might have dropped it while climbing. The same sheet came flying near her; she took the sheet to return it to the person climbing up the stairs. She quickly came near the staircase, and looking up at him, she called 'Hello!' but he climbed without responding.

Anu climbed the stairs and saw him climbing the last floor. She came climbing quickly near the last-floor corridor. Suddenly, a strong breeze passed her and she covered her face to protect her eyes. A little later, she uncovered her face as the breeze slowed down. She rubbed her eyes to see him and she walked quickly to approach him, but to her surprise, she could not see him. The surroundings became misty and she began turning in all the directions to find him. A little later, she heard a mesmerizing romantic tune never heard before and her mind had begun to vibrate, and to her, everything looked strange. Following the music to find its source, she blindly ran. The volume of the music increased and she suddenly stopped, realizing that the music was coming from a classroom whose door was partly open. Breathing hard, she came slowly near the door and peeped through the partly open door. She opened the door slowly and the music stopped suddenly. She entered the classroom and to her surprise saw no one. The whole room was very dusty; looking around curiously, she came near the front bench and saw the wording 'I love Kirthi' carved on it. There was an old violin and three to four cassettes scattered in the corner. Curiously, she came near it to see the cassettes. She took them and they were unlabelled. She thought for a while, came near the carved bench, and sat on it. She kept the cassettes on the bench, and looking at the carved words, she prayed, 'Oh God, please help that girl, happily let their love flourish forever,' and dreamily, moved her fingers on the carved words. The door banged suddenly; she saw the person coming who had climbed the stairs earlier, and he stood near her.

Anu looked at him curiously. Tears were rolling down his eyes with depression on his face. With a heart filled with pity, she passed the sheet to him; while passing it, she saw bold letters written in red, '**LOVE NEVER DIES EVEN IF THE WORLD DOES**', which resembled the carved words on the table. Curiously, she said, 'Oh! You are Kirthi's boyfriend. Why are you crying? Has anything happened to her? I pray to God that your love should succeed and remain forever.' She was surprised when she saw him smiling a little but he gave no response, so she said, 'Hi, I'm Anu, what's your name?' He immediately went outside without giving any reply. Quickly, Anu took those cassettes and rushed outside to look for him. Soon she saw a sheet was flying in the air and was about to go into the open space. She jumped to catch and caught it. To her surprise, it was the same sheet that she had returned, and she saw the words written on it: 'Thank you.' She kept it safely in her bag along with the cassettes and went downstairs.

Sandhya saw Anu coming down. 'Hello, instead of searching you could have stayed down here to wait for me,' she said, but ignoring her, Anu was looking around to see him again. 'Hello, listen, what are you looking for? Today no classes, inauguration has already started, come fast,' Sandhya said and dragged her outside. Sandhya saw a big board near the front entrance with 'WELCOME, FRESHERS' but Anu was looking out for the person, and both entered the huge auditorium. All newcomers were seated and Anu looked around to find him.

The hall was almost filled with new students and some were busy introducing themselves. The seniors had begun to perform a cultural programme, and Anu signalled at Sandhya, asking her to come out. A few minutes later, 'It's boring, let's move,' she said.

'*Shh*, it will be over, shut up,' Sandhya replied. Anu could smell the flavour of spices that was coming from outside and pulled Sandhya. 'Let's go, they might have arranged lunch for us,' she said.

The buffet was arranged and servers were making arrangements to serve after the programme was over. The spicy flavour tempted Anu and she pulled Sandhya's hand again to go near the dining hall. A little later, both came near the table and saw a cook who was holding a big bowl that contained hot vegetable biryani. Looking at it, Anu's mouth was watering. 'Uncle, can you please give us some biryani to taste?' Anu asked politely and the cook smilingly gave them some. He looked at Anu to know her opinion on biryani preparation, as she was hogging the food.

'Superb, uncle, never tasted like this before, can you please tell me how to prepare?' she asked and he took five minutes to explain.

Sandhya patted Anu on the back and said, 'If you'd like to be a cook, then simply why attend college?' Anu looking at both, replied, 'You know, even cooking is an art and a profession as well, right, uncle?' and nodding his head proudly, the cook smiled.

Meantime in the auditorium, the seniors' programme ended. Thereafter, the vice principal Mr Subhas Karuna came to the podium and he addressed them: 'Dear students, I'm announcing with regrets . . .'

Arun looked constantly towards the female students who sat on the chairs reserved for them, and he was hoping to find Anu. His attention was diverted as he heard bad news from the announcer, and he looked at the dais.

'Our college has lost a brilliant final-year BA student, Spandan,' and hearing that, Arun jerked, condoling in his heart, and keenly began to listen about the deceased person. 'He actively participated in many social activities; he raised his voice against the corrupt society and fought against the antisocial elements by sacrificing his life. Spandan is no more but his memories will be with us forever. Let all of us observe a minute's silence to pray for his soul, please stand up.' Everyone stood up and prayed for his soul.

Everyone sat after praying and Mr Subhas Karuna announced, 'I request the police commissioner for presenting the medal to their parents as a sign of gratitude and love,' and invited the guest. Later, the programme ended. Finally, he invited everyone to have lunch at the dining hall. Anu and Sandhya joined the line and both had their lunch.

Later, Anu and Sandhya left earlier than the other students did. Sandhya and Anu sat on the vehicle and Sandhya rode. Suddenly, the surroundings turned breezy; Anu closing her eyes, extended her hands sideward, screaming happily. 'I know he must have seen some beauty and fallen in love by now,' she said.

'Idiot, stop illusory thinking about him, otherwise that could lead to your mental imbalance and you will become a subject for psychiatrists' study. You stop mixing present reality into your illusory thinking,' Sandhya said loudly as she was riding and hearing Anu becoming a little dull.

'Sandhya, stop here, I don't want to go home so early,' Anu said dully and got down. Sandhya cautioned her to be ready at around 7 a.m., and left. Sandhya stopped near the signal and turned back to see Anu. She was surprised, as she saw Anu was walking along with an old man and holding some luggage of that man. Tapping her head, she murmured, 'She will never change.' Later, they reached home.

Anu reached home, peeping, entered inside slowly. She confirmed that no one was there and moved fast towards her room.

Suddenly, Shwetha came running from the back door, caught her hands tightly, 'You devil sis, I was punished in the class since I was late to school because of you, I won't leave you,' she said angrily and called her mother in a high voice.

Their mother came quickly, looking angrily at Anu, 'You have grown up like a donkey . . . you still behave like a child. Stop going to college if you want to dress up like this,' she said, and Anu, instead of getting serious, came near Shwetha and whispered in her ear, 'I know you like the bathroom very much—that's why I locked you inside.'

'Wait! I have already told Daddy and you will have it nicely from him,' Shwetha angrily replied, and hit her. A little later, looking at Anu, Anu's father called her to his room.

Before entering his room, she applied quickly some talc powder on her face, combed her hair and as she entered, 'What's this, being such a grown-up girl, can't you understand how to dress up? Everyone will watch you, dress up neatly, don't spoil my image and get some water, go,' their father said harshly.

With tears filling her eyes, Anu went to the kitchen and took a glass of water; instead of giving it to their father, she drank it herself. She went to her room dully.

Shwetha was reading; she saw tears in Anu's eyes and said, 'Didi, I don't understand why you won't dress up well for going to college. All the neighbours dress up so well, you know some even have boyfriends,' she said with sympathy, and Anu reacted seriously.

'Stupid! Mind your own business, you're insisting for me to dress up well and have a boyfriend,' she replied angrily.

'I didn't mean it in that way,' Shwetha said in a convincing manner.

'Shut up! You haven't reached that age to speak like this, be in your limits,' Anu said in a sharp voice.

Same day in the morning, Vishaal was tense looking at his watch and asked his mother to serve his breakfast quickly. His mother was watching a serial and applying jam on a bread slice as well. He grabbed the bread slice from her, stuffed the slice into his mouth, and chewed it hurriedly. He looked at the mirror to see how he looked; a little later, he went, swinging his bag, and saw his friend Prashanth, who resided near his house, was sitting on a bike. Vishaal sat behind him and asked him to start the bike. Laughing at him, Prashanth said, 'Hey, dude, it's your bike, mine is in the service station,' and Prashanth sat at the back of the seat, allowing him to ride.

'Wait, dude, I forgot to pull my pants' zip,' Vishaal said and was a bit embarrassed.

'I was sure that something will go wrong with you, as you were looking at the mirror for such a long time, pull it fast, dude,' Prashanth said, laughing.

Fuming at him angrily, Vishaal replied, 'You rascal, I'll kill you,' started his bike, and moved fast to reach Stephen's College.

Prashanth was a habitual Eve teaser and teased many girls before reaching his college. Vishaal and Prashanth reached Stephen's College around 9 a.m. It was a very big and reputed college in Bengaluru. Most of the bureaucrats, officials, and the rich business class's children preferred to join this college. Only those who came out with good percentage were able to get their admission. Ragging by the seniors was common here. Vishaal and Prashanth entered the college field, after attending their orientation programme. Both heard a huge roar from the seniors. Tensely looking at the seniors, Prashanth said, 'Dude, better let's escape from here, sure they'll rag,' and pulled Vishaal's hand.

'Dude, be cool, if not today, surely tomorrow they'll rag more severely, let's face them,' Vishaal replied, and both went near the seniors but Prashanth was not much convinced.

'It's better to get out,' tensely he said and, moving backwards, stared feverishly at the seniors. Vishaal walked slowly towards the seniors and then tried to move a bit faster away from them.

Looking at Vishaal, one of the seniors called him loudly, 'Hey, you come here!' and asked his name as he approached them. He replied in a relaxed way, and as they were about to unbutton his shirt, he folded his arms, looking at the seniors.

Vishaal pointed at Prashanth. 'Sir, that guy is not willing to come,' Vishaal said deliberately. They asked his name.

'He's Prashanth,' Vishaal replied politely. Most of the seniors walked quickly towards Prashanth, with added enthusiasm. He ran in rocket speed when he saw them approaching him, and the seniors chased him.

Looking at the chase, Vishaal laughed and sat on his bike to start. Meanwhile, Deepthi screamed at the seniors to stop chasing Prashanth; hearing her scream, they stopped chasing and looked at her. Panicking Prashanth didn't stop running. Prashanth came running right opposite to Deepthi; she stopped him from running and offered him water quickly. He thanked her and saw Vishaal getting down from the bike, and Prashanth hit him with his bag angrily. 'You scoundrel!' he said.

'Cool down, dude, I got my revenge,' Vishaal replied, winking his eyes.

Meantime, Deepthi argued with the seniors, showing some note, and succeeded in convincing them not to rag. A little later, looking at Prashanth, she said seriously, 'You must say sorry to my friend since you teased her near the traffic signal.' He pretended to oblige and folded his hands, looking at her friend whom he had teased.

'Extremely sorry, Hilfiger, nice to meet you,' he said smilingly and offered a handshake. Deepthi and her friend Shruthi gave an angry grunt.

Looking at Deepthi, Vishaal asked curiously, 'OK, by the way, miss . . . how did you stop them from ragging?' And Deepthi gave the same note to Vishaal; it read, 'According to law under section . . . ragging is a punishable offence.' After reading it, Vishaal raised his eyebrows. Deepthi softly said, 'You know, guys, this is my dad's signature, I just lied to them that he's a judge.'

A little later, they started to introduce themselves; looking at Deepthi, Vishaal said, 'I'm sure that I saw you several times in many functions.' Even Deepthi was nodding affirmatively; they exchanged their parents' names and learned that their fathers were friends. Later, all of them sat on their bikes.

'Bye, Deepthi. Bye, Hilfiger,' Prashanth said smilingly and Vishaal giggled. Shruthi gave an angry grunt at Prashanth. Deepthi controlled her laugh and pretended to be serious. Later they all left to reach their homes.

Next day in the morning, Anu got up early to get ready for college. She looked very gorgeous, as she wore an attractive designer dress. Shwetha gaped with eyes wide open. 'Wow!' she said. Anu's mother saw Anu was dressed well and was happy. She then saw that Anu's hair was wet and told her not to tie it.

'Why are you going in a hurry?' her mother asked suspiciously, because Anu was early and also because, unlike every day, she wore a very attractive dress.

'It's already six forty, the bus arrives at seven twenty. If I miss that bus, then I have to catch two buses, OK bye, Mom,' Anu replied and left in a jiffy.

Anu reached the bus stand and she was waiting alone. Later, a person passed near her; he said softly, 'Hi, babes.' A little later, another person came near her and watched her constantly. She prayed tensely, 'Please come, 36, 36, 36,' and thanked God as she saw the bus arriving. With a sigh of relief, she boarded the bus. She peeped outside to see whether the person was still standing there. She was relaxed when she saw him standing at the bus stop. She reached the college finally. To her surprise, very few were present.

Anu felt restless sitting alone and she began thinking about the person whom she had met yesterday. She went towards the art section's entrance to reach the last floor and saw there was no one to guard. She reached the same classroom and entered slowly. She saw the person whom she had met yesterday, and he was setting the violin strings. Smilingly, she greeted him, 'Hi!' and he gave a short smile but didn't react much. Anu continued to talk. 'Don't you remember me? Yesterday, I met you. I'm Anu,' and she went near him. He didn't speak a word and played the violin to try some tunes, without looking at her.

Anu was hearing the tunes. 'Wow!' It's very nice, if you don't mind, could I know your name? Yesterday, I looked all around the college but could not find you. Don't you get bored being alone? OK, now I understand, the one who truly loves from their heart chooses to be alone, dreaming about their loved ones when they are not around. In fact, they have nothing except their hearts are filled with love for their loved ones,' Anu said emotionally. He gave a pleasant look at Anu and smiled but she didn't realize that he was smiling at her and continued expressing her views about true love: 'One day or the other, I'm sure that I'll learn about your love story. Don't hesitate to reveal it to me. I will definitely help you out if needed,' she said.

'Thank you,' he replied softly and left the room.

Anu followed him quickly. 'Hello! Which class are you in?' she asked in a high voice, and without responding, he was walking away in the corridor. She asked him to stop and he turned towards Anu and said, 'I love Kirthi!'

Anu gestured at him to wait and came near him. 'Don't worry; your love will succeed!' she said, showing her thumbs up, and saw tears rolling from his eyes. Waving his hands, he replied, 'Thanks a lot,' and moved backwards, looking at her.

'Wait, I'll help you if your love is true!' she said. A strong breeze suddenly passed her, everything looked blank for a moment, and he wasn't there when the breeze stopped. The atmosphere had turned dark with clouds and soon it started drizzling. Surprisingly, for a while, thinking about that person's strange behaviour, she looked around to see if she could find him but she couldn't. A little later, she went down the stairs and leaned against a pillar in depression. She exposed her face for falling raindrops and she felt quite relaxed as raindrops fell on her face. Thinking about Vishaal, looking at the falling raindrops, she prayed, 'Let God give you wonderful love, Vishaal, all the best!' and blew on her palm pointing towards the sky. At the same time, Vishaal was riding his bike and felt some kind of chilling sensation within. Suddenly, he applied brakes.

It was the same day and Arun woke up early to reach his college. Looking at Arun's enthusiasm, Nirmala was surprised and asked as to why he was going so early. 'Didi, yesterday I made new friends, we have decided to play basketball before the classes begin,' Arun replied hesitatingly, with a lie. He finished his breakfast quickly and left for the college. Nirmala came outside quickly to give him the lunch box. 'Oh, sorry, Didi, I forgot,' he said and she smiled, waving her hand.

Arun rode his bike fast to reach the Srinagar bus stand and looked around if he could see Anu around the bus stand since he thought that Anu might be waiting for a bus to reach her college. Seeing that she wasn't there, he moved to next bus stop to see if she was waiting there and covered nearly six bus stops. While riding his bike, he looked around the footpaths, applied sudden brakes several times to avert collisions with other vehicles, and was scolded by other people on the road. Ignoring them, he drove his bike towards the nearby colleges to look for Anu. A little later, he looked at his watch and it showed eight fifty. Still ten minutes were left for the main gate of his college to be closed. He rode his bike fast to reach his college and saw the security guard was closing the gate. 'Wait!' he said in a very high voice. He drove the bike very fast inside the college and parked his vehicle quickly to reach his classroom.

It was still drizzling; Arun began searching for his classroom, and some distance away, he saw a beautiful girl with soaked hair, leaning against a pillar. Though he recognized her, he wanted to make sure of himself again; he ran like a sprinter towards the arts section. Breathing hard, he slid behind a pillar.

'Hey, how amazing, she's Anu!' his eyes spoke and he became breathless looking at her.

Looking at the rain, Anu opened a mint wrapper dreamily but the mint fell down and she looked disappointedly at the fallen mint since that was the last one left with her. She moved dully from that place to search for her classroom. Arun, with some mints in his hand, followed her quickly; his heart had begun to beat faster, and swiftly moving, he took a long step right opposite to her, stretching his hand. 'Want to have a mint?' he said smilingly and Anu was shocked seeing him.

'Hello, Arun, did you join here, which course have you taken?' she said smilingly and took a mint from his hand.

'Science bio, what about you?' he asked excitedly.

'Even I took the same course,' she replied.

'But how come you're here in the arts section?' he asked curiously.

'I'm looking for my friend,' she replied with a lie.

Arun and Anu searched for their classroom, and both were in the same section. Arun becoming happy, looked towards the sky. 'Oh, the book of miracles, thank you,' he spoke to himself.

Sandhya saw Anu along with Arun entering into the classroom, and Anu introduced Arun to Sandhya later. After introduction, Arun went and sat in the last row. A little later, a boy came, sat next to Arun, and introduced himself as Madan. Both shook hands and Arun introduced himself. Anu and Sandhya found enough space to sit together later. A little later, looking at Anu, Sandhya asked curiously, 'How come you know him?'

'You know, once I told about Ooty guy . . . tea garden . . . his cycle,' Anu briefly said and Sandhya, recalling quickly, said, 'Ha ha, got it.' Meantime, Arun was looking dreamily at Anu; he began recalling his memories that he had with her in Ooty. Everyone was waiting for the professor's arrival to start the class.

The professor entered the classroom; introducing himself, he said, 'I'll give chemistry classes. How many of you have a desire to grasp this subject?' Nearly half of the students raised their hands, and Sandhya and Anu exchanged looks but Arun was soaked in the happy moments that he had spent with Anu. Madan distracted Arun by pulling his sleeves and he began to hear the professor's talk.

'As you all have taken the science course, it's not that simple subject to mug and throw the book aside. This subject has no limits, and if you understand clearly, that'll remain forever in your mind. How much you read daily is not important, how much you are able to grasp is all that will make the difference. I am hoping that all of you have understood what I have said and wish you all to move on the right track,' and Arun listened seriously. A little later, the professor began to explain the introduction of the subject.

Arun stood up a few times to have a look at Anu, pretending to clear his doubts, but to his disappointment, Anu didn't turn back even once. After explaining, the professor, pointing at Anu, asked, 'What's the forward reaction of $CuSO_4$+?' and she was a bit confused to answer that, although she knew it. Sandhya whispered the answer but she ignored her. 'Very bad, this must not be the case with you, be prepared for tomorrow, I will ask you again,' the professor said, and after the class ended, he left the classroom.

During lunch break, Anu and Sandhya sat together to have their lunch. 'You look so gorgeous, hope nobody made eyes at you today,' Sandhya said.

'Not only eyes, I even faced words.'

'What happened?'

'A guy told me, 'Hi, babes".'

'It's common, don't take that into your mind,' Sandhya said, consoling her. 'I threw those into the gutter,' Anu replied and Sandhya giggled. Both finished having their lunch, and they moved towards the corridor. Arun was standing leaning against a pillar and was busy talking to his new friends. Anu imagined Vishaal standing with them and dreamily said to herself, 'Vishaal, you should have joined here.'

Looking at Arun and his dressing style, some girls were admiring him. He felt irritated, as some girls were throwing looks at him and he left that place. Later, everyone went to their classes.

In Stephen's College, Prashanth was busy in taking some notes and pulled Vishaal's shirt to clear his doubts. 'Wait, Arun,' he replied absent-mindedly, and Deepthi looked back at him, surprised. Shruthi expressed her surprise to Deepthi, as he mentioned the name Arun.

'Yah, I heard, we can find many guys bearing Arun as their name,' Deepthi said, ignoring her, and later, the classes came to an end.

After the classes were over, Arun introduced his friend Madan to Sandhya and Anu. They all sat together to speak for a while about the coaching and Sandhya pulled Anu, indicating that she had to attend her tuition. Everyone left except Arun and sat alone to revise the day's portion.

Arun reached home and Nirmala asked curiously about the coaching. 'Fine, oh, I forgot, fantastic. I told you in Ooty that I met a friend; she's studying in my college and is my classmate as well. Her name is Anu,' he blabbered blindly. Meeting Anu had made him energetic.

'As far as I remember, you told me that your friend was a boy, on the phone. How come *he* has changed into *she* so fast?' she asked with a smile and moved her hand on his hair. Arun told her everything about what had happened in Ooty, and Nirmala laughed.

'Sorry, Didi, I lied to you,' he said regretfully.

'Come on, that's OK,' Nirmala replied.

Sandhya dropped Anu at her house. Anu had her food in a hurry. She went to her room and felt that studying the science course was tough so she would require a fixed schedule for studying. She took a notepad, 'From now onwards I shouldn't be disturbed by thinking so much about him,' she thought and started scribbling on a notepad: 5.00 p.m. to 7.30 p.m. study, 8.00 to 9.00 p.m. watching television, 9.00 to 10.00 p.m. writing, 10.00 to 11.00 p.m. thinking of him. 'I must avoid thinking about him in the college,' Anu said to herself.

Shwetha wondered why Anu went to her room so early and silently entered the room to see what she was doing. She saw the written pad, read it loudly and curiously asked, '10.00 to 11.00 p.m. thinking about whom?' Anu gave a nervous look.

'Stupid, don't you know, thinking about God and doing meditation,' she replied.

'Didi, if you stop fighting with me, it is as good as praying to God.'

'Even gods will fight,' Anu replied with a smile.

Next day in the morning, Sandhya came to Anu's house to pick up Anu to go to college and called her to come quickly, as it was getting late. Anu came out quickly, wiping her mouth, as she had her breakfast in a hurry. They both reached the bus stop. Anu got an assurance from Sandhya that she would not give Anu's address or phone number to any of the boys, including Arun. They both boarded the bus as it arrived, and Anu was shocked as she saw the same guy entering the bus who stood in the bus stop a day before.

'Did you work out maths problems?' Sandhya asked.

'Yeah, I did, except the last problem.'

'It's OK, even I didn't.'

'Hey, look at that guy,' Anu said, pointing at the guy, but Sandhya ignored her. He slid behind a passenger, as Anu pointed at him.

Arun reached the college early and he was playing basketball with seniors. Each time, after shooting the ball into the basket, he looked towards the main gate, expecting Anu's arrival. A little later, Arun saw Anu and Sandhya entering and walked fast towards them. Anu ran towards the arts section entrance, and the guard near the entrance of the arts section asked her to show her ID card for checking. After checking it, he didn't allow her to enter the arts section, as she was a science student. 'Hello, it's me, Anu, please come down, I want to meet you!' Anu called the person in a high voice.

'Whom are you calling? It's arts section,' Sandhya asked curiously.

'Oh, I forgot to tell you, my mother's mom's father's great-granddaughter is studying, exactly, even I don't know. My grandmother has told me to enquire. She has given me some details of her,' Anu said in a humorous way and laughed.

'You liar, I can't believe that. You're up to something, be sure that I'll find it out,' Sandhya blasted her but Anu ignored Sandhya's comments. Seeing them arguing from some distance, Arun came near and asked, 'What's the argument?'

'Nothing, we were discussing about the maths problem, can you solve this?' Sandhya replied with a lie, but ignoring Sandhya and looking at Anu in a helpful manner, he asked, 'Anu, did you get all the problems right?' And Anu, without realizing what Arun asked, she was looking around the field to find the guy.

Showing fake anger at Arun, Sandhya said, 'Hello, I'm the one who is asking you to solve it, not her,' and pulled Anu's sleeve, looking at Anu. 'Hey, you dumbo! He's asking you,' she said and Anu turned towards Arun.

'No, I didn't solve it,' she replied. He took a workbook quickly from his bag and began explaining to them how to solve the problem; meantime, some girls came near him curiously and said, 'Hi, Arun' in a romantic voice. 'Hi,' Arun replied casually and continued to solve the problem, and the girls who came got involved to solve the problem.

Madan saw six girls grouping around Arun. Feeling himself as unlucky, cursing, he said to himself, 'Shit, since morning, only a fellow has noticed me but there, already six girls have grouped around Arun.' And he came near them and greeted them, saying, 'Hi, guys,' but none of them responded as they were concentrating on solving the problem, and everyone solved it except Anu. She put her workbook aside and was busy looking at a corner where there was some greenery. Arun saw her looking elsewhere, and to confirm that she had understood the solution to the problem, he asked, 'Did you understand?'

Sandhya saw that Anu was not responding to Arun, she tapped Anu's head and said, 'Hey, dumbo, see here. Where is your concentration?' and Anu turned towards Arun.

'Yeah, no, I didn't understand properly,' Anu replied and again Arun started explaining.

'Fine, now I got it, thanks Arun,' she said smilingly. Sandhya tapped Anu's shoulders and said, 'No need to have formalities between friends.'

'You're absolutely right,' Madan replied.

Later, Anu ran towards the greenery. Arun followed her curiously. Anu touched a tree trunk that had something carved on it and slowly moved her fingers on the carvings. After clearing the waste from the carvings, she saw that 'I love Kirthi' was carved on the tree. Seeing her near the tree trunk, Arun asked, 'What happened?' sounding a bit suspicious, and she pointed her finger up but continued to look at the carving.

'What?' he asked again. She pointed out a nest on a tree.

'Which bird's nest?' again he asked but her eyes were fixed on the words written. Realizing that she was busy in her dreams, Arun wished her goodbye and left the place to reach home. After a while, Anu went back near the classroom to see the board on which the practical schedule was put up; after looking at it, she went to bus stand to reach home.

After attending their colleges respectively, Prashanth and Sandhya were attending the Pragathi tutorials at Wilson Garden. Nearly, twenty pupils were coming for the first-year science group. Ever since they joined the tutorials, they had not spoken to each other. She was quite good at learning and also a soft-spoken girl. Prashanth was familiar to everyone as he looked very funny and used to crack jokes in the tuition class. Prashanth liked her behaviour and began showing interest in her. He succeeded in tracing her house and he learned that Anu was her best friend when he followed Sandhya and saw them several times together.

It was Sandhya's birthday and she looked very charming. Anu saw her coming on the Scooty and wished her well as she came near. 'Arun wished me a happy birthday, early morning itself,' she said proudly.

'So what? Go and put a crown on his head. By the way, how come he knows your birthday?'

'I told them since I felt like taking you all out for a treat.'

'Did you go to the tuition yesterday?' Anu asked.

'Oh! Don't ask me, I sat helpless in the house like a ghost as it was raining. I went outside after the rain stopped. The streetlights went off suddenly and I had forgotten to wear my glasses. A person stopped his scooter near me, he was wearing a helmet. I thought he was Ajay. "How's your girlfriend Sahana?" I asked him, tapping his shoulders. "Hello, Sandhya," he replied, removing his helmet. To my bad luck, he was Ajay's father. "Sorry, uncle," I told him but he didn't reply and left hurriedly. I went to my neighbour's house. I played chess with a fourth-standard kid and lost my game since I had not worn my spectacles to see the pawns clearly. Yesterday was my terrible day and today I called up Ajay to invite him for a treat but he didn't receive the call. My guess would be that he must be angry because he might be receiving a treat from his father and I'm wondering how to face him again,' Sandhya said dully.

Anu asked Sandhya to stop her Scooty just opposite to a shop near the bus stand, and she stopped. Anu crossed the road, and Sandhya looked at her restlessly as Anu was buying something in the shop. Sandhya thought that she was going to surprise her with some beautiful gift. Sandhya ran blindly, crossing the road as soon as Anu called her, and Anu blasted her for carelessness. Sandhya stretched her hand to receive the gift but it was a chocolate. 'Is this a surprise? Get lost,' Sandhya said with disappointment and didn't take it since Anu said that she would surprise her. 'OK, give it to me, though it may be small, we must take it, a gift is a gift,' she said after a few minutes.

Keeping her face doubtful she said, 'Sorry, Sandhya, I swallowed it, you're too late and I couldn't control my temptation, actually I kept a small piece but it fell down.'

'Where did it fall, into your stomach? I know you very well, idiot!'

'Sorry.'

Later, Anu and Sandhya entered the college, and a little later, Arun came near Anu. 'Boom!' he screamed near her ears. 'I didn't hear you, sorry. Did you say something?' she said. Arun turned towards the other side, closing his eyes tight with a smile, and Anu giggled. Arun and Madan gave gifts to Sandhya, wishing her happy birthday. Anu asked Sandhya to open the gift and she did. Madan had given a beautiful crystal vase, and Arun gave two teddy bears holding a bunch of flowers with some wording written below ('Friends are forever') and Sandhya felt very happy as she saw the gift.

'Sandhya, let's see what Anu has gifted you,' Arun asked eagerly.

'Oh! She said that she will surprise me and then she gave me just a chocolate. I didn't take it. After a few minutes, not to disappoint her, I asked for the chocolate and she said it was already in her stomach.' Arun laughed hearing her reply and

Sandhya continued, 'But she's simply superb. I saw her distributing chocolates to poor children and asked her curiously why she did things like this. "Even they have to enjoy your birthday. Instead of giving them money, sharing happiness with them is just amazing, you know. By giving them happiness, they would feel quite satisfied," she said, pinching my nose. I'm lucky to have such a sweet friend.'

Arun's eyes gradually slid towards Anu. Some of the girls greeted him but his eyes were fixed on her and he did not respond to any of the girls. 'I don't know when you will slide me into your heart. You have impressed me a lot, you are great, Anu,' he said to himself.

After the classes, Sandhya invited Anu, Arun, and Madan, 'Let's all go to Pizza Corner today, it's my treat,' but Anu refused to come and told the three of them to go.

'If you really want me to eat, get it parcelled, keep it in a freezer, and bring it here tomorrow to have it,' Anu said in a swinging voice.

'Stop it; we're not going, OK, guys, bye. Come, Anu, I will drop you back home,' Sandhya said angrily.

'No, just for my sake don't cancel it, please carry on, I won't mind at all,' Anu said, convincing her.

'I know why you are not coming, just because of your father, right? OK, I'll call your mother to ask permission,' she replied, and Anu tried to snatch the mobile from her but she had already dialled the number. Anu became tense as Sandhya was speaking with her mother.

'Hello, aunty, can I take Anu out for a treat? Please, aunty . . . OK, aunty, I'll drop her . . . Aunty, is Shwetha there?' Sandhya spoke with respect. Anu grabbed the phone as she was about to speak with Shwetha.

'Hello, Shwetha, did Mom really say yes for the treat?' she asked in a tense voice.

'Yes, she agreed, Didi, enjoy, even boys are joining for the treat, right?' Shwetha asked in a low voice.

'No, only girls.'

'OK, you swear on Mom, and tell all your friends who are going with you for the treat to speak with me right now. Don't try to fool me, I want to make sure that all are girls.' Anu covered the speaker of the mobile, and looking at Arun and Madan, she said, 'She wants to speak with you guys to clarify that I am not going out with boys. Please speak in a girl's voice. If she knows that I'm going with boys, then she will start blackmailing me,' and passed the mobile to Madan to speak with Shwetha.

'Hello, Shwetha,' Madan spoke in a girly voice.

'What's your name?' she asked suspiciously.

'My name is Madhumitha . . .' Meanwhile, Arun grabbed the mobile from Madan, and he spoke in his own voice, 'Hello, Shwetha.' As she heard Arun's voice, Shwetha opened her eyes wide and asked his name. Anu's eyes met Sandhya's with a shock.

'First tell me your best friend's name,' Arun replied.

'Suma.'

'Have you ever gone out with her?'

'Yah, many times.'

'Yah, similarly, with the same feeling, even your sister is coming out with us, all right? Do you understand?'

'Understood, yah, sorry, enjoy your day, bye.' Shwetha sounded friendly and ended the call.

Tapping his shoulders, Sandhya said, 'Cool, Arun.' Anu started biting her nails, looking at her.

'Trust me, Anu, nothing will go wrong,' Arun said convincingly but Anu, still having some doubt, looked at them. 'If my dad comes to know, I'm sure he won't let me step into this college again,' she said.

'OK, anyway you cannot step into the college again, at least come for the treat with us as a memory,' Madan replied with a smile and she chased to hit him.

'Stupid, that means you've already thought that it's my last day in the college, OK, come, let's go, let the hell fall on my head. I'll face it,' Anu said with frustration.

Later, all of them reached Pizza Corner and entered. Sandhya asked them to order their favourite pizza. Anu read the menu with a flummoxed look. 'Cheese cap will be nice,' Arun said, looking at the menu, and Anu took the menu card from Arun to glance at it.

'No, I don't like that,' Anu said since she had never tasted pizza before, and pretended she was fed up with pizzas.

'Stop pretending, liar,' Sandhya said softly. Arun smiled, hearing their talk. He looked at Anu constantly as she was looking at the menu card, turning the flower vase that was kept on the table.

'Butter ropes will be better,' Anu said, passing the menu card back to Arun. Hearing this, Madan stuck his tongue out.

'As you wish,' Arun said smilingly and called the server to place the order.

'Gone, I'm sure you won't eat that,' Sandhya whispered in Anu's ear as they were served and felt awful as Anu took a bite. Arun's eyes slowly slid towards her.

'Wow, tasting really nice,' Anu said, biting the pizza. She ate hardly a quarter piece of it; that too was swallowed with difficulty and she left the remaining. After some time, as soon Sandhya ate her last piece, Anu said hurriedly, 'Hey, come on, it's already late; I have to reach home fast,' and pulled Sandhya's hand.

'OK, guys, bye,' Sandhya said to Arun and Madan after paying the bill.

Arun waved at them. He pulled Anu's plate slowly and started eating. He chewed the pizza, closing his eyes with a complete feel. Madan looked at Arun and Anu's plate up and down twice. He kept his face closer at Arun's mouth.

'Are you all right?' Madan asked with a fishy look. Arun pushed his face and stood up.

'Hmmm, it's my favourite from now onwards,' he replied, stretching his hand sideways.

Tapping his head, Madan said, 'You're really crazy,' and both left the restaurant to reach their homes.

Anu's mother was waiting restlessly as Anu arrived at 7 p.m. 'Mom, since it's evening, it was crowded, so we waited for a long time to find a vacant dining table,' she said.

'Don't lie, hardly anyone visits before 9 p.m. except on weekends,' Shwetha whispered in Anu's ear.

'Shut up, I beg you, please,' Anu said pleadingly to Shwetha and went to her room to change her dress. Shwetha followed her curiously to ask about the treat. Anu questioned Shwetha how come she knows the exact rush-hour timings.

'My friend told me that her father is working as a main in-charge in one of the Pizza Corner branches,' Shwetha replied.

Arun reached his home and told Nirmala that he had birthday treat at Pizza Corner. After some time, she called him to have dinner but he refused, saying, 'My stomach is full.'

'The food will simply be wasted, should've informed me before about your treat,' Nirmala said.

Later, Arun was thinking; he suddenly got up from the chair and told her to pack the food in a container.

'For what?' Nirmala asked curiously.

'I'll tell you later,' Arun replied and told her to get ready for going outside with the food packet.

Nirmala packed the leftover food and Arun told her to sit on the bike as she came out. The time was around eleven o'clock. They stopped at the corner of the footpath after driving through the main road. They saw many people including children were sleeping, except a small girl who was crying with hunger and her mother was tapping her back to make her sleep. Nirmala looked at the small girl with pity and gave the food container to her mother.

The mother opened the container quickly to feed the small girl. Folding her hands, the mother thanked Nirmala, as the small girl began eating. Arun started his bike, riding in a zigzag way. 'Woohoo!' he screamed happily, looking at the stars in the sky.

Nirmala was surprised looking at his enthusiasm and happiness. She wondered how come he was showing so much concern for the poor and saw a change in his attitude as he was not like this before.

'How come you're so happy?' she asked in surprise.

'Anu has brought a change in my attitude. She's stupendous, I felt happy just because I shared my happiness with the small girl.' He sounded a bit emotional.

'I think she's quite interesting, I want to meet her. Can you introduce her?' Nirmala asked and he nodded his head approvingly.

Dussehra festival holidays had begun. Arun called Sandhya and asked her help to him speak to Anu.

'Come on, try this, it will really work. Just close your eyes, and abracadabra, you can not only hear her voice but can even see her as well,' Sandhya said, giggling, and ended the call.

Bitten by love bugs

At the beginning, Vishaal thought Deepthi was somewhat egoistic and seemed to be pampered by her parents, but he changed his perception after he met her frequently in the college. Both were attending the same tuition in Koramangala.

It was Vishaal's birthday, he looked very cheerful, and he invited his friends, including Deepthi, for a treat at Coffee Day. He was walking impatiently, as nobody turned up but Prashanth. Although he was sure that all would turn up, he looked tense.

'Don't worry, dude, you know girls, right? They are latecomers so there's nothing to be worried about,' Prashanth consoled him.

After a few minutes, both saw Deepthi getting down from an auto along with her friends. Vishaal stood near the entrance to welcome them. Deepthi wished him a happy birthday and gave a gift while others gave him flower bouquets.

At the same time, Anu brought back her sweet memories into her thoughts, recalling her expression of love to Vishaal on his birthday.

After having snacks and drinks, everyone left with smiles on their faces after wishing the birthday boy well. Prashanth sat behind on Vishaal's bike, carrying the bouquets that covered his face. As Vishaal started his bike, Prashanth struggled to hold the flower bouquets. Prashanth got down near Vishaal's house, wished him well, and started walking to get to his house. Vishaal was parking his bike and an old man came near Vishaal.

'Has someone passed away in this area?' the old man enquired curiously. Vishaal gave a confused look and turned back. His eyes were left wide open as he saw the whole road was filled with flower petals, and he turned back to see where Prashanth was. Prashanth started walking a little faster away from him when Vishaal began chasing him.

Finally, Vishaal was able to get hold of Prashanth from the back and angrily asked, 'Hey, Monk . . . what's all this?' Prashanth turned back to Vishaal with a little struggle.

'Dude, be cool, keeping these flowers in the house until they dry up and become rubbish demeans their purpose. Instead, try to open the gift that your darling gave you, standing amidst these flower petals. Surely that enriches your feelings and joy,' he replied smilingly and left after wishing him well again.

Vishaal ignored what he had said and entered his house. The sun had already begun to set. At the same time, Anu entered the veranda, thinking about Vishaal and looked at the sky with tears filling her eyes. 'Wherever you are, be happy—happy birthday, Vishaal,' she said emotionally and blew on her palm pointing at the sky. As soon as she blew, the flower petals near Vishaal's house began swirling with a strong breeze. Vishaal saw them, in surprise, through his window and felt a strange feeling. Thinking about what Prashanth had said, he hurried to open Deepthi's gift, and some petals fell on his face. He dropped the gift as his heart shivered and he kneeled on the ground, looking up at the sky.

'This is strange! The moment I was about to open the gift, my heart is reacting,' he said to himself and took the gift to open it slowly. It was a cream-colored college bag with black stripes. Looking at the bag, he said in an emotional voice, 'Oh, Deepthi, you are the one who's thinking about me all these days, thanks!'

and jumped with joy, hugging the bag. He got ready to attend the tuition classes later.

Next day, Anu went to Sandhya's house to meet her and get some help to complete the science assignments. Sandhya informed Anu about Arun's wish to speak with her; meanwhile, Sandhya got a call from Arun, and winking her eyes, she passed the mobile to Anu to let her speak with Arun.

'The Airtel number you are trying to reach is currently not reachable, please try after some time,' Anu said and disconnected the call.

'Stupid, it's Spice!' Sandhya said, laughing, and Anu bit her tongue, raising her eyebrows.

Arun called Sandhya again and asked, 'When did you change your connection from Spice to Airtel?' and sounded a bit flummoxed.

Anu grabbed the mobile quickly from Sandhya after hearing Arun's voice. 'Hello, uncle, my Didi is not feeling well, please don't disturb,' Anu replied in a kid's voice and they both burst out laughing. He didn't call up again.

'OK, tell me, do you love Arun?' Sandhya questioned her.

Anu opened her eyes wide open. 'Shut up, you very well know whom I love. Of course I'm sorry for Arun. I think it is better to tell him soon so he will not get disappointed. He's just a good friend of mine,' she replied seriously, looking at Sandhya.

'Sorry, Anu,' Sandhya said, and both started with their assignments.

After finishing his assignments, Arun wondered why Sandhya didn't speak to him on the phone. He called up Sandhya after an hour and Anu signalled her to speak. 'Hello, sorry, Arun. I couldn't attend to your call, I was not feeling well, my cousin received the call,' Sandhya said softly.

'What about the Airtel connection?'

'No, Arun, mine is the Spice connection why?' Sandhya replied and continued, 'OK, forget it, tomorrow our college opens after two long weeks. Did you finish the three assignments?'

'No, Sandhya, it's four, PCMB,' Arun interrupted and he heard somebody saying loudly, 'Oh! Biology we forgot.'

'Who else forgot?' Arun asked curiously,

'It's Anu,' Sandhya replied, muted the mobile speaker, and tensely looking at Anu, she replied worriedly, 'Oh, we forgot the biology assignment. Oh shit! We don't even have the question paper with us . . .' Anu grabbed the mobile quickly and turned on the microphone.

'Hello Arun, please bring your biology assignments early to college tomorrow so we can copy it. We will be there at seven sharp, don't miss, OK, bye,' Anu said hurriedly.

Tapping Anu's head, Sandhya said, 'You idiot,' and grabbed the mobile to disconnect.

'Oops! What's wrong with me? I spoke with Ar—' Anu said tensely as she realized that she spoke with Arun in an untimely situation.

'Forget it, we will manage something,' Sandhya said, consoling her.

At night, Arun thought about Anu. 'Oh, Anu, it was you who spoke right at the last minute. Your voice has brought back my breath,' Arun said to himself and lay on the bed.

Next day, Anu woke up around 5.40 a.m. and got ready to go to college. Anu and Sandhya reached the college early and saw that Arun was waiting. He waved his book as he saw them. 'Hi, Arun, sorry,' Anu said in a sweet voice. Arun gave a sharp look and smiled at her.

Both started copying the biology assignment; they had completed almost half of it. Suddenly, looking at Sandhya, Anu said, 'Hey, keep writing, I'll be back in five minutes,' and before

Sandhya could realize, Anu left the place quickly to reach the arts section.

'Where, why are you running away like that?' Sandhya asked in a high voice. Arun looked at Anu in surprise. Turning her face towards Sandhya, she replied, 'I'll tell you, I'll be back soon,' and went hurriedly towards the arts section. A little later, Sandhya asked for Anu's pen as he was writing Anu's assignment. 'Sure,' he replied and gave it to her.

'Sandhya, please give back that pen, it's the first thing I've ever touched that belongs to Anu,' he said emotionally. Sandhya paused helplessly and felt sorry for him, looking at Arun.

Anu entered the strange person's classroom and she saw him looking up, thinking deeply, holding his violin. 'Hi, spectacles, nice to see you after a long gap,' she said smilingly.

Looking at her, he replied with a smile, 'Hi.'

'Tell me about Kirthi,' she asked desperately.

'I need to go, bye,' he said and got up to go.

'At least tell your name,' Anu asked but he went near the corridor without responding.

After walking some distance away from her, he turned back and a bit loudly said, 'Spandan . . .' Hearing his name, she walked towards the corridor, but to her surprise, he disappeared in front of her eyes. Unbelievingly rubbing her eyes, she said to herself, 'Is he a magician or what?' and turning back, she saw Arun and Sandhya coming as she heard their voices.

Looking at Anu, he asked curiously, 'What are you doing here?'

'I . . . I . . .' she stammered.

Looking at her watch, Sandhya interrupted hurriedly, 'OK, there isn't much time, only fifteen minutes left,' and pulled Anu's hand. Anu left with them and turned her face to look for Spandan but couldn't find him. Later, they entered into the classroom after completing their assignments.

In the classroom, Arun sat next to Anu and she turned her head away from Arun with frustration. A little later, looking at Arun, she said, 'Why don't you go back to your place?' She sounded a bit angry.

'It's not much comfortable there,' he replied smilingly, and Anu was seriously looking at him.

'But I'm not comfortable sitting here,' she said angrily and went to sit on Arun's bench.

Fa-thud. Anu was on the ground since one of the legs of that bench had broken. Arun went quickly to help her and lend his hand so she could get up.

'Wow! What a great fall,' Madan said, giggling.

'Thanks for your comments,' Anu said, laughing as everyone laughed, and she asked Sandhya to clarify her doubts in physics later.

'It's better if you ask Arun, for doubts in physics,' Sandhya replied.

Anu turned her face towards Arun with a smile, but her smile faded as she saw Arun was gazing at her. Turning towards Sandhya, she said, 'Hey, look at Arun, he's gazing at me,' and Sandhya turned her face towards Arun.

'No, it seems he's thinking deeply but he looks like he's gazing, let's make sure. You move slowly to another bench, and if his eyes stay where they are, he's not gazing at you,' Sandhya said like a psychiatrist. Anu moved slowly towards the side bench but Arun's eyes stayed where they were. Looking at Anu, Sandhya gave her opinion.

'Yes, I was right, he's thinking something.' But Anu looked bewildered when he smiled, gazing at her again, and continued to write when Sandhya saw him again.

During lunch break, four of them sat in a circle. Anu didn't bring her lunch, Sandhya shared her lunch with Anu, and others also shared their lunch with her. 'Why did you go to the arts section early in the morning?' Sandhya suspiciously asked Anu in a low tone.

'Oh, I met a guy when you went to see your grandmother on the first day of college, his name is Spandan. Whenever I meet him, I feel he's . . .' Anu's words were unclear as her throat was choking. 'Whenever I question him, he dis— Today also the same thing hap—' she said in a struggling voice, and in the meantime, Arun went to buy some mints from the college canteen. A little later, he came and offered a mint to Anu. Anu took it with a broad smile. Later, the practical classes came to an end for the day.

Vishaal called up Prashanth to ask his opinion about calling up Deepthi. 'Tomorrow you may as well speak to her in the college. If you still wish to call her, it's left to you,' he replied and Vishaal ended the call with frustration. Later he decided to call Deepthi and dialled her number.

'Hi! I was also thinking of calling you.' Deepthi sounded in a better mood. Vishaal felt very happy; she continued to speak as he asked about some doubts. 'Brainless, you could have told the formula. It is so easy. At least when sir asked you to solve $ax + bx$ . . . the reason why it comes in this form is that if we simplify this problem, we will get that formula. OK, have you revised physics and those problems? Oh, my goodness, what about Newton's law? Those problems are so difficult . . . I have completely gone mad; chemistry is OK . . . and my biology . . . Don't ask for heaven's sake. I'm fed up with those diagrams . . . hello, Vishaal, are you there? Say something. Why are you so quiet?' Deepthi didn't give him a chance to utter a word. Vishaal jerked his head as he was fed up with hearing her endless speech. 'Hello, Vishaal,' she said a bit louder as she didn't get any response from him.

'Ha, what else?' Vishaal asked in a tired voice.

'Yah, that's it and complete your physics record without fail, fine, bye.' Deepthi ended the call finally.

Later, Prashanth called Vishaal. 'I spoke with her, dude, she told me that she missed me and the college a lot,' Vishaal said casually with a lie.

'I told you, dude; you could have spoken to her tomorrow at college, anyway, how did you enjoy her class?' Prashanth asked with a funny giggle.

'How come you know, idiot?' Vishaal asked in surprise.

'Even I had called her up just before you. She was about to begin with her class and told me to hold my call, that she was getting some call from the landline. I was thinking who might be that lucky chap to hear that lady's speech patiently. Who else could it have been? And I was sure that it must be you only,' Prashanth burst out laughing and ended the call.

Later, Vishaal got a message. 'Good night; let your dream girl come in your dream . . .' It was Prashanth's message.

After an hour, he sent another message, 'She should take such a prolonged class that all your hairs must wither like leaves from your head,' but Vishaal ignored the message.

Prashanth's father shifted his residence from Koramangala to Hanumantha nagar, as it was strenuous for him to travel to his shop, which was located near B. T. Road, every day. Prashanth was a little hesitant about shifting the residence since it would mean that he would have to get up early to reach his college. 'Sandhya stays near Hanumantha nagar. Moreover, I can meet Vishaal in the college and also the tutorial is nearer than before.' Prashanth thought that it would be better in some way and stood near the bus stop to reach his college. To his surprise, he saw Anu and Sandhya were standing at the bus stop. Sandhya met his eyes.

'Hey, look at him, he's Prashanth, he comes to my tuition. One day, sir gave us some problems to solve, and later, sir saw that he had not even solved the first problem though everyone completed solving all the given problems. "What's wrong with you?" sir asked him. "Sir, I lost my mobile. If my father gets to know this, he will blast me," he replied. "You rightly deserve to be punished. Why do you want a mobile phone at this age, to show off?" sir asked, and can you believe he replied, "For emergency, sir, and for safety as well . . ." Oh my God, we all couldn't control our laughs, hearing his reply,' Sandhya said, pointing at him but Anu couldn't recognize the guy as there were many people standing alongside.

Pointing at him, Sandhya said, 'Very funny and smart as well, see, he's wearing blue shirt with cream stripes.'

Arun entered his classroom after seeking permission from the physics professor, as he was late for the class. His friends wondered why he was late. Sandhya asked him the reason during lunch break. 'My sister is not feeling well, she has fever,' Arun said dully.

'Why, your mother should have taken care of her,' Anu interrupted before he could say anything further.

'Actually, my mom is . . .' He could not answer further and left the place, walking some distance away.

Madan, looking angrily at Anu said, 'Idiot, I was hinting to you people not to ask him. You know his mother passed away when he was just five years old. He has a sister and he treats her like his mother.' Hearing this, both were shocked.

Anu went hurriedly towards Arun and, to comfort him, kept her hand on his shoulder. He turned slowly and pretended was fine, hiding his tears.

'I'm extremely sorry, Arun.'

'That's OK.'

'Even Sandhya has lost her mother; her mother expired because of blood cancer. She often feels lonely but you have a sister who takes care of you like a mother, she will recover soon, don't worry,' Anu said and his eyes were almost filled with tears.

Never had he felt so relaxed as he felt after hearing Anu's words, and both joined them later.

He looked at Sandhya. 'See, God has bonded both of us into perfectly matched friends, we both are sailing in the same boat,' Arun sounded emotional. Sandhya's eyes were filled with tears as she was serving food for him, and he continued, 'You are never alone, we all are with you forever,' and tapped her shoulder.

They all shared their food and later had ice cream as well. Anu applied ice cream to Sandhya's spectacles and Sandhya chased her. All of them enjoyed forgetting their hardships.

Next day, Sandhya called up Arun to ask about his sister's health. 'She's improving but she is not eating properly. When I had high fever, she served me rasam and rice that reduced my fever. I'm planning to give her the same,' Arun said in a pleased voice.

'You mean you will cook yourself, great.' Sandhya sounded surprised.

'Yeah, could you please tell me the recipe?' Arun asked.

'Oh my God, I've no idea at all, I think Anu is fond of cooking, especially rasam, just hold on. I'll call her from the landline, be prepared to take note of the ingredients when I repeat them,' Sandhya said and immediately called Anu.

'Hi, Anu, I'm coming tomorrow.'

'Sorry, I'm going out tomorrow,' Anu replied in a dull voice.

'It's OK; can you please tell me how to prepare rasam?'

'Aha! Am I speaking to Sandhya, how come you are asking about cooking?'

'Come on, friend, so what? I was able to smell rasam flavour from neighbour's kitchen. You see, I can't go and ask them often. Not good for my reputation, you know. Anyhow it's a holiday, so I thought it's better to try out and prepare it myself,' Sandhya said restlessly.

'OK, make a note of it, first cut two ripe tomatoes, then boil tamarind, put some chillies, garlic . . . After that . . .' As Anu started to tell them the names of the ingredients, Arun started writing on a notepad, and Anu explained in such detail that it seemed like a cookery show was going on in front of his eyes. Both said thanks together after her explanation was over. 'Oops!' Arun said.

'Sandhya, who's that male voice?' Anu sounded suspicious.

'No, dear, can't believe you get doubts like this, he's our neighbour boy who thanked me for a nail cutter that he borrowed, OK, bye,' Sandhya said in a hurried voice and ended the call. Arun giggled after hearing the reason given to Anu by Sandhya.

'Stupid, you always put me into trouble. Anyway, all the best for your rasam; I hope your sister gets well soon, bye,' she said and cut the call.

Arun started preparing rasam by following Anu's recipe, he felt as though she was still in front of him, explaining. He added less salt as a precaution. After the rasam preparation, he added some salt to taste, after tasting the rasam, and the rasam flavour filled the place. Anu lifted her thumb with a cute smile in his imagination and he bowed.

Later, Arun helped Nirmala to sit comfortably and gave her some warm water to drink. She was in a sleepy mood and he fed her hot rice with rasam from a spoon. After tasting it, she took the bowl from him to eat quickly since her taste buds had become active. She could not swallow and he gave her water. She asked him for more rice with rasam and he served. A little later, he gave the medicine and made her wear a blanket. Nirmala caught his wrist and pulled him near to kiss on his forehead when he turned to leave. He tapped her shoulder and went to the veranda. He looked up, facing the sky with a dreamy look. 'Thanks, Anu,' he said to himself, closing his eyes with a smile.

Next morning, Arun was surprised when Nirmala got up and was preparing breakfast. 'Why did you come, how are you feeling now?' he asked anxiously, touching her forehead.

'The rasam with rice that you served was so delicious, you fed me with affection and love and the fever vanished just like that. Last night I did sweat a lot and my fever is now gone. Now I'm completely fine, today I'll attend my office,' Nirmala said and hugged him affectionately. Later, after both had their breakfast, Nirmala packed her lunch and got ready to go.

'Didi, I have some doubts in maths and a lesson in physics as well,' Arun said.

'Don't worry, I will help you out in the evening, I'll be free at that time, bye,' Nirmala replied. She went outside carrying her handbag and files.

Deepthi became restless, as she didn't receive a call again from Vishaal. 'I never knew these kinds of guys can be seen in the world,' Deepthi said angrily to Shruthi. After a few hours, she got a call from Vishaal and he invited her along with Shruthi to watch a movie in PVR cinemas, as he had already reserved tickets for the weekend show. Deepthi couldn't hide her joy. 'Woohoo!' she exclaimed and jumped with joy. She immediately called Shruthi. They both managed to get permission from their parents.

On the weekend, Vishaal and Prashanth reached the PVR an hour before the show could begin. Vishaal had dressed up more smartly than the way he usually did, and a girl stared at him admiringly. Seeing her admiring him, he said, 'Yes . . . I'm sure Deepthi will like my dressing style.' Prashanth turned towards the other side and giggled. Later, Vishaal saw Deepthi and Shruthi coming.

'Hi, Vishaal you are looking cool,' Deepthi said with a bit of excitement. He felt as though he was flying in air and all of them greeted each other.

Everyone entered the cinema hall to take their seats, and Prashanth told Shruthi to take her seat bearing the number 8— next, Deepthi at 9, Vishaal at 10, and 11 for himself, and he didn't forget to tease Shruthi. Looking at Shruthi, he said smilingly, 'The fat ones deserve fat number 8,' and she gave an angry look, raising her hand a bit. Even Sandhya was coming to PVR cinema along with her father to watch the movie for a second time. She was very excited as she was coming with her dad after a very long time. She began to tell the story of that movie while her father was driving and she told him up to almost the ending part of the story. They reached the parking place of the PVR cinemas. 'Since you've almost told me the story, complete it, there's no point in seeing the movie, let's go back home,' Sandhya's father said and she kept quiet.

They entered the cinema hall and as the movie started, she said with more excitement, 'Dad, the photography is really magnificent. Thank God you have a holiday to see such a great movie.'

'Will you allow me to watch the movie silently or shall we go back from here?' her father asked and warned her not to speak while watching the movie.

In the cinema hall when the movie started, Deepthi asked Vishaal, 'Are you seeing this movie for the first time?'

Intervening, Prashanth replied, 'No, twice.'

Looking at Vishaal, she said seriously, 'Twice, if you see like . . . my goodness, it's bad for your eyes, it strains your eyeball, then headaches and you have to miss your classes, you will fall sick . . . your future . . . *interval*.'

'Dude, the comedy was so nice, did you enjoy it?' Prashanth teased Vishaal.

He looked at Prashanth. 'Idiot, you're being the reason to create such nonsense, I warn you, be careful before uttering her a word, you stupid,' he sounded softly but in a grudging voice and was pressing his forehead, as it was paining him after he heard her lengthy advice, and both exchanged their seats later.

During interval, in the cinema hall, Sandhya got up to get some snacks; it was very crowded near the counter, everything looked like a blur to her as her spectacles fell on the ground and she had to ask someone to help in finding her spectacles. Prashanth saw her kneeling down to find it. He rushed towards her and gave her the spectacles.

After wearing her spectacles, she said in surprise, 'Thanks . . . Prashanth,' and he introduced her to Vishaal as he came near them. A little later, they all entered the cinema hall. Prashanth felt very happy as she spoke to him and keenly looked at her to see where she was sitting. Vishaal had a closer look at him to read his mind.

'How do you know her?' Vishaal asked curiously.

'She's a Presidency College student, she comes to my tuition,' he replied and continued gazing at her.

Shaking Prashanth's shoulders frequently, Vishaal said smilingly, 'Hello, dude, the movie is over.'

'Oops, my neck,' Prashanth yelled, looking at Vishaal; he caught his neck and turned it to the right side since he was constantly turned back left to see her. He rushed fast towards the escalator to see her but she had already gone.

Tapping his shoulders, 'Better luck next time,' Vishaal said.

'Where is Deepthi, by the way?' Prashanth asked.

'They have already left and Deepthi told me that she has to study chemistry for tomorrow's test,' Vishaal said and both left to reach their houses.

One Sunday at around 5 p.m., Anu got ready for going to temple along with Shwetha, but Shwetha was not interested to go to temple for praying. 'See, Mom, she's not willing to come and so even I won't go,' Anu said restlessly.

Her mother angrily stared at Shwetha and said, 'The priest has told me that today is a very auspicious day for praying. Both of you shall go to temple, or else. Shwetha, be prepared to face your dad's scolding,' and cautioned them to be careful about the 100-rupee note that she had given.

'Mom feels as if it's a 1,000-rupee note,' Shwetha murmured. They both went and boarded the bus to reach the Lord Ganesha temple. After praying, they came out from temple, bought an ice-cream cone and roamed around the market to buy some hairpins, hair bands, etc.

'Didi, let's go by auto it's already seven thirty, I'm very tired.' Shwetha sounded very tired. Anu tried to stop many autorickshaws but none of them stopped, she got frustrated and saw an auto stood without the driver. They both sat inside and waited for the driver to come.

Carrying a box, the auto driver, with a tense look, came hurriedly from an electric shop and began ratcheting to start the engine. He didn't notice the girls sitting in his auto.

'Uncle, Srinagar main road.' Anu said her stop and the driver, looking at Anu, said surprisingly, 'No, it's engaged, I didn't see you girls, please get down.'

Anu looked around. 'Uncle, how come it's engaged? There are no passengers around here.' She sounded a bit curious.

'OK, OK,' he replied, tensely looking around, and moved very fast. He took a left turn instead of right.

'Uncle, why are you taking a left turn?' Anu sounded a bit tense.

'The right-side road is blocked,' he replied restlessly but she looked at him suspiciously. They approached the signal and the fast-moving wheels of the auto gradually slowed down. Her tension increased, as the driver got down from the auto, carrying the box. She saw two women dressed in saris with flowers on their head. They waved their hands at the auto man, and looking around to confirm that nobody saw him, he quickly went near them to hand over the box. He came back hurriedly towards the auto after giving it. Anu was sweating tensely as he entered the auto. Tapping Anu's hand, Shwetha asked curiously, 'Who are those girls?'

'Shut up, we have to get down here only,' she said softly in a hurried voice but the auto moved very fast before they could get down. Immediately, Anu loudly said to stop the auto but he didn't listen and drove fast. A little later, he stopped near the Nagasandra road signal and both immediately got down without telling him anything.

Seeing them getting down from the auto, the auto man asked in surprise, 'Why did you get down suddenly, you wanted me to drop you at Srinagar, right?' but Anu ignored him. She paid the auto fare and hurriedly walked towards the other side of the road.

'Didi, what's wrong? Why did we get down here,' Shwetha questioned.

'Stupid, we would have gotten ourselves in danger if we wouldn't have got down,' Anu said and started wiping her sweat with her dupatta.

'What danger?' Shwetha asked curiously.

'Oh, you are too young to understand all this, you'll become aware of it as you grow up, don't tell Mummy about all this,' Anu replied worriedly.

'Don't worry, I won't tell her,' Shwetha said in a serious tone.

Next day, Anu reached the college hurriedly, as she wanted to share the incident yesterday with her friends.

Arun excitedly jumped from the step, out of breath as he saw her, and greeted her, 'Hi, Anu.'

Ignoring his greeting, she asked a bit tensely, 'Has Sandhya come?'

'No, why, what's the matter?' Arun asked curiously.

'No, nothing,' she replied.

Arun saw the college captain passing near him. 'Hello, Karthik, how come you're so early today?' Arun asked.

'I have a special class today,' he replied casually and left the place. Meanwhile, a person came driving a scooter and Anu saw him. 'Oh no!' she said out of fear and moved backwards with a scared look. Arun went near her, wondering, and she blindly ran, pulling Arun's hand, to hide behind a tree. He gave a perplexed look; she was looking very nervous. She peeped tensely at the person who was speaking with senior students.

'Tell me, Anu, what's wrong with you?' he asked anxiously.

'Yesterday, I had been to temple and . . .' She told him the incident that had happened last night.

'Are you sure this person is the same person riding the auto?' he asked doubtfully.

Madan came near them. 'Hey, what are you both doing here, planning up to climb this tree or what?' Madan asked funnily.

'Shh, just wait,' Arun said and continued to look towards the man.

A little later, Sandhya saw them peeping from behind the tree, came near them, and curiously asked, 'What? You guys are playing hide-and-seek?' Anu told her the incident that happened the day before.

Sandhya looked at Anu. 'Really? Have you gone mad? Do you know who he is?' she said unbelievingly and continued, 'He's the vice principal and most senior professor of arts, Mr Subhas Karuna. He's next to the principal and all his students respect him a lot. Maybe you are mistaken, that auto driver must have resembled him, that's all.' Sandhya sounded disbelieving.

'No, I'm damn sure, believe me,' she replied seriously.

Looking at Anu, Madan said, 'It's better if you have a closer look.'

Anu thought for a while. 'My doubt is that he's up to something. I think he wants to attract the students initially and later is probably planning to betray them,' Anu said, using her logic.

Later, they all went near the vice principal, Mr Subhas Karuna, to have a closer look at him for confirmation and to read his reaction when Anu met his eyes directly. They wished him good morning. 'Good morning, new faces, I believe you are all science students, am I right?' the professor replied casually and moved away without reacting to them.

'Are you sure?' Sandhya asked tensely.

Looking at Sandhya, Anu replied with confidence, 'Yes, it's him, I'll lodge a complaint with the principal and I'm quite sure that I'll unearth his true colour.'

'OK, Anu, wait,' Arun said.

'Why?' she asked impatiently.

'Let's attend the classes now and later we can have discussion about this,' Arun replied. Agreeing, they went into the classroom, but all of them lacked concentration as they were thinking about the vice principal, Subhas Karuna.

After the classes, Anu and her friends gathered, breathing in fresh air in the open ground. Anu saw some of the girls from the arts section. They were discussing what to do next. 'See those two girls, I'm sure that they are the ones who took the box from him and waved,' she said in a high voice and ran towards the girls.

Sandhya, seeing Anu running at them, tapped her forehead. 'She is definitely a gone case, she's pinpointing everyone in the college,' she said.

'Hello, girls, please excuse me, I saw you both yesterday near the Nagsandra circle, you both were dressed up in blue and red colour sari, am I right?' Anu said in a determined way.

'No,' both said together and exchanged serious looks with a slight smile.

'You liars!' Anu said in a high voice and everyone turned their faces to look at them.

Realizing the situation, Sandhya came running near Anu, looking at the girls. 'Sorry, girls, she meant us,' Sandhya said, pulling her, and both came near Arun.

A little later, Arun saw Karthik and he thought that it would be better to reveal to him beforehand the incident that Anu came across yesterday before complaining to principal since he was a college captain. 'Hello, Karthik, please, can I have a word with you?' he asked softly.

'Yeah, sure,' Karthik replied and Arun took him to a corner.

'Today we learned from our friend Anu that our college vice principal Subhas Karuna was doing some immoral activities by involving some female students. Last night, she saw him doing that, with her own eyes. We have decided to lodge a complaint to the principal so he can be interrogated regarding his activities,' Arun said seriously.

Karthik caught Arun's collar, and seeing that, Karthik's friends came closer to him. 'What nonsense are you talking about?' Karthik asked angrily in a high voice.

Anu moved quickly towards Karthik and pulled Karthik's hand from Arun's collar. Looking angrily at Karthik, she said,'Your civics professor Subhas Karuna is a brute, I saw him with my own eyes, don't support him,' and explained in detail what had happened.

Hearing Anu, Karthik gave a dreadful look at her and all his friends came near as though they were about to hit them but Madan came between them.

'Wait,' Karthik said, realizing the situation and all of them immediately stopped. Anu walked away some distance towards the principal's room and looking at her friends, said in an angry voice, 'Come on, guys, let's go and complain, he must be expelled from here for his dirty deeds and we shall see him getting imprisoned,' and her friends came near her.

Karthik and his friends grouped quickly around Anu and her friends, looking seriously at her. 'Shut your mouth, what exactly do you know about him?' Karthik raised his voice and continued, 'Please listen to me patiently. You are all unaware of what really he is. You guys are experts in solving problems using equations and doing experiments in a laboratory, that's all. After that, you people will be promoted as doctors and engineers. You will then find a nice job and get a good salary to lead a comfortable life, which is your aim of life. You all are ignorant about the sufferings of people and the problems which the society is facing,' he said emotionally and continued, 'It's enough, don't interfere in the matters of our vice principal, otherwise get ready to face severe consequences,' said in a sharp voice with a sharp look at them.

Hearing his views about the present generation of college students' attitude, everyone turned silent.

Anu looked seriously at Karthik. 'You can convince anyone but not me. If we won't complain, then we really have to face our conscience,' Anu said, raising her voice, but Arun gave a confused look, trying to read Karthik's mind. He looked towards the other side to control his anger.

'You all think that we'll shut our mouths if we get scared,' Sandhya said, looking at the arts students who circled around her. A little later, Anu and her friends moved a little forward but nearly ten arts students blocked them.

'Please don't stop us from going,' Madan requested and they ignored his request, remaining silent. A little later, Sandhya succeeded in diverting the attention of some of the art students, and Anu and Sandhya ran quickly towards the office. Some of the girls who stood among them chased Anu and Sandhya while others stood near Arun and Madan. Madan looked at the arts students who circled him. 'What? Do you all think of yourselves as dons or what? We don't get scared of anyone, whatever the situation may be,' Madan said in a grudging way and Karthik blew a whistle to call his friends back. Anu and Sandhya also came back; they were out of breath and Madan gave them water.

'Tell me, what are you guys planning for?' Arun asked, raising his voice after a long pause.

Looking at Arun and his friends, Karthik said emotionally, 'Please don't reveal or complain about this matter to anyone, please trust me, he's really a dynamic person, does nothing wrong. I assure you all, please just wait for few days. You guys will soon get to know about his noble task.'

Meanwhile, Anu was looking at the girls whom she saw the day before, to read their faces and to conclude whether they were genuinely engaged in some noble task.

'So that he can escape, that's what his task is, right?' Sandhya gave a slow reply and one of the female arts students, who knew Sandhya, looked at her. 'Sandhya, you were asking me why we often get holidays, right? It's just because of our professor. We know that he's doing the right thing, but as of now, we can't reveal any details. You'll definitely come to know the truth in future, please trust me,' she said.

'Please, guys, keep this a secret at least for a few days, don't reveal this, or else you all will have to face the music,' Karthik said warningly.

Arun gestured at his friends to move out. The sky looked almost dark as everyone left the college.

Looking at Anu, Sandhya said restlessly, 'Oh God, my tuition, it's late, I can't go today,' as both crossed the main gate of the college. Both reached their homes later. Anu was very tired and fell on the bed after having dinner. Prashanth couldn't find Sandhya at the bus stop and wondered why she didn't turn up to attend the tuition class.

Next day, Anu's mother woke Anu up. Anu was watching the TV news while getting ready to go to college. She became curious as she watched *NDTV Live & Exclusive*, Vandana reporting from Bengaluru: 'There was a blast near Lalbagh road, in the Charu hotel. Unconfirmed report says at late night, three people have died and five are injured, including an independent MLA, Siddharaju. We are not yet sure of whether it was a terrorist attack and the police are yet to confirm it. The injured have been admitted to Deepa nursing home. The whole area is cordoned off and the police have begun to investigate. The dog squad is already inside and around to find the clues about the blast.'

Anu was watching with a curious look. Suddenly the TV reporter's voice rose with an excitement.

'Here's breaking news, the police have found an underground room inside the hotel premises. Please turn the camera quickly,' the reporter asked in a high voice, and nearly twenty teenage girls aged between fifteen to eighteen years were coming out with the help of female police staff. The reporter asked a girl about the incident and the girls looked very tired.

With tears rolling down, a girl replied to the news reporter, 'They locked us in the underground for the past seven days and were planning to send us this evening to Mumbai, to engage us in prostitution. They had kidnapped us. I reside near Hosur in Tamil Nadu.'

'Do you have any clue about those who might be involved in this blast?' the reporter interrupted.

'No, we don't but we are thankful to whoever manoeuvred this blast, they have indeed rescued us from hell.'

Even Arun, Sandhya, and Madan watched it eagerly and praised the person who rescued them.

Anu got ready to reach the college quickly without having her breakfast and she entered the bus. Meanwhile, Prashanth ran towards the bus to call Anu and ask about Sandhya but the bus already moved. 'Why didn't she come? Maybe she's not feeling well,' he said to himself with disappointment.

Anu entered her college and reached the arts section but the security guard was already there. Realizing that she would not be allowed, she went through the science section staircase. Looking around, she carefully jumped over the small gate to reach the arts section. She often looked back to check whether anyone, especially a security guard, was watching her. She saw that all the classrooms were closed except one at the top floor. Anu saw a girl coming out and she was a prefect of the arts group. Anu immediately hid behind a pillar before the prefect could see her. A little later, she peeped to confirm that the prefect was gone and slowly went near the room. Looking around, she came near the window, which was ajar, and peeping, she saw the students were sitting with their eyes closed. They were meditating, and she saw a photo frame which was not fully visible and ducked her head quickly as their eyes opened. After meditation, Karthik stood up to address the students.

'Give a round of applause to our professor. He rescued many girls from entering into the life of hell,' he said in a high voice and all of them clapped. She again peeped to have a clear glimpse of the professor but she couldn't see him. She hid behind a pillar when they all came out from the classroom, and Subhas Karuna wasn't there.

She peeped to see the photo frame as Karthik came out holding it. Her eyes widened with shock, her lips started shivering, and she couldn't speak out as she saw the person's photo in the frame. She sat down, leaning against the wall, and everything looked blank. She was frozen. All left the place except Anu, and tears were rolling from her eyes. A little later, with a sudden rush of blood, she ran towards the classroom where she usually met Spandan and entered. She touched the words 'I love Kirthi', which were carved on the bench and her eyes were filled with tears. 'Oh, it's Spandan—unbelievable. I could have helped you by convincing her if you had shared her details and the obstacles that prevented her from loving you. You missed the joyful experience of love, hard to believe that you're no more,' she spoke to herself, resting her head on the bench. After a few minutes, she left the place to reach her classroom, with a difficult feeling.

Later, Anu went down the stairs and wiped her tears as she saw Karthik. 'Karthik, Karthik,' she called loudly and he turned back. She ran near him. 'I am so sorry I hurt you. Please can you tell me what happened to Spandan? I saw him a fortnight ago, how did he die?' she asked sadly.

He looked at her seriously. Removing his spectacles, Karthik asked, 'How come you saw him about a fortnight back? He died long ago,' he said and continued to walk.

'Please stop, I won't believe,' Anu said in a high voice and he turned back.

'He died ten months ago and don't ask me any further details. It's true, bye,' he said and left the place. Anu could not control her crying; still unbelieving, she sat leaning against a pillar.

Madan saw her crying and kept his hand on her shoulder. 'Anu . . . Anu, tell me what happened. Why are you looking so depressed?' Madan asked worriedly. Immediately, Madan called Arun and he came running.

'Tell me, tell me what happened,' Arun asked, caressing her cheeks but she did not respond. He immediately took water and sprinkled it on her face. She nodded her head slowly and got up to reach the classroom. In the classroom, she rested her head on the desk, and Sandhya looked at Anu anxiously.

'What happened?' she asked, tapping Anu.

'Sandhya, leave her alone,' Arun said dully. Madan told Sandhya that Anu was a bit depressed about something she was not willing to share.

'I've no idea what's troubling her mind, she often feels that others' worries are her own, it's her strange attitude,' Sandhya said, looking at them. Arun listened keenly in trying to understand Anu deeply.

Sandhya put her arm around Anu's shoulders. 'Hey, you'll become mad if you start taking others' matters so seriously. Let me know what happened,' Sandhya asked.

'Don't get disturbed because of others' matters, relax,' Madan said, and Anu nodded her head slowly.

That day, during lunch break, Arun and his friends sat in a circle. Arun was looking at his friends. 'I'm certain that all have lost concentration for the past four days. I see no point in wasting our time like this, and I urge each one of you . . .' Arun gave a deep stare at Anu because what he said so far was meant for her and continued, 'If there is any stress in your mind, please check it out and divert your attention towards the books.'

Looking at Arun, Anu asked with frustration, 'How's it possible?'

'OK, try to solve six maths problems now, the remaining during free period since we don't have physics today, and I'm sure you can work it out if you concentrate,' Arun replied to Anu but looking at Anu, he was still thinking.

'OK, it'll be better if you relax, close your eyes for about five minutes,' he said and insisted that she close her eyes.

As she closed her eyes, Spandan came and opened her eyes immediately, looking at Arun

'Oh no, I can't,' she said in a crying tone.

'OK, it's all right. Anu please read the problem,' Arun said. After she read the problem, Arun asked whether she understood.

She gave a hesitating look at him and read it again.

'Anu, try to concentrate and understand my explanation, don't bring unwanted thoughts into your mind, all right?'

Arun said in a sharp tone with a sharp look. He sounded like a hypnotizer and explained the problem and its solution in detail.

Anu started showing interest to solve the problems and asked Arun, 'How can you take acceleration into consideration?'

'See you can take the mass but—'

Looking at Arun, Anu said, 'Yeah, now I got it,' with a smile as she understood and proceeded to the next problem by making her mind strong enough to stop thinking about Spandan.

Later that day, Anu's friends had learned from Anu about the truth behind the activities of Professor Subhas Karuna, and soon, Arun and Madan went to express their apologies to Karthik.

'Your friend has already apologized,' Karthik said smilingly and went away after wishing them well.

'Oh, our energy was wasted taking a long walk from the classroom up to the field,' Madan said, bending and stretching his body in scorching sunlight, pouring sweat.

Sandhya asked Anu, 'Where have these specimens gone, leaving their bags on the floor?' Anu wondered, looking around in the corridor. Sandhya laughed at Anu as she carried their bags, and both went downstairs to look for them.

'How come you are so concerned about them that you are carrying their bags?'

'They are my good friends forever.'

'Oh! You're praising them a lot, today not even a single leaf would wither from the trees,' Sandhya said, laughing, and Anu ignored her comments. When they met Arun and Madan, Anu handed over their bags to them. Taking his bag from Anu, Arun looked at her in an affectionate way, and later, all of them left to attend their practical class.

After the classes were over, Sandhya and Madan went to see the noticeboard and Anu and Arun stayed back in the class.

'By the way, do you believe in life after death?' Anu asked suddenly, and it looked as though she had forgotten to ask this important question before.

'I believe in the life before death, it's a gift from God, and don't believe in life after death. It just doesn't make any sense.'

'No, even I had the same view before but after learning something that is true, it is making me think otherwise,' she replied, spontaneously looking outside, and got up to go but he caught her hand to stop her.

'Can you tell me what is that "truth" which you have learnt and which is making you believe in life after death?'

'Oh, you won't believe, I am sure,' Anu replied with a forced smile and went away near the corridor, looking dully towards a tree where the words 'I love Kirthi' were carved.

'When will my feelings touch your heart and when will I be able to understand you completely?' Arun asked himself.

Looking at the noticeboard, Sandhya was excited since the college had put up an educational trip for three days to visit the botanical garden. Enthusiastically she came running with Madan and informed Anu and Arun.

Looking at them, Sandhya said, 'OK, fine, the three of us can go.'

'Why three? Even I will be coming,' Arun replied seriously.

'You are already included in the count, sir, I excluded "Anu the great",' Sandhya said, pointing at Anu.

'Why?' he asked curiously.

Looking at Arun, Sandhya replied, 'You know what, it's hard to even imagine or even dream that she would be joining us for a trip. It's better to forget it,' and insisted Anu should try to convince her parents at least this time and get permission to go for the trip. Anu nodded her head in affirmation. A little later, all of them reached their home.

At her house, Anu was trying to get consent from her mother about the college trip and said, 'Our college has put up a three-day educational trip to visit a botanical garden, and tomorrow is the last day for nominating ourselves. This trip will definitely help me gain practical knowledge about the rare plants.'

'Let it be any place, we can't send you alone,' her mother replied sharply.

'You don't worry, let us all go to some place this weekend, all right?' Her father was trying to convince Anu but she was disappointed, as she did not get permission to go with her friends.

Sandhya called up Anu to ask if she got permission and learnt that she didn't. Sandhya was disappointed and called up Arun to let him know.

In Arun's house, Arun's happiness of getting permission from her sister to go to the trip turned into frustration after Sandhya's call. Arun looked at Nirmala. 'We all are going on an educational trip, to gain knowledge. Why don't a few parents trust us?' he asked with frustration and told her that Anu's parents were not sending her for the trip.

Tapping his shoulders, Nirmala said, 'Parents have their own fears, they think differently.'

Next day, Sandhya reached her tuition. 'Hi, Kalpana, sir has not come yet?'

Ignoring Sandhya's question, she started murmuring in Sandhya's ear, 'You know what, sir has taken his mobile to teach him a lesson.'

Prashanth looked at Sandhya, as she looked at him, and turned his face towards the board.

'Kalpana, do you have the important questions of quadratic equation?' Sandhya asked her.

'Sorry, I didn't bring that book,' she replied, and Sandhya's eyes turned towards Prashanth slowly.

'Hello . . . Hello,' she called him but he doubted whether she was addressing him, replied very innocently after the third call, 'Yeah, what?'

'Please, can I get your book for copying yesterday's questions?' she asked. He gave the book and his heart started ticking. The lecturer came after a few minutes and started his class. Prashanth was very happy talking to Sandhya. The class was almost over; Sandhya went near the lecturer and said, 'Sir, I'll not be able to come for the next three days, since our college has arranged an educational trip.'

'OK, have fun and make sure that you gain knowledge as well. Just don't waste your entire time in spending time with your friends,' the lecturer advised her. Sandhya was so excited and forgot to return the book to Prashanth. He was very upset as she went without wishing him goodbye. He wore back the footwear blindly and left for his house disappointedly.

'What is this?' Prashanth's mother asked, pointing towards his feet, as he had worn his footwear on the right leg and somebody else's on the left, and meantime in his tuition, his lecturer was searching. 'Where's my other footwear?'

Next day, the biology professor asked all those interested to go on the trip to nominate themselves. Arun looked at Anu angrily when his eyes met hers and turned his face away. After the class was over, all students went to the practical lab.

'Everyone listen, be careful while handling the concentrated solutions,' the chemistry professor warned the students.

'How come yours has changed into pink so quickly?' Anu asked Arun, as she saw him completing the process of chemical reaction in a test tube.

'Oh no, take that solution, stir it well.' Arun, instructing her, added some concentrated sulphuric acid into her test tube to convert that into a pink solution. After pouring concentrated sulphuric acid, with a hiss, Anu gave a painful sigh.

'I am really sorry,' Arun reacted tensely.

'What happened?' the professor asked loudly.

'Nothing, sir,' Anu replied with pain and Arun pulled her to give her first aid.

'Stop it . . . We can do it after the class . . .' Anu whispered and he looked very upset. The professor instructed Arun to collect the records later.

'Yes, sir,' he said and called Sandhya immediately.

'Take her quickly, apply the blue-tube ointment that's in the first aid box,' Arun whispered in her ear. Both hurried out of the lab.

'Ouch,' Anu shouted as Sandhya applied ointment on her wrist. Madan came near them and helped in dressing the wound.

'Where's Arun?' Madan asked Sandhya.

'I think he's still in the lab. Can't you see that door is open?' she replied.

'Oh fine, you're the right person to show us the unknown places clearly through your four eyes,' Madan said, laughing, and she hit him on his head with her bag.

Madan entered the lab. 'Arun . . . hey, what's wrong with you, man? Idiot!' Madan said in a high voice tensely and went near him as he saw him sitting on the floor holding his leg, in pain. Madan went downstairs quickly and took the ointment and cotton from the first aid box. He came back to the lab and dressed the burnt skin of Arun's feet.

'I'm sure that you hurt yourself to avoid coming for the trip and to stay with Anu alone,' Madan said, winking his eyes. A little later, looking at his leg, Sandhya enquired of Arun regarding how he got hurt.

'It's just a small burn,' he replied casually.

Nearly twenty students didn't turn up to go for the trip, and the professor instructed them to attend the classes as usual. After the day's classes were over, Anu ran towards the corner of the field, as it had begun to rain and wrote on wet mud 'Spandan, be happy wherever you are' using a small piece of bark.

Pulling Arun's hand, Madan warned, 'It's raining, your leg will begin to swell, dude,' but Arun ignored him and looked towards Anu. She was looking at the moving clouds with depression, as it stopped raining. Arun and Sandhya came near her.

Tapping her shoulders, Sandhya asked Anu, 'What are you thinking, looking up?'

'I don't know, whomever I like they will stay for a while and move away like these clouds,' Anu sounded depressed. Sandhya saw Arun, and both saw Anu as though she had lost some valuable thing. Sandhya, trying to comfort Anu, shook her shoulders and said, 'Come on, lady, it's getting late, we have to go.'

A little later, Madan came near them; he said, looking at Arun, 'Let's go,' and pulled Arun's hand to go home but Arun could not hear him and stood like a statue. He took the bike's key from Arun's pocket to ride his bike and drop him since he had hurt his leg. A little later, Arun came near his bike and sat back but his eyes were fixed on Anu as she was walking towards the bus stand to go home. Madan rode the bike and both reached home.

Nirmala saw Arun coming inside, limping with Madan's help.

'What happened?' she asked when she saw him suffering to remove his socks. She went quickly to get the first aid box and dressed the burn.

Arun saw tears in her eyes. 'Oh, Didi, come on, please don't cry. If you cry, my pain will increase,' he said. She immediately wiped her tears off and went to the kitchen to serve him food.

Next morning, Arun got ready to go for the trip. Nirmala cautioned him to be careful and instructed him to carry the painkiller tablets with him. He looked very cool in casual dress and had worn a red cap. He boarded the bus arranged by the college for the trip and took his seat.

Sandhya's father had also come to bid her farewell. Sandhya sat next to Arun. 'Wow, you're looking so cool. What's the secret . . . is it because you're hurt?' she said and giggled. She took his cap to wear it. 'Mister, I will take the window seat.' And peeping out of the window, she looked at her dad. 'OK, bye, Dad,' she said. Arun smiled and both exchanged their seats later.

That morning in Anu's house, Anu requested her mother, 'Please, Mom, I'll be back in thirty minutes, let me go and at least bid them farewell.'

'You can bid them farewell on the phone itself,' Shwetha interrupted.

'Shut up, Shwetha! Mom, please,' Anu requested again, and her mother finally agreed.

'Fine, go, but come back quickly before Dad wakes up.'

Anu quickly went to the bus stop, boarded the bus which went to her college as it arrived, and often looked at the time on her watch tensely. Meantime, Sandhya was thinking about Anu.

'At least she could've come here to bid us farewell,' Arun murmured, looking outside the window, hoping Anu would come.

'Hello, don't have such an expectation of that peculiar creature, otherwise you'll go mad.' Sandhya sounded angry. He leaned back against the seat dully, saw Nirmala suddenly, and saw that she sat on the ground, holding her head. 'Didi!' he came out shouting and offered her water quickly. She was half-conscious and he lifted her up with others' help. Meanwhile, Madan got an auto. Sandhya helped Nirmala to get into the auto and came forward to get into the auto, to accompany them.

'No, Sandhya, you guys please go, I can manage, bye,' he said firmly and Nirmala rested her head on his lap.

'Don't worry, dude, take care,' Madan said dully and the auto moved quickly.

Meanwhile, Anu got down from the bus, walked as fast as she could, and reached the college but the bus had already started moving. 'Stop, stop!' she shouted, cursing, 'Oh, I should've come earlier, bad luck.'

Arun became frustrated as there was a traffic jam and was looking around to find a way to reach the nursing home quickly. He was sweating with tension. He took a deep breath as the traffic was cleared and turned towards the other side. His eyes widened as he saw Anu but he was so exhausted that he couldn't even call her and he waved his hand at her but she didn't see him.

Arun immediately got down near the nursing home as they reached it and got Nirmala admitted. He sat waiting for the doctor to know about her condition. A few hours later, she looked better after getting the treatment.

'Nothing to worry about, Nirmala, it's just weakness. Iron content is less,' the doctor said, looking at her medical reports.

'Why did it happen like this suddenly, doctor?' Arun sounded very upset.

'Don't worry, boy, you can take her home today evening, nothing serious,' the doctor assured him.

Here, Prashanth was disappointed, as he could not see Sandhya in tuition for three days. He thought that instead of expressing his love to Sandhya directly, it would be better to first speak with her best friend Anu, and he asked Vishaal's suggestion in this regard.

'Brainless, you have to express your love in person to your loved one and not anybody else. OK, fine, tell me, what if her friend is stubborn and arrogant?'

'No, dude, I can't,' Prashanth sounded nervous.

'Go to hell,' Vishaal said and left the place after wishing him goodbye.

Next day, Anu woke up very late. Her mother was surprised as she was having her breakfast very slowly because by that time (actually, an hour before that time), Anu would usually run to the bus stand.

'What happened to you today?' her mother asked Anu.

'I'm not feeling like going since very few are attending the classes,' Anu replied restlessly and later went dully. She stood in the bus stand and missed two buses on purpose.

In Arun's house, Nirmala said dully, 'Come on, don't miss your classes, go to college instead of sitting here idly. Even I'll go to sleep after some time. The maid will look after me, in case I need something. Now I'm absolutely fine.' Arun left the house half-heartedly to reach his college.

'Hey, is this my dream?' Prashanth said as he saw Anu at the bus stand and ran towards her, 'Hi, I'm Prashanth, nice to meet you, actually . . .' Anu became tense as he spoke, and turned to the other side, but he continued to speak. 'Sorry, I'm in Sandhya's tuition, and please, can . . .' He was not able to complete his statement.

Anu looked at him. 'Please, I'm extremely sorry and I can't speak in public like this,' Anu replied and pretended to read a board. She boarded the bus quickly as it arrived.

Arun reached the college, and one of his classmates enquired about his sister's condition. 'Well, she is much better now,' he replied and looked around the field to find Anu.

'Classes have not yet started—that's why we are wandering,' one of his friends said and Arun walked quickly into the classroom to see Anu but to his disappointment she wasn't there either. He walked down the field and sat dully on the stairs next to the ground, where they used to sit regularly.

Anu entered the college and looked at the stairs of the college ground thrice. She scratched her head and wondered, 'How come I am able to see Arun sitting over there? All three have gone to the trip, right?' And to clear her doubt, she pointed at Arun and asked a girl, 'Excuse me, is there a guy over there sitting on the third step?'

'Yes, you are right, he surely is one good-looking guy!' the girl replied, smiling.

'OK, OK, thank you,' Anu said with excitement and was surprised.

'Wait, I'll surprise him,' she thought to herself and slowly walked towards him. 'Boo!' she cried, jumping up from behind to frighten him.

'Did you say something?' Arun asked, and she looked at him angrily. He pretended to read, and as Anu snatched his book, both smiled at each other.

'How come you didn't go?' she asked in surprise, and he narrated yesterday's incident.

'Oh, I am sorry! How is she now?' she enquired in a dull voice.

'Yeah, better, but I can't sit relaxed here knowing that she is not feeling well and is also alone,' he said in a worried tone and continued, 'Fine, let's finish our physics record,' and even she started writing.

'Why did Prashanth approach me, and what was he trying to say?' Anu was thinking deeply and Arun tapped on her head.

'Where's your mind gone? Bring it back here,' he said, pointing at her book, and she started writing.

'Oh, we have English now, let's go to the classroom,' Arun said.

'Oh, I thought I could be alone in my own world, this fellow won't leave me,' Anu thought and went along with him but suddenly she changed her direction.

'Anu . . . Anu!' Arun called her and she came near him with frustration.

'Why are you going there?' he asked curiously.

'Please, will you leave me alone, got to tell you everything?' she replied angrily.

'OK, OK, fine! I'll be in the classroom,' he said and left the place quickly. Anu changed her mind and went to the classroom. He was writing physics and she looked at him angrily as he was writing without looking at her. All of them waited for fifteen minutes but the English teacher had not turned up and everyone left the classroom one by one. Arun went to the staffroom to enquire, and Anu was sitting alone, thinking deeply.

Arun got a call from Madan and Sandhya. They enquired about Nirmala's health. 'Idiot, why did you go to the college instead of looking after her? How you could be so careless?' Sandhya asked angrily.

'Oh God, she shouts at me if I stayed back there and you guys are shouting here because I didn't stay back home. What do you think? Am I a throw ball?' Arun replied seriously.

'OK, it's all right, by the way, how's your leg and my Anu?' Sandhya asked.

'Yeah, she's OK,' he replied dully and walked towards the ground.

A little later, Anu came near Arun. 'What's that?' she asked him looking curiously at a gift box in his hands.

'I've got to tell you three things about . . .'

Caressing his cheeks, Anu said curiously, 'Carry on.'

'Firstly, they assured me that they'll give back half of the trip amount.'

'That's good.'

'Secondly, the English teacher will not be coming and thirdly—' He gave a pause, giving a keen look at Anu, as she was expecting him to talk about the gift.

'When I was at the office, suddenly a girl came near me and introduced herself as Shailaja studying commerce in our college. After presenting this gift, she left the place immediately,' he said and sat on the steps restlessly.

'Did she say anything?' Anu asked curiously.

'No, nothing, but she smiled, looking back at me several times while she going. I called out to her thrice but she didn't respond.'

'No doubt, she must be in love with you,' Anu said with a naughty smile and took the letter affixed on the gift. 'Come on, let me open it,' she said and went forward to open the gift quickly.

'I think she has given it to me,' he said, turning his face towards the other side with a smile.

She pulled back her hair. 'Oh yeah, I am sorry! OK, you read it,' she said and returned the letter along with the gift.

'Let me make her feel jealous,' he thought to himself and started reading the love letter.

'Stupid, you didn't tell me how she looks,' Anu sounded curious.

'Yes, it's working,' he thought and continued, 'Oh yeah, she is very good-looking.'

'If she's beautiful then why can't accept her proposal?' she asked and grabbed the letter. Arun stared at her seriously.

'Sorry! I mean first and foremost, you have no idea regarding how to read a love letter. Firstly, you have to imagine as though she's in front of you. This isn't a book and aren't the words either that are written in ink, it's her inner voice and feelings that emanated from her heart and passed through the pen and landed on this sheet as words. Must read it with a feel, man,' Anu said emotionally. Arun's hands were on his forehead with disappointment, as she was not jealous, as he thought she would be. Anu began to read the letter.

'Dear Arun, I love you very much. I've no guts to stand right opposite to you to express my love—that's why I have written this letter. The truth is that you are my life. Your presence gives me a thrill, your happiness is my fragrance of love, your tears are my blood which makes my heart burn, I love you so much . . .' Anu read it emotionally.

'Wow! She's written so well, I'm sure she truly loves you. OK, let's go, I'm damn hungry,' she said and handed over the letter. Arun was stunned and gazed at her as they strolled. He felt as if every word had come from Anu's heart, and he thought how well she understood the feelings of the one who loved. As she was busy ordering snacks, Arun looked at her and thought when the time would come to express his love to her.

After having snacks, Anu saw some of the students were playing basketball and even she joined the game. While they were playing, the ball fell on a girl who was passing by. She turned back angrily and Anu immediately pointed at Arun.

'What?' he gave a confused look at Anu. 'OK, sorry, Shailaja, it was . . .' Arun stammered.

'It's all right, bye,' she replied with a smile and went away. He chased Anu to hit her, and she ran quickly to escape. He caught her wrist tightly after chasing.

'OK, sorry! But see, you got a chance to speak to your lovebird and that's *only* because of me.'

'Better be in your limits, mind your words. Please don't take her name again.'

Looking at his watch, she said, 'OK, OK, it's already late,' and went to the bus stand after wishing him goodbye.

Next morning, Anu came near the bus stand. Prashanth saw her and walked towards her quickly. Seeing him, she had already crossed the road and had gone near an old lady who was selling onions. 'How much do you want? One kg is only fifteen rupees,' the old lady asked Anu, and Prashanth came near the old lady, following Anu.

Looking at the old lady, Anu asked, 'Does anyone say onion rates in public?'

'Then where shall I speak to you, on the phone or what, have you gone mad? If you want the onions, buy them, otherwise get lost,' the lady replied angrily.

Looking at Prashanth, Anu said, 'You come near the college around eight o'clock in the morning tomorrow, I'll buy the onions there, understand?' and he nodded his head smilingly, indicating that he understood.

'Hey, you, what are you saying? I am not your servant, get lost,' the lady grunted angrily at Anu. Both went to attend their college later.

That day, after reaching his college, Prashanth blabbered to Vishaal about what had happened near the bus stand. He praised her intelligence as she spoke with him indirectly. Since Prashanth had missed his classes frequently, Vishaal advised him, 'Dude, be punctual and attend all the classes, you have no idea how it affects your studies in future.'

That day, Anu told her mother that she hardly had any classes tomorrow.

'OK, then don't go tomorrow and instead you can help me here.'

'No, I have a very important class to attend tomorrow, I just remembered,' she said, remembering about Prashanth. Anu went upstairs on the terrace and began to speak, looking at the moon.

'What about my Vishaal, is he fine, when will I have a chance to see him?' Anu was thinking about him.

At the same time in Vishaal's house, 'Oh, it's unbelievable. Deepthi, I'm sure that you're the one who is creating the wonderful feelings in my heart,' Vishaal said to himself as he felt a chilling sensation in his heart.

Anu felt a cool breeze across her face and said bye to the moon. She came down and began to study. Later, she lay down on the bed, carrying deep sleep in her eyes.

Arun recalled each and every scene of Anu that he enjoyed in the college. Her voice was still echoing in his ears. Lying down on the bed, he felt quite relaxed imagining her.

Next day, Anu got ready and went to the college without carrying a lunch box. 'Go fast, the classes have already started,' the security guard said. Anu went anxiously towards the classroom but it was empty. She thought it might be a special class for the arts students and looked at the door. To her disappointment, it was closed except for a few windows.

Siddha gundaraju was in hospital. Later, he was arrested for his involvement in human trafficking and flesh trade. He was a rowdy before entering into politics and had control over many slums. Later, he became an independent MLA by virtue of money and muscle power. He had the support of the ruling party since he supported them in the assembly; he managed to get the bail and went underground. Subhas Karuna got the information about his movements. He planned to trace him and his activities thereon.

In the classroom, Subhas Karuna gave final instructions to his senior students after manoeuvring a plan to trace Siddha and his men. 'Pramila, Anthony, Gopal, Rashid, and Partha, wait near this signal. I'm having some doubt there, just act as if you're among the public. I hope you all got it. OK, fine, any doubts?'

'No, sir,' all of them replied together. 'Wish you good luck, Karthik,' the professor said.

'Thank you, sir,' he replied in a sharp voice and all of them stood up as the professor left the classroom. Anu saw them coming out with enthusiasm and their faces looked very brave and daring.

That day, Prashanth came near Anu's college and was surprised that the gate had not opened yet. 'Show your identity card,' the security guard asked.

Anu looked towards the gate and came running near the gate. 'Hello, brother, thank God that you brought my notes, sorry for troubling you. You have not seen my college, right? Please come inside and I will show you our college,' Anu said, and Prashanth gave a bewildered look. The security guard opened the gate and said, 'Come back within fifteen minutes.'

'Oh! Tell me, what's your problem and which college are you from?' Anu asked curiously.

'Stephen's College.' And he continued, 'sorry for troubling you, I want to speak about Sandhya with you, actually I love her,' he replied innocently.

'She's not here.'

'I know, please can you tell her about my feelings?' Prashanth pleaded with her.

'Sorry, I can't. What if she says no? I'm very much sure that she'll say no to your proposal and then what will be your next plan?' Anu asked him in a sharp voice. After a pause, she continued, 'Am I right that you try another one?' and he looked at her angrily. She continued looking at him. 'See, man, a person who falls in love must keep their heart always soaked in love forever—that's the true love and should not be feared. I want that kind of person to enter in Sandhya's life, bye.'

Anu went forward but Prashanth gave no reply and she came back near him. 'Please think whether you love her sincerely, but just proposing and going away with disappointment won't make any sense. Just spending money on costly gifts, using Dad's money, will never impress the one who wants to love you truly. You can impress her by presenting even a very small gift from your hard-earned money.' She stressed the words 'earned money' again and continued, 'Why I am telling you all this is just that you must try to understand my friend's life—that she has lost her mother and has to enjoy each and every moment with you if you become her true life partner. Look, I'm really not bothered about asking who you are and where you are from, but I'm very much concerned about your character. I hope you understood what I am trying to say.'

'Hello, come out,' the security guard screamed at Prashanth, and Anu stopped speaking. He walked away without speaking a word.

'Hello,' Anu called him and he stopped without turning back. 'All the best,' she said with a dull smile and he went away.

Thinking about Arun, Anu sat on the steps of the college grounds and wondered why he had not yet come. 'How he would look differently today to impress Shailu, oops, Shailaja,' she giggled by herself. As soon as she saw Arun coming near, she said excitedly, 'Hi.' He gave a grudging look at her and didn't reply.

After a pause, he was staring at her angrily. 'Have you got any brains? How can you give her my number without my permission? This morning, Shailaja called me up to ask my opinion. My sister came to know about this. You brought the college matters into my house unnecessarily. Idiot, all this is your mistake. It's all just because of you,' he blasted her without giving a gap and left the place to reach his classroom.

Looking up the sky, Anu said, 'Oh God, today is not my day.' Suddenly she heard, 'You're sick! When you gave me his number to call him, I was not able to stand on my feet out of joy, but I never thought that it is just an ill design for trapping me until I called him this morning to know his opinion. Very cleverly, you made him feel that he cannot bear me. For sure, even you'll face the same failure like me in future, it's my curse,' Shailaja said angrily and went cursing her.

'Oh no, I never thought that your love should end in this manner and that too with my friend. You don't know that I have suffered a lot facing a failure in love and that is why I try to help others who fall in love,' she said to herself, and her eyes were filled with tears.

Later, Anu entered the classroom dully and saw Arun sitting on the front bench. The chemistry professor told her to sit next to Arun. He moved to the next bench as she came to sit next to him.

'OK, you tell me about the phosphor sulphate reaction,' the professor asked her.

'I don't know sir,' she promptly replied.

'OK, fine, this has become a routine with you. Write this reaction fifty times and show it to me today itself,' he said angrily.

'Yes, sir,' Anu replied softly and sat. The class ended for lunch break. She took her bag and went to the last floor immediately. She started writing the reaction in her rough book.

Later, Arun entered the basketball court.

The college captain saw Arun and said, 'Hello, Arun, I saw you playing the day before. It was very impressive. You joining our team will definitely help. Will you join our team? Today there are no classes as well for the science branch.'

Arun gave a pause and later said, 'OK, I'll join your team.' He played well and made five baskets. They all stopped the game to have their lunch. Arun opened his lunch box and heard a voice.

'Hi Arun, you played really well, that was cool,' Prerana, his classmate, praised him.

'Ha, that's nice to hear. Do you know where Anu is?' he asked.

'I think she must be writing on the last floor,' she replied.

Closing his lunch box, he said, 'Oh thanks,' and ran upstairs.

Anu was on the last floor and Arun saw that Anu was quickly trying to complete the detention.

'Oh God, this detention has made me sick, hope this will end in ten minutes. Professor Chandra Shekar, why haunt me only? Can't see others?' Anu was murmuring to herself and continued to write. Arun came near her silently and hid behind a pillar so she could not notice him.

'Arun, you called me idiot. OK, but surely it's you who is the idiot, since you only made me believe that she's supposed to be your future darling. In order to promote that and that too because you are my friend, I thought I would mediate between you guys, hence I gave her your number so she could directly speak with you. It's really sad that you failed to understand my intention although you are my friend. Fine, your reactions show that you don't like her but I'm sure some day you have to fall in love with someone. At that time, who do you think will help you? Remember that it's going to be me only.' Anu spoke angrily to herself, and holding her stomach, she said, 'Oh God, I'm so hungry.' Arun smiled and also felt pity on her. She then got up and went to the staffroom.

'Excuse me, sir, may I come in?' Anu asked softly. The professor nodded his head to give permission, and she entered the room. After seeing her book, he warned her, saying, 'Next time, be careful and don't take another chance like this. You may go now,' and Anu went to her classroom. She was very tired.

A little later, Anu entered the classroom and rested her head on the bench. 'Arun is stupid. I am sure he will nicely be hogging lunch alone and making me feel hungrier. Oh my God, I didn't get my lunch today.' As she was murmuring, she heard, 'Anu,' and she lifted her head and softly said, 'Hi, Prerana.'

'Come on, have this,' Prerana said and gave her a warm foil-covered container.

'What is this?'

'Today's my treat, even I didn't get my lunch,' Prerana said, and Anu opened the container and took out the vegetable burger to have before saying anything further. Hiding behind the classroom door, Arun smiled, peeping, and Prerana turned back to see him and winked an eye, showing thumbs up. He went back to the field and opened the lunch box to have his lunch but didn't feel like eating it because he had hurt Anu's feelings. He closed the lunch box and gulped some water. He then went to play the game.

Anu got down the stairs and looked around for Arun. He saw her but pretended that he didn't. She restlessly walked out towards the gate and slowly turned back to see him again, but he continued to pretend. She went away with disappointment. A little later, he went into the classroom and sat. Dreamily looking at the blackboard constantly, he said to himself, 'Oh my God, let all my thoughts move away from me for a while,' and took his physics textbook to study.

After some time, he left the classroom. Arun rode his bike and stopped near a small boy who was sitting at the corner of the road. He opened his lunch box and gave him the food. The boy started eating quickly, and he left the place with a bit of satisfaction.

Sandhya in the botanical garden was thinking about Anu and Arun. 'I'm missing them a lot, Madan, it's boring without Anu,' Sandhya said, plucking the leaves and flowers and writing their features in detail.

Anu sat on the sofa reading some magazine; *tring tring*, the phone rang. Her father picked up the phone, and after he learnt that it was Sandhya's call, he asked, 'Hello, beta, how's the trip?'

'Fine, uncle,' Sandhya replied.

Anu came quickly and took the receiver. 'Hi, Sandhya, how's the trip?' she asked excitedly.

'It's boring without you, by the way, how is Arun?' Sandhya asked dully.

Looking around, she said softly, 'Yeah, he's fine.'

'OK, fine, we are leaving tomorrow night. Wait, Madan wants to speak to you,' Sandhya said, giggling, and gave him the cell phone.

'Hello, Anu,' said Madan, but Anu had already hung up the phone.

'She disconnected the call,' Madan said with a tangled look.

'See, I was right, I told you that she will not speak,' Sandhya said, smiling.

'Oh no, I so wanted to speak with her. You know what, something went wrong between Anu and Arun,' Madan said seriously.

Arun entered the house and as soon as he saw Nirmala; he was upset, recalling Shailaja's phone call. Nirmala saw Arun entering upset; she called him and made him sit beside her. 'Don't be so upset about the girl's call this morning,' she said, serving him some snacks with coffee.

'You know what, I blasted Anu. It is because of her that girl got the courage to call up my home. After scolding her, I didn't even speak to her in order to punish her, but after seeing her in tears, I'm feeling as though I'm punishing myself. I realized that her intention was to only make me feel happy and support me,' Arun said and his eyes were filled with tears.

'Arun, don't worry, sometimes fighting with friends will only make your friendship stronger. Go and apologize, I am sure she will understand and forgive you. Now relax and forget it,' Nirmala consoled him.

Late in the evening, Arun took his bike in order to buy few things. He stopped at a huge junction near a signal and saw a beggar wrapped in a torn rug around. The beggar knocked on the window of a car and pleaded for money, saying, 'Sir . . . sir . . .' He then showed his leg to the person in the car and said, 'Sir, look, I'm handicapped, please give me some money, sir.'

The car's window opened slowly and five persons were seated in it.

'What's your name?' a person who was wearing sunglasses asked the beggar sharply.

'My name is Govinda,' the beggar replied.

A person who sat next to him took out a book and that book had the details of persons' names along with area name, written in a list. He went through the list and nodded his head with a serious stare at his boss.

Pointing at the beggar, the boss said seriously, 'Catch him quickly, don't leave.'

Arun heard this conversation and feverishly spoke to himself. 'He-he's, I think I have . . .' Suddenly, four men came out of the car and started chasing the beggar. The beggar quickly ran towards the other side of the road, snaking through heavy traffic. Arun followed him on his bike with full speed and stopped near the beggar.

'Come on, sit fast,' Arun said hurriedly. The beggar jumped immediately on Arun's bike and covered its number plate with his torn rug. Arun rode very fast, and people who were chasing the beggar failed to chase the bike. He stopped his bike after he thought that it was safe then.

'Thanks, Arun.'

'Oh, Karthik, why are you disguised like this, what are you up to?'

Putting on his spectacles, Karthik replied, 'Please don't ask me anything, I can't reveal anything now,' and corrected his clothes.

As he continued to walk, Arun asked seriously, 'I should know this.'

'Don't worry; I'll let you know in future. In fact, the less you know us, the better it would be for you,' Karthik replied and went away.

Anu was not feeling like going to college the next day and hence told her mother not to wake her up early in the morning. She quickly fell asleep and, after a while, got up suddenly and said, 'Oh my God . . . no . . . it shouldn't happen that way,' because she had just dreamt that Sandhya slapped Prashanth.

Next day in the morning, Arun woke up around 6 a.m. He exercised in the gym for about ten minutes and got ready quickly. He stuffed a few spoons of lemon rice in his mouth, took his bag, and zoomed, riding his bike. He reached his college and honked at the gate so the guard would open it. 'Don't you know it's very early to open,' the guard said.

'I know, but just allow me to sit inside, actually I have to wait for someone to come,' he said sharply.

'No, the gate will be opened at seven sharp only,' the guard replied.

'See my ID card, can't you trust me?' he said seriously. The security guard allowed him inside and he felt restless sitting alone, looking at his watch. 'By this time, Anu should have come, why has she not come yet?' Arun murmured and looked at the gate with frustration.

He waited for a long time and it was time for his class. After the first period, there were no classes and he called his sister. 'Hello, Didi, I will go mad staying here.'

'Why?'

'Didi, only few students have come, that is why we don't have classes for the rest of the day.'

'Are you sure?'

'Yes, Didi, I'm quite sure.'

'OK, fine, just wait and I'll send Lokaiah along with a leave letter.'

After an hour, Arun got the letter from his driver Lokaiah. Taking the letter, he went to the office to get the permission for leave. After getting permission for leave, he went to his favourite park. The security guard at the park smiled, wishing Arun well. He walked inside the park and entered inside the fencing where the security guard's quarters were located. Nearby, there was a huge tree; the security guard had made a small platform and a small hut (like a machan) on it for viewing the whole park. He had made a ladder out of rope, using coconut fibre, for climbing to reach the platform.

Arun often visited the park for reading. He had befriended the security guard. Sometimes, he was also teaching the security guard's daughter. He climbed to the treetop to reach the hut, using the rope ladder and the view looked quite pleasant with greenery all around. None of them were allowed to climb the tree to reach the hut on the treetop except Arun. He had hidden Anu's photo in the hut and took it out. He dreamily looked at it and a pleasant breeze made him sleep. A little later, he woke up. He immersed his mind in the books for almost couple of hours and later played his favourite tunes on his mobile to relax.

Arun reached the house around 7 p.m. and Nirmala was waiting impatiently. 'What do you think of yourself? Where have you been for so long?' she blasted him as soon as she saw him. He felt as though his sister had turned into a dragon.

'You know what, I have been to my favourite park. I just wanted to stay alone for some time,' he casually replied without being tense.

'OK . . . OK . . . from next time, always inform me and then go wherever you want to,' Nirmala said angrily. A little later after having his dinner, he fell asleep.

The same day in the morning, Prashanth had been to the college but Anu's words were still echoing in his ears. He began to think about love seriously which was only fun for him before he heard Anu and her words made him realize what true love is.

'What happened?' excitedly Vishaal asked.

'I told her and she has asked for some time to think,' he replied casually with a lie.

He bunked off his classes and made his mind strong to express his love to her. He sat on a bench in a nearby park and began thinking, 'What to do, getting flowers from dad's money will not give any value for love.' Later, he wandered until evening to look for a small job but couldn't find one, as he wanted to earn some money to buy flowers for expressing his love to Sandhya since she would be coming back from the trip the next day and he rang up Vishaal immediately.

'Hello, dude, I'm searching for a night job. My dad won't believe me, so just inform him that I'm having group studies with you tonight.'

'Dude, are you all right? Why did you bunk off the classes without telling me? Has something gone wrong with you? Has your pocket gone dry? If that's the case, dude, don't worry, I can lend you some money.'

'No, dude, it's not about the money. I'll tell you later, please do this favour,' he said and disconnected the call before Vishaal could speak further.

Prashanth entered a park and sat on a bench after wandering for a few hours. He fell into thoughts about how to earn some money and saw an old man digging the ground so he could plant saplings. Prashanth went near him and asked whether he could work for him to plant the saplings.

The old man, laughing at him said, 'You look like an educated person. Why do you need to do this kind of a job, huh? This kind of work is meant for illiterate people like us. But still, if you really want to work, then join me.' Prashanth nodded his head in affirmation and started ploughing the ground, and the old man showed him how to plant. He worked until midnight and later slept in the park itself.

That evening, Anu was washing her face. She looked dull, as she had to wear a sari to attend a marriage reception. Her mother helped her to dress, and she was dressed up but again looking dull. 'It's always the case with you, you're so beautiful and look great when you dress up well but you still look like a sad doll,' Shwetha commented on Anu.

Anu didn't speak a word. They all got ready and went to attend the function.

In the reception hall, Anu looked around and she felt very awkward as someone was staring at her. The mother looked very happy, as their relatives were showing interest in Anu and they enquired about her studies.

'After her second year PUC if we find a suitable guy, we'll definitely think about her marriage,' Anu's mother said to her relatives. Anu gave a grudging look at her mother. After the reception was over, they all went home.

Next day, Prashanth got up around 4 a.m. and the old man told him to water the plants. After watering the plants, he carried manure and mud to pin the plants. It was about 6.30 a.m., Prashanth was sweating even in the cold. He wiped the mud off his face and dusted his clothes. The old man removed a fifty-rupee note from his pocket to give it to Prashanth.

'Thanks, grandpa, but can I take those flowers instead?' he requested. The old man smiled and tapped his shoulders. He plucked all varieties of flowers and gave it to him. Prashanth said bye and left the garden.

That morning, Shwetha saw Anu praying in front of God's photo.

'Oh God, help Prashanth, let him do something wonderful to impress her.'

'Didi, without brushing your teeth, you're praying,' Shwetha said, giggling and showing her thumbs down. 'I'm sure your prayer will go for a tussssss . . .' she said.

'Great prediction, shut up,' Anu said and got ready for college. Same day in the morning, Arun was getting ready with not much energy.

'Today all your friends must be coming, then why are you looking so dull?' Nirmala asked him.

'Oh yeah, you are right,' Arun said with a smile and hurried off to the washroom to get ready.

Later, Anu reached her college and began to think how Sandhya would react to Prashanth's proposal. Arun saw Anu and he ran towards her. Even she came running and both were breathing fast.

'You know something superb?' She sounded excited as she was expecting that Prashanth would come here to express his love to Sandhya since she was coming today.

'What's superb . . .' He was puzzled and offered her some mints.

'Just wait, keep watching and see what's going to happen,' she replied and took some mints. 'Oh God, I'm feeling so nervous, I hope nothing goes wrong.' She sounded very excited and went around the field to look for other friends.

Looking at her, Arun said to himself, 'Thank God she is not angry at me anymore, my girl has a peculiar attitude,' took his bag, and followed her.

'Oops!' Arun shouted as Madan jumped on his shoulders and hugged him from behind. Madan looked at Anu after greeting Arun.

'Hi, Madan,' Anu greeted him.

'Hi, Anu, great to see you, Sandhya was upset without you,' he said. As Anu was listening to Madan about the trip, Sandhya jumped from behind on Anu and loudly said 'Hooo' in her ear and they hugged tightly.

'Stupid, couldn't call me even for one time? Just one call, Anu,' Sandhya said.

Meanwhile, holding a bunch of flowers, Prashanth stood under a banyan tree and was sweating badly as he walked very fast from the garden where he worked since yesterday and which was about three kilometres from Sandhya's college.

'Guys, come on, let's go to our class,' Arun called them but Anu often looked back towards the gate.

Looking at the gate, Madan said, 'Hey, look at that guy near the gate holding some flowers, the security guard is not allowing him to enter.'

Anu saw and ran quickly towards the gate.

Looking at the security guard, Anu said, 'Hi, I know him . . . Please allow him.'

'All the best,' she whispered in his ear, and everyone's eyes were perplexed as she was coming along with him.

'He's my tuition mate Prashanth,' Sandhya said to Arun as she saw him coming near her. Prashanth began shivering as he approached Sandhya and Anu came near Arun after tapping him. Arun met Anu's face with bewilderment and Sandhya moved towards Prashanth.

'Hi, sorry, you have come here for the book, right? I should've returned the book, but I . . .' she said regretfully and gave a pause, looking at the flower bunch curiously.

He kneeled in front of her suddenly and stretched his hands, offering her flowers. Sandhya froze and couldn't speak a word.

'Sandhya, I love you,' he said and stood up firmly, with sweat running all over his face. There was complete silence and nobody spoke. Anu's heart started beating faster with tension.

'Wow!' Madan said and started clapping his hands.

Tensely biting her nails, Anu reacted. 'Stupid, she didn't say yes yet.' He stopped clapping immediately.

Looking at Prashanth, Anu asked, 'Why is your shirt so wet and why do you look so tired?' .

'Sorry, I can't give a reason, but a great person has told me that taking Dad's money and spending for loved one is not great. I swear I bought these flowers with my own earning,' he replied and turned towards Sandhya. He continued, 'Please listen, Sandhya, whatever my heart says, I'll follow and I am ready to do anything for you. I don't know whether I will be able to accomplish it but I'll promise you that I'll remain with you forever.' He sounded very emotional.

With tears rolling in her eyes, Sandhya said in a very angry tone, 'Shut up, just shut up. Just because I am keeping quiet, do you think that you can speak whatever you want?'

'No, Sandhya, I'm speaking truly from my heart.'

'Go to hell, is this the age to go through all these?' Sandhya shot back angrily.

'Love has no age, it's a feeling that comes through our heart and it's gifted by God. I have to—sorry, I mean we have to accept it,' Prashanth spoke in a shivering voice.

'I can't understand all this, please go, get lost,' Sandhya said and pushed him. He sat on the ground, and after a pause looking at him angrily, she said, 'OK! You do whatever your heart says is right. In my opinion, love is merely a waste and is suitable for only those who have no responsibility and dedication. If you really love me, show me that you are sincere in your studies.'

Madan, tapping Prashanth's shoulders, said, 'Look, brother, if you secure high percentage in your exams, she will definitely accept your love. Take it as a challenge and prove that your love is real.' Madan deliberately said this loudly so that Sandhya could hear, as she had gone a little distance away. Hearing this, Sandhya turned back, gave a grudging look at Madan, and walked away.

Anu gave a water bottle to Prashanth but he kept the bottle aside and put his head down restlessly.

'See, Prashanth, be ready to fight for your love, her challenge is nothing in front of your love. You know, why Sandhya has told you to show more interest in studies is that she wants you to get through in both. Try hard to secure high marks. Your love should inspire you to work hard, and I'm sure that this act of yours will definitely win her heart. Come on, cheer up,' Anu said and patted him on the back, consoling him. He took the water bottle and drank the entire bottle at a stretch.

'Anu, your advice has given me hope and belief in my love, thank you,' Prashanth said in a determined tone.

'Bye, all the best.' Madan and Arun wished him well and he left after wishing them goodbye.

Sandhya started shivering as Prashanth left and Anu rubbed her hands. 'You're shivering for this, just for this, you scary chick,' Madan teased and burst out laughing. Even Arun giggled, tapping on her head. A little later, they went to their classroom, their half day was spent in dealing with difficult lessons, and Anu had to clear some doubts through Arun. Sandhya at lunch break started shivering more.

'What happened?' Anu asked and touched her forehead.

'Ho! It's so hot.' Anu sounded worried and took a plain paper sheet to write a leave letter for Sandhya. After writing the leave letter, she asked Sandhya to sign on it. Arun went quickly inside the staffroom with the letter to get permission for leave. Meantime, Madan called an auto and Anu helped her to get into the auto.

Anu also entered the auto but she stopped her. 'Don't come with me by taking this as an excuse to bunk off the classes,' Sandhya said in a tired voice and suddenly vomited. Even Anu's dress got dirty. She ran towards Madan, grabbed the water bottle to help Sandhya wash her mouth, and made Sandhya have some water. The auto left immediately. Anu looking at both, said, 'I'm scared whether she will reach home safely,' and cleaned her dress.

Tapping her shoulders, Madan replied, 'Don't worry, she'll be OK. She will give you a call as soon as she reaches home.'

Arun, pressing his fingers, was thinking about Sandhya. Anu grabbed the mobile phone before Arun could speak, as the mobile beeped. 'Hello, Sandhya, thank God you reached home. Did you consult your doctor? Don't worry, don't think of anything, go to sleep,' Anu said dully.

'Yes,' Sandhya replied very slowly.

'OK, don't speak now, don't forget to take tablets, OK, bye,' Anu spoke in a hurry with worried voice and disconnected the call.

Looking at her anxiety and concern for Sandhya, Arun murmured to himself, 'You are showing as much concern as her mother would have shown if she was alive. She's very lucky to have such a sweet friend.' Looking at her, he said, 'Anu, what's your problem? She'll be fine, relax,' as she was thinking deeply again about something.

'No, not that, can you help me?'

'Yeah sure, tell me?'

'Please can you give your notes to Prashanth? It'll be helpful for him so that he can understand the lessons easily, fine, bye,' she said and went in a hurry without hearing his reply. Arun tapped his head and could not understand her. He felt strange about her behaviour and later joined his friends to play basketball.

Anu reached home quickly and lied to her mother that she was going to temple for praying. She soon reached Sandhya's house, saw Sandhya's father had not come yet, and entered the kitchen to prepare rice and dal soup, and while preparing it, she added garlic, pepper, etc. Anu fed Sandhya since she was tired and sleepy. She gave her tablets with hot water and later covered her with a blanket. She left after saying bye, and Sandhya fell into a deep sleep. Anu came back to her home; after studying promptly, she went to the terrace. She was looking dull. She tried, but couldn't see the moon. This added to her dullness. She then sat leaning against the wall and looked towards the sky dreamily.

Next morning, Prashanth reached his college. 'Hey, dude, why are you looking so dull?' Vishaal questioned him curiously, but he didn't answer. He left the place and sat on a bench. Deepthi and Vishaal came near him. She offered him some juice to drink. After drinking the juice, he went to the classroom without speaking much.

In the classroom, giving a confused look at Prashanth, Shruthi said to Deepthi, 'These days he's acting very strange.' After the classes were over, Deepthi came near Prashanth. 'Hello, stop dreaming, what's wrong with you, huh?' she asked seriously.

'Nothing, I'm completely fine, can you teach me mathematics and physics?' he asked and took out a textbook from his bag.

'Oh sure, I just can't believe this,' she said and started explaining.

Seeing that Prashanth was actually studying, Vishaal was flummoxed. Looking at him, he said, 'How come, dude, you've become so serious in studies? Very surprising.'

'No, dude, nothing much, my casual approach towards studies has resulted in poor marks in my tuition tests, so I thought of putting in some more effort,' he replied dully and continued to refer to the book. After the classes were over, he went home.

It was late night and Prashanth was studying in his room. Prashanth's mother saw his room's light was switched on and knocked on the door curiously.

Looking through the window, she asked, 'What are you doing?' and was surprised to see that he was studying. She said, 'This is unbelievable. How come you're studying, do you have any exams tomorrow?'

'No, but next week I do, in our tuitions.'

'Oh my God, you usually touch your books just a day before your exam. How come you have become so sincere towards your studies? Let's see your performance in the coming exams,' she said and left the room.

Vishaal also got added inspiration from Prashanth and even he began to study more seriously. He got help from his brother's wife to learn drawing some diagrams in order to draw these more neatly.

The doorbell rang; Nirmala opened the door and was surprised to see who the guest was.

'Hi, Siddharth, what a great surprise, come in,' she invited him with a smile and called Arun immediately. Arun was thinking something deeply, and as soon as he heard his sister's call, he suddenly got up from the chair and came down the stairs.

'Hello, sir, nice to meet you,' Arun greeted as he saw Siddharth.

Tapping his shoulders, Siddharth asked him, 'How are your studies going on?'

'Quite OK,' he replied firmly.

Nirmala arranged for the dinner and Arun felt very happy seeing his sister enjoying the dinner with her college friend Dr Siddharth. He was a specialist in brain surgery and a psychiatrist as well. Later, Siddharth left after wishing them well and Arun went upstairs. He called up Sandhya immediately and asked, 'How are you feeling now?'

'Quite better now, I'm even sweating and all this is just because of Anu's magic hands, she fed me some dal soup with hot rice,' Sandhya replied.

'OK then, you need complete rest, so take complete rest and also good care of yourself,' he said and ended the call with a sigh. 'I should have been in your place,' he thought and fell asleep.

OPERATION SPRAY

*I*n the Presidency College, it was a very busy day for the office bearers of the old students association, since they were discussing about arrangements to felicitate Professor Subhas Karuna on the eve of his twenty-fifth anniversary of his service as a professor. They arranged to display the list of programmes on display banners, sent invitations to the old students who held high positions in various government departments currently and to all the members of the old students' association. The students were very enthusiastic to perform various cultural programmes on the eve. Finally, the awaited felicitation day had come and the volunteers decorated the college nicely. They built a huge spectator area with seating arrangements. As expected, the maximum number of invitees gathered, and their mood was upbeat since they met their old friends after a long gap.

The programme began with a welcome speech, and everyone gave a standing ovation when Professor Subhas Karuna ascended the dais. The students performed cultural programmes with enthusiasm. Everyone's eyes widened as the anchor announced, 'We welcome Professor Subhas Karuna to come on the podium for giving a speech.' He walked towards the podium, waving his hands at the crowd smilingly, and began to speak, 'Dear students, friends, I'm overwhelmed by your love and affection showered on me, I thank you all for your contribution and participation in various programmes so far. I never had a flake of hope at the beginning that we would achieve this to this extent. Our college has become a breeding ground for soldiers, police officers, intellectuals, scientists, journalists, etc. and it's a proud moment to all of us as we are getting an opportunity to serve our country selflessly. Our elders have achieved the independence with utmost difficulty, their sacrifice and efforts shouldn't go to waste. Even after fifty years of our independence, we have much left to achieve by eradicating poverty and antisocial elements from our society. Evil minds have no caste or creed so we shall fight it in unity. The gap is widening between the rich and poor. Political parties and corrupt government officials exploit the poor. Many parties are dividing our society on the lines of caste and religion. All the political parties are corrupt in one way or the other. There may be some honest politicians whose hands are tied because of various reasons as well as pressures within. I urge all the old students who are serving in the government to be honest and try to put their efforts for the system to function correctly without any bias, to provide justice to all the sections of society. Please don't be a mute spectator by watching the system fail. There isn't much to tell since you're all well aware of every aspect of our country. All the political parties are engaging in mud-slinging at each other to get political advantage. In some cases, many ministers have failed to take action against criminals and rapists who have political background by fearing it may be a deterrent to their political future or their party and personally as well. They have become broad-daylight looters of our country. I dream of a prosperous and peaceful India. Also, wish to see a casteless society and everyone as an Indian. I wish everyone success in their life, thank you all. Jai Hind!'

Everyone stood up clapping hands to give a thunderous applause. Later, many intellectuals and old students spoke about their experience and moments they had in the past with Professor Subhas Karuna. They promised their honest commitment for the society. The old students carried Professor Subhas Karuna on their shoulders and took him around the gathering.

After thanksgiving, Karthik announced, 'Dear friends, lunch has been arranged on the top floor by the old students association. The old students after lunch can interact with our beloved Professor Subhas Karuna. Please gather in the conference hall at 4 p.m. Kindly have your lunch, thank you.'

The old students hugged each other while greeting their friends; some of them were laughing at each other by recalling their golden days spent in the college. The whole atmosphere was filled with happiness and excitement. The present prefects served the food to the old students, and everyone had their lunch. Karthik gave instructions to the volunteers to do various tasks.

At 4 p.m. in the conference hall, nearly a hundred old students from various walks of life had gathered to interact with their honoured Professor Subhas Karuna. Everyone stood up as the professor entered the hall. A little later, Karthik announced, 'Those who want to interact with the professor, please give your names to the volunteers waiting to take them.' About fifteen persons gave their names.

Karthik handed over the mike so the person whose name was at the top of the list could speak, and he took the mike and said, 'Sir, it's my pleasure to speak with you. I was your student in the year 1980, my name is Shyam Sunder and I'm very much moved hearing your speech. In what way can we help you to bring about changes in our society? At present I'm serving as DIG in Tamil Nadu.'

'Ha, very good, Shyam Sunder. I think you're a black-belt holder in karate, am I right?' the professor answered.

'Very correct, sir, thank you for remembering that.' And the professor continued, 'Look, our country has the political system, the judicial system, and the administrative system to run the country smoothly. Now these systems act fast only for the high society by virtue of influence and media attention, whereas for the middle and deprived classes, these systems act very slowly with negligence leading to denial of justice to them. Criminals with political connections will go scot-free even though they are proven guilty. Some officials and lawyers are taking advantage of some loopholes that exist in our system. Politicians change like a chameleon according to the situation. All of you can help each other by passing the information about the criminals, corrupt people, rapists, and murderers who escaped from the system with the influence of politicians, high officials, and judicial loopholes. This will enable us to destroy their criminal and illegal establishments indirectly and also provides the authentic and solid proof to the system so that they can't escape from the eyes of law. Suppose someone amongst yourselves provided the information about a dreadful criminal, you can encounter them at the spot where he is operating. Hope you got my point.'

'A very good suggestion, sir, I got it and I'll co-operate,' Shyam Sunder replied.

'Next in line is Mahesh,' Karthik announced.

'Sir, I was your student in the year 1983. Now I'm practicing law, my question is, isn't it unethical and wrong to punish a guilty person without going through the judicial system? Our judicial ethics say, "Leave ten guilty persons but do not punish one innocent." If we take law into our hands in our own way, what will be the guarantee that we will punish only the guilty? Our profession code says, "We should argue and defend in favour of the guilty until he's proven guilty" May I know your viewpoint on this sir?'

Mahesh took out a swirling question out of his mind. Professor Subhas Karuna gulped a glass of water and everyone laughed.

'You have put up a good point really. Yes, it is unethical and wrong to go against the system as you said, but those acts that you are speaking of are outdated. It is irrelevant to the present situation of our country. In the past, majority of administrators were honest and efficient. Now politicians, big industrialists are looting our country's resources for their personal gains in the name of development and the poor people are left with nothing except mere assurance during elections. Have you ever argued for the poor without taking remuneration? Some famous lawyers argue in favour of the poor only if it is sensational or a much-publicized event. Popular and professional lawyers will gang up to argue in favour of rich industrialists and politicians. They try to their level best to protect them from the clutches of law by hook or crook and thereby take advantage of loopholes that exist in the judicial system, thus denying the justice to the affected. I was denied justice for various reasons. Though the justice was favourably delivered, it was never implemented although my father was a freedom fighter and I knew highly placed persons. The system had let off the guilty, because of pressure and political reasons, and then you think, what about the illiterates and poor people? They can't even dream of getting justice. There is a lot of bias between poor person's guilt and rich person's guilt. I have decided to frustrate the evil people present in our society after my horrible experience with the system by giving back to them in the same manner what they gave us. Our foundation volunteers are working very hard to wipe out cruelty in our society, causing damage indirectly to their illegal establishments since they cannot complain to anyone legally. Sorry, Mahesh, if I have hurt you by commenting about your profession.'

The professor's words had aroused him.

'No, sir, not at all, what you're saying is right, sir,' Mahesh replied calmly.

The remaining thirteen students asked various questions to clear their doubts, and the time was around 7 p.m. At last, a student stood up, raising his hand. 'Sir, I'm Manikantan from Kerala, I heard everyone's views, sir, the bad elements in our society are like insects and if we leave them they will multiply manifold. My only suggestion is, sir, that we have to wipe out such bad elements like we kill the insects by spraying them to protect ourselves from diseases. Our Baba Vishwanathan knew your father very well, sir. I'm quite sure he gives very good suggestions to plan your programmes without risking anyone.' He spoke firmly and Professor Subhas Karuna nodded his head with affirmation slowly.

'Definitely I'll meet him, even I heard about him before. You can meet me later to discuss about visiting him,' the professor said. Everyone left the place after greeting the professor with a handshake.

A few days later, Manikantan and Professor Subhas Karuna went to the Anaimalai Hills adjoining Kerala and Tamil Nadu states. Manikantan escorted the professor deep inside the thick forest by walking and they both walked about fifteen kilometres. They then climbed a hill; both were exhausted as they reached a small ashram. Both saw guru Baba Vishwanathan watering the plants. They came near the guruji and touched his feet to seek his blessings. The baba offered seats on the wooden benches and they sat.

The baba went inside to get some fruits and offered them the fruits to eat. Manikantan introduced his professor. 'Babaji, he's our professor, Subhas Karuna, vice principal of our college in Bengaluru. I think you even know his father and you told me long before that he was a freedom fighter.'

'Ha, I remember, Karuna Prasad is your father, how is he?' Baba asked.

'Yes, Baba, you're right but he passed away about six years ago and he told me long ago that he had a best friend who stays in Kerala. He neither mentioned the name nor address in detail,' the professor replied.

'We both participated in the freedom movement. He saved my life while a bullet was about to hit my chest but he becoming alert pushed me quickly and it went through his hand. He was very courageous, never cared for his life. He organized many demonstrations very effectively. Sorry to hear that he's no more. By the way, may I know the reason behind your visit?' Baba questioned Subhas Karuna, but he gestured at Manikantan to answer.

'Babaji, his father and you fought against the British rule. For the past twenty-five years, my professor Subhas Karuna has been fighting against the evils of our society. He's creating fear in the minds of criminals, corrupt people and running a foundation to fight against the cruel people. Its volunteers have destroyed the illicit liquor factories, saved many girls from entering into flesh trade, and informed whereabouts of the criminals to honest officials to take action against them. He's the inspiration for thousands of students,' Manikantan replied.

Baba said, 'We used to fight only against the British rule. Now I know how much difficult it is to fight against the corruption and the criminals. Only the rich and the middle class are reaping the benefits of country's freedom. The politicians couldn't eradicate poverty even after fifty years of independence. How much ever the country has progressed, was done at the beginning. Crores of people still don't have proper shelter and food. Only the rich are enjoying our country's freedom. I cannot tolerate the hardship faced by our people, especially in rural areas and therefore decided to live here,' and after a pause, Baba asked, 'Tell me what I can do for you,' looking at Subhas Karuna curiously.

'Babaji, although my foundation is working quite effectively, a few ministers and MLAs have their own illegal activities such as illicit liquor manufacturing, operating human trafficking in an organized way. The government is sitting helplessly without initiating any action on them since they will lose their majority to run the government if they take action, hence they are doing these activities openly, rapes and extortion have become daily news, and it is spreading like a deadly disease. Manikantan told me that you know the secret of rare herbs which kill a person gradually without harming organs inside the body,' the professor said and Manikantan, looking at Baba, said,

'Sorry, Babaji, I told him this without seeking your permission. After hearing the dreadful incidents happening in our country, I could not control myself and told our professor about this, so he can use it against the culprits,' he intervened.

'That's OK, you have told your professor with good intention,' Baba replied and looked at Subhas Karuna. 'Subhas, the rare herbs he spoke about is very dangerous. The person dies after one or two years with a torturing pain in their internal parts without giving any clue as it disrupts the functioning of the organs slowly. It is impossible to find out the reason even after going through lab tests and also it's impossible to find out from which herbs it's prepared even if they detect its substance. Only our guru's ancestors knew about it, my guruji was well experienced in the Ayurvedic medicines. One day, while looking at some medicine bottles, I took out a very small bottle and that had "Mruthyu moolika" written on its label. I curiously asked my guru regarding its usage. "It's used to kill," he replied and continued, "It was used by the kings to kill their enemies and traitors without a clue, using a small pin. First, the pins were coated with the solution and were fixed to their rings in such a way that the pin came out from the ring to pierce the enemy's hand when the fingers were pressed while shaking the hands. It slightly pierces the enemy's hand as the enemies shake their hands. Just a slight pierce is enough to kill them. That's how they were used to kill them." My guruji handed over all the medicine bottles to me before he passed away, but I'm not sure whether that bottle is still there. In my opinion, it is wrong to kill a person in that manner but I know that you are helpless. I'll agree to give it to you if I find the bottle only because you're Prasad's son. I'll trust you and I am quite sure you won't misuse it.'

'OK, Manikantan, show the garden to your professor,' Baba said and went to prepare food.

Manikantan and Subhas Karuna began to roam around the garden. He showed some rare herbs to his professor and explained their uses as well.

'Sir, look at this plant. The hairs won't grow forever on the cheeks by applying the juice of those leaves.'

Subhas Karuna laughed.

'Then we can avoid our shaving expenses. There are so many secrets hidden in nature, proper research shall be done to the benefit of mankind,' the professor said, and later, both entered the ashram.

They saw that Baba himself was cooking food. He prepared boiled rice and sambar with vegetables. He served them and the food was simple and tasty. Later, looking at each bottle's description on it, Baba started searching for the bottle. Finally, he found a very small bottle and the words written on it were not clearly visible. He took the bottle carefully and went in an open area to read its label; it had 'Mruthyu moolika' written in very small words. To his surprise, there wasn't any solution left in the bottle except black stuff less than half a pinch. He opened the lid carefully and added ten to twelve drops of some solution into it. He closed the lid quickly and packed it in a box.

Giving it to Subhas Karuna, Baba said, 'Luckily you got it. It's enough to send fifty people to hell. Be very careful. Just coat it on the tip of a pin by inserting the pins into the bottle, and don't look at it directly.' Both thanked Baba and left the place.

After a few days, the college had announced the first term exam results in the third week of October. Arun topped in all the subjects. Anu didn't score good marks, especially in mathematics and science subjects. Arun was disappointed after looking at her answer papers and advised her to concentrate more on studies. He also told her to get her doubts cleared from him as and when she had difficulty following something. Anu nodded her head dully, and the classes were conducted only half a day on that day.

Anu reached the bus stand and saw the bus moving. She saw two children and a lady who came near the bus stop to beg. Anu fell into thoughts: 'Why do children beg around? Why is the government not showing much interest about these children? Even we have to do something for the poor children. At least they should get basic education so that they can do some job instead of begging.'

After a few days, her college was conducting some programme on Children's Day. Her mind flashed an idea about conducting a programme on Children's Day. As she was thinking deeply, she said, 'Shit, I should have taken arts instead of science. I took science just to have Sandhya's company, which is really foolish. Tomorrow, I will put a letter in the suggestion box. Let's see whether the college programme committee considers my suggestion,' and boarded the next bus.

Shwetha knew that Anu's first-term exams results were going to be announced today. As soon as Anu entered the house,

Shwetha asked loudly, 'Didi, today's first-term result, show your answer papers. Let's see how much percentage you've scored.'

'They have postponed it, we will probably be getting it in the next week,' Anu replied and murmured, 'I must hide my answer papers, this idiot won't spare me,' but Shwetha didn't believe her and kept an eye. Later, through the window, she saw Anu was hiding the answer papers. Anu was looking quite tense. She then took a book to read.

Anu's father entered the house and everyone sat to have dinner later. Shwetha ran silently into Anu's room and took the answer papers. Holding the answer papers behind, she came near her father. English 85, she began to read. Anu came rushing to snatch the papers but Shwetha moved swiftly to other side and began reading.

'Anu, don't chase her, let's know your marks, why are you looking so tense?' their father asked angrily and Shwetha continued to read Anu's marks.

'In physics 43, chemistry 41, biology 45, and mathematics 40,' Anu looked at her grudgingly and warned her by showing fingers.

Anu's father seeing her expression, said, 'Why don't you tell me your marks yourself? Be serious in your studies. Only if you secure good marks in your final exams can you can continue your studies further. Otherwise what's the use of you getting such low percentage?'

Looking at Anu, her mother said, 'If you get just passing marks in second PUC, surely we'll look for a groom to get you married.' Shwetha laughed teasingly at Anu, and Anu, giving an angry look said, 'Stupid, if you score lower marks, even you'll be married soon after your tenth itself, me at least after couple of years later than you, so better mind yourself.'

'I'll score well, don't worry,' Shwetha said with a serious smile.

'Let's see,' Anu replied and their parents laughed hearing their arguments.

Next day, Anu dropped a letter into the suggestion box, hoping they would consider her idea. Two days later, a college staff member came to her class and called her name. Everyone looked in surprise at Anu, including the lecturer, and he informed her that after the classes, the principal wanted to meet her. Arun and Sandhya exchanged confused looks, and Anu gestured at them to wait. Later, Anu entered the principal's room and saw the principal, the vice principal, and Karthik. All of them smiled at her as she entered the room and offered her a seat. Looking at her, Professor Subhas Karuna asked her to elaborate her concept.

'Sir, our college has been distributing books, clothes, sweets, etc. on the eve of Children's Day every year and this can be done by any other charity institution. Those poor children require basic education, which will prevent them from begging and getting involved in antisocial activities, and they can do some jobs with dignity. They should learn at least how to read and write and know basic mathematics, but their parents are not sending them to school to learn, because of their poor financial condition. We have to make them realize the importance of education for their child's future, through direct interaction and by showing them through cultural programmes during Children's Day,' Anu said.

'Very good idea, but how to organize, I mean do you think all the children can be covered?' the principal asked with a little excitement.

'My suggestion, sir, is to let some of the volunteers visit their homes to inform them about the programme that we conduct and convince them to attend by inviting them. There is no need to collect money from the public to arrange funds for the programme. We should run a collection campaign inside the college premises and convince all the students to contribute voluntarily. Say, three days of their pocket money how much ever they get. This creates awareness among the students to do something for the needy people and my suggestion is that our college canteen should be closed for three days so that no one will be able to buy within the college premises,' Anu said with a little smile. Everyone laughed, clapping their hands; all of them agreed to appoint Karthik and Anu to organize the programme.

Next day, they held a prefects' meeting. Arun and Sandhya were among the prefects and were seated. Anu had informed Sandhya and Arun before the meeting about the programme to be conducted on the eve of Children's Day. They were very happy and appreciated her idea. Anu introduced herself, looking at the prefects. 'Friends, we need a minimum of five volunteers from each section. The prefects of the respective sections shall have the responsibility to collect the amount but please don't force anyone. Convince them, organize the cultural programme from each class, only two weeks left. There are five slums around this area, let's form five groups to visit those places and convince them to attend the programme,' she said and explained in detail about organizing the campaign.

After Anu's speech, Karthik stood up to speak.
'Friends, for three days, there will be no canteen in the college, that is, from Wednesday to Friday. The canteen management has agreed to close it. All the prefects shall inform the students to bring their lunch from home and also tell all the students to share their lunch to those who cannot bring because of inconvenience. It's a great opportunity to be a part of this movement, hope everyone co-operates with dedication. Thank you all.'
After the meeting, Karthik told some prefects to prepare banners as Anu handed over the caption 'Just save three days' pocket money to educate the poor'.

'You always hope for the good in others' lives, you're amazing,' Arun said to himself, looking dreamily at Anu, who was busy discussing with other guys.

Karthik collected money from the prefects. Later, Anu came to join him after the classes were over. They saw the canteen staff coming towards them. Anu bent her head down feeling guilty, as the proposal to close the canteen for three days was hers and thought that the staff might lose their wages but they came smiling near her to donate money.

'Thank you, madam, we are getting three days' leave as well as salary because of you. Our owner has arranged three days' trip for all of us and he is bearing the expenses himself,' one of the canteen staff said smilingly. Anu and Karthik smiled at each other and received the amount from the canteen staff. After Karthik collecting the money from prefects, Anu issued vouchers for that.

Anu was busy looking at the dance practice sessions and corrected the dance steps. Looking at her expression, Arun felt as though a lovely peacock was dancing.

In Anu's classroom, everyone discussed about the programme to be performed and some came out with different suggestions but Anu didn't feel that it was unique.

'See, all others are performing dance, it's better if we do something differently which entertains everyone, especially the children. How about doing a puppet show with dance?' Anu gave her opinion.

'Who will play it?' somebody asked.

'Nobody knows,' another person said.

'No problem, after all, it's a song and play mixed together, if we practice to pull the threads properly, that's sufficient. I have some experience, I'll show you all how it's done.'

'What will be the storyline of the play?' Arun asked.

Anu began thinking deeply and everyone started murmuring. After a few minutes, she asked whether someone had created the storyline but no one had it. Later, she said, 'Yes, I got it,' snapping her fingers; everyone looked at her and she started telling the story.

'See, guys, imagine a paddy field. Many villagers, including children, are working in hot weather, with sweat dripping. A small girl will be holding a ripe mango and watching them doing work. A monkey from the tree gets down suddenly, snatches the mango from her, and climbs up on the tree. The small girl cries for the mango, pointing towards the monkey. The children holding sticks will come to gather around her and disguise like dolls covering leaves. A boy climbs up the mango tree and plucks the mango to give her. They all will start dancing and even the small girl joins them. Meanwhile, an elderly villager gets down from a bullock cart and starts calculating the money with his fingers and looks at the paper sheet given by the paddy buyer with confusion. He won't be able to understand what's written, he will scratch his head and show it to his son but he also will not be able to understand. Later, the son passes the paper to his son and even he will not be able to understand. Everyone looks at the sheet curiously but none of them can make out what was written on it. They will all look at each other, twisting their hands towards the other side. A schoolteacher passes by and questions them about their worry. They will show the paper sheet, he will then explain them how to calculate and the elderly man will thank the teacher. Then they will explain to the audience through a song: "See your children and grandchildren should not fall into trouble like this, send your children to study, knowledge is more than wealth." Later the sun rises with chirping birds. The teacher will take rest under a banyan tree, as he shall be waiting for the children to come. Still they all have not turned up. He will hear the footsteps. All the children will be seated and he will happily dance with the children in the end.'

After hearing the story, everyone agreed to perform the play with some changes. Later, Anu explained and demonstrated how to play it scene by scene. She informed her friends to bring colour papers, cardboard, thermocol sheets, paints, and other accessories to decorate the sets. Everyone left the college after doing some practice.

Next day, all the prefects and volunteers came to college a little early. Karthik had made five batches to visit the slum areas. Arun and Sandhya were in Anu's batch. Anu had chosen to visit the Kannan slum area since she knew it very well. Everyone was surprised when they saw many slum dwellers knew her and spoke freely as they visited their houses. They listened patiently to what she said and the students invited them to attend the Children's Day programme. Anu informed them to bring along other people whom they knew. The volunteers visited nearly 750 houses in two days.

Looking at Anu, Arun asked in surprise, 'How come you know these people so well?'

'Three senior citizens are conducting classes for these children, along with me but I conduct classes only during weekends and holidays,' Anu said, pointing towards the shabby children who were playing in the muddy water.

'Why didn't you tell me this, how many more secrets are you hiding from us?' Sandhya asked in shock.

Anu smiled and took them near a room where the classes were held for the slum children. She introduced the three senior citizens to her friends. Later, they left the place to reach the college. 'How come your father does not have any problem sending you alone to teach those children?' Sandhya asked curiously.

'Oh, one of the volunteers is my father's uncle. He picks me up and drops me back when I have to conduct classes,' Anu replied.

In the college, all the volunteers were engaged. Many of them were drawing designs to make the screens and some others were making the dolls. The art teacher saw these and wasn't impressed much about their work.

'Guys, it's better to call my old student, she's an expert in the artworks. I am not sure that she can come here and help you out, since she got married recently. But nevertheless, we can still give it a try. Let's hope for the best,' the arts teacher said.

After the classes were over, Arun revised the portions and the clock struck five. Arun saw Anu sitting some distance away from him and she was restlessly plucking the grass. He decided to leave her alone and left the college to reach home.

After learning about Spandan's death, Anu wondered how she was able to see him and was yearning to meet him again. She thought that she must know Spandan's love Kirthi and at least their story. The time was six o'clock in the evening; the special classes for the below-average students were almost over. It was cloudy and dark all around. She ran upstairs breathing hard and there was no sign of him on the last floor. Frustratedly, Anu looking up, thought, 'My friend, where are you? I want to be your friend forever, if you're feeling my thoughts really, then show yourself,' and shouted, 'Spandan, Spandan' and her words were echoing. The atmosphere around her had turned into complete silence. 'Anu,' she heard suddenly from behind, and as she turned, giving a jerk, Spandan was standing there with a broad smile.

'Oh, you listened, thank God at least your appearance proved my humanity,' Anu said in a low tone with tears rolling down her eyes, and she touched his cheeks. He was cold, very cold.

'Are you a ghost really?' Anu asked him and he burst out laughing. Anu smiled dreamily, looking at him. After a pause, Anu questioned him curiously, 'Spandan, how's it possible that only I can see you?' and he became completely emotional.

'Your true friendship and affection on me has enabled me to show my appearance since you never showed any fear or hesitation to meet with an eternal person like me. Undoubtedly, you have some special power,' he said.

'Spandan, where is Kirthi? Did you express your love to her? Please tell me, I want to know,' she asked eagerly.

Tears rolled down his face but he smiled, looking at Anu. 'I came from a village and joined this college, my parents were from a very poor background. I was a very shy person and everyone in the class used to tease me except Kirthi. She proposed to be friends with me. She was the one who changed my attitude and helped me to strengthen my willpower. She encouraged me to participate in many seminars, debates, and that inspired me to win. I fell in love with her without my knowledge but I feared to express it, thinking whether she would accept, and also feared that this act of mine might make me lose her presence, I mean her friendship.'

'What does she look like?' Anu asked, looking at him curiously before he could continue further.

'Oh, she's like a beautiful mermaid with brownish eyes, she looks like a golden deer. I stayed in my sister's house. Once she happened to came to my sister's house. I was surprised, as I had not given my address to anyone, and she gifted me a beautiful painting. I asked the reason with more surprise and she wished me happy birthday. My heart drowned in a deep sea of joy. It was the first time that someone greeted me on my birthday, and since I had been lifeless before, I felt that I was reborn with joy when she greeted me. I was curious to know how she got my birth date and I asked. "I went through the admission register book in the office," she replied. All had gathered around us as she opened a box, and it was a cake beautifully decorated. She put that on a table and fixed candles to light. After she lit the candles, everyone sang the birthday song. It was an unforgettable moment in my life, and I felt that I want to spend the rest of my life with her, forever,' he said emotionally.

Continuing, he said, 'Kirthi used to love music, especially violin, hence I took violin classes and learnt to play it well. Whenever I saw that her mood was dull, I played violin to make her happy. When I was alive, I created many tunes and recorded them in the cassettes for gifting on her birthday.'

'Oh, sorry, I took those cassettes out of curiosity, since I saw the label "With love to Kirthi". My sole intention was to give them to her,' Anu said, feeling guilty.

'It's OK. My soul is unwilling to leave her memories until she is alive; I want to see her happy forever.'

Anu, wiping her tears, asked in a puzzled way, 'How did you lose her? How did you lose your life?'

'I became a police informer when I was in the final year. One day, I gave a video clip of a dreaded goon with others murdering a person to the police department. Later, I had become a witness in the court against him, and the court had passed a judgment to hang him. Later, his brother with other goons killed me. I left the material world with many of my wishes unfulfilled. I want to know what she feels in her heart about me,' he said desperately.

'Definitely she feels for you, good hearts never repel, true friendship and true love always attracts the loved one,' Anu said with emotion.

He waved his hands smilingly and disappeared. Anu, realizing that it had almost become dark, ran down the stairs to reach the main gate quickly, and the security guard near the gate shouted at Anu to come fast as he saw her coming. Anu reached home thinking about Spandan.

Looking at Anu, her mother asked in an angry tone, 'Why are you so late?'

'Special classes,' she replied curtly and went to her room.

Anu couldn't sleep as Kirthi was haunting her mind. 'Where she might be living, oh, I forgot to ask him,' she thought and restlessly was turning left and right on the bed. She began speaking to herself, 'Ho, Spandan, since you're an eternal person, you can show me Kirthi in my dream, please don't disappoint me,' and gradually fell asleep. In her dream, she saw a beautiful lady with curly hair, dressed in traditional sari, and she was lighting mud lamps. The light was about to go out from wind, but she covered the lamp using her hands. 'Kirthi,' she could hear someone calling and the lady turned back.

Anu woke up immediately and stammered, 'That . . . that . . . the voice sounded like that of Spandan. It means that you showed me Kirthi to recognize her and that she is very near, and if miracles do happen, show me tomorrow itself.' Suddenly recollecting the dream, she thought, 'Ha, she lit the lamp in a temple, which temple was that? Yes, thanks a lot,' and happy tears rolled down her face.

Anu woke up early in the morning and planned to visit temple since that day was a government holiday. 'Where are you going so early in the morning?' her mother asked in surprise after she got ready to go out.

'I'm going to temple,' Anu replied casually.

'Oh, nice that the God only has driven you to visit him,' her mother said and was very happy to see her daughter going to the temple.

'Oh, it's senseless for me to hope to find her in a temple just because I saw her in the dream. It's an illusion surely, but what will I lose if I try? Miracles do happen sometimes,' Anu thought and went to the temple. For about an hour, she watched the devotees who came into the temple, expecting some miracle to happen. She was looking at God frustratedly.

'Oh God, I have gone real crazy, oh no, which god did I see in dreams? Ha, I saw a saint, he's Raghavendra, ha, Sri Guru

Raghavendra swami.' She recalled her dream slowly and said to herself, 'Ha, today is Thursday, since this day is relevant to that god, I'll go to that temple right now. Oh God, please let me see Kirthi there.' She prayed to God and reached the saint's temple. She entered the temple; after praying, looking around, she sat leaning against a carved pillar.

That day in Vishaal's house, 'Bhabi, I'm ready,' Vishaal called Kirthi. She was his elder brother's wife. She came quickly, as he started his bike and sat behind him. He spoke about Deepthi while riding but she was listening quietly with not much reaction. The surroundings became breezy suddenly, as he came near the temple. Anu felt some kind of shiver in her heart.

'Bhabi, I think God is welcoming you,' he said, stopping his bike near the temple and Kirthi called him to come inside but he prayed from outside.

'Sorry, Bhabi, it's getting late, bye,' he said and rode his bike to go.

Looking at the god, Anu got up with disappointment but she didn't see Kirthi entering the temple. 'It's my bad luck, let me try next time. Oh, I came so far, let's wait outside at least five more minutes.' Murmuring, she blindly walked out and stood outside near the temple's door. A little later, she heard the temple's bell sound and turned towards the idol. Her mouth was wide open with a stunned look as she saw Kirthi praying to God. 'Oh God, thanks a lot,' she said in a breathy voice. After finishing her prayers, when Kirthi came near the temple's main door, Anu saw that she was wearing the Mangala Sutra around her neck and realized that she was married already. For a moment, Anu thought about whether or not to disclose Spandan's feelings towards her but Spandan's depressed face appeared right in front of her and then she made up her mind to reveal it and followed her blindly. Kirthi gave a confused look at Anu, as she sensed that she was being followed by Anu, and went walking very fast. 'Kirthi,' Anu called her name loudly. As she suddenly turned back, Anu ran towards her.

'How do you—' Kirthi asked in a perplexed way and Anu hugged her. 'Oh, stop it, sorry to ask you, who are you?' she asked seriously but Anu smiled. Kirthi got frustrated as she didn't get a reply and began to leave the place.

'Spandan,' Anu shouted loudly as Kirthi moved. She gave a sudden jerk and ran towards Anu.

'Yeah, yeah, how come you know Spandan?' She sounded very excited.

'He always speaks about you,' Anu said with emotion and Kirthi offered a handshake. 'Fine, I'm Anu.'

'Our bad luck he left all of us,' Kirthi said with deep emotion.

'But sorry to tell you that you've lost a great person who truly loves you. He loved you so madly that with the fear of losing you, he did not even express his love to you.' Hearing this, Kirthi was paralyzed and started sweating.

'I'm sorry to share this with you though you're married but there is no other way. You're living in his soul even now, just imagine how much he loves you and he's around us, thinking every second that you should be happy. Suppose Spandan had proposed to you, be frank, what would have been your reply?' Anu firmly questioned her.

Kirthi sat on the steps with a shock and began thinking deeply. A little later, she said, 'I treated him as a good friend but perhaps if I could have continued my journey with him, I would have got the feeling of love.' Kirthi sounded dreamy and completely drowned in Spandan's memory, with tears rolling down her face.

'I am sorry if I have hurt you,' Anu said and continued, 'Spandan had a wish to gift you on your birthday with his cassettes that contained many violin tunes created by him only for you. He will definitely be happy if you take those cassettes. Please meet me in the college to collect them,' Anu said.

'May I know which college?'

'Your college . . . Spandan's college . . .' Anu said, at which Kirthi, wiping her tears, said, 'Sure, I'll come tomorrow to take those cassettes with pleasure,' and left after wishing Anu goodbye.

Later, Kirthi reached home but her mind was disturbed. Thinking about Spandan, she sat on sofa and gave a call to her friend.

Kirthi's mother-in-law shouted, 'Kirthi, what's wrong with you, can't you hear the cooker's whistle?' But Kirthi was emotionally thinking about Spandan in her heart.

'Sorry, Ma, I'll shut it off, one minute,' she replied and continued to enquire about some address with her friend on the phone.

Later, she got ready to go out.

'Ma, I'm going out for shopping,' she said to her mother-in-law and left the house. She drove her vehicle for about forty-five minutes and reached a graveyard. She came near the gate to open it but it was stuck. She was trying to push it hard; an old man passing by helped her to open it. She entered slowly and most of the graves were covered with dry leaves. As she looked around, the surrounding became very breezy and the dry leaves began to swirl well above the ground. Using her hand, she covered her eyes for a while, and as the breeze stopped, she uncovered her eyes. Right opposite to her, she saw a carved gravestone which read, 'You will remain in our hearts forever Spandan.' Looking at it, her heart began to beat fast and she came near Spandan's grave. Trembling, she sat near it and tears rolled down from her eyes.

She wiped the gravestone using her dupatta and placed a bunch of flowers on it. 'Spandan, I had a feeling for you as a true friend. You know how much respect we had towards our friendship—that forced us not to express the feelings with each other openly. My heart will always love you forever,' she said and kissed the stone after putting a wrapped painting on it. She wept for a long time and didn't realize that it was drizzling. Her mobile started beeping; she opened her eyes slowly and stood up to go. She walked out dreamily and turned back to look at Spandan's grave. She saw her dupatta was stuck to the gravestone; she freed her dupatta and left the place to reach home.

On Kirthi's arrival, her mother-in-law asked, 'Why so late?' But Kirthi went to her room without replying and took a cold shower. Hardening her heart, she continued as usual.

After some time, Kirthi received a call. 'Hello.' She was surprised to hear her arts teacher's voice.

'Hello!'

'Am I speaking to Kirthi?'

'Yes, who is this?'

'Hi, Kirthi, it's me, Mohan Kumar. How are you?'

'I am fine, sir; it's a pleasure to talk to you again. How are you, sir?'

'I am fine, Kirthi. Just needed a favour from you, we are celebrating Children's Day, so I want your help in doing some craft works, can you help us?'

'Definitely, sir, it would be my pleasure to be of some help. Thanks a lot for remembering my arts work and me. When do you want me to come?' On hearing her teacher's answer, she replied, 'Sure, sir, I will be there tomorrow, bye,' and on her teacher's affirmation, she disconnected the line.

Anu took Spandan's cassettes curiously and was about to play them. She suddenly thought something and decided not to play them, because Spandan wanted to present them to Kirthi and listening to his cassettes like this would not be good. She then wrapped the cassettes using a gift wrapper neatly and wrote

'With love from Spandan' on a small greeting card and pasted it on the gift wrapper.

Next day, Anu reached her college very early and ran upstairs very happily to see Spandan. To her surprise, she heard heart-touching violin music she had never heard before. She entered the classroom and clapped her hands as she saw Spandan playing violin. Seeing her, he came closer to Anu and kissed her forehead. Anu felt it like the touch of air. Looking at her, he said happily, 'Anu, now I came to know my love is worthy. Thanks a lot, you're my sweet friend forever.'

Anu, looking at him, confusedly said, 'I've no idea why you're thanking me.' He smiled and showed her a painting wrapped in a transparent cover. It was magically hanging in air. Anu wanted to touch the painting and tried, but her fingers rather went inside the painting. She suddenly pulled back her hand. Spandan smiled at her, thinking that she was rather getting scared.

He then told Anu everything about Kirthi. While talking about Kirthi, he unfolded the transparent cover of the painting. It was a painting of a beautiful woman who looked exactly like Kirthi, presenting flowers to a handsome man wearing spectacles, who looked exactly like Spandan. A little later, he opened a letter, showing it to her. The words of the letter were floating in air. Anu couldn't believe what she was seeing. The letter read: 'If God gives me another life, I shall be yours and keep your love in my heart forever, I missed you so much. This is my last farewell to you, bye.' Anu read the letter and tears rolled down her face. She then happily offered a handshake to Spandan, who acknowledged it.

'Though I'm satisfied now, I shall remain until she is alive, my soul is not accepting to leave,' he said emotionally and disappeared.

Anu came down the stairs hurriedly since her classes were about to start. She tapped her head as she forgot to tell Spandan about Kirthi coming to college for the cassettes. Feeling restless, she murmured to herself, 'Oh God, he missed such a nice opportunity to see her,' and ran towards the staircase quickly. To her disappointment, the guard was already standing there and did not allow her to go upstairs. Looking up, she said in a high voice, 'Kirthi is coming today, see her!' and some of the students looked towards her in surprise. She reached the classroom with frustration; Karthik was waiting for her impatiently and he felt a sigh of relief when she came. 'Anu, our art teacher has told me that an old art student is coming now. Come, let's go to receive her near the gate,' he said and both reached the gate quickly.

In some time, Kirthi arrived and got down from an auto. She looked very gorgeous. A strong breeze had begun to blow, as she entered the college main gate. The branches of the trees had begun to swing and the flower petals and dry leaves fell from those trees. The dry leaves rose above the ground, swirling, and it looked as though these were dancing in the air. Anu and Karthik came near Kirthi and offered a handshake. Anu was surprised. While introducing Kirthi, Karthik said, 'She's Kirthi, our college ex-student and a great artist.'

'Ahem, thanks a lot for coming to help us,' Anu said with an innocent smile. She offered a rose and also gave the gift box containing cassettes. As Kirthi received the gift, Anu heard melodious violin music and felt that the music was coming from the top floor. Anu looked up and saw Spandan was playing violin with complete emotion. Seeing Anu looking up, Karthik looked at the same direction curiously; to his surprise, he saw nothing and he gave a confused look at her. The breeze slowed down but Anu was looking above constantly.

Looking at their attention on something else, Kirthi asked a bit loudly, 'Karthik, how are you?'

Karthik jerked and replied, 'Fine,' and they went to meet the arts teacher.

Seeing Kirthi, Mohan Kumar greeted her and introduced the students who were busy painting. All of them got completely involved in making changes to their paintings and crafts work as suggested by Kirthi. Anu made a dreadful female mask and showed it to Arun. 'Very beautiful,' he said. Madan closed his eyes and murmured something in Arun's ear.

'What happened?'Anu asked curiously.

'I pray that he should get a person whose face looks exactly like the one in that mask, as his life partner,' Madan replied laughing loudly but Arun ignored him.

'No, he will get a very beautiful wife,' she said smilingly. Arun gave a keen look at her and smiled looking at the ground, feeling shy. After learning the crafts work from Kirthi, all the students left the college.

Prashanth took his studies very seriously since he had exams in his tuitions and Anu had given him Arun's number to clarify any doubts he had. Prashanth took Arun's notes to read them during holidays. He was often meeting Arun to clear his doubts in mathematics. He became so serious in studies that sometimes he even ignored Vishaal's invitation to visit malls and cinemas. He attended tuition classes regularly; even the teacher was surprised to see his serious involvement in studies.

Prashanth was left with only a couple of days for his exams. 'The positive terminal has . . .' He was studying physics. He opened his notebook as he saw Deepthi and showed it to her.

'I got that complex problem which you asked,' he said and she gave an astounded look.

'OK, let's see how you have solved the problem,' she asked and he solved the problem. 'Quite nice, you really got it,' she said.

'OK, but this credit goes to my friend, he's the one who taught me to solve the problem,' he said promptly.

'That's OK, at least you understood, all the best for your tuition exams.' She wished him goodbye and left.

Prashanth reached his home and later got a call from Arun. 'Hi, dude, I was about to call you up, I solved all the problems that you told me to and got them correct,' he said with enthusiasm.

'Good, but you need a lot of concentration to make your exams easier, listen carefully . . .' And Arun continued to give him advice. After telling him what to do, he disconnected the line. Prashanth became more focused and he started doing meditation every time before he could start studying, as advised by Arun.

On the day of exam in Prashanth's tuition, all of them were writing their exams seriously.

'Hey, dude, fourth one,' a boy whispered with a gesture at Prashanth and asked him the answer. Prashanth leaned forward to answer but the invigilator's eyes caught him gradually.

'Hey, you, what do you think you are doing? Get up, I said get up,' the invigilator said angrily, pointing at Prashanth.

'Sir, I . . . I actually . . .' he stammered.

The invigilator shouted at him, 'I don't want to hear any reasons; this is the hardest paper I'm giving you all. Let me see if you can solve this, and if you fail, just quit this tutorial. I don't want to see such cheating business again, go to the next room to solve this paper.'

As Prashanth was going out of the classroom, he passed by Sandhya, who clenching her teeth said, 'Shameless,' and he went to the next room dully.

Sandhya's tuition exams were over. Next day, she reached the college early and ran towards Arun to wish him well.

'Fine, how did your exams go? And how did he do it?' he asked.

'Disgusting,' Sandhya replied and said what she thought Prashanth did in the tutorials and gave a frustrated look towards the side.

Madan, looking at her, said, 'Hi, four-eyes, don't tell lies, who knows, probably you would have asked his help to know an answer. Don't trust her, dude,' and she went chasing him. Arun giggled, looking at them. She stopped chasing as she saw Anu coming and hugged her. Arun and Madan joined them later.

Sandhya, looking at Arun, asked him, 'Please, Arun, can you teach me chemistry and mathematics portions which I have missed? We anyways don't have classes from today onwards.'

Anu tapped Sandhya and asked her, 'Hey, Sandhya, can I ask you something? Please don't get irritated.'

'OK, carry on,' she replied and Anu continued, 'If Prashanth secures better marks than yours, will you accept his—'

'I bet he won't, not even in his dreams,' Sandhya replied and left the place angrily.

Anu, looking at Arun anxiously, asked, 'Arun, are you sure that he has done his exams well? We haven't spoken to him for the past many days, how about calling him now?' He immediately took the mobile and started dialling the number but the line was busy.

Later, all went to the arts class and got busy making masks, and Sandhya also joined them. Anu showed how to pull the strings for the puppet show to her friends, and everyone practiced very hard. Anu felt satisfied, looking at their practice, that they learnt it completely.

Karthik came near Anu hurriedly. 'Sir, is calling you,' he said. A little later, both entered the principal's room and saw that the principal and the vice principal were having a discussion.

Looking at both, the principal said, praising her, 'You both have done a very nice job. Anu, your ideas are very creative in that they have an emotional touch, and everyone is pleased with your dedication towards the poor and needy people. Karthik told us that you're running classes and a handicrafts training centre for the slum and handicapped children with the help of some senior citizens.'

'We all are interested to visit that training centre now. Can you take us there?' Subhas Karuna sounded very keen, and Anu replied, 'With pleasure, sir, I teach only during my holidays, the retired uncles are handling the coaching centre mainly, sir.'

Later, all of them went to visit the place, Anu introduced the retired persons. 'In what way can we help your centre?' the principal asked one of the volunteers.

'It's a rented building, we need to do a lot here and the building owner is planning to sell. He's asking us to vacate the place, otherwise we have to give him ten lakh rupees if we are planning to buy it ourselves. We have collected nearly about six lakh rupees, we are hoping for the best to happen and trying to find some sponsors,' he replied.

Assuring them of their commitment to help in a best possible way, they watched their activities with an impressive note later and then left the place after wishing them well.

On the eve of Children's Day, a large number of children along with their parents had gathered at the corporation community hall located near the college. Volunteers had come early to make necessary arrangements to conduct various cultural programmes. Arun and Sandhya were helping to arrange the snacks and sweet boxes, which were meant to be distributed to the children. Later, they came near Anu and helped her to tie strings for the puppet show. Madan also joined them later.

'Do you know, Ms Nirmala the great architect and Dr Siddharth the famous surgeon are the special guests for this event,' Madan said excitedly.

Anu, looking at Madan, replied, 'So what's the highlight in this? Their achievements have helped only the rich community and I see nothing great in that.'

'Hey, Siddharth is great! He is the best neurosurgeon in town. He treated my grandmother in Nanda hospital,' one of her classmates said.

Anu was looking at them. 'OK, OK, tell me something, has he given any free treatment to the poor? And if he has, then I'll regret that I had a bad opinion about him.' Anu sounded emotional.

Hearing the reply, her classmate's face fell and she continued, 'That lady Ms Nirmala—it seems that she's a great architect and a builder as well, did she lend her services freely for constructing houses or hospitals to the poor? Why can't she do that? Hmm. Why . . .'

Meanwhile, Subhas Karuna saw them discussing seriously and he went down the stairs with a smile. 'To me, they're just viewers, the ones who care for the poor, they are the real guests. Those are the people who are serving the poor selflessly,' she said and then pointing at the retired uncles, who were distributing joker caps and clothes to the children, she said, 'See, look at them, they're the real guests.' Hearing this, Arun's face fell as she commented on his sister and turned his face away. Later, Anu and her friends practiced for the puppet show they were about to put on. The programme started after a welcome speech.

The children were enjoying the programme, and it took them to a different world, bringing broad smiles to their faces. Anu was looking tense as the puppet show event was the last one. Arun counted all the strings before the show, and a string was missing. She became tense as her event was getting closer and prayed to God before performing.

Arun and Anu were in tribal outfits and he pulled her towards the stage. Both were ready and they appeared like dolls behind a transparent screen. They danced like dolls; all the children enjoyed the show, and they were on their feet to dance while the show was on. The show was over after twenty minutes. They both were alone behind the stage curtain, and Anu was looking at Arun.

'Thanks, Arun, it's because of you the show went on well, otherwise my programme would have flopped miserably,' she said, showing her thumb down, and he stared at her with a smile constantly.

'I will love you until my last breath, Anu,' he said in a breathy voice and pulled her hands closer. Anu was almost paralyzed; she pushed him and walked away without reacting. She came near the children and they gathered around her. 'Anu Didi, Didi,' they shouted.

Later, the principal, the vice principals, and the chief guests took their seats on the dais. The principal stood up to begin his speech.

'Dear students, all of you have done a marvellous job with dedication. It's hard to believe that our students contributed so much by engaging themselves in the social service. I'm very happy to announce that the excess amount left will be donated to the training centre run by Mr . . .' The principal announced a few names and continued, 'They're helping the Kannan slum area's poor people by training them in various fields so they can earn their livelihood, thank you.' The principal ended his speech and took his seat.

'Next, I call Karthik on the stage to speak,' the announcement came. He spoke as to how each and every one can contribute in the progress of the society in removing the poverty and improving their living conditions. He criticized the politicians: 'They are the ones who are looting our country and denying social justice to the poor.' Karthik ended his speech.

The announcer asked Dr Siddharth to speak a few words.

Arun stood up and went near the mike quickly, looking at the guests. 'Please wait, sir, sorry for not allowing you to speak first,' Arun said and continued his speech, looking at the audience. 'Good afternoon to everyone. Many great achievers are here, but in my opinion, achievers are not only those who achieve success in their respective fields, but those who ensure their success also helps the poor. I'm sorry to say that you all might be worthy to your family and the rich but not for the poor who are struggling with pain. I request specialist doctors to provide their treatments to the poor freely or by charging them much less. Similarly, engineers and architects shall find some way for constructing cheap and best roofs over the heads of poor people. Lawyers, teachers, and other professionals can help the poor by charging them a lower amount than those who can afford. I don't have any intention to insult anyone but am just saying that we all need to come forward to help the poor in one way or the other. I am sorry if my words have hurt somebody's feelings. Thank you.' He looked around for Anu as he finished his speech and left the stage immediately, ignoring huge applause from the audience.

After the programme was over, Arun whispered in Nirmala's ear, 'Sorry, Didi.' She hugged him and tears rolled down from her eyes. Everyone exchanged surprised looks among them, as they learned that Arun was her brother.

Subhas Karuna and the principal tapped his shoulders but Arun's eyes were at the corner of the hall looking around for Anu. Looking at Sandhya, he asked in a sharp voice, 'Where is she?'

'I don't know she may be upstairs.' She sounded doubtful and he ran upstairs but couldn't find her. He got down the stairs and gave a tired look towards Sandhya and Madan.

Coming near them, Kirthi asked in an energetic voice, 'Where is our Anu doll?'

'I think she's gone,' Madan said dully.

'Today, I could see millions of smiles in the hall but that is only for today, from tomorrow, they need to suffer the same old pain.' Anu was thinking and sat in the bus, leaning against a window dully.

'OK, bye, guys,' Arun said disappointedly and left the place. He went riding his bike slowly, looking around if in case he could find Anu.

Later, Anu reached her home tiredly and fell on the bed.

'Didi, call for you,' Shwetha called loudly, and she came walking restlessly and picked up the receiver to hear 'Stupid! Where did you zoom away without saying anything? We all are upset that you were not around to hear all the praises that were showered only on you and you missed that . . .' Sandhya said angrily with a loud voice, and Anu rubbed her ear using her little finger.

'Sorry, sorry, I was feeling dizzy, that's why,' she replied softly.

Sandhya said, 'Stupid, you missed interesting events, especially the last one that Arun—'

'Sorry, please tell me that tomorrow in the college if you don't mind, I'm dead tired,' Anu replied and ended the call.

Arun massaged his head using pain balm, as he was strained thinking about Anu's peculiar attitude.

Next day, Anu reached her college and heard some voices as she was passing by some students.

'It is amazing, you know, he spoke so strongly and stood for what is right. He didn't even think that it might go against his own sister . . .' Anu gave a sudden jerk as she heard and turned back. She went near those students so she could hear more clearly. Looking at her, one of the students said, 'Oh, Anu, your friend spoke just wonderfully,' and Anu smiled. She went and sat on the ground. Later, she turned back as someone's hand rested on her head and it was Arun's. He lifted his eyebrow with a smile and stretched a helping hand to make her stand but she gestured at him to sit. He sat beside her and she took out a sheet from her bag, wrote something, and handed it over to him.

'I don't know how to thank you by expressing my praises for you, because you'll get more excited and concentrate more on me rather than my praising words. That's why I don't want to express anything.' He read it smilingly and turned towards the other side. A little later, she wrote another note, and leaving that note, she got up to go. Arun took it curiously and read, 'I strongly believe that I'm the reason to disturb your mind and heart hence I'm punishing myself. I won't speak with you from now onwards but my silence will. I've freedom for having your friendship but not your love.'

After reading, Arun smiled, giving a deep look at her and he got up immediately as Sandhya and Madan came near him.

'Dude, that was really great,' Madan said, giving him a hug, and after a pause, he saw Arun's eyes, which were focused on Anu and Sandhya, as they went walking some distance away. Madan tapped Arun's shoulders.

'Oh dude, what did your lovebird say, I mean, what praising words did she have to say about you?' Madan asked in an energetic voice.

'I don't have an answer yet,' Arun replied, dreamily looking at Anu, and both went to their classroom later.

With no other option left, Anu had to take Arun's help for understanding the lessons since the portions to study were a bit challenging. Without speaking, she managed somehow but Sandhya gave a suspicious look at her. 'It seems to me that you're not speaking with Arun, tell me the truth. Is it so? And why?' Sandhya asked when Arun was discussing about some lessons with Madan.

'Now who on earth told you that? I'm definitely speaking with him,' she replied casually and started writing notes in the record book.

'If you are really speaking, then swear.' Sandhya sounded like a father, as though Anu had to swear an oath.

'Even though I don't speak with my mouth, my mind definitely does,' she said to herself in her mind and swore to satisfy Sandhya.

'Oh, I forgot to tell you people, tomorrow are my results,' Sandhya said a bit loudly and Madan coughed as he heard. Arun and Anu exchanged surprised looks.

'Why are all of you wrapped in silence, is anything wrong?' Sandhya asked, staring at everyone, trying to read their minds.

'Oh, nothing at all, by the way, how were your exams?' Arun asked.

'Oh yeah, quite better, I might lose ten marks in physics and mathematics,' Sandhya said disappointedly.

The classes ended for the day. Anu and Sandhya went walking towards the main gate. Looking at Anu, Arun hummed a romantic song.

'Why are you leaving me, sweet mermaid, as you go farther from me, I feel like coming nearer like a dolphin,' he dreamily said to himself, and both had already left. He ran outside the gate immediately. 'Anu,' he called loudly. She gave a jerk and looked back at him with puzzlement.

Coming near Anu, he said in a dreamy voice, 'Even I will come with you.'

'What's wrong with you?' Sandhya asked, lifting her nose.

'Oh no, nothing, I mean, I'll join you guys and come along up to the bus stop, I need to buy something there, can I?' he asked.

'Yeah, sure,' Sandhya replied. He went along with them and looked at Anu constantly, but she was walking blindly. As they reached the bus stop, he went towards the shop that was right opposite.

Waiting for the bus, Anu and Sandhya stood near the bus stop. Anu saw a schoolkid carrying a bag that was similar to the bag that Vishaal carried, and she smiled at the kid and touched his bag, giving him a chocolate.

'Hello, what do you want?' the shopkeeper asked Arun but he was looking constantly towards Anu standing right opposite to her.

'Come on, let's go,' Sandhya said and pulled Anu's hand as the bus arrived. They both boarded the bus and Anu put her head outside, looking towards the boy.

Sandhya, pulling her shoulder, asked curiously, 'Hey, Anu, I came to know that Arun has expressed his feelings to you, right?' but she smiled dully and turned towards the window.

'Anu, one day or the other, you will definitely understand his feelings for you,' Sandhya thought to herself and there was a pause.

'I'll get down a stop earlier,' Anu said.

'Why?' asked Sandhya.

'I feel like walking alone.' She gave a sharp reply and got down from the bus without speaking a word.

Anu was walking, finally reaching a children's park, and she sat there thinking. 'Arun, soon you shall understand me and I shall be your friend soon,' Anu said to herself and looked towards the sky. It started drizzling and she quickly walked to her home. Meanwhile, rubbing his hair, Arun looked towards the drizzling sky with a smile and dreamily walked towards the bikes' stand.

Arun could not solve some of the problems in mathematics and he looked at Nirmala frustratedly. 'Better solve your mind's problem which is troubling you, then only you can solve this problem,' she said sharply. He gestured that he understood and she explained to him how to solve the problem. He took a longer time to understand than usual. Looking at him, she said seriously, 'Nowadays you're losing concentration, it's better that you shell that out from your mind if you've some worry, so you could get back to be normal.' He worked out the problems until late night and fell asleep.

In his college, Vishaal saw that Prashanth sitting alone and he was revising the day's lessons. He came near him and tapped his shoulders. 'Why, dude? Your tuition exams must be over, right? Even then you're stuck to your books? Is it to impress your loved one?'

'I don't know exactly, but her friend has opened my eyes and made me realize that responsibility is as important as loving someone, she's just marvellous.'

'Oh, I forgot, when will your tuition results come?' Vishaal sounded curious.

'Tomorrow maybe.'

'Good luck, dude,' Vishaal said and left the place after wishing him goodbye.

That day, Anu stood in the veranda and looked towards the empty sky, 'Oh, it looks empty like Sandhya's heart; tomorrow the sky will be filled with glittering stars, similarly, I hope that her heart will be filled with Prashanth's love. Hope that soon he shall win her heart.' Anu's heart spoke all these. Later, she went back to the room and fell asleep.

Next day, Anu woke up lazily, around seven o'clock, and said, 'Oops.' She opened her eyes widely, looking at the clock. She got ready quickly to reach the college as fast as she could and was breathing hard as she reached it. She saw Arun coming near and grabbed the water bottle from him blindly to drink.

'Hi, Arun, please call up Prashanth immediately,' she said, forgetting that she had stopped speaking with him and he immediately dialled the call smilingly.

'Hi, Prashanth.'

'Hi, Arun, today is my result, I feel like speaking to Anu,' he said in a breathy voice.

'Oh yeah, just a second.' Arun looked at her but she gestured no, and he gave a perplexed look at her and said, 'Sorry, dude, I thought she had come.'

'OK, I'll call you later, bye,' Prashanth said and ended the call dully.

Looking at Anu, Arun said with excitement, 'You spoke with me!'

Anu with a pleading look, 'Now I'm beginning to trust you, and as a friend, I want to share every feeling with you. At least, let our friendship survive and it is in your hands.' She sounded very emotional and continued, 'I hope you understand me,' and took his hand in hers. He nodded his head, and a little later, Anu went towards the classroom.

'You can force me to shut my mouth but cannot command my heart,' Arun said to himself and joined her in the classroom.

That day, during lunch break, Arun got a call from Prashanth.

'Yeah, Prashanth . . .'

'Did Anu come?'

'No.'

'OK, fine, I'm feeling tense, bye,' Prashanth said tensely and cut the line quickly. He walked towards the library and met Deepthi.

'Hi,' she greeted him. Prashanth sat on the chair dully.

'Will I achieve?' he asked himself.

Deepthi rested her palms on his shoulders. 'If you have put an effort sincerely in any work, I'm sure that you'll get a good result out of it. OK, fine, tell me, have you worked hard?' she asked and he gestured dully at her that he did.

'Fine, then why are you worrying? Forget it, I think today is your result, buck up,' she said convincingly and later, they both left the library.

'Oh God, even if I don't get good marks, no problem, but at least not less than that fellow, or else I just can't imagine,' Sandhya was thinking while riding her vehicle to reach her tutorials. Everyone's faces looked like they were fried, as the professor entered. Looking at his pupils, the professor said, 'Good evening, all of you,' and continued, 'compared to previous . . . all the students of course,' and took answer sheets to read out each student's results. Sandhya's and Prashanth's hearts were beating faster as he announced each student's marks and announced all the students' marks except Prashanth's and distributed the answered papers. Prashanth gave a serious look at the professor. Sandhya had scored really well and she gave a serious smile, looking at Prashanth.

A little later, the professor continued, 'I see a great miracle, it is totally unbelievable . . .' and removed his spectacles. The professor stared at Prashanth, as he was sweating with tension. 'To make myself sure, I need to give him another test. Prashanth, come here,' the professor called, and all of them gave a curious look.

The professor wrote a difficult problem on the blackboard. Giving him a chalk, he said, 'Come on, solve this.'

Even Sandhya couldn't understand the problem that was written on the board. Prashanth started writing on the board, and tears rolled down his eyes as he solved the problem slowly. He checked many times and turned to the professor slowly with a smile. The professor tapped his shoulders. 'He's secured the highest marks in all the subjects and it is just unbelievable. Keep it up, Prashanth. I saw students progressing day by day but I haven't seen scoring the highest in such a short period, how did you achieve it?' he asked.

Sandhya was shocked as all of them were discussing and she didn't move her eyes that were frozen at Prashanth. Prashanth looked calm instead of getting excited.

After the tuition classes were over, all of them wore their footwear. Looking at Prashanth, one of the guys said, tapping his shoulder, 'Great, dude, really.'

Looking at Sandhya, he said, 'No, dude, the credit goes to that angel.' She gave a sudden jerk and went down quickly.

'What do you mean? I didn't get you.' Prashanth just nodded his head and went down the stairs. She saw him through her vehicle's rear-view mirror and he was looking dried completely.

Prashanth started his bike and straightaway went to Arun's house. Prashanth hugged him as he opened the door.

'Dude, good news, I topped in all, and this credit shall go to both of you,' Prashanth said and Arun punched his stomach lightly, with a smile.

'Let it be, but where's the party?' he said.

'Oh sure, dude, I want to share this sweet moment with you before it descends, let's go right now,' Prashanth replied and both sat on the bike. Arun couldn't believe that Prashanth had proven his true love.

Prashanth screamed, 'Woohoo, never in my life have I felt so good, it is just mind-blowing,' he said, stretching his arms completely.

Seeing him happy, Arun said, 'If you're feeling so thrilled, even I'm feeling desperate to get into this same feeling.'

After a few minutes, they parked their bike and entered the Coffee Day restaurant and sat.

Prashanth looking at Arun, said, 'At first, I was thinking that the love will lead us to pain and depression. Later, I learnt it even gives joy. It is just a wonderful feeling but I feel sorry for Sandhya since I have disturbed her mentally by proposing to her without knowing its repercussion. She could have scored high marks if I had kept my feelings within me and I hope she understands me soon. I would have been much happier if Anu had been with us for celebrating. Can I give her a call if you don't mind? Can you?' Prashanth said, passing his mobile to Arun. Instead of taking it, Arun turned towards the other side and giggled. He gestured with a short smile, indicating that it was not possible.

'Why?' Prashanth asked seriously, and his smile made him perplexed.

'I don't have her number, I mean, I don't know?'

'Hey, come on, please don't fool me, dude.'

'You won't believe, never in my life has she called me up.'

'What do you mean, never in your life? You guys met just about a year ago, right?'

'Yeah.'

'In future, in case she calls up, then the world will come to its end,' Arun said with a broad look, and his mobile started ringing.

'See, what I told you is absolutely true,' he said and answered the call.

'Hello,' he said in a puzzled voice as it was an unknown number.

'Hello, Arun.' As he heard the voice, his heart started bouncing and his eyes were sparkling with surprise.

Turning to face other side, he said softly, 'Yeah, I am speaking.'

'Sandhya is not answering my call; I don't know what's wrong with her. Can you call her up and ask her to call me back. Oh, I didn't realize, when she's not willing to speak to me only, how come she will speak to you? OK, call up Prashanth and ask him about . . . Arun . . . what happened?' Anu cut the line as she did not get any response. Prashanth overheard Anu's voice and understood that she only gave the call to Arun. He raised his eyebrows, looking at Arun, but he dreamily smiled with his eyes wide open. The weather suddenly became breezy and all the windowpanes started banging. One of the windows broke and scattered glass all over. Prashanth, looking at that, said 'Oh God, I need to survive in this world and spend at least an hour with my loved one. If the world comes to an end after that, it doesn't matter, please,' and looking up, Prashanth prayed. Arun gave a guilty look and then smiled, looking towards the ground.

Later, both left the restaurant to reach their homes. Prashanth dropped Arun at his house. Arun had not come out from the shock yet. He could hear only Anu's voice even in that breezy weather.

Meantime, Anu went walking to her home after calling Arun and she was a bit confused and was thinking, 'Why didn't Arun respond properly? And even Sandhya didn't receive the call. What's wrong with these guys? Hmm, got it, I think Prashanth would have scored more marks than she would have. I hope that my guess would be right,' and she reached home.

Sandhya didn't sleep that night and, for the whole night, was thinking what might happen in future. 'Why did I challenge him or did I love him spontaneously? I will leave my destiny to God.' And she fell asleep almost around early morning.

Next morning, Arun was the first person who came to college and Anu came later. She ran towards him as she saw him, caught his collar and said, 'Stupid! Why didn't you speak clearly when I called you? OK, tell me, did you call up Prashanth? Oh, come on, reveal it now, I can't hold on this suspense anymore.'

Arun smiled looking at her. 'He won, he's secured the highest,' he revealed slowly.

'Woohoo!' she screamed happily with excitement.

'The next step is to convince her. Is it fine?' she asked.

'Done.' He sounded energetic, and Arun got a call from Prashanth as they were discussing regarding how to convince her.

'Hello, Prashanth, you must not come to meet us for a week and we will keep informing you what to do. Actually this is the message from Anu.'

'Oh, one week . . . fine,' he said, breathing hard. 'OK, how did Anu react?' he asked in a desperate voice.

'She is really happy, more than us, I believe,' Arun replied and cut the line. Surprised, he looked at Anu. 'I don't understand why he should be away and wait for a week,' Arun said in a pained voice.

'As things go farther, they get closer—this logic applies for love,' Anu said smilingly. Arun smiled and went along with her.

Sandhya got up later than her usual time and rushed to her college. Arun saw her coming dully. Anu told everyone to be as usual.

'Sandhya, come here,' Anu called and she joined them.

After the classes were over, all of them gathered in an empty classroom. Anu looked at Sandhya.

'You're very lucky, such a dedicated person has expressed his love to you,' Anu said but Sandhya left the classroom angrily; Anu followed her, and Madan and Arun also joined them.

'Listen, Sandhya, just imagine if some other person was in Prashanth's place—that person would have ignored you and would have gone to propose to another girl,' Anu said in a high voice.

Madan, looking at Sandhya, gave his opinion. 'He is an honest person, or else probably he would have put some effort and got some better marks but not put so much effort and get such good marks that he topped the class.'

Sandhya, becoming angry, looked at Arun. 'Come on, maybe even you want to comment something on this topic. Everybody else has, so go on,' Sandhya asked angrily, and Arun, giving a serious look at her, replied, saying, 'I don't know about all this but he truly loves you.'

'OK, Sandhya tell me one thing, just one, has he got any negative attitude?' Anu asked.

'He told me that he realized his mistake and hurt your feelings by proposing to you. He's left it for you to respond,' Arun said in a very strong voice.

Sandhya widened her mind, trying to recall if he had any negative attitude.

After a pause, Anu was looking at her. 'OK, he expressed his love, falling in love is not a mistake. Please note that he is not like other guys who, just to flatter girls, make unreal promises that they are ready to give their lives. Giving life is not a true love, you know what Prashanth told you—that throughout his life, he's ready to dedicate anything to make you feel happy. It sounded as though it was his heart which was speaking and not him.' Anu sounded emotional and continued, 'We are not compelling you, it's your wish. All we can say is that at least once, think positively about him before you make a decision,' and everyone left the place to let her think alone.

Later, Sandhya went home riding her vehicle very slowly, and a schoolkid giggling overtook her even though he was cycling. She parked the vehicle and blindly entered her house, thinking about Prashanth. The landline phone started ringing as she entered, and it was a call from her father's native place near Dharwad. They informed Sandhya that her grandmother had passed away and told her to inform her father immediately since they could not get him on call. She called her father immediately and informed him, 'Dad, Grandma passed away; just now I got a call.'

'Oh no, you pack your stuff fast, I'm coming.' Her father sounded upset. Sandhya started packing and got ready. She informed the neighbours as well and both left later. She sat leaning against a window in the bus, and the bus moved. Her mind also gradually leaned towards each and every moment that she had with Prashanth. She realized, and tapped on her forehead, she had left her mobile in the house.

Later, Sandhya reached her ancestral house and she was looking at her grandmother's body, thinking how she had ill-treated her mother. Her aunty consoled her but she didn't have any feelings for her grandmother's death. She got frustrated and went to a nearby paddy field to feel better.

Next day, Anu as usual reached her college. To her surprise, Sandhya had not come. 'I think she must be disturbed,' Anu said anxiously.

'I will call her,' Arun said and he gave a call to Sandhya quickly but the mobile was only ringing. Arun thought about why she didn't receive the call, disconnected it dully.

Arun gave a call to Sandhya again at late night but there was no response. Next day, hearing this, Anu was disappointed. After a couple of days, Anu went to Sandhya's house to enquire her whereabouts. She felt relaxed after hearing the news from Sandhya's neighbours that she went to her native place, attending her grandmother's cremation.

Almost five days had passed and Prashanth gave a call to Arun, enquiring about Sandhya as she had not attended the tuition. Arun informed him about her grandmother's death; hearing that, he felt a bit relieved and put down the receiver dully.

In the college, Deepthi asked Prashanth, 'Why are you looking so dull? Tell me.'

'Nothing' he replied.

'You have scored the highest marks, you must feel proud, instead . . .' she said. Meantime, Vishaal came near them.

'No, madam, I'm tired—that's all,' Prashanth said.

'Oh, he's tired of convincing his loved one,' Vishaal said laughing. Prashanth threw a grudging look at him.

'OK, bye, take care,' Deepthi said and left the place after wishing them goodbye.

In her native place, Sandhya became restless. 'Dad, please, I'll miss my classes, I have to go.'

'Oh yeah, dear, now all rituals are over. My boss called me and even I can't take leaves anymore, let's move tonight.' Her face blossomed as she heard her father's reply. She called up Arun at night and informed him that she will reach Bengaluru by tomorrow. 'OK, bye,' he said in a sleepy mood and cut the line as it was eleven o'clock in the night.

Next day in the college, Arun said to Anu, 'Sandhya will come today.'

'How come you know?' she asked in surprise.

'Yesterday she gave me a call but I'm not sure whether she will come to college,' he replied. During lunch break, Arun got a call from Sandhya.

'Oh, she might have reached by now, OK now, all of you please don't say anything about Prashanth,' Anu said before Arun could receive the call.

'Hello, Sandhya, where are you? Why didn't you come?' he asked.

'We reached home late and I was tired, I'll see you tomorrow, OK, bye.' Sandhya ended the call.

Arun gave a call to Prashanth after the classes were over. 'Prashanth, you need to come to our college immediately,' he said and ended the call quickly. Prashanth felt very surprised.

Madan was looking at Arun. 'You guys are confusing me. What's going on here?' he asked, scratching his head.

'Just wait,' Anu replied with a smile.

Sandhya felt very restless. 'I'm yearning to see you right now, Prashanth, I understood how much you love me,' she said to herself and tears rolled down her eyes. Later, she got a call.

'Hello, Sandhya, come to college right now, it's serious, or else you will have to miss something which is really valuable,' Anu said and disconnected the call immediately. Looking at each other, Arun and Anu laughed.

Madan looked at Anu with confusion, trying to know their plan.

'Prashanth came,' Madan said curiously, as he saw Prashanth entering the college.

'Hi, Anu,' Prashanth greeted her with excitement as he came near her, and she gestured at him with a smile.

Meantime, in Sandhya's house, Sandhya tensely searched for her vehicle's keys all over the place as she had forgotten where she had kept it. A little later, it flashed in her mind that she had kept it in the college bag, and she zoomed to her college as fast as she could.

In the college, everyone was looking at the gate, expecting Sandhya coming, except Madan, and a great confusion was running through his mind while wondering what was going on here, but he pretended that he was aware of it. No one was in the college grounds except the four of them and Prashanth was wandering around the field, thinking about Sandhya. Anu saw Arun as soon she heard Sandhya honking while she entered the gate. Sandhya straightaway drove her vehicle into the college grounds. Prashanth was about to run as he saw her, but Anu caught his wrist immediately and gestured at him to go near her. Arun tapped on his shoulders encouragingly. Looking at their gestures, Madan scratched his head again with more confusion. Sandhya left the vehicle just like that as she saw Prashanth, and she went running towards him. He saw tears rolling down her face as she came near and she threw her arms around him.

'Yes!' Seeing Sandhya kissing Prashanth's forehead, Anu hugged Arun excitedly and left him immediately. She started biting her nails. 'Oh no, why did I hug him? That was just a friendly hug but he will think something else,' she thought and immediately hugged Madan.

'Great, my friend,' Madan said, patting her on the back and seeing that Arun became a bit disappointed.

'I think she must be a love goddess,' Madan said, leaning against Arun. A little later, Sandhya came near Anu, hugged her, and kissed on her cheek. Meanwhile, Arun and Madan plucked some flowers from the nearby shrubs and they gave these to Sandhya. Looking at her, Madan said teasingly, 'Sandhya, now you must propose, hugging is very easy but proposing is very hard,' and looking at each other, he and Arun laughed loudly.

'Idiots, being my friends, you all support him,' she said and chased them as they were escaping from her catch. Looking at their chase, Anu and Prashanth burst out laughing and he thanked Anu. She felt very happy to see their love flourishing victoriously and her eyes were filled with tears of joy. As the sun had begun to set, they all left the college.

That day, recalling the incidents that happened in the college, Arun reached home and couldn't hide his excitement with his sister. 'Didi, I never knew such a wonderful relationship would emerge in my life, and that has become possible having friends like Sandhya, Madan, Anu, and now, newly, Prashanth. Especially Anu, she is such a sweet girl.' He was sharing all his feelings with his sister. While listening, she was giving an anxious look at him. 'I hope they all must be my friends forever. What's your opinion about love?' Arun finally asked.

'I don't have a clear idea, but my friend once said that love encroaches into our hearts blindly, so we can blame neither love nor our heart,' Nirmala replied.

'Do you support this?' Arun asked.

'Why?' Nirmala questioned, giving an astonished look.

'No, nothing, just like that,' he replied.

'No, tell me, you're hiding something,' she said in a sharp voice. He told her everything about Sandhya and Prashanth's love, and how Anu brought their hearts together.

Nirmala was shocked listening to him.

'Didi, she's completely different from others, I hope you would soon meet her,' he said dreamily and walked into his room.

Nirmala made conclusions on his thoughts. 'Arun seems to look very disturbed. I think he's completely involved in that girl's attitude. Is he? No, no,' Nirmala thought to herself and walked into his room. She saw him lying down on the bed and his eyes were opened. Giving a deep stare, Nirmala sat near his legs and he suddenly sat leaning against a pillow. Nirmala enquired about his study schedule for the exams and spoke about some of her projects, but a little later, she saw that he had already fallen asleep. 'I hope you haven't fallen in love, I trust you, good night,' Nirmala whispered in his ear and left the room.

Next day in the college, with Madan's help, Sandhya was arranging a flower bouquet. 'Hi, Arun,' she screamed happily.

'Hi,' he replied dully.

Pulling her ear, Arun asked, 'What's the matter with you? Yesterday, for nearly one hour, your number was engaged.'

Hearing Arun, Madan pulled his ear and asked, 'Hey, Arun, what's the matter with you, why didn't you pick up the phone?'

'Oh, my day went very badly, my sister is somewhat suspicious of me, and I came without having breakfast,' Arun said and he looked completely disappointed.

'Oh is it, but careful, huh, in that anger, don't empty my lunch box,' Sandhya said and hid her lunch box.

'Oh, come on,' Arun said, giggling.

Madan, hogging a chocolate, asked Arun, 'All that is OK but why she is suspicious?'

'I told about Sandhya and Anu's help,' Arun replied.

Hearing that, Sandhya said, 'Stupid, can't you hold anything in your stomach, you are ridiculous,' and threw an angry look at him.

A little later, Anu came and they greeted her. Arun saw that Anu was hiding something behind her and curiously asked, 'Anu, what's that you're hiding?' and she said, 'Nothing.' Immediately, she ran towards the conference hall, and unnoticed, he followed her quickly. He saw her entering the hall and peeped through the window curiously. He saw her sticking Kirthi's paintings and placing a flower bouquet. Anu started dancing with a feeling, and she met Arun's eyes while dancing.

Surprisingly, Anu came near him and asked, 'Oh my God, what are you doing here?' She sounded a bit tense. Arun smiled and entered the hall.

'You dance so well.'

'I don't know, these paintings arouse a feeling of joy and inspired me to dance.'

'Why all these decorations, is there any programme?' he asked.

'Oh yeah, today a Carnatic music group will be coming to perform,' Anu replied and left the place immediately. Later, the class ended with boring biology, and all the students came out of the classroom restlessly. Arun and his friends gathered on the college grounds.

'Hey, Arun, tomorrow is your birthday, right, shall I tell her?' Madan whispered in his ear.

'No, dude, let it be a surprise,' he said. Sandhya and Anu said bye to them. Mandan opened his mouth to tell them that the next day was Arun's b'day but Arun closed his mouth, nodded his head, gesturing goodbye. Looking at Arun's action, Anu and Sandhya smiled and went away. Madan pushed Arun's hand hard.

'Tomorrow is Arun's birthday,' Madan screamed, and Arun saw both of them were walking some distance away. Anu turned back slowly and smiled.

'Yes, she heard it,' Madan said, and Arun gave a grudging look at him.

That evening, Sandhya called up Arun and asked in a humorous way, 'Hello, birthday boy, did your sweetheart call you, are you in this world or not?'

'Please, for heaven's sake, don't psyche me in Anu's matter like this. I'll fly in the sky if she's going to be my girl, and if she won't, then I can't imagine what will happen to me. You know I already expressed my feelings towards her but there was no expression in her appearance,' Arun said frustratedly and rubbed his nose with his pointed finger.

'Fine, sorry, why are negative thoughts entering your mind? Don't worry, trust your love,' she said, consoling him. He cut the line and threw the mobile on his bed.

Nirmala was busy cooking; touching her shoulder, Arun said, 'Didi,' but she ignored him and continued with her work. 'Didi, please, I'm not able to bear this, don't stare at me like this. I'm feeling insecure. I will not do anything which is wrong and anything which will hurt you,' Arun said pleadingly. Smiling slowly, Nirmala looked at him. 'Come, let's have dinner,' she said and he gave a sigh. They had dinner together later.

Next day, Nirmala showed him a rich brown jacket. As Arun wore it, she lifted her eyebrows.

Looking at her happily, he said, 'Thanks, Didi, it's really cool.'

'I think you must feel warm, right,' Nirmala said. He smiled and hugged her. He then left in a hurry to receive first wishes from Anu and forgot to carry his mobile phone. Meanwhile, Anu was in a deep sleep; she woke up suddenly, had a quick look at the clock, and moved like a rocket towards the washroom.

Arun parked his bike. Sandhya, Madan, and Prashanth were waiting for him in the college grounds and he saw them as he came near the gate. He felt a bit disappointed because Anu wasn't there. Deliberately, he stood outside, waiting for Anu, and a green-coloured paper airplane fell near his feet. He narrowed his eyes at that and took it, to read, 'Don't worry, let your sweetheart wish you happy birthday first, we won't greet you until she does, with love, your enemies.' He lifted his head after reading and all were giggling as he looked towards them. A little later, Anu came walking very fast, entering the college main gate. Throwing the paper airplane aside, he looked at her and pretended to walk towards the gate. After seeing Arun, Anu came running towards him,

'Happy birthday, Arun,' she said, excitedly offering a handshake and Arun watched her gesture admiringly. Seeing Anu and Arun, all came near.

Prashanth greeted him and Arun snatched the gift from Sandhya's hand. She tapped his head and greeted him.

'Why did you switch off your mobile? I couldn't greet you,' Madan asked deliberately so that Anu could hear.

'Shut up,' Arun whispered in his ear.

'What shut up?' Madan repeated loudly. 'Ouch . . .' Madan said when Arun pinched his back. As usual, all the classes ended for the day and all of them rested in the college field.

Anu, sitting on the ground, was thinking something dully. Looking at her friends, she recalled Vishaal giving birthday bumps to his friends by swinging and throwing on the ground, and all others were giggling and teasing. Arun came near her and looked into her eyes; 'Anu,' he said and touched her shoulders. 'Yeah, what?' she replied, giving a jerk.

'Can you stay back for a while?'

'Yeah sure,' Anu replied and turning to the others, she screamed with a small curve on her lips, 'Why don't we give birthday bumps to Arun?' Everyone screamed and came together to give the birthday boy birthday bumps. His eyes were fixed on Anu, as they were swinging him and they threw him hard on the ground.

Later, a rich violet car entered the gate. The driver came with a cake box and gave it to Arun. 'Yeah, meet my friend Lokaiah,' he introduced his driver to his friends. Sandhya opened the box and it was a big chocolate cake. Arun cut the cake and all of them wished him a happy birthday. Madan stuffed the cake into Arun's mouth and applied some cream on his face. Meanwhile, Anu saw some poor children watching from outside the gate.

'Arun, if you don't mind, can I take some cake for distributing to those children?' she asked and he nodded his head in affirmation. Arun saw Anu distributing the cake pieces and chocolates to the children and he looked at the children with pity.

Anu waved her hands at the children and came towards Arun.

Madan looking at her, said, 'Anu, you didn't feed him the cake, so this is a chance to dump the whole cake into his mouth,' winking his eyes at Arun as he was wiping the cream off his face.

Hogging the cake happily, Anu said, 'No, it's his birthday; he's fed up eating so much, don't worry, Arun, I won't feed you.'

'Oh shit,' Madan said disappointedly.

'My bad luck,' Arun said softly with a sigh. All of them waved their hands at him and left the college.

Alone with depression, Arun kneeled on the ground, 'Oh, Anu, why you don't react as per my feelings? Is it that I appear so bad or is it that you have someone else in your mind? Oh no, that's impossible; otherwise, Sandhya would have definitely told me. What's stopping you from loving me, when will you accept my love?' he murmured and lay on the ground. The driver understood that something was wrong with him so he went away without having a word.

Later, Arun left the college alone and blindly walked on the footpath to reach the park. He recalled Anu greeting him, his past turned blurry, and the place was crowded. He turned towards the main road, and looking at that, he was shocked. Jumping over the jammed vehicles swiftly, he blindly crossed the heavy-traffic road. 'Hey . . . He . . . what you,' Arun screamed at the guys who zoomed away in a car. Looking around the place frenetically, he saw a stone, picked it up quickly, and threw it hard towards the car's glass. The car's glass broke into pieces, they threw a boy out from the car as green signal appeared, and drove very fast. Arun immediately caught the boy, whose head was bleeding, and carried him on his shoulders. He ran towards a nearby auto quickly and got inside the auto along with the injured boy. 'Nanda Hospital, Jayanagar fast,' he screamed and cried, as he had never seen a life suffering so much. 'Don't worry, you will be all right,' Arun said and made the boy lie on his lap. Searching his pockets, he said to himself, 'Oh, I forgot to carry my mobile phone,' and was cursing. Later, the auto reached the hospital.

In Nanda Hospital, 'What has happened to the patient?' the receptionist asked. Arun reacted at her angrily, 'Doctor must say that, that's why I have got him here, fast he is bleeding,' he replied. The receptionist called the nurse quickly.

Looking at the wounds on the boy's body, the nurse said, 'This is a police case.' Arun snatched the receiver from the receptionist immediately, as she was holding the receiver to call someone, and he dialled to Dr Siddharth quickly.

'Uncle, my friend got injured badly, they're telling me it's some police case,' he said in a hurried voice, and passing the receiver to the receptionist, he said sharply, 'Dr. Siddharth is on the line, he wants to speak with you,' and she spoke with the doctor immediately. She called the nurses and they took the injured boy inside quickly. A little later, a doctor came and took the receiver to speak with Dr Siddharth hurriedly.

'Mr Kshethram, please cooperate, it is my request,' Dr Siddharth said as he was the head of the Nanda hospital. The doctors started giving the treatment immediately, and after an hour, the doctor came out with some positive hope.

'Now he's OK but he's to be kept under observation, to be on the safe side,' Dr Kshethram said to Arun and left the place quickly to check other patients.

Later, Dr Siddharth arrived and saw the injured boy. 'Ha, Arun, I know you're backing up something and I'm sure he's not your friend. His appearance looks like he is a beggar, and how come you got him here?' the doctor asked and threw a detective look at him. Arun was silent and sweat was running all over his face. After a pause, 'Now don't create another lie,' the doctor said, and after tapping his shoulders, he left the place. Arun's lips curving slowly, he gave a call to his sister immediately and told her everything what had happened.

'Fine, stay there,' Nirmala said and disconnected the call.

Arun was thinking, 'I can't leave this boy alone here and go to college. They might have traced us the minute I took him.'

Arun felt tense again, when the nurse informed him to meet Dr Siddharth and she took him to his cabin. 'Arun, this is not an accident, it's a murder attempt. The boy is suffering from severe damage to his spinal cord and on his head. It's better you move away from this case because it is a lot of risk,' the doctor said seriously.

'Yes, sir, sure, but not right now, I'll let you know tomorrow, sir. Please don't tell my sister about the murder attempt,' he requested and left the room. He started thinking what to do with the boy, and finally, an idea flashed into his mind. He gave a call to Subhas Karuna immediately and briefly informed him about the incident that happened. Later, Karthik came and Arun, introducing him to the doctor, said, 'From now on, he will handle the boy, sir. I shall see you tomorrow, sir,' and left with a bit of relief in his mind after wishing them goodbye. He reached home.

'How is he?' Nirmala sounded worriedly.

Brushing the bloodstains off his shoes, he replied, 'Yeah, he's out of danger now.'

Next day, Arun reached the college early to speak with Subhas Karuna. He told him everything that had happened to the boy, in detail.

'You managed the situation well. This evening, you speak to the boy if he's conscious and ask him in detail about his whereabouts and the attackers. I'll call Karthik to handle the boy until he recovers,' Subhas Karuna said.

'Thank you, sir,' he said and left the place. In the evening, he directly went to the hospital from college. He reached the ICU, tried shaking the boy's hand slowly in an attempt to wake him up, and asked his name. The boy opened his eyes slowly.

Folding his hands, he slowly replied, 'Mariyappa.'

'Don't move, relax. Listen, he's my friend Karthik, he will look after you from now onwards. You tell him everything in detail, why they attacked you and who those persons are. Don't worry; soon you will come out of this painful problem. Do you understand?' Arun sounded anxious, and the boy gestured, indicating that he understood.

Karthik fed some soup to the boy so he could drink it easily. Arun and Karthik left the ICU room; Arun asked about their activities. Karthik just gave an outline of their programme, and Arun becoming inspired, came out with an emotional outburst and said, 'I'm very much eager to join your foundation for punishing the criminals of our society.'

'No need for you to join, we have enough volunteers to take care of, please don't get involved in this. I know you're a topper, we need doctors, police officials, etc. who have tough, passion-filled in their attitude to serve the poor and downtrodden. This will help us to serve the society in a better and effective way. From this day onwards, you forget everything about what had happened, and we will take this up,' Karthik said, and Arun nodded his head.

'Bye,' Arun said and left the place.

Next day, Karthik went to the hospital, and the boy smiled as soon as he saw. The boy was out of danger and recovered well. He had taken some light food.

'How are you?'

'I am OK now.'

'Who hurt you? Tell me in detail about them,' Karthik asked and the boy fidgeted.

'OK, don't worry, the reason I am asking you all this is to throw out your nervousness and help bring back your normal life . . .' Tears rolled down the face of the boy. 'Mariyappa, why are you hiding, who are behind all this? Don't panic, we want to protect you,' Karthik asked softly.

'Anna, I don't know those people, I'm an orphan, and my elder sister looked after me so well until I was ten years old. Later, I came to know that she was not blood related to me, one day she vanished and I searched everywhere but I couldn't find her.'

'Where were you residing after she left?' Karthik asked.

'I lived in a slum along with other children. One day the city corporation people came and smashed everything, as it belonged to the government. We were pulled to roads. We formed a group and we were doing part-time jobs, and many a time we were left with no money to buy food. One day, a man who looked tall told us that he's going to give us food and money if we work daily at regular timing. We all agreed to do the work; he took all of us in a van, provided lunch for us, and we were very happy. Next day, he took us to some strange place, and we saw plenty of dusty rooms. A little later, the tall person took us one by one into a room, and the other person injected some fluid into us. After few hours, I opened my eyes when I began feeling some pain and everything looked dark. I saw my leg was dressed with bandage, and it was paining me like hell. I looked around, frenetically shouting, and there was a small girl who had come along with me. They had wrapped a bandage around her eyes. 'Prabhavalli . . . Prabha,' I called her loudly. 'Anna, what has happened to my eyes?' she cried. I went crawling on the ground towards her, and I consoled her as she was crying. That whole day, we were left in darkness, and they were throwing food at intervals. After a week, a man who covered his face came and removed the bandages. I screamed when I saw her blind and my broken leg in the light. "Hey, now go around streets for doing your work," the tall man demanded. "What work?" I asked him. "Beg around, beg and collect at least 100 rupees to give to me daily, and if I get less than that amount, then your pain and punishment will become more, which will take you to the extent of death. If I see anybody escaping or complaining to the police, then you all need to face hell," he said with an angry smile. Prabhavalli had become blind, and I was suffering with a dreadful pain. We had to beg around in the hot sun, and we thought of escaping, but at each point they had kept a person for observation.'

After a pause, 'Why did they want to kill you?' Karthik asked.

'One day, I was caught escaping. "How dare you escape? Yesterday we killed a boy, next time if you try, then you will be the next victim," he threatened me. I was put on with a broken stick. Three years had passed with torturous life. I thought that even God could not see us, even he might have lost his eye—that's why he's keeping quiet. They were giving sleeping pills to make small babies to fall asleep whenever we beggars take them carrying to beg. One day, a granny came out with a question about my lost leg, and I couldn't hold my pain. I revealed everything just like that, and she told me to inform the police. Once, I planned and moved forward according to her suggestion. I went to a police station, meantime they saw me, and they pushed me into a car after following me for some distance and hit me with rods. They were about to poke me with the knife. I couldn't see them, as they had covered their faces, and I met a signal at the junction road luckily. I think someone shouted and threw a stone at the car's window. A little later they threw me outside,' the boy said.

'Do you have a stain of clue left in your mind about the criminals?' Karthik asked anxiously.

'No, I don't know,' the boy replied quickly.

'Do you know about their location?' Karthik said with little hope. There was a pause.

'Yeah, I remember, six months ago I went to Kalappa colony 5th cross. There's an old building just opposite to an arrack shop and beside there is a main sewage canal. I heard from an old drunken man saying that some criminals had gathered in that building. They held a party on new moon day, and he also used to say that those criminals will meet regularly on every new moon day at different places. That's all I know,' the boy replied.

Tapping the boy's shoulders, Karthik said, 'Take rest, I'll see you tomorrow.'

Later, the nurse came and informed Karthik that the doctor wanted to meet him quickly, and he entered Dr Kshethram's cabin.

Looking at Karthik, the doctor said firmly, 'He's getting better, and our security guard told me that some persons were roaming around the hospital suspiciously. This morning, a person enquired from the security guard about the boy and tried to enter into the ward. It's better to move the boy out from here.'

'OK, doctor, we won't put you in trouble. Tomorrow, he will be moved safely,' Karthik said and left the place.

Later, Karthik gave a call to Subhas Karuna. 'Sir, the boy's life is in danger, and we have to shift him to some other place.'

'You meet me at late night, we shall chalk out some plan,' the professor said and disconnected the call. He met Subhas Karuna at night, and they manoeuvred to shift the boy from the hospital. In the end, 'Karthik, I'm cent percent sure that this racket is run by Siddha only, his hooligans bear a scorpion tattoo on their left hand. Use his name as I mention, even be prepared for anything as per the situation,' Subhas Karuna said in a sharp voice.

'OK, sir, I got your words, thank you,' he said and left the place.

Next morning, Karthik disguised himself as a police officer. He saw there were six policemen patrolling in the hospital. The nurse covered the boy's face fully with bandage, leaving some space for breathing, and made him lie down on a stretcher. A little later, a mortuary van stood at the back gate of the hospital, and the staff moved the stretcher from the ward. Seeing the stretcher, five to six goons rushed quickly towards the stretcher, showing knives, as Karthik moved along with the stretcher, and they came near it to uncover the body and verify whether it was the boy they were looking for.

'Wait,' Karthik whispered, and he himself removed the cloth to show them. 'He's dead, Siddhanna has sent me. The policemen are watching, move away fast,' he said softly, and meanwhile one of the goons observed a Scorpion tattoo on Karthik's left hand.

'Anna, why I haven't seen you before?' the goon asked, surprised.

'I'm from Kerekatte area, Raja,' Karthik whispered in the goon's ear, and the policemen watched the goons as they were enquiring of Karthik. Those policemen came rushing towards them, and the goons moved away quickly.

The nursing home staff pushed the stretcher into the mortuary van immediately, and the driver drove the van swiftly. Karthik removed the boy's bandage and his police uniform quickly. A little later, the mortuary van stood near a car that was parked a few furlongs away from the nursing home, and he shifted the boy into the car quickly. He drove the car towards the opposite direction and saw the goons were riding on their bikes to look for the van after they learned that they had been duped. Those policemen were none other than the senior students who wandered inside the nursing home, giving cover to Karthik.

Sandhya wondered why Prashanth had not attended the tuition classes for the past three days nor given a call. Becoming frustrated, Sandhya called Prashanth at night, but his mobile was switched off. Next day, the news channels aired the death of a Stephen's College student called Jyothi, who hanged herself in her house. Her parents, talking to the reporters, said, 'She disappeared about three days back, but we had not given complaint to police as it would pave a way for others to think badly about our daughter's character. She came yesterday night, but her face was looking frightened and depressed as though she had lost everything in her life. We questioned her, but she told us that she would explain everything in detail tomorrow. We made up our minds for the next day to know the reason by looking at her condition, but it was too late and we are now looking at her dead body. God only knows what went wrong with her,' and they wept. The police came and asked several questions. Later, the police asked them to search for any suicide note left from her, but her parents couldn't find any. After taking the statement from parents, the policemen took the body for post-mortem.

Stephen's College had declared holiday for a day; Prashanth and Naveen were very upset. Jyothi was a distant relative of Prashanth, and she was Naveen's best friend. Prashanth and Naveen had come to know that she was missing, and her parents had requested Prashanth to find her without much publicizing. Jyothi did not even have a mobile phone since her parents couldn't afford it. He informed Naveen about her disappearance. They enquired from her friends indirectly and searched for her.

After Jyothi's demise and cremation, the whole world looked empty to Naveen. He sat in his house dully and tears were rippling in his eyes. Later, the postman rang and dropped a letter. He came near the door; sweat ran along his face as he took the letter, and it was from Jyothi. He ran into his room to read it immediately.

'My dear sweet Naveen, I'll not be alive while you are reading this letter. You may be wondering why I have ended my life without a clue. It's rather bad luck and hard to imagine how you will handle yourself after my death.

'What happened was that, on Friday, after the classes were over, I stood waiting near the bus stand. It was raining heavily. A few minutes later, a car stopped near me and a person in the car asked me to get in, but I refused. He was Jagath. "It's getting dark, raining heavily, I'll drop you. Don't you trust me? Come on, friend," he said, opening the car's door, and laughed innocently. "He's studying in our college. Why shouldn't I trust him?" I thought to myself and got inside the car. To my surprise, another person was already seated in the car and I felt very uneasy. He introduced him as Rathan. "The rainwater is falling inside," his friend said and closed the car's window. A little later, something was piercing my hand, I don't know exactly what it was and I was not completely conscious. I felt like I was flying in air. When I became completely conscious, it was morning. I was lying on a bed, I don't know which place it was, and everything was looking weird. It's very painful to tell you that there were five persons in the room and they gang-raped me for three days. I felt like killing myself and I pleaded them to kill me. Jagath warned me, saying, "Hey, you, if you open your mouth and tell someone about us, beware, by now you very well know who I am. What kind of people I have. I know that you have a sister, if you complain to the police, I assure you that your family would be in danger. It's better that you erase all these from your mind. If you wish to die, you can, but better not leave any clue about us. If you plan something like that, then your family will land up in danger," he warned me. Later they tied cloth over my eyes and left me on the Tumkur highway road. Naveen, I love you so much, I'm carrying your memories along with me to the eternal world. Please don't reveal this to anyone, burn this letter. My soul will never forget you; I shall remain in your heart forever. I hope you won't lose your heart. Goodbye, Naveen.'

After reading the letter, Naveen was spilling over with a grudge, his blood started boiling, and at the same time, his heart was pounding. Prashanth reached Naveen's home to console him. As Prashanth entered Naveen's house, Naveen's mother invited him in and showed him Naveen's room. The room door was ajar. Prashanth entered and saw Naveen holding a letter, with tears rolling down his eyes. His eyes had turned red, and he was looking up constantly, Prashanth shook his shoulders and curiously took the letter that he held. He read the letter, and he was shocked. After a pause, Naveen hit the windowpane hard with his bare hands frenetically, and it cracked. His palm started bleeding and Prashanth immediately wrapped his palm tightly using a cloth.

Giving him water, Prashanth said, 'You need to harden yourself to be avenged on those rogues.' Naveen gulped the water with anger but to Prashanth it seemed that his thirst wouldn't recede unless he saw the blood out of those dreadful guys.

'Everything is over, those bas—. I'm helpless, I can't put them to an end,' he said tightening his fists. Prashanth tried to calm down his emotions by hugging him and made him lie on the bed while consoling him. Naveen kept on murmuring and later Prashanth left the place.

That day, Prashanth gave a call to Sandhya.

'Oh, Prashanth, I was eagerly waiting for your call. What's happened to you? I heard that a student, Jyothi, committed suicide.' Sandhya sounded anxious.

'Yeah, she's my relative, I was not in a stage . . .' He sounded emotional.

'Oh, sorry, can you tell me the reason behind her death?' Sandhya asked.

'Even I don't know,' he replied curtly and ended the call quickly.

While passing, a few days later, the police investigated the suicide case. Jagath's father was a minister and he was a goon before entering politics. Jagath told his father about the rape he and his gang committed, and his father, being a minister, used his influence to close the case. The police closed the case by stating, 'The cause of death is suicide due to depression,' in the report.

A few days later, Prashanth met Sandhya in her college. Arun and Anu came near them as they saw.

Looking at Prashanth, Arun said consolingly, 'Hi, dude, I heard from Sandhya that . . .'

'What's the reason, what did the police say about . . .' Anu asked seriously, posing him many questions.

'The police have come to the conclusion that because of depression she committed suicide,' Prashanth replied casually. A little later, Anu and Sandhya left the college after wishing them goodbye.

After seeing them going near the gate, Prashanth looked at Arun. 'I want to say something, dude, I got frustrated after learning that the incident was so horrible beyond anyone's imagination—that's why I don't want Sandhya and Anu to know, as they are very sensitive. Actually, the reason behind this incident was that five senior guys of our college, including a minister's son . . .' He told the complete story and ended with 'That's how it happened, I'm not able to see Naveen in this condition. He is becoming mad day by day unless I do something.' He sounded very upset.

Arun thought for a while and tapping Prashanth's shoulders, he said consolingly, 'Calm down, we can find some solution for this,' and as he saw Karthik was coming near him, he continued, 'Oh yeah, now I got it. We can definitely find some solution from that person who is coming near us, just wait, I'll introduce you to him.' Arun introduced him to Karthik, as he came near. Prashanth shared the painful incident with Karthik, and his face turning pale after hearing of the incident, Karthik looked at Prashanth. 'We shall find some way, let's take a suggestion from our professor, I'm sure that he will show us the way. Will you come to meet him? Those rapists shall be punished severely,' Karthik said.

'Yes, thank you but let's meet him tomorrow, please let me bring my friend here who was much closer to that girl, and it would be much consoling for him. His name is Naveen, we will surely come tomorrow,' Prashanth said and, with slight hope, left the college after wishing them goodbye.

Next day, Prashanth and Naveen came to Arun's college. Karthik took them and introduced them to Professor Subhas Karuna. Naveen offered a handshake and gave him the letter that Jyothi wrote. The professor read the letter, and his eyes turned dreadful as his past nightmares once for all became alive in his mind. Karthik had never seen his professor turning so wild; after a pause, looking at them, the professor asked in a strong voice, 'What about the cops, did they come up with something?'

'They have already closed the case, sir, saying that it is a suicide,' Prashanth replied but Naveen was left silent without any hope.

'Then we can't take the action legally,' the professor said thinking and Naveen's eyes widened and the professor continued, 'We will plan something, I think their bad time will start very soon, Karthik will discuss with you further for manoeuvring their punishment as early as possible,' the Professor sounded aggressive. Naveen became more aware and both left the room after wishing them goodbye.

Later, Subhas Karuna and Karthik discussed what course of action should be taken.

'Varsha will accompany you for manoeuvring this further,' Subhas Karuna said finally.

Two days later, Prashanth and Naveen sat discussing in a hotel since Karthik had told them that he would meet them in that hotel for discussion. 'They are helping, now I'm ready for any risk including my life,' Naveen firmly said. A little later, Karthik came walking along with a young lady and she was looking quite smart but at the same time wild.

'Hi, both of you, she's my classmate Varsha, black belt in martial arts,' Karthik introduced her and came out with a serious question immediately. 'Do you know where the minister's son is usually found?'

'Yeah, I heard he and his friends often visit the Rock nightclub, he's a drug addict, they're very dangerous,' Naveen replied.

All of them discussed and manoeuvred a plan to trap the minister's son. Finally, looking at them,

'Varsha, you act as Naveen's girlfriend, both of you be there at this weekend. Hope we trace him soon,' Karthik said hopefully and they all left the place after wishing.

On Saturday night, Naveen and Varsha entered the Rock nightclub and she looked very attractive with her shorts. Everyone's eyes were fixed on them, as they were not regulars and they straightaway went near the club manager. She winked her eyes at him, as he looked at her constantly.

'We want to enrol for the membership, dude, before we have been at Remos, want to have some change,' Naveen said jovially and the manager gave permission after collecting the charges.

The whole atmosphere was filled with smoke. Naveen and Varsha danced. After a few minutes, they managed to get some space to sit, and many of them were smoking heroin. They were pretending they were drug addicts by inhaling some powder. They joined others to have a small chat with them later. They were disappointed as Jagath didn't turn up, and meanwhile, Jagath's friend saw Naveen and Varsha in the addicts group.

Later, he gave a call to Jagath, 'Hello, dude, I saw your classmate with a girl, she's really hot. They have smoked some stuff and the manager said that after enquiring, they have booked the space for two days. They may again hang out tomorrow,' Jagath's friend said.

'OK, fine, let's cover them up and tell others also to come. I shall see you tomorrow,' Jagath replied and cut the line.

Next day, Naveen and Varsha came early to the club, eagerly waiting for Jagath's arrival. Half an hour later, their eagerness came to an end, as they saw him with his gang. Jagath and his friends looked at Naveen and Varsha. They never imagined that he was with such a beauty and came near Naveen.

Jagath looked at Prashanth, 'Hi, dude, it's surprising how come you're here, you didn't look like this in the college.' Jagath sounded surprised.

'Policing in the college, dude, my spot was Remos, meet my babe Jenny,' Naveen said, introducing Varsha to them. She came forward and offered a handshake to all of them. Provocatively looking at Jagath, she said, 'Hi, smarty!' pulling his head, and kissed him on his cheek. He felt certain that he would have her today.

A little later, She asked, 'Got any stuff?' winking her eyes, and Jagath turned back with a question. The peddler had gestured that he'll deliver to him the next day.

'No, babe, tomorrow,' Jagath said in a dull voice and Varsha laughing loudly, said teasingly,

'What guarantee I live until tomorrow?'

Naveen, looking at her, said a bit angrily, 'Babe, don't tease my friend, you stingy cat,' and continued, turning towards Jagath, 'Dude, she has rare stuff, she's keeping it herself.'

'Stupid as—, don't blabber, I'll give you some,' she said angrily and took a small bottle and disposable syringe from her purse. She tore the syringe wrapper and injected the liquid into Naveen's hand.

Licking their lips, Jagath and his friends looked at her curiously and Naveen took the same syringe to inject back to her. Pushing his hand, she said, 'No, who knows, you might have HIV.'

'Cute bi—, don't you trust me?' he said in a funny tone and everyone laughed. Naveen took the wrapped syringe from her purse and injected the liquid to her hand.

She turned towards Jagath and his friends. 'Sorry, guys, it's very new stuff, got to have guts, and if it starts, it kicks up to the moon. No compulsion, guys, if you all want no issue in giving,' she said and pinched Jagath's cheeks. Naveen and Varsha laughed, dancing, clapping their hands. Jagath and his friends exchanged unsure looks with each other and finally they agreed.

Jagath, stretching his hand at her, said, 'OK, babe, let's try this stuff.' She took the wrapped syringe, which was coated with Mruthyu moolika, and injected the liquid into Jagath and his friends by using the separate syringes for each one. A little later, she said in a dragging tone, 'I don't like this world, guys, I put this stuff for taking you all up above the sky to fly and it reacts slowly. Better to move out to a lonely place,' and Jagath holding her hand, excitedly asked, 'Babe, I got a separate flat, shall we go there?'

Winking her eyes, she said, 'No, smarty, I'm alone, sure you'll have my company but you all have to come to my place,' and all of them left the club.

Jagath was completely activated. 'Bi—, she thinks I'm an innocent and I'll show her what I am,' he murmured to himself, giving a sharp stare at her.

A little later, Naveen and Varsha rode the bike. Jagath and his friends followed them and they came to a resort on the city outskirts. Jagath and his friends entered her room. Cracking jokes at each other, she sat in between Jagath and Naveen. A little later, a room boy knocked on the door and he entered.

Looking at Varsha, he asked, 'Madam, is anything required?' and the room boy was none other than Karthik.

'Yeah, two full Chivas Regal and dry spicy foodstuff of your choice,' Varsha replied in a dragging voice.

'Thank you, madam,' he said and left the room. The symptom of the injected drug had already begun and their heads were reeling. They felt a terrible headache and they looked at Varsha with a question mark.

'Don't worry, guys, new stuff, you know, right? It'll settle after boozing,' she said, laughing loudly.

After half an hour, Karthik entered carrying the liquor bottles with glasses and served them. They gulped quickly to get relief from the headache. Keeping close to their lips, Varsha and Naveen made them believe that they were consuming liquor. Later, the heads of Jagath and his gang had begun to reel severely and they fell unconscious. The resort belonged to Karthik's friend and he had instructed the manager to inform those guys that she already checked out, in case they asked. Karthik came and took Jagath's and his friends' cash and their valuable stuff. Naveen handed over his watch and money pouch, and Karthik and Varsha left after wishing Naveen goodbye.

Next morning, Jagath opened his eyes and was in half-consciousness. He looked at Naveen and his friends lying down. He went slowly to the washroom and vomited. A little later, he saw everyone lying down and he came near Naveen to wake him up.

Jagath shook Naveen's shoulders, asked restlessly, 'Where's the babe, I can't see her, bi—?' and looked at his wrist to see the time. His watch was missing and he checked his pockets.

Meanwhile, Naveen in half-opened eyes, 'Jenny babes, hug me,' he murmured, pulling him. Jagath became frenetic.

Shaking Naveen's shoulders with some force, he said in an angry tone, 'Hey, Naveen, the bi— she's robbed us of all our stuff, man, everything is missing.'

Naveen got up and pretended to check his pocket. Looking bewildered, he said with feeling, 'Dude, she's cheated us, I met her a week back in Remos. She had told me that her father had fixed up a marriage but she was not satisfied with that guy's attitude, so she left the house, taking lots of money and jewels.

She acted nicely. Don't worry, I'll make up your loss, actually for all of you, sorry, dude.'

Meanwhile, everyone became conscious, and Jagath, catching his shoulders, said, 'It's OK, dude, it's our bad luck, that's it, but one thing that bi— she's clever, cheated a guy like me. Don't tell anyone that we have been fooled,' and they all enquired from the manager about her later.

'Sorry, we don't have her details, she stayed for a week,' the manager replied.

'It's OK, she's left her ring, you can inform me in case she comes back again to stay here, take my mobile number,' Naveen said and gave his number. Looking at Jagath and his friends, Naveen said, 'Sorry, guys, bye,' and rode his bike. Stopping his bike on the highway road, he murmured, 'Now I'm feeling satisfied; now I hope your soul rests in peace. I love you, Jyothi,' looking up at the sky with a short smile.

Next day in the college, Jagath and his friends had turned weak and pale. Naveen pretended to act very tired along with the gang.

'It's better to have a check-up, dude, I don't know what the bi— has injected. I'm not able take up,' Naveen said deliberately with a restless look.

'Yeah, even I think that we have to, we all are feeling the same,' Jagath replied angrily. Next day, Jagath and his friends underwent a medical check-up and the result came as normal. As Naveen met them, he said deliberately, 'I had a check-up, it came back as normal, dude.'

'Even our report came as normal,' Jagath replied with a sigh.

A few days later, Naveen called Karthik. 'The stuff what we had injected is showing very good result. Their symptoms are growing day by day darker with pain. Can I join with you as a volunteer?' Naveen asked.

'OK, fine, I will let you know,' he replied.

Later, Subhas Karuna asked about the condition of the rapists when Karthik met him, and he said, 'Yesterday he and his friends were in the hospital for treatment, sir, the medicine is really working. One more thing, sir, can Naveen join us? He's showing some interest.'

'Why not, he handled the situation very well, we can take him,' the professor said.

A little later, Karthik gave a call to Naveen. 'Naveen, you can join us, meet me tomorrow . . . There's an important job for you to do,' he said.

Next day, Karthik took him to Kalappa colony. He showed an old building and the nearby arrack shop. He told him a few details about the illegal activities happening there and gave some hints about the goons. 'Find out the details of their activities completely and their movements. The building must be under your surveillance, so be careful. The success of our operation lies in your hands. The punishment we gave for those rapists is also to be given to these cruel vultures. Firstly, you give priority in getting a part-time job in that arrack shop, all the best,' he said and saw confidence in Naveen's eyes and left the place after wishing him well.

Next day, Naveen wore old clothes and came near the arrack shop around evening. He saw a woman selling boiled eggs and other eatables. He came near her. 'Sister, give me vada for five rupees,' Naveen asked and sat on the stone block that was near her. He started eating slowly, looking at her. 'Vada is very spicy, sister,' he said and she smiled broadly at him.

'Where do you belong, why did you come to this area?' she asked curiously.

'Sister, I'm Hanuma from Kemanna doddi near Ramanagar. I'm jobless and my friend has told me to come here. I'm waiting for him and even he works somewhere here,' he replied innocently.

The time was 7 p.m.; the arrack shop's lights went off suddenly. The shopkeeper shouted to call the electrician immediately. Time had passed for fifteen long minutes and the electrician hadn't turned up. Naveen thought for a while, looking at the arrack shop as some idea emerged and turning towards the woman, Naveen said with a pleading look, 'Sister, I know electric work, I can repair it, please tell the owner, I'll get some money.'

'OK,' the woman said and entered the arrack shop. 'Anna, there's a guy sitting outside. He says he can repair, he's jobless. Shall I call him?' the woman asked the owner.

'OK, what's there, I want the work to be done right, call him,' the owner replied.

Naveen entered the arrack shop and wished the owner well. He asked for a torch, screwdriver, and other tools. The owner provided the tools, and he checked all the wires and corrected the fault. The lights came on and the owner asked how much to pay.

'As you wish, Anna.' Naveen sounded very polite, and the lady interrupted him from speaking further, looking at the arrack shop owner.

'Anna, he's from Ramanagar, he's jobless. Even you told me to find someone for working at night, I think this boy is suitable for the job,' the lady said approvingly.

The owner came out with the same question and asked, 'Are you interested to work at night?'

'Yes, Anna, I'm interested,' he replied.

'OK, I'll pay you 100 rupees daily. Your work timings are from six o'clock in the evening up to twelve midnight and you have to stay here until morning. Thereafter you can go home. Be punctual,' the owner said in an authoritative voice.

'OK, Anna, I'll join right now,' he said politely and started his work by serving the customers.

Naveen had completed working for three days in the arrack shop. He had lied to his parents that he was doing group study with his friends in the hostel at night. Watching at the old building, he could see daily that someone got inside the building and for hours together stayed inside and later came out. An old man came dawdling towards the arrack shop to have liquor, and Naveen caught hold of him before the old man fell; he made him sit and heard some words as the old man was murmuring. Pouring liquor into the old man's glass, Naveen asked him, 'Come on, grandpa, you're so lucky to have a life like this, you're enjoying it, right?' and looked at the entrance door whether the owner came back as he had gone outside. The old man stared at him seriously, hardening his face; he gulped the liquor. Naveen provoked him to speak.

'Are you lonely or do you have children?' Again he posed a question and the old man's eyes turned red. Again gulped as he could not hold on to his questions, 'Ha, you think my life is enjoyable, no, not at all . . .'

Naveen's ears widened and the old man continued, becoming wild. 'I had a son of your age. The Mada gang killed my son in front of my eyes. That building belongs to Siddha and my son had worked for him. Now that bas— has joined hands with Mada, rogues—they will even sell their mothers if they get any benefit,' the old man said in a high voice and Naveen's eyes were glancing outside as the old man was getting emotional with his rising voice. 'I don't care for anyone. My life will be over in a few days,' he said in a receding voice with a feeling at last.

Naveen, tapping his shoulders, said, 'Calm down, grandpa, God won't let them go free, they will be punished when their time will come,' and gave a grudging look towards the building.

Later, the old man left the arrack shop and fell on the ground as he was walking towards the old building. Naveen ran towards him and lifted him up. Looking at Naveen, 'No god is there, no, he is . . .' the old man murmured to himself. Holding the old man's shoulders, he helped him to walk up to the building, and its main door was locked. Slowly turning around, he saw a washroom at the corner of the building and there was no light. Looking at him, Naveen asked softly, 'Grandpa, can I use the washroom?'

Tapping Naveen's shoulders, the old man replied, 'Oh sure, the whole world is yours.' He was completely drowned in his own world, and doddering, he caught an old pillar. Naveen came near the washroom and it was filthy all around. He observed the old building completely, and its main cable wire was running towards the street pole with numerous joints. Looking at it, some thought emerged in his mind that it might help him in manoeuvring the punishment plan, and the whole building's electricity power went off after he pulled the cable wire hard. He saw the old man had fallen down because he had drunk heavily. He went to the arrack shop hurriedly before its owner could see him not being in the shop.

A few days later, one among Siddha's goons entered the arrack shop and Naveen saw the scorpion tattoo on his left wrist. He came near the goon, pretending to clean the table and his ears became alert for listening to the goon's conversation as he was speaking with the arrack shop owner.

'How are you, Puttanna, how's your business running?' the goon asked.

'OK, it's running as usual. What's the matter? You remembered me after a long time,' the owner replied.

'Anna, Siddhanna is arranging a big party here; you send your staff to clean the building. There's no power in the building, get that set right. Anna has given the food menu for the party. Get these liquor brands a day before and the food by Saturday evening. Only two days left,' the goon said seriously. The arrack shop owner gave him a whisky bottle to drink. Glancing at the goon's face, Naveen served fried groundnuts to him, and he went inside the room to serve others later.

Next morning, Naveen met Karthik and informed him about the goon's conversation with the owner. Naveen and Karthik discussed with Subhas Karuna about it in detail, and finally, they manoeuvred the plan to enter the old building. That night, Naveen saw the students who wore turbans, and they looked like painters and construction workers. They entered the arrack shop and bought two bottles of arrack. They came outside and pretended to be drunk. Naveen, looking at the persons, gestured with his eyes directed at the old building. They moved around the old building to inspect and dumped some stuff behind the washroom. Naveen saw them dumping and they went away later.

The arrack shop owner instructed Naveen and the other guy to check the electric switchboard of the old building and gave them the keys of the main door. They entered the old building, and while inspecting the switchboard, they saw many sockets and plugs were burnt from high voltage. They both returned to the arrack shop.

'Anna, sockets and bulbs have already gone. It's looking very filthy with lots of dead bandicoots and the walls are very dirty,' the co-worker said. The shop owner gave 2,000 rupees to his worker Chenna and told him to bring paint, paintbrush, and some electric items after taking the list from Hanuma. Later, Naveen prepared the electrical spares list and gave it the co-worker. Chenna came near the owner with the list, to have permission for going outside to bring the items.

'Chenna, immediately look for the painters, some painters were here half an hour before. They may be somewhere around, boozing, and after the closure, start the cleaning work immediately. Bring the items quickly,' the owner said after looking at the items list and went back to do his job. Half an hour later, Naveen saw his co-worker carrying the paint and other materials accompanying the students who were disguised as painters. The co-worker showed them the building and took them near the owner to fix up labour charges. They both agreed to paint the building after some bargaining and started painting.

Next day, Subhas and his students gathered in a hall for discussing the plan to attack Siddha and his men. After manoeuvring the attack of the dangerous criminals, Karthik said, 'Guys, it's a very big operation and risky. Here is the building sketch, ask these guys to clear your doubts. They know the whole building area,' and pointed at Naveen and two other students who painted the old building.

Looking at his students, Professor Subhas Karuna said in a strong voice, 'Split into two batches for entering inside the building from front and back. There's heaps of rubbish lying at the back of the building and a main sewage canal attached to the building. Karthik and I will take on the front to attack them, and don't hesitate to hit them. They are murderers and rapists. They have ruined hundreds of lives. Chop their arms and legs but leave them alive. Nobody must escape from us.'

After entrusting a task to each one, Karthik said in a sharp tone, 'Guys, any doubts?'

'No,' everyone said firmly.

It was Saturday evening; Naveen came early since the arrack shop owner had insisted that Naveen come early, as some more electric work was left pending, and he started fixing the sockets and tube lights. Meanwhile, Siddha's men entered the building to inspect and saw Naveen working.

One of the goons came near him. 'Who called you up to work here, where's our regular electrician?' he roared at him.

'Anna, Puttanna has sent me to work here, I'm working as server,' he replied.

'OK, finish your work quickly and move,' the goon shouted.

'OK, Anna,' he replied and completed the work. He reached the arrack shop later.

Around 6 p.m., nearly twenty students walked into a narrow lane of a slum. They had worn khaki-colour shirts and shorts and were holding long sewage pipes and tools. They reached near the old building from the back and hid sharp weapons in the pipes. They pretended they were going to do some sewage work.

Siddha's men checked the whole building. 'Don't allow any outsiders.' The senior goon had instructed other goons to guard in all corners of the building. Nearly fifteen goons stood guarding all around the building.

A little later, Naveen had managed to steal the back-door key that was kept under a cupboard. The arrack shop owner told Naveen to deliver thirty carton boxes containing liquor bottles and some eatables. He carried a box on his shoulder, and as he came near the gate, one of the goons stopped him.

'Allow him inside, he's Puttanna's man,' the senior goon shouted at him. He entered the room that had the back door of the building and kept the box. He placed all the boxes in such a way those boxes covered the back door, leaving a narrow passage behind the boxes. He pretended he was adjusting the boxes and he quickly opened the door lock while the goon's attention was distracted as someone conversed with the goon who was guarding.

Disguised as labourers, Subhas Karuna and his students, including females, came near the arrack shop and they purchased arrack. Naveen showed thumbs up at Karthik, and Karthik responded, gesturing. They sat on the sewage wall holding arrack bottles. The time was around ten o'clock at night. The goons were roaming around that area to look for anyone moving suspiciously.

The students had decided not to use mobile phones for contact. The criminals and gang leaders from different areas started arriving. Since it was a secret meeting, their car drivers dropped them and checked out from that place immediately.

Some distance away from the old building, the female students had kept mud utensils using bricks. They put the firewood sticks in between the bricks, and it was a part of the plan that when they lit the firewood stick, then it was an indication for the students to attack the goons. The arrack shop was closed earlier than usual time, and the owner left the place after locking the door. The goons closed the main door of the old building to begin the party. Subhas Karuna and his students were waiting a furlong away from the building. The whole street was deserted except for noises from the building. Some students went through the sewage canal, passing iron rods and sticks to Subhas Karuna.

Most of the criminal gang leaders had gathered. Siddha stood up and came near the rival goon leader. Tapping his shoulders, he said to the invitees, 'Mada is not only my friend, now onwards he's more than my brother. Our friendship will remain forever, I became MLA because of his support,' and hugged him later. After a pause, he continued, 'But one thing I have got to tell you everyone that we have to be very careful from now onwards. Some groups are keeping a closer watch and they have escaped from us narrowly.'

Meantime, Naveen saw that the workers had already slept and all the lights were switched off. He slowly got up and went inside the arrack shop's kitchen. He burned a matchstick to see the time on his watch, and after looking at the time, he opened a small window. Karthik anxiously looked at his watch, and the time had reached five minutes to twelve at midnight. Naveen stretched his hands outside from the window and caught a thin long copper wire to pull it. The other end of that copper wire was delicately tied to a four-inch cable wire and that cable wire had been fixed by him in the street-pole fuse box for providing the electricity power to the old building. This was done while repairing the switchboard of the old building.

Lifting a glass of whisky, Siddha announced, 'Soon they will be caught, let's celebrate this occasion, cheers,' and the lights went off in the old building since Naveen pulled the thin long copper wire, which disconnected the power supply from the street-pole fuse box. The female students who were stationed at some distance away from the old building saw that the lights went off in the old building, and they lit the firewood sticks which they had kept earlier in between bricks.

Subhas Karuna and his students saw the firewood burning near the old building and they rushed towards the front gate of the building, and they hurled gas shells all around the building. They attacked the goons who stood outside the building, using iron rods and sticks. The whole area became smoky; the students chopped arms and legs of the goons and threw them in the sewage canal. Subhas Karuna locked the front door of the old building. Karthik heard shouts coming from inside the building and the goons screamed to turn on the generator. They heard the sound from outside and tried to open the doors. The students who were disguised as sewage workers tried to enter through the back door. Though Naveen had opened the lock, the door got stuck since it wasn't opened for a long period, and they finally broke the door to open it. Meanwhile, the goons in the building were able to run the generator, and the building lights came back. The students rushed inside from the back door of the building and hurled the liquor bottles that were in carton boxes at the goons. All the students turned very violent against the goons and they blindly attacked the goons using sharp weapons and rods. Siddha rang up the police commissioner and asked for help.

'Hello, wrong number,' the police came out with a simple reply and ended the call.

'You ate my shi— and still you bas—. Ho no!' One of the students had hit him. Everyone joined together and attacked the goons wildly. Some of the goons were trying to escape but could not, since all the doors were locked from outside. Some goons succeeded in breaking the front door and tried to escape. They rushed outside to escape, but Karthik and other students were waiting to attack them.

Meanwhile, Subhas Karuna fell on the ground, as one of the goons had hit him on his head. Seeing it, Karthik carried Subhas Karuna immediately through the sewage canal. Students were carrying other injured students on their shoulders. They were almost succeeding in their plan. Siddha and Mada were severely injured with broken legs and hands. Some of the female students were injecting needles coated with Mruthyu moolika in all the goons who fell down as a result of getting injured.

Karthik took Subhas Karuna to Nanda nursing home quickly and the other injured students reached the college hostel. There was a doctor already waiting and they were given first aid treatment. The doctors nearly took three hours to complete the operation on Subhas Karuna's injured head. Many students stayed in the hospital, waiting tensely to know the condition of their beloved sir.

Later, having a smile on his face, Karthik called up from the public phone booth. 'Hello, please send ambulances to Kalappa colony . . .' The injured goons were treated in the government hospital later. The TV channels aired the incident live by terming that incident as a gang war. Hooligans, using that opportunity, went on a rampage, destroyed public property. Many persons were killed and hundreds of people were injured. The chief minister promised to enquire into the matter, for taking necessary action.

Karthik and other students were very disturbed, as Subhas Karuna was not responding well to the treatment, although the doctors told them that he was out of danger. The doctors had confirmed that he had lost his memory and couldn't speak because of malfunction of his vocal cords. A few days later, he was able to see and move his body. After further treatment, he was responding to sound and movements. The students decided not to engage in activities related to criminals for the time being.

Many days have gone; Arun became frustrated as Anu and Sandhya couldn't interpret the lessons properly. He cautioned them as they were lacking in their concentration and he prepared a timetable for studying the portions since only forty-five days were left for the first year final exam. Anu walked dully, rolling the studying schedule sheet, towards the bus stand along with Sandhya. That day, Anu studied until twelve o'clock midnight.

Next day, Anu came and sat next to Arun. 'Hi,' he greeted her with a brightened face. 'How come you're looking so bright? Anu asked Arun.

'Once you told me that we won't have the same feeling forever, so I was upset yesterday, and now I'm fine. Give me your book,' he said and grabbed the book. Anu was looking at him constantly, trying to read his problem.

'Which problem?' he asked, turning the pages.

'Oh, on page number 173,' Anu replied and Arun taught her how to solve the problem.

The days went on just like that, and the looks and stares from Arun were decreasing day by day. Calls from Sandhya were also very few for a week, and playing basketball in the college stopped completely. Sandhya had warned Prashanth not to call her until the exams were over. Everyone had a hard time facing the exams, and finally, they landed into the examination hall after a long studying schedule. The exams were over, except the last days, and they had zoology. After the exam was over, Anu was with her friends.

'I found difficulty attempting most of the questions correctly,' Anu said dully.

'Anu, don't worry it's not the end, put your effort in the second year final exam,' Arun consoled her.

In Stephen's College, Vishaal asked Prashanth, 'Did you meet your friend?'

'No, dude, I'm counting hours, 672 hours plus 30 minutes.'

'What you mean by 30 minutes?' Vishaal asked.

'By the time I reach her college, it takes half an hour,' Prashanth replied.

'OK, dude, bye,' Vishaal said and left the place after giving a hug to Prashanth.

In the Presidency College, Arun and his friends had decided to stay until evening, and everyone sat in a circle for discussion, on the college grounds. Prashanth came near Sandhya.

'Can I be a part of this round-table conference?' Prashanth asked. Looking at him, Sandhya exclaimed, 'Oh, Prashanth,' and threw her arms around him.

'Idiot, after how long am I seeing you? I felt sick with your absence. At least now you could have called me,' he said in a tired voice.

Holding his wrist, she said, 'Oh, sorry, I'm extremely sorry.'

'OK, during all these days, did you think about me at least one second, just one second?' He threw another question.

'Yeah, thousands of seconds,' she said, hugging him.

Anu was looking at them, feeling happy. 'I was strained with some suffocation, now looking at these lovebirds, I'm feeling relieved as though fresh air is around,' she said to herself with a cute curve on her lips, and the atmosphere really turned cool with a sudden breeze. Arun threw a sudden surprised look around and turned slowly towards Anu as she was discussing the question paper with Madan. After that, 'We all will have contact through phone but you have contact only with Sandhya, how will Arun— sorry, I mean how will we meet?' Madan asked Anu.

'Sandhya will let you know,' she answered in a casual way.

'That's what he will do,' Madan murmured to himself, looking towards Arun with pity.

'Oh, it's getting late. OK, guys, meet you all soon. Bye, Prashanth. Anu, come,' Sandhya said. Waving her hand, Anu looked at everyone with a smile. Arun's face turned pale, and Madan, seeing Arun becoming pale, said with frustration, 'Dude, it's intolerable seeing the same old expression of showing your pale face.'

'How many days I have to suffer like this, dude?' Arun asked him resting his forehead on Madan's shoulders.

'Sixty long days,' Madan replied, patting him on the back. Arun, after looking at Anu walking some distance away, ran behind her.

'Anu . . . Anu.'

'What?' Anu turned back immediately.

'I'm going to miss you so much.' Arun sounded very depressed.

Looking at Arun, Anu said, 'Relax, what is this, you are acting so strange, as though I won't meet you forever. Just two months it will be over within no time, and I would like to be back in the college,' and reached the gate.

Arun, becoming heartbroken, said, 'Then my heart has to suffer sixty long days on a thorn, yeah, I'll reach you soon, my girl,' and kneeled on the ground. As she heard him saying so, Anu turned and hid behind the gate wall to peep at him. Looking at his depression, she leaned against the gate wall, becoming depressive.

'Not seeing my Vishaal so far was effecting horrible pain in my heart and I got addicted to it, it's like a hell bound that I can't come out of, but this idiot, even he's trapped in that hell by thinking about me and that is effecting the pain in his heart,' Anu thought, with compressed feeling. Sandhya gave a suspicious look at her, trying to read her mind.

The days went on; Arun sat watching the television dully.

'Hey, why do you look so dull? Must look happy since exams are over, ha. By the way, there is some good news, the government has sanctioned the plan for constructing our project.' Nirmala sounded very excited showing a building plan. He threw his arms around her to behave normally. 'Congrats,' he said with not much energy.

One day, Arun gave a call to Sandhya, enquiring about Anu. 'Can you convince her to see me?'

'Come on, Arun, can't you be strong enough to forget her just for a few more days, why do you worry? She will, however, come to college on the day of result,' she replied. He ended the call, looking towards the sky dully.

The exams' result day had come, and the results were put on the bulletin board in the college. Anu and Sandhya came to the college early. Looking at her result, Anu gave a deep sigh. 'Ha, 61 per cent, thank God.'

Sandhya, looking at her result, exclaimed, 'Yesss, 88 per cent.' She jumped, and hugged Anu. Looking around, Sandhya said with disappointment, 'Those guys haven't come yet.'

Meantime, Arun had his breakfast in a hurry. He took his bike to reach the college, but on the way, he got a call from the doctor to come immediately and he quickly reached the Nanda hospital.

'Where's the doctor?' he enquired of the receptionist, in an anxious voice.

'Hello, Arun,' the doctor said and was right behind him. Tapping Arun, he continued,

'Your professor is out of danger, but he has lost his memory completely, no hope is left of returning to normalcy.' Arun became upset on hearing this, and after a pause, the doctor continued, 'It would be better for the professor's health if he stays in a calm atmosphere surrounded with greenery. Karthik has given a letter to you.' The doctor gave him the letter. Arun read, 'Arun, some goons are looking out for me, hence I am underground. Please take care of sir and take him to the address mentioned below at the earliest. I can't contact you through the phone, as the police would have tapped my mobile for the leads.' Arun informed the doctor that he would take the professor with him tomorrow. After thanking the doctor, he left the place to reach the college quickly.

Later, Arun went inside the college and looked around for Anu. His classmates, circling around, lifted him up and shouted congrats as he was the topper, but he looked around for Anu anxiously.

Madan, patting him on the back, said softly, 'Come on, dude, let's move, you're too late,' and Arun, becoming disappointed, sat on the bike dully.

'You're in no mood, let me ride,' Madan said and took the keys from him. Arun slid to the back seat, and Madan dropped him home.

In the state of Karnataka, the election commission had announced the dates for conducting the assembly elections. All the political parties were preparing for the elections. Anu gave regular classes for the slum children since it was summer holidays.

In the Kannan slum area, a local leader named Kanda swami had directed his men to put banners all around the main circle, where the training centre for the slum children was located. Being a corporator, he was also the right hand for the sitting MLA.

After winning the election, the MLA hardly visited the slum. He was appearing in the slum when the election was near. He came this time and saw nearly fifty children were studying at the learning centre. The MLA's face hardened as he saw the study centre.

'Kanda swami, come here,' the MLA shouted.

Kanda swami came quickly and asked, 'What, sir?'

'Why are you allowing these guys to run the study centre for these children, you shouldn't have allowed outsiders to mingle with our people, we shouldn't give room for our people to question us in future, they shall remain illiterate forever, otherwise this could lead them to turn against us and we lose their votes. Give them a day's time to close the centre,' the MLA said sharply.

'OK, sir, I'll close up everything,' Kanda swami replied with a grudging smile. Giving some instructions, the MLA spoke for half an hour with him about the election campaign.

Later, Kanda swami entered the study centre with some hooligans, and looking at the volunteers, he said in a threatening voice, 'We don't require a study centre in our location run by outsiders, vacate this place by tomorrow, it's the MLA's instruction, don't put yourselves at risk.'

One of the volunteers dared to speak against him. 'At any cost we won't leave this place,' he replied firmly.

'OK, let's see.' Kanda swami gave a final warning and left the place. Anu wasn't there in the centre at that time, as she had gone to Ooty to visit her relatives.

Next day, Kanda swami came to the study centre with ten hooligans. The volunteers were teaching the children as usual.

They pulled the children outside, smashed the furniture, training equipment, computer, etc. and threw them outside. The volunteers tried to resist the hooligans, but they could not hold the situation, as the hooligans were hitting them with sticks and rods.

With a cruel look, Kanda swami said, 'I warned you all, see what happened. Don't come again in our way, I mean not to this place again.' Kanda swami stressed the last word.

After three days, Anu returned from Ooty; she came to the study centre to teach the children and saw the whole building had turned into a political party office. Many persons were packing and distributing the posters, banners, etc. A girl came running as soon as she saw Anu. With fear in the girl's eyes, she pointed at the hooligans.

'Didi, those people threw all of us out, and they smashed everything. They even hit our teachers, and they warned them neither to teach nor to step into this place. We all want to study,' the girl said in a whispering voice.

Tapping her shoulders, Anu said firmly, 'Don't worry. I'll teach you all, tell everyone to gather in the field,' and she left the place.

Later, Anu visited the volunteers' houses and enquired about their condition. Some were with bandages, but they had recovered from the injuries. The volunteers held a meeting for discussing, and, Anu looking brave, said in a sharp tone with a strong will in her mind, 'They threw the stuff outside but cannot throw our willpower. Let us teach the children in the field.'

'OK, we will also come,' they said and Anu felt more confident, with hope twinkling in her eyes. Later, they entered the slum and the people saw them with bandages, and an elderly person came near them and asked, 'Sir, how is your wound? All those cruel . . . definitely, we will send our children for studying.'

A little later, Anu and the volunteers reached the centre portion of the slum. It was a large area left for garbage dumping, and a vacant field was left for parking the lorries. Anu carried portable blackboards, and there were slum children waiting for them. Anu and others began teaching. At the same time, Kanda swami came near the field to address the election meeting. He saw red as he saw Anu and the volunteers were teaching. Holding swords and rods, the hooligans circled around them. All the children ran away, bringing their parents. Nearly a thousand people had gathered, looking anxiously at the volunteers, fearing what might happen to them.

Looking at the volunteers, Anu said softly, 'Don't move, let's face them.'

Looking at the crowd, Kanda swami addressed his people, 'Dear elders, brothers and sisters, I'm born as your boy, and with your wholehearted support, I reached this level for serving you all. See, these people are interfering in our matters. They are up to something bad, but they are making us believe that they are doing well. They take our children for slavery, and you all have experienced this in the past. They are here to fill poison in your minds, don't trust them, I'm giving protection to you all. Many slums have vanished, but our MLA is protecting this area from being acquired. What these guys know about us, let them answer.'

'How much you know about these people, can you tell me how many people do live here?' one of the volunteers asked, raising his voice.

Kanda swami was shocked at his question. 'Approximately how many?' he asked one of his goons, and people started murmuring to each other, guessing what reply might come.

After a pause, Kanda swami replied doubtfully, 'Six thousand four hundred approximately.'

'It's a wrong number. I'll tell you how many. Nearly 1,750 males and 1,700 females aged above 50, 2,580 males and

2,500 females aged under 50, 1,800 boys and 1,200 girls, 800 handicapped people, 460 males and remaining females, 100 males and 64 females are educated, totally around 12,500 and are striving their lives with pain, Kanda swami.' As the volunteer spoke, Kanda swami was paralyzed hearing those figures. Occasionally, he visited the slum and lived in a posh locality having two wives, keeping them separately.

Murmurings began in the crowd. Looking at the crowd in a convincing manner, Kanda swami addressed the gathering.

'These people have come with some plans, don't believe them, see they have gathered such detailed information.'

But another volunteer said in a rising voice, 'We have gathered information about you also, mister,' and continued, 'You are collecting nearly three lakh rupees monthly from these people as protection fee, 50 per cent you're giving to the money collectors. You're having five shopping malls getting rents, about five lakhs a month, you have three big houses, and your MLA has given you one crore now for this election. Is this information enough?' And Kanda swami started sweating a bit.

Anu looking at the crowd, said in a high grudging tone, 'For securing your votes, they're protecting you all without improving your lives. They don't want your children to get educated. They want your future generation also to remain as their slaves. We are not politicians, and we come here with a good intention. If you all feel that we don't need to show you all some good way, then we won't step into this place.'

'No!' hundreds of voices emerged from the crowd at once.

Seeing this, the MLA's cousin screamed, 'No, they are lying!' and holding a sword, he rushed towards Anu. Suddenly an elderly woman came rushing in between, protecting Anu.

Seeing that, Kanda swami screamed, 'Stop!' running towards the old woman but she was hurt badly while protecting Anu, and that old woman was none other than his mother.

His mother, with a wild look, said, 'Scoundrel, it's my sin that I gave birth to you, she's like my daughter. You never cared for me and left me here, alone! You are least bothered about me, not even bothered to know whether I'm alive. These people provided me medical treatment; these are my actual children who are better than the ones who are blood related. It's better to leave this world instead of seeing you like this,' and Anu quickly wrapped the wounded portion using her dupatta tightly to check the bleeding. The volunteer rushed to bring the vehicle for admitting her in the hospital.

Meantime, Kanda swami stood like a statue, and all his past deeds were rolling in front of his eyes. Some elderly persons who were locals came near him and threw some mud, cursing, 'You're worse than a beast, God won't forgive your sins,' they said. Pulling his hair, Kanda swami sat on the field and screamed, facing towards the sky. A little later, he ran towards the elderly people, and catching their feet, he said, 'Sorry, I regret what I have done so far. I'll never trouble anyone, from now onwards, I'll serve my people. Please forgive me,' and looking at the crowd, he addressed them. 'I'm resigning from the party. I'll work for your better future, it's my promise.' Everyone exchanged smiling looks and he rushed to the hospital later.

After summer holidays, the colleges reopened. Arun zoomed to the college but Anu had not come yet. Arun gave a call to Sandhya and said, 'Hello, Sandhya, will she exist for or exit me?' he asked restlessly.

'Oh, you're in the college so early, sure you might have jumped from bed to the college without having a bath. Come on, she will come or else I'll kill her,' Sandhya replied and disconnected the call.

After a few minutes, 'Hi, Anu,' Arun greeted her with a broad smile as she came near.

'Hi,' she said, giving a cute smile.

Arun turned to the other side. 'Ha, after seeing you, I got a new feel as though the wings of my heart are fluttering widely for reaching your heart,' he said, moving his hands like wings. Anu turned back at him but suddenly rubbing his palms, he looked towards the gate.

Anu's eyes moved towards the gate and she saw Sandhya was coming with Madan, and Anu threw her arms around Sandhya immediately, as she came near.

'How come both are coming together?' Arun asked bit curiously.

'I was waiting in the bus stand, he was coming on the same way, and I came on his bike,' she replied in a casual way.

Looking at Arun's face, Anu asked Sandhya, 'Why Arun is looking somewhat distressed?' Seeing her concern for him, Sandhya's face blossomed. Later, they all entered the classroom.

In the classroom, Madan pleaded, 'Dude, I had a dreadful dream early morning. You were in the mental hospital with unshaven face, practicing how to propose to Anu and you had gone mad. At least today, make up your mind to express your love. Please, man, early morning dreams are bound to happen.'

Seeing Madan speaking, the professor blasted him. 'You in the blue shirt get up, right in my first class, you can't disturb, and Arun, how can you encourage this? Both of you get out!' Madan gave an innocent look towards the girls. Some were giggling but Anu and Sandhya exchanged bewildered looks. They both went out and leaned against a pillar.

Madan, pleading, said, 'Dude, please, if we face even more weird punishments, also no problem but don't turn my dream into truth. I beg you,' and nearly touched his feet, but seeing the professor coming out of the classroom, he pretended to be tying Arun's shoelace.

Looking at that, the professor asked, 'Why, sir? Can't you tie your lace yourself? Need an assistant for that?' giving a serious stare towards Arun, and he went.

'Sir . . .' Arun had not realized and showed his wrist to hit Madan after seeing him escaping from there. Arun chased Madan and both ran inside the classroom. Anu laughed, looking at their chase.

Breathing hard, Madan stopped. 'If you hit me, I'll tell Anu about the dream,' Madan whispered in Arun's ear and Arun stopped hitting him.

After the period was over, Sandhya came to know what Madan was up to. Sandhya and Madan came near Arun, as Anu wasn't with them at that time.

'I know everything about Anu personally. I hope her life will change in your company, carry on and propose her,' Sandhya said encouragingly and Arun was bewildered.

'Dude, I'm fed up looking at this same expression for the past year,' Madan said.

'No, dude, I don't have the strength,' he said restlessly.

'OK, then have my lunch for regaining strength,' Madan said and offered his lunch box.

'Shut up, it's not an easy job, it's hard,' Arun said. Sandhya, looking at their arguments, consoled Arun, 'That's why we are telling you to take out that heavy burden from your heart which is troubling you a lot, and your life will go on smoothly.'

'You people can't understand, I have already expressed myself, I can't disturb her again and then she will abhor me forever.' He sounded worried.

'Dude, I'm sure this time the luck will turn to your side,' Madan said smilingly, and Arun gave a grudging look at him.

'All right,' Arun said and left the place.

In the next period, Anu smiled at Arun and continued to write something in the classroom. 'I want you to smile like this forever in my company, I just can't imagine you turning against me.' He said all these to himself dreamily, looking towards the blackboard, recalling her charming smiles. Sandhya was trying to speak through signs with Arun but he did not give any response and Anu gave a confused look at him. After the classes were over, Anu walked out of the classroom along with Sandhya dully. Anu reached her home.

That night, on her terrace, Anu was speaking alone, looking at the moon. 'Oh, moon, I know all of them are up to something. Arun is trying to express again, oh my, how should I make him understand . . .'

Next day in the college, Anu sat on the college grounds steps alone and saw Arun coming with Prashanth and Madan together. Anu pretended to act as though she was normal and turned towards the basketball court immediately. They came near her.

'Hi,' Prashanth greeted Anu.

'Hello,' Anu replied and understood about their visit together. Prashanth, showing thumbs up, was pushing Arun.

'Where is Sandhya?' Anu asked Prashanth.

'She's not well so she didn't come, OK, now bye,' Prashanth gave a quick reply and hurried off towards the gate.

A little later, Madan said, 'Sorry, I have games practice session,' and left the place immediately.

'OK, even you want to go. Now what reason do you have?' Anu asked Arun and he turned towards the other side tensely.

'Nothing,' he said and sat next to Anu, giving her a deep stare as she was murmuring to herself, turning the pages roughly, and then looking at Arun.

'Why is everyone acting so peculiar, including you?' she asked and continued, 'That Prashanth, just to say three words, he came so far? This is sick . . .' she said frustratedly, and holding his wrist, continued, 'Swear to me and reveal the truth, what? Are they forcing you through warning looks?'

He closed his eyes tightly to charge his braveness and opened his eyes slowly. 'I don't have such a big heart like you to read others' minds and understand. Even you know what's running in my heart but . . .' Arun again turned towards the other side to recharge and stood up immediately. 'I love you, love you so much,' he sounded in a tired voice, and a small curve on her lips appeared.

Arun was almost stunned, excited, perplexed; all kinds of feelings were running in his mind.

Anu with a pale smile, said dully, 'Arun, you think this smile is giving you the answer. No, your expectations are wrong, please.' Anu continued smiling, and he gave a tired look towards the other side. She continued, 'I should have spoken earlier, I'm too late.' Her eyes were filled with tears. 'Please wipe out that kind of feeling in your heart, I know it's very hard but there's no way. Immerse yourself in my valuable relationship called friendship, not that the other one.' She had a very bitter feeling in her heart and she walked away. He stood like a rock and kneeled down on the spot. His eyes were soaked with tears.

Seeing him kneeling, Madan came running towards him. 'Arun!' Arun didn't say anything, got up, and walked into the classroom.

Next day in the college, Arun didn't speak a word with Sandhya and Madan.

'Oh shit, I think our plan didn't work. Even Anu has not come today. He's not speaking with us,' Sandhya said tensely.

'Don't worry, problems like this will always arise and these will get solved later. Even your case was more critical and serious. It's common in love matters,' Madan said as though he was well experienced. They came near Arun later.

'Arun—'

Before Sandhya spoke further, Arun said with a smile hiding his depression, 'It's enough, you are both happy now; please stop giving suggestions or ideas. I was hiding my feelings, looking at her happiness, and it was absorbing all my stress but now I don't have that chance also. Thanks a lot, guys,' and he left the place.

'Shit.' Madan hit the pole. Sandhya walked towards the classroom dully.

Arun dully sat on the sofa with his book opened but kept his mind closed. 'You can study in the room,' Nirmala said, changing channels on the TV and he stared at her seriously.

'No, I can't concentrate, today I'll take a break,' he said in a tired voice.

Next morning, Nirmala, holding a coffee cup, called, 'Arun, your coffee is ready, come fast,' and meantime she got a call.

'Didi, I'm in the park just to relax, I'll go to the college directly, bye,' he said and ended the call.

'He's sick,' Nirmala murmured to herself frustratedly and she drank the coffee.

Arun reached the college and saw Sandhya and Madan. 'Hi,' he said and smiled, and both of them exchanged looks with guilt.

'We are extremely sorry, Arun,' Sandhya said as Arun turned to move away. 'Hey, why are you telling him sorry? Facing the negative at the initial stage would definitely pull them to the positive finally,' Madan said, and hearing that, Arun smiled more broadly. And he went to a nearby pole to lean and became dull again.

A little later, Sandhya said, 'Hey, Anu is coming.' Arun's eyes were pulling towards her, but his mind controlled his eyes and prevented him from looking at her.

'Hi,' Anu greeted Madan.

'Hi,' Madan said, looking towards Anu. Sandhya caught her shoulders and Anu smiled. Seeing Arun near the pole, Anu went right to the back of his shoulders. 'I'm not able to solve the mathematics problems, just because he's creating a problem. He only has to solve both of my problems. Will he?' She spoke but Arun didn't turn back, since he was feeling guilty with a heavy feeling. After a while, he turned back but was late in responding, and Anu had gone walking towards the first floor. Seeing Anu climbing the stairs, he ran quickly.

'I'm always willing to help you, Anu,' Arun said in a high voice with his eyes soaked in tears. Anu, looking back at him with the same expression, gestured with tears filling her eyes.

Those who were in the corridor looked at them with surprise. Both went together into the classroom; Anu asked him to clear all the doubts and Arun solved them. 'Thanks a lot,' Anu said and left the bench.

'You are making me feel that we have a formal relationship now, by saying thanks,' he thought in his mind.

'Acting formal with you, I have to control this friendly relationship or else your feeling will arouse more in me,' Anu said to herself but he felt very uneasy in his heart and they both joined with others later.

VISHAAL AND DEEPTHI

*I*t was Sunday morning; Anu was immersed in her sleep and the clock struck seven. *Tring tring*, the phone rang and Shwetha answered the call.

'Hello.'

'Hi, I'm Tanuja, can I speak to Anu?' Tanuja sounded very bubbly.

'I'll call her, hold on,' Shwetha replied and loudly called Anu, saying, 'Didi, call for you, come fast . . . Tanuja on line.' Anu jumped out of the bed as she heard Tanuja's name and rushed towards the phone to talk to her schoolmate.

'Hi, Tanuja! How are you? You are calling me now? Stupid, do you realize it was last summer you called me up, and out of the blue, you have turned up now? You know what? I tried calling your number many times but got a response saying that the number didn't exist. By the way, what are you doing? I mean which college are you in?' Anu spoke without a pause.

'Whoa, whoa, whoa! Relax, dear . . . First of all, I am really sorry for not contacting for so long, OK? And regarding your questions, I'm in Stephen's College and I have taken science stream. Now tell me, Chennai Express, what about you?' Tanuja asked.

'Presidency College, science . . . Now forget that, do you realize that I saw you last summer . . . Where did you hide after that?' Anu asked desperately.

'At Madiwala, OK? Fine, tell me how's college life, huh? Do you have something exciting that is going on?' Tanuja asked.

'Nothing much, but if I compare, I feel that our school days were simply great and more exciting . . . Remember how we and Vishaal used to play together and enjoyed forgetting ourselves?' Anu sounded very excited and, at the same time, felt that she had lost something now which she had before.

'Hey, I forgot to tell you, guess what? Your Vishaal has appeared again and even he is in Stephen's College science stream . . .' Tanuja said.

Anu raised her eyebrows with happiness and felt as though colourful butterflies were flying around. Her heart started beating faster. 'At first even I didn't recognize him. He was acting as though he has landed from the States and pretended that he didn't recognize me. Finally, stupid liar recognized me when I called out his pet name Shawl.'

'Did he ask about me?' Anu asked eagerly.

'No, friend, I know how much you liked him, but he didn't. You know boys' mentality, right? They forget easily,' Tanuja replied angrily.

Anu's heart yearned to know more about Vishaal. She suddenly thought of a plan and said, 'Tanu, I'll bunk off my half-a-day classes tomorrow. Shall we meet at the school? It's a long time since we met, right?' Anu asked softly.

'Stupid, that's the exact reason I called you. Tomorrow, even I don't have any classes. I'll come around 10 a.m. to the park which is just beside the school,' Tanuja said with enthusiasm and ended the call.

Anu called Sandhya immediately after speaking with Tanuja and said, 'I'll come to know about Vishaal. Tomorrow is going to be a great day, thank God,' in a breathy voice.

'What? You got some news about Vishaal? That is simply great! Hope you will soon get your love, dear, all the best,'

Sandhya replied, and thinking about Arun, said to herself, 'I feel sorry for you, man,' and ended the call.

Next day, Anu got up very early. After waiting for the sun to rise, she quickly got ready and left the house. She boarded the bus to reach the park beside her school; recalling her beautiful past moments with Vishaal, her heart was filled with joy. She got down a stop earlier and walked towards the park. She recalled Vishaal cycling on the street and, while doing so, turning back, waving his hands with his cute smile. After entering the park, she sat on a bench and recollected Vishaal's activities in the school. As she was thinking about Vishaal playing cricket, a ball rolled near her; she looked at the ball dreamily. A small boy came and he asked for the ball, snapping his fingers. She woke up from her beautiful dream, passed the ball to the boy, and pinched his cheeks.

A little later, 'Hi,' Tanuja surprised Anu, hugging her from behind. Looking at Anu, she saw that Anu's eyes were red.

'Looks like somebody didn't sleep the whole night,' Tanuja said. Ignoring Tanu's comment, Anu asked, 'How are you, anything exciting?' and patted her on the back.

'No, friend, this is not the time to think about it. For now, we should concentrate on completing our studies to get a good job, which will make our future bright,' Tanuja replied like a philosopher.

'By the way, how's Vishaal?' Anu asked curiously.

'Oh yeah, he is fine, but—' Tanuja gave a pause. In reaction to that, Anu desperately asked, 'Don't hesitate to tell whatever you know about him, has he fallen in love?'

'Yeah,' Tanuja said dully, nodding her head.

'Wow, that's great, tell me when did he see his love for the first time, do you know how he ventured into loving her? Are they happy together?' Anu seemed very curious and Tanuja's hands were on her forehead. After seeing that, Anu said dully, 'Then my predictions are wrong.'

'Come on, stop shooting questions at me. Allow me to speak, will you? But, oh God, how should I tell you, huh? OK, fine, your imagination might be true that he's fallen in love, but I'll tell you how much I know of their love,' Tanuja said with boredom.

Anu gave a broad smile, 'Did he propose? And did she say yes?' Anu asked, closing her eyes.

Seeing Anu's excitement, Tanuja said, 'Oh, don't be so excited. You know what? The way he proposed to her was like he almost surrendered himself completely. He had actually misread her friendly approach as love. When he proposed to her, his timing was damn wrong. She was actually in a restaurant with her friends at that time. She had never imagined something like this and could not say a word. Maybe she was embarrassed in front of her friends. In reply, she asked for some time. In the meantime, he began capturing snaps of her with his mobile. His parents accidentally saw her snaps in his mobile and took away his cell phone from him in order to stop him from getting into these things at this age. Becoming tense, he started smoking. Even her parents got to know and she didn't attend college and tuition as well for a week since both were attending the same tuition. Looking at his behaviour, she finally spoke to him and accepted his love but all of her friends were saying that she's accepted it superficially and not truly from her heart.'

'What's her name?'

'Deepthi.'

'Oh! I never dreamt that he would smoke, idiot.' Anu sounded frustrated and Tanuja continued, 'At the beginning, they were fine but as days went on, on some occasion, the whole class had arranged a party in a mall. In that party, a guy called Shravan invited Deepthi to dance and she accepted his invitation as she is open-minded. After some time, Vishaal joined the party; seeing her dancing with his friend, he didn't mind and he also joined them. After some time, his friends teased him as they were drunk and challenged him to have a drink in front of her to test her patience. Accepting the challenge, he gulped down a glass of beer. Deepthi saw that and she slapped him. After that, Vishaal became wild and seriously argued with her. Not realizing what he was saying in that drunken state, he blamed her for dancing with another guy. She could not take that rubbish and left angrily.' Before Tanuja could say anything further, Anu became restless.

'Stop it, please, it is enough, I don't have strength to hear this anymore. How could he do this?' Anu said, crying, and sat on the ground.

'Relax, Anu; we never expected that our friend would do this,' Tanuja said sadly and there was a pause.

'Now what's their situation?' Anu asked in a sharp tone.

'Next day, she came to college as usual. She met him and told that from that day onwards, she would never have a relationship with him and they stopped talking to each other. Both of their parents were close family friends and even they broke up because of this incident. They have put her in some other tuition and she changed her class section as well. All these incidents happened two months ago. I recently heard that Vishaal couldn't control himself, and he secretly went to see her a week back. He's becoming more depressed day by day,' Tanuja said.

Anu, becoming more depressed, leaned against a tree and began to think emotionally. Seeing that, Tanuja said, 'I never thought you would react like this,' and started to walk. She slowly turned back as Anu caught her hands.

Controlling her tears, Anu asked, 'Please tell me if what I heard is true?'

'It's true,' Tanuja replied in a sharp tone and left the place, as even she could not watch Anu in depression. Anu's heart was deserted because the image she had built about Vishaal in her mind was that of a dream hero who had all the good qualities and character. Realizing about Vishaal's actual nature, she was hurt badly, actually worse than knowing the fact that Vishaal loved Deepthi. After some time, Anu left the place and reached her college, as some schoolchildren curiously watched her.

Anu reached the college at around four o'clock and sat on the college grounds staircase. 'Hi, Anu,' her classmate greeted and came bouncing the ball towards her but she didn't reply.

In another corner of the college grounds, Arun said, 'Thank God, I finished all the equations,' closing the chemistry workbook. He was wondering, saying 'Why didn't Anu come today?' He turned towards the other side of the ground and said to himself, 'What is wrong with me? If I can see those steps, I can definitely see Anu. Can it be hallucination? No, it is not, she is actually there. But, how come she's here at this time? Oh God, I have to control my senses.' A red long dupatta flew over beside him, and holding it, he called, 'Anu,' loudly. Looking at the steps, he said in surprise, 'Oh God, it's Anu,' and ran towards her.

Anu had rested her forehead on her knees and she looked almost exhausted. He lifted her head and saw her half-closed eyes. As he shook her shoulder, she neither spoke nor moved, and becoming tense, he sprinkled some water on her face. She became conscious and looked at him. Throwing his arms around her shoulders, he asked, 'What happened to you, huh?' and she suddenly moved away, wiping her mouth. 'What's wrong with you? All these days I controlled myself, stop hiding, and tell me what happened,' Arun painfully asked. It sounded as though his heart was speaking. He moved her hair back from her forehead and consolingly tapped her shoulders. 'Come on, don't hesitate to tell me what happened, please,' Arun asked sadly.

'He has completely ruined his own heart,' Anu replied with tears rolling from her eyes.

'Who . . . about whom are you speaking?' he asked tensely. She wiped her tears and seriously looked at him for a while.

'It's Vishaal, my friend,' she replied, crying, and it started raining. Arun became depressed after hearing the name of her friend that he wasn't aware of.

'He proposed to a girl and she accepted, although not truly. But now, their love has broken,' she murmured.

Arun, becoming relieved, said angrily, 'Stop, what if they break up? Why are *you* so worried?' and both stood up.

'I have already lost my heart for him, I don't want him to fall in pain forever like me,' Anu said and walked away crying without looking at him. It started thundering, and again becoming depressed, he closed his eyes, facing towards the sky.

Anu reached her house; she was completely drenched. Seeing her, her mother asked tensely, 'Oh no, what is this?' grabbed a towel and came running to pat her dry. After a while, Anu lay down on her bed, covering herself with a thick rug, but she was shivering, and a little later, Shwetha gave her tablets.

Arun also reached his house and dully got down from his bike. Nirmala came running towards him with a towel and started to dry his hair.

Next day in the college, when the professor called Anu and Arun's names, he heard, 'Absent, sir.' Sandhya and Madan exchanged confused looks. Later, Arun gave a call to Sandhya informing her that he had fever and he would come the next day. He asked her to come a little early in the next morning to college. Next day, he reached the college early and started practicing basketball. It was drizzling.

A little later, Sandhya came running with an umbrella and opened it to cover his head. Looking at him angrily, she said, 'Stupid, you have fever and you're playing in the rain.' He seriously stared at her and threw the ball aside angrily.

'Answer my question first,' Arun said seriously.

'You have really gone mad . . . OK, fine, I'll answer, but first, let us move inside, OK, not here,' she said, looking up at the pouring clouds.

'Anu had already fallen in love, right?' he asked, but ignoring him, Sandhya pulled his shoulder, and as she got a jerk, she stopped pulling him. 'Tell me, why did you hide all these from me? What's your problem, huh?' he asked angrily, pushing away the umbrella and continued, 'OK, at least when I made up my mind to express my love again, you should have stopped me and told me everything, but no, you had to spoil everything by not letting me know that she was already in love with somebody.'

'Shut up, Arun, what do you know about her? I was her friend since the eighth grade. She has told me everything about her love. Do you know who her love is? A boy called Vishaal, a schoolmate who studied with her up to the seventh grade.'

His ears stretched as he heard the name Vishaal.

'He later moved to Mumbai along with his parents, as they got transferred. Idiot, she lost her heart for him when she was just in first grade, believing him as her dream hero. She started chasing her own shadow, trying to catch it. Several times, I told her to forget him, thinking of him as a dream. You very well know how stubborn she is. She came to know that he is back from Mumbai, only a day before, from her schoolmate. I don't know what news she heard from her friend,' Sandhya said in an angry tone and he was completely shocked hearing about Anu's childhood.

Sandhya continued after a pause.

'Think practically and tell me something. Had you known all this before, were you in a state where you would have erased all your feelings for her from your heart? Tell me if you would have done so, I am ready to punish myself.' Arun didn't speak and she continued, 'This is life, Arun, not a paper where you can write, erase, and rewrite on it. I thought your love would be like an oasis in her desert-like life. But now everything is over,' Sandhya sounded emotional and left the place.

A little later, she got a call from Anu. 'Hello, Sandhya. How is Arun? He was very upset yesterday just because of me. I had flu, so couldn't come to college, now it's better and I want to speak with him,' Anu said.

Sandhya had turned on the loudspeaker on her mobile and Arun pretended to act normal. His eyes slowly moved towards the mobile but he ignored it.

'I don't know what it was that had driven my mind and heart to share my intimate feelings with him.' Anu sounded very depressed and Arun was very pleased hearing her words. Sandhya stretched her hand to give the mobile but Arun immediately left the place.

'Anu, he's not here,' Sandhya said and ended the call.

In the classroom, Madan came to know from Sandhya that Arun didn't speak with Anu. 'Why dude? Why didn't you speak to her?' Madan asked.

Arun closed his eyes and bit his lips. 'I lost all my strength of voice,' he replied. Sandhya was also sad looking at his depression and later didn't even have her lunch.

Near Stephen's College, Prashanth saw Vishaal smoking near the college canteen. Vishaal had not shaved, wore untidy clothes, and looked very depressed. Prashanth came near and said, 'Dude, I can't watch you being so depressed. See, love matters take their own time to settle, life does not end here itself, you have a long way to go, better you concentrate on your studies and give some pause to your love matters.' He sounded like a philosopher. A little later, Prashanth got a call.

'Hello, Prashanth, Anu and Arun are very depressed, everything went wrong, meet me at evening. I'll tell you later,' Sandhya said and ended the call.

'Shit, oh, only good people face the litmus test.' Prashanth sounded very frustrated.

'What happened?' Vishaal asked.

'Yeah, firstly listen about my love and that has turned unbreakable. I feel that way every second when I meet my love. All this has become possible because of Sandhya's friend.' Prashanth sounded dignified, giving a keen look towards the ground. Vishaal's mind was not much present and immediately got back listening to his words and he continued, 'She's amazing, I might have had just a touch of attraction to Sandhya, but her friend has made me realize what true love is. She has got such a power that she can give life to a lifeless love.' And further, Prashanth told him every mannerism and attitude about Anu.

After that, Vishaal deeply went over his words. 'OK, bye, dude,' Prashanth said but Vishaal was left in silence and slowly got up from the bench. The sun had almost set and he blindly went walking on the footpath, thinking about what Prashanth told him. Some kind of positive feeling entered his heart.

'Will we both get together again; will you understand me and come back?' Vishaal questioned himself, and at the same time thinking about Vishaal, Anu felt somewhat uneasy in her heart and walked towards the window. She opened it, and seeing the sunset, she said in a breathy voice, 'I think even your heart right now is exactly feeling what mine is. Don't worry, soon your love will rise like the rising sun and you must show it to the world. If you prove your love to your girl, that's like proving it to the whole world.'

In Vishaal's house, his mother knocked on the door to call him for their dinner but he didn't respond. Getting worried, his brother hardly hit the door with his shoulders and it broke open. They were shocked to see that Vishaal's eyes were closed and his eyelashes were wet. Everyone tried to wake him up but their attempt went in vain. They immediately rushed him to the hospital. Later, they came to know that it was due to weakness that he had fallen unconscious, and the weakness was because he had not taken proper care and food for months now. He slowly opened his eyes after the intravenous glucose was started as prescribed by the doctor. His mother cried looking at his condition. His father, who was looking at him, standing outside the ward, came in and shouted at him.

A little later, Vishaal's grandfather came, looking at Vishaal; he said, 'All of them say that you're like me but I wasn't depressed like you for any matter. I used to take things challengingly. No, Vishaal, prove yourself in a positive way to everyone, especially to your girl. Don't hurt others' feelings and make them cry by putting yourself in the trouble of depression.' Vishaal slowly nodded his head. His grandpa then shared some incidents about his love venture, about the time when he was young and Vishaal giggled hearing it.

A few days later, Anu recovered and was desperate to see Arun. Looking dull and pale, she entered the college and walked towards her friends. Seeing her in that condition, all of them were surprised. She came near Arun. 'How are you?' Anu asked sounding very concerned.

'I'm fine, actually I think I should be asking this to you, how are you?' While Anu's friends were wishing Anu well, Prashanth came walking towards them.

Giving her a bunch of flowers, he said, 'Anu, my wishes for good health and happiness,' and wished everyone well. She accepted it, and after a while, he left the place to reach his college.

It was Sandhya's birthday. All her friends wished her a happy birthday and gave gifts, except Prashanth. She was impatiently expecting a call, and everyone teasingly laughed at her, as she was looking restless. Arun received a call from Prashanth, and he purposely turned on the speaker.

'Hello Arun, how are you?' Prashanth asked, and Sandhya heard his voice and murmured, 'He is such an idiot; he has even forgotten my birthday. Instead of calling me, he called up Arun.'

'Everything is ready, dude,' Prashanth said softly. A little later, all the students who were on the college grounds raised their heads excitedly looking towards the sky and shouted, 'Wow!' they saw a huge balloon hanging in the sky behind the college. The balloon rope was tied to the college terrace railing.

'HAPPY BIRTHDAY SANDHYA' these words were boldly printed on the balloon and Sandhya gazed in surprise at the balloon. A little later, Prashanth covered her shoulders from behind and turning quickly to him, she said, 'Oh! Prashanth, it's so thrilling. You are such a darling, this is the most wonderful birthday I ever had,' hugging him tightly. She kissed his forehead, and all her friends clapped. Anu was very happy, looking at Sandhya's excitement.

Giving her a bow, Prashanth presented to her a cell phone and she felt very happy, as it was latest one available in the market. Her friends came near and greeted her. Madan snatched the cell phone from her and started taking snaps of Prashanth.

'Hey, Madan, please don't take my snaps. I don't want her to land in trouble in case her father gets to know,' Prashanth said quickly.

Tapping his shoulders, Madan said, 'Look, guys, see how he cares about her now itself, it is just great.'

Looking at Prashanth and Sandhya, Anu dreamily said, 'I hope I shall see them soon like this,' thinking about Vishaal, and at the same time, with tears rolling from his eyes, Vishaal was holding hard against his chest the returned cell phone that he had gifted to Deepthi.

Anu walked some distance away and stood thinking alone. 'Hi, Vishaal.' Prashanth got a call from him.

'How's your day? You didn't come to college,' Vishaal asked dully.

'Superb, dude, I never imagined my love would climb this height. Today, I gave her a surprise on her birthday. I never had any idea that surprising the loved ones would bring unimagined happiness,' Prashanth sounded very emotional, looking at Sandhya's smiling face.

'How is your love's friend?' Vishaal asked, and Anu felt suddenly some kind of jerk in her heart. 'Did you think of me?' Anu spoke to herself, looking at the ground. Vishaal asked Prashanth, 'Dude, I am thinking of getting help from your love's friend to solve my love problem.'

'Oh, I forgot to tell you, I don't think that it is a good idea because she hates to speak with guys. At the beginning, even I had a problem getting help from her. Firstly, she sees whether the guy is fit to fall in true love. Only then she does take a step forward to help them. OK, let me see, I will try to insist and see what happens. Don't worry, everything will turn out fine.'

Hearing this about Sandhya's friend, Vishaal didn't feel disappointed at her attitude and a small curve on his lips appeared slowly. 'You sound so different from other girls,' Vishaal said to himself, smiling, and Prashanth ended the call. Prashanth had not mentioned Anu's name to Vishaal; he thought it would be better to reveal her name after speaking with her.

A little later, Prashanth's cell phone beeped; it was a message from Vishaal, and it read, 'Dude, looking at your success in love, I am feeling a bit confident that I can regain my love, thanks! I'm feeling better now.' He smiled looking at it and continued explaining features of the cell phone to Sandhya.

In the college canteen, Sandhya's friends enjoyed the ice cream treat the birthday girl gave. After that, everyone sat in a circle on the college grounds, having a chat. Their chat was a blend of argument, shouting, cheering, laughing, and they were chasing one another finally. Arun went chasing Sandhya and Madan.

Prashanth was dully looking at their chase.

'Are you fine?' Anu asked him.

'Yeah, I'm fine.' He spoke in a jerky voice. Anu got up to go, looking at her. 'Anu, one minute, I want to speak with you,' Prashanth said softly.

'Yeah, tell me,' Anu said and sat down again. Arun came back breathing very hard after chasing Sandhya. A little later, Sandhya invited all her friends for a birthday party at Café Coffee Day.

Madan got a call from his mother to come back soon. 'OK, it's my mom. Sandhya, I'll join you guys tonight, bye, guys,' Madan said, and even Anu got up since it was getting dark. Prashanth was disappointed and could not speak about Vishaal with Anu. She said bye and left the place. Later, they all landed up in the restaurant except Anu. After a while, their party was over.

'Arun, I need to talk with you and Anu, I'll meet you tomorrow in your college,' Prashanth said after the party.

'About what?' Arun sounded curious.

'Tomorrow I'll let you know when I meet you,' he said and left the place.

That night, Anu studied for three hours, as she had warnings from Sandhya. After that, she was fed up with physics and closed the book. Later, she went to the terrace. 'Hi, sweet friend, right now my wish is that I want him next to me so that I can tell him how to convince his love,' Anu said, looking at the crescent moon and continued, 'Oh, girl, why are you troubling my boy? Maybe he didn't know how to handle the love matter. Surely, he will prove that he truly loves you and will love forever. Oh, moon, please send this message.' And she blew on her palm pointing towards the moon. As she blew, *whoop . . . whoop,* Deepthi coughed constantly, as she had some spicy food.

Next morning, Prashanth got up. 'Oh! My God, never in my life have I taken a bath so early in the morning when it is so damn cold,' he said, shivering, and got ready quickly. At the same time, Arun was holding his brush and, instead of brushing, blankly looking at his image in the mirror. He suddenly realized that he was getting late and got ready quickly around 6.30 a.m.

Anu remembered that Sandhya had called her the previous night about Prashanth coming to college to talk to her. 'Oh no . . .' Anu said and ran to freshen up.

Later, Arun gave a call to Prashanth: 'I'm leaving right now.' Arun reached the college a little earlier than Prashanth and started practicing basketball. A little later, Prashanth came near him and greeted him.

'What's the matter, dude?' Arun sounded curious.

Looking towards the gate, Prashanth replied, 'No, wait, let Anu come.'

Arun was increasing the distance for throwing the ball into the basket after earning a basket and was looking at the gate after earning each basket.

Seeing Anu, Prashanth said, 'Hey, she came,' and ran towards Anu. Meanwhile, Arun had successfully thrown the ball into the basket, and he turned smilingly to greet her.

'Hi, Anu, let's go there,' Prashanth said, and they reached a corner of the college grounds, near the steps.

'Yeah, tell me,' Anu asked.

'Please, can you help me?' Prashanth said in a pleading manner, and Anu gave a perplexed look.

Looking at him, Arun asked, 'What?'

'My friend is facing some problem in his love, that's . . .' Prashanth slowly revealed.

Arun felt restless and turned towards the other side.

'His condition is growing worse day by day.' Prashanth sounded as though he was explaining a patient's condition to a doctor.

'Of course anybody's condition would grow worse day by day especially in our mind, it's nothing new,' Arun said, meddling in their talk, and Anu gave a serious stare at him.

'Why does he need my help? I think you yourself can help him,' Anu replied.

'It's a big story to tell you,' Prashanth said, breathing hard.

'OK, OK, please don't tell that story,' Arun said.

Anu looked at Prashanth. 'Sorry, I helped you just because you loved my friend and that necessitated me involving myself, and at the same time, I found truth in your love.'

'Please listen, I can surely tell you that he loves her truly, I swear, just meet him once and you will understand. Anu, please,' Prashanth pleaded.

Looking down with uneasiness, Anu thought, 'Oh, what is this? I have my own tension about Vishaal and now,' and seeing that, Prashanth asked sharply, 'Are you not willing to help him?'

Anu tensely looked towards Arun, but he ignored her; after a pause, looking at Prashanth, she replied seriously, 'OK, wait, Prashanth, if I find something wrong in him then I have to break the link with you, remember.'

'I think this is right,' Arun said slowly.

'Yeah, fine, I've no objection at all,' Prashanth said.

'And you, Arun?'

'Yeah, it's OK,' Arun replied.

Prashanth offered her a handshake. 'Thanks a lot, you know he will feel so happy when I tell him about this,' Prashanth said with a smile.

'Wait, but on a condition that you shouldn't reveal my name or any details about me to him,' Anu said in a sharp tone. 'I promise you, bye,' he said and left the place. He walked towards his bike.

Arun looked at Anu. 'Oh, this is what he wanted to say. I thought something else,' he said.

'Me too,' Anu replied and said, 'Hey, OK but . . .' and ran towards Prashanth's bike, as he walked some distance. Anu came near him, as he was about to start his bike.

Removing his headgear, he asked, 'What, Anu?'

'I forgot to ask his name,' Anu sounded in breathy voice.

'Oh yeah, even I forgot, he's Vi—' As he stammered, Arun came walking towards Anu. 'Vishaal,' he said very clearly, and hearing this, she went backwards, not noticing Arun, and leaned on him shockingly.

Coming near her, Prashanth asked, 'What happened?'

'Idiot, what did you tell her?' Arun asked loudly.

'I just told her my friend's name is Vishaal,' he replied. Arun, who was holding her, suddenly left her shockingly.

Looking at them in surprise, Prashanth said anxiously, 'What is this? You both are reacting as though you heard the name of a terrorist.'

Arun, becoming aware, replied, 'Nothing, dude, she will be fine, we were shocked for something else,' he replied and felt certain that his friend Vishaal who studied in tenth standard was Anu's schoolmate. Somehow, he convinced Prashanth to send him. Prashanth looked at Anu twice while going and was trying to read her face.

As Arun stretched his hand to Anu, she held it, got up, and smiled with tears. Holding Arun's wrist, Anu said, 'Oh, see, he's coming to get my help. Fine, Arun, can you come and have a talk with me?' They immediately caught an auto, and tensely looking around, she showed the direction to the auto man.

After alighting from the auto, Anu said, 'Arun, you follow me, if known people see us together, it will be a problem,' but none of her words had reached him, and he blindly walked behind her.

They entered a vacant field covered with grass, beside a lake. 'You know why I got you here, I need your support for helping Vishaal, please, can you?' Anu pleaded with him.

Giving her an astonished look, he asked, 'You love him, right? Anu, have you gone crazy?'

'Yeah, that's why I'm looking forward to help him,' Anu replied with a dreamy smile.

'How can you think like this? I'm not able to get . . .' He gave a pause and continued, 'He loves somebody else, not you.' Arun sounded very upset.

'That's mere love, but a life which strives hard every second for another life's happiness, to make every moment special forever, and is ready to take any kind of risk for the loved one's happiness—that kind of love is the best love,' Anu spoke dreamily, looking at the lake.

'What, you're calling that one as love? But everyone says that it is sacrifice,' Arun said.

Turning towards him, Anu said emotionally, 'No, it's not sacrifice, it's the true love, this is an opportunity for expressing my love heartily in this way.' After a pause, she asked, 'So what's your reply?' but Arun remained silent and both walked along the lakeside.

'I can see true love in your heart, but I'm not lucky to feel it,' Arun murmured. A little later, smiling at her, he showed his thumbs up.

'Thanks a lot,' she said in a breathy voice. Both got into the bus and reached their college later.

Arun was thinking about how to convince the physics professor, as they had bunked off the first period and both entered the classroom. Luckily, the professor was not there, and all of them looked at them as they had never seen both together coming after a period. Looking at Arun, Madan asked in surprise, 'Where have you guys been?'

'Forget that, what about the physics class?' Arun asked.

'First answer his question,' Sandhya said.

Meanwhile, the physics professor entered the classroom. 'Oh, hello, guys, I was held up with some important work, I'll take the third hour,' he said and left the classroom. Later, the bio professor entered the class, and they waited with complete patience until the classes were over.

Anu told them everything that Prashanth said, and Sandhya was surprised hearing that. Madan stared at Arun to see his reaction and at the same time, he was hearing Anu's talk.

'So what have you both planned?' Sandhya asked.

Looking at Sandhya, Madan asked, 'What? Prashanth is hiding a lot from you?'

'I told him that I'm least bothered about the unwanted secrets,' Sandhya replied.

'That's right,' Arun said with a smile.

'Oh, now I have to think how to contact him without revealing my name,' Anu said dully.

'Then how can you help him?' Madan asked, and Anu took Arun's cell phone from his jacket. Looking at that, Sandhya asked, 'What if he recognizes your voice?'

'No chance. It is really a long gap since he heard my voice, he heard me in my childhood. It surely sounds different now,' Anu said and continued, 'You know my full name is Anushika, and he doesn't know my full name since my dad had mentioned my name as Anu only in the school records. So you guys call me by my full name when he calls up,' Anu said.

'OK, fine,' Arun said.

'You're going to meet your love in this way finally, all the best,' Sandhya said and kissed her forehead. All of them wished her well and left the place.

Prashanth reached his college and saw Vishaal was sitting alone on the stairs. He came near and greeted him. 'Vishaal, I met her and told everything about you. She has agreed to help you but be careful, dude, she's very sensitive. Hope good time starts from now onwards,' he said.

'Thanks, dude,' Vishaal replied and feeling better, he massaged his face a bit using his palm. After giving Arun's cell phone number, Prashanth said, 'Dude, call her up only during morning and evening when required, it's her friend's cell.' He dully looked at the number, thinking about the girl's attitude.

That night, Anu could not sleep as the clock was ticking for her to hear dream boy's voice, and she went upstairs as usual but couldn't see the moon. 'Oh, I'll talk to him tomorrow, I'm feeling so excited,' she said and turned back with astonishment as she suddenly felt someone standing behind her.

'Anu, your immaculate advice helps solve problems for those who are having some issues in their love matters and that's because you understand them. You're so wonderful, it's my wish and I'm gifting you that your love shall reach its highest peak. Bye,' Spandan said. He tapped her cheeks and vanished immediately.

Vishaal came near Anu and hugged her tightly. She immediately woke up from the sleep. 'Oh, Spandan, if his love reaches to a great success, it's like my love reaching to its destination. Don't give these wishes to me again,' she thought and fell asleep.

Next day in the college, Arun got a message around 7.30 a.m.: 'Please can I call you now, my friend?' He gave a surprised look at the message, and in a moment, he saw Anu coming near the gate.

'Hey, Anu, come quickly, what a coincidence, just now he sent a message, he will call you right now if you reply,' Arun said in a hurried voice, and she sat next to him.

'How can . . .' Anu said and gave a pause.

'Come on, buck up, you need to feel great to speak with him now.' He sounded cheerful and continued, 'I have sent him the reply, he might call you now,' Arun said and she caught his wrist tightly.

'What is this? My heart is beating very fast, I'm sure that I won't be able to speak a word,' she said tensely, and the mobile started ringing. Anu became more tense. 'You speak first,' she said in a breathy voice.

'Hello,' Arun said, unwillingly fearing that Vishaal might recognize his voice.

'Hi, I'm Vishaal,' he said softly. Arun said, sounding a bit differently, 'Hold on, I will give it to her, here you go,' closed the speaker, and looked at her. Anu took the mobile and his eyes spoke. 'Come on, speak . . .'

Anu realized that she received the call. 'Hello . . . I am Vishaal, I want to know your good name. Please may I know?' After a pause, he again said, 'Hello . . . is somebody there?' and her eyes were in tears. She could not speak, as her depression and anxiety were absorbing all her energy. Arun stood up to go, but she caught his wrist tightly.

'Hel . . . hello,' she said in a very low tone.

'Hello! Hey, thanks a lot for your response,' Vishaal replied softly.

'My name is Anushi . . . Anushika,' she stammered.

'I'm Vishaal. How are you, Anushika?' He sounded very dignified. 'Hello . . . Hello . . .' She ended the call and started weeping.

'I still can't understand. Is this your happiness or depression?' Arun said to himself.

'Something went wrong, might be some signal problem, it won't be nice if I give another call,' Vishaal thought to himself.

A little later, after sipping some water, Anu said, 'Why am I feeling so emotional? This surely won't help him.'

Time went by and around four o'clock, Vishaal came out from the classroom and sat alone, thinking about Anu.

'Hey, look at him, it's really surprising, you know, remember how he used to stare at you, but now how come he looks like he's least bothered,' Deepthi's friend told Deepthi as they both passed by Vishaal.

Looking at Deepthi from afar, he thought to himself, 'Let me call now,' and gave a call.

'OK, he's called again . . .' As Arun said so, Anu felt very thrilled and she grabbed the mobile from him as he was about to say hello.

'Hello, Vishaal,' Anu said in a jerky voice.

'Hi, Anushika,' he greeted her, giving a broad smile.

'So how's your loved one?' Anu asked.

'Yeah, I think she's fine, very happy without me,' he said in a casual voice, and there was a pause between them.

'One minute, Vishaal.'

'Yeah, sure.'

Anu went to the edge of the field, and wearing the earphone, she said, 'Yeah, tell me, how she is reacting now?' She sounded curious.

'She does not show any kind of reaction at all. It is as though I don't exist at all. I am no more to her, you can say that according to her, I am dead already,' he replied dully.

'Vishaal, listen to me carefully . . .' She gave a big lecture for about fifteen minutes and concluded saying, 'See now, she will come to know that you're quite alive. Do this, all the best!' After speaking to Vishaal, she told Arun about the advice she gave him.

'A great idea,' he replied, and after a while, they both left the college.

Next day in Stephen's College, 'Answer it, Vishaal, what's the result of this reaction,' the chemistry professor asked.

'It turns pale blue, sir.' He gave a sharp reply.

'Perfect! You are alert today,' the professor said. Later, Prashanth called in a loud voice from the college grounds as Deepthi and her friends were walking in the first-floor open corridor,

'Chandana, where are my papers, could you please get them right now? I won't be here later.'

Chandana nodded her head in affirmation and suddenly said, 'Oh no, this fellow, hey, Deepthi, can you please come along?' she requested.

'Sure,' Deepthi said.

They both went down the stairs; they saw through the classroom's window and it looked empty. 'Oh, I think all of them must have gone to play volleyball,' Chandana said and looked at the door, which was ajar.

Looking at the door, Deepthi said, 'One minute.'

Chandana, peeping through the door, said, 'Hey, it's Vishaal,' but Deepthi didn't react. 'Wait, I think that fellow must also be there,' she said and peeped again.

Vishaal was sitting alone and was speaking. 'Deepthi, it is only now that I am realizing how much pain and insult you had to bear because of me and my behaviour. I am extremely sorry; I know it won't cure your pain. However, I promise that how much pain you had to bear from me, I will bear more than that now. Actually, I wanted to express all this to you directly but did not get an opportunity to do so. So I am imagining you and expressing my repentance,' he said emotionally and wept, not realizing that he had to say all this after getting Prashanth's missed call as planned by Anu and Prashanth earlier, but he expressed it without waiting for the signal. But he expressed all this truly from the bottom of his heart, unaware that Deepthi was watching him.

After hearing him, Chandana said, 'Oh my God . . .' and took her head out of the doorway to see Deepthi but she had gone upstairs quickly. She immediately took out the sheets from her bag and started continuing with her assignments. She did that just to erase that scene from her mind, and Chandana came with excitement for speaking about it.

Closing Chandana's mouth, Deepthi said in an angry tone, 'Whatever you're trying to say or you have seen, better don't tell me. Just forget it right away, that's it.'

Later at her house, although Deepthi decided to ignore Vishaal's feelings, whatever he had expressed was echoing in her mind and she could not concentrate. She threw the book aside and started playing with her cousin.

Next day, Anu didn't feel like getting up early since the weather was cold, but thinking about Vishaal's call, she got up hurriedly, and after she got ready, she went to the college. A little later, Arun reached the college.

'Did he call up?'

'No.'

'Thank God,' she said and widened her dupatta to cover her shoulders, as she was feeling very cold. She looked up at the foggy sky and hummed her favourite tune. The phone started ringing and she immediately received the call but was disappointed, as it was from Madan.

Later, they got a call from Vishaal, and Arun immediately passed the mobile to her.

'Yeah, tell me,' Anu sounded very energetic.

'Anushika, I really don't know whether she heard my intention or desire of love, but I came to know each and every mistake that I have done and understood the pain she underwent. I think it's a curse which I'm ready to accept, Anushika . . .' Vishaal said with a heavy feeling, and tears rolled down her eyes. Arun gave a confused look at her.

'Thank you, thank you so much,' she said.

'For what?' Vishaal replied; he was puzzled.

'Because you understood her so much, bye,' she replied and ended the call.

As soon as the class ended, Anu took Arun's mobile and he gave a fishy look. 'Oh, I'll just give a missed call,' she said and gave a missed call to Vishaal, but since the class was going on, he could not realize his mobile was beeping.

Madan, seeing them together, whispered in his ear, 'Hey, Arun, it's good that you are helping that guy. At least in this way you both can get closer.' Arun stared at him.

'You're expecting a lot,' he said with a little smile.

In Stephen's College, Vishaal saw Deepthi going on her Scooty. 'Bye, Deepthi,' he said in himself and took his mobile. Looking at the missed call, he exclaimed, 'Oh, it is Anushika.' Giving her a call, he said hurriedly, 'Hi, Anushika.'

'Vishaal, how are you feeling now, I mean, is your mind calm?' she asked.

'No, but some space is left in my mind for preserving your words, please tell me,' Vishaal said in a very dignified way. Feeling pity on him, she gave a pause. Arun patted her on the back, as she was dreamily looking at the ground. Realizing, she jerked.

'Vishaal, listen, just taking her to a gift gallery for purchasing an expensive gift, using your father's hard-earned money, and gifting her will not impress her or make her feel really happy in the true sense. You must express your love in a way that makes her feel unique. Her heart must pop out with happiness and she should thank God that such a wonderful person has entered in her life. You need to struggle and do something different for her to make her feel special. I hope you understand.'

Her words almost touched Vishaal's heart and he could not speak a word about her point of view since he had earlier spent his father's money for presenting a mobile to Deepthi. Anu's attitude surprised him. She immediately ended the call without waiting for his reaction.

That night, Vishaal without blinking his eyes was thinking about what Anu told him and almost couldn't sleep the whole night.

The days were passing by as usual. Vishaal was calling Anu regularly and she was asking Deepthi's reaction all the time to know her exact intentions on him. One day, as he called Anu, she insisted, 'Vishaal, be in front of her, let your eyes be fixed on the book,' as he was listening through the earphone of his mobile. A little later, Deepthi passed across them but ignored him. A little later, Prashanth spoke.

'OK, Prashanth, did she see him?' Anu sounded desperate.

'No, she didn't see,' Prashanth sounded restless and continued, 'But she was looking down constantly and I couldn't read exactly what she was looking at.' He sounded doubtful.

'Give it to Vishaal,' she said in hurried way. 'Vishaal, tell me where exactly you were standing,' she asked.

'Right opposite to her but I don't think she saw me,' he said softly.

'Oh, surely her eyes were on you and you went a step ahead in your love, congrats,' Anu said in an excited way and ended the call.

Vishaal gave a confused look at his mobile.

'Yessssss,' she said and spun round, widening her arms.

Seeing her happiness, Arun gazed at her with a slight blush. 'How's that possible?' He came out with the question.

'Prashanth said that she was constantly looking at the ground, it means actually she was looking at his shadow, I mean she saw him,' Anu replied.

Hearing their conversation, Madan said, 'Wow, you brilliantly caught her sight.'

Anu pulled Sandhya's hands as she came near her, and they both hurried off towards the gate to reach home.

Looking at her, Arun said dreamily, 'Anu, I can't desist anymore from loving you, I don't know when it will reach your heart.'

After some time, Vishaal gave a call and Arun didn't receive it, but the mobile started beeping again. With no other option, he received the call. 'Hello, I'm Arun, Anushika's friend, she left long ago,' he said, speaking in a different tone for hiding his identity.

'Oh, my schoolmate's name was also Arun but I lost his contact,' Vishaal replied and Arun gave a pause.

'Anushika is your best friend?' Vishaal asked but Arun didn't respond.

'Great, you're lucky to have such a friend.' Vishaal sounded very bubbly.

'Yeah,' Arun said but with not much energy.

'OK, bye, Arun,' he said and ended the call.

A couple of months were left until Deepthi's birthday, and Vishaal thought about whether he could be the part of that occasion, and at the same time, Anu's mind was running into different thoughts: 'Will she change her opinion?'

'Hi,' Arun greeted her, giving a bright look at her, before she could greet him back, his mobile started ringing and it was Vishaal's call. Anu took the mobile with a broad smile and spoke at length for about half an hour.

Becoming restless, Arun ignored her and carried on with his bio diagram. She gave back his mobile and got up to leave the place but he caught her hand. 'I think it will distract his study schedule,' he said, biting his lips.

'No, not at all, he will study with more concentration as soon he gets into a love track and it will boost him to study harder.

Take for example Prashanth himself,' Anu replied with a smile and slowly dressed her hair as it was breezy.

'The way you're healing the depressed hearts is really amazing. When will you cure my depression?' Arun said to himself and continued revising lessons.

Next day, Vishaal straightaway went to Deepthi's classroom and said hi to everyone. Without noticing, Deepthi replied hi and looked at him angrily.

'Hi, guys, I won't trouble anyone from this moment on, no past issues. Thanks for giving me a chance to speak out,' he said and left the classroom without looking at her. Later, she angrily stared at him while coming down the stairs but Vishaal pretended that he didn't see her.

Next morning, not noticing the time, excited Vishaal called Arun and heard 'Hello.' It sounded like Anushika's voice for him.

'Hi, Anushika, you know what? Deepthi said hi to me! She replied to my gesture after such a long time, I'm really feeling great.' Vishaal sounded very energetic and he heard, 'She is really brilliant.'

After a pause, 'Hello, hi, Vishaal,' Arun said.

'What happened? Why did Anushika pass the mobile to you?'

'Anushika, no, it was my sister.' Arun said on a casual note.

'I am really sorry, I was so excited that I blabbered to your sister just like that . . .' Vishaal said in a tired way.

'What? Oh shit,' Arun replied.

'Sorry, actually . . .' Vishaal continued.

'Oh no, forget that, congrats anyway, bye,' Arun said.

'Sorry, bye.' Vishaal sounded exhausted and ended the call.

Pouring milk into a glass, Nirmala asked, 'When did you all start the mediating business?' and Arun threw a guilty look towards her.

'No, it's a godly business, helping to erase the misunderstanding between friends earns smiles of God, I mean, God feels happy,' Arun said, looking up towards the roof.

'You're sounding like a philosopher, I think Anu's training must be very advanced,' Nirmala said, but ignoring her, he watched the television.

Nirmala pulled his collar. 'OK, anyways, will she come for your birthday party tomorrow?' she asked. Arun coughed hurriedly as he was sipping coffee slowly and smiled at her.

'What do you mean by that smile?' Nirmala asked him, giving a perplexed look.

'Oh God, she won't come to a nearby restaurant with her friends for birthday treats then how can she turn up here, in our home? No way, she won't speak with me or with any other guys in the public places except in the college, you know she won't even come in dreams.' Arun sounded a bit frustrated, and Nirmala laughed, hearing about her peculiar behaviour.

Next evening, in Arun's house, Nirmala was receiving the guests, and all the invitees had gathered. 'He would have felt very special if Anu had joined,' Madan said, giving a dreamy look at him, and Sandhya got a call from an unknown number. Hearing Anu's voice, Sandhya sounded excited.

'What a pleasant surprise! Hold on, I'll give him the phone.' Sandhya went near Arun to give the mobile.

'Who?' He just made a gesture and Sandhya winked her eyes with a smile.

'Happy birthday, Arun,' Anu greeted him, and his heart felt like flying.

'Anu, I would have felt much happier in your presence,' he said in a dreamy voice. Anu stared at the phone, nodding her head with a smile and ended the call.

Next day, in Stephen's College, Vishaal was thinking how to execute Anu's plan. 'The next plan is quite hard.'

And at the same time in the Presidency College, Anu was hogging Arun's birthday cake. 'Why he hasn't called up yet?' Anu asked.

'Ten minutes left for the classes to begin,' he replied and got up to go. As she caught his hands, he felt as though the fragrance of love was arising in his heart and he turned. 'Why hasn't Vishaal called yet?' She sounded like a small kid.

'Relax, he will call up in the evening, stop thinking, otherwise you won't be able to understand the lessons,' he replied and she dully nodded her head.

In the Presidency College, classes were ended for the day, and all of them left, except four of them, who were sitting on the steps of the college grounds. Anu was waiting for the call.

'I'm fed up, I'm going,' Sandhya said and left the college along with Madan.

'Oh, he didn't respond to my missed call, better you only call him,' Arun said with a little impatience, and Anu nodded her head.

'There is another way,' Anu replied and closed her eyes.

Arun became curious. 'What are you doing?' he asked, giving her a keen look.

'Ha, wait, he can sense my words,' she said in a sharp voice.

Arun asked, smiling, 'How is that possible? Ridiculous.'

Touching Arun's chest, she said, 'If there is true love in anybody's heart,' and he felt as though he was floating in air and she continued, 'the experiment that I do will work,' and her words really touched his heart. He looked at her beautiful eyes. 'Oh, don't disturb, shh,' Anu kept her pointed finger on her lips and closed her eyes again.

'Please, Vishaal, call me, I want to speak with you,' Anu said softly.

'No, no,' Arun murmured, smiling. A little later, he asked, 'Did you finish sending the message?' and Anu smiled.

'Just wait for a few minutes.'

'Let's see how your experiment works,' Arun replied, looking at his watch. 'Five minutes more . . .' After four more minutes, he said, 'Only one more minute left.' And he looked at Anu. 'Oh, your magic went wrong,' he said funnily.

'I think something must have gone wrong, OK then, bye' Anu said dully.

'Even this time, your heart is telling?' Arun said teasingly.

'Yeah,' she said dully and went walking.

Meanwhile, Arun got a message, 'Sorry, Anushika, I called you three minutes back but my currency was over, I shall call you tomorrow, bye.' As he read it, he was frozen. Seeing her walking near the gate, he went running towards her.

'Anu . . . Anu!'

'What?' she asked.

'Are you not feeling bad that he didn't call you back?' he asked for knowing her reaction.

'No, I felt consoled at the last minute, thinking that he's not in a position to speak, maybe some problem, ha. One more thing, please read this letter whether my suggestion will do him good and send this letter to Vishaal if it is OK. Look, Prashanth has come, I saw him parking his bike outside,' Anu said, giving a letter to Arun, and left the place.

Arun started reading the letter; her advice concluded by saying, 'Vishaal, the step that I have mentioned is tough, but in future, it will turn out to be wonderful, be strong-hearted, with a strong mind. I hope you will do it. All the best,' and Arun felt that her suggestion to Vishaal was good. Prashanth came near Arun, after wishing,

'I'm fed up dealing with Anu, dude.' Arun sounded frustrated.

'Why?' Prashanth asked.

'She kept on guessing about Vishaal's girl whenever she looks at some couples together. She even asks me to guess how she looks like.'

'Oh really, actually I'm getting that girl's photo tomorrow,' Prashanth said.

'What! Don't ever do that or else I'll kill you,' Arun said.

'No, dude, actually I told her to come to college itself for seeing her secretly, but she didn't accept and asked me to bring her photo,' Prashanth said.

'Oh is it, I am sure that she will start writing a book on her after looking at the photo, oh God,' he said, looking at the sky. Later, he gave him the letter to be passed on to Vishaal.

Prashanth went to Vishaal's house and gave him the letter. 'It's from Anushika,' he said. Vishaal went inside hurriedly without speaking.

'Oh, her letter is more important than calling me inside, stupid,' Prashanth said to himself and left the place.

After reading the letter, Vishaal said to himself, 'Oh, Anushika, you have really inspired me; I think there's only one way for this. Fine, I will follow your suggestion.' Later, he called Prashanth, asking for some suggestions.

'Wait, dude, I'll connect to my dad's phone, he knows well about that,' he replied.

'Hello, good evening, uncle,' Vishaal greeted him and asked for the suggestions.

'It's good you have made up your mind to start earning from now itself, but why?' It's quite risky, you can't cope with your studies and work as well,' Prashanth's father said.

'Sorry, uncle, I can't tell you the reason but I can really manage both,' he replied, looking at Anu's message, which he had pinned right opposite to him.

'OK, Vishaal, the work that you want to find is not so hard, you just have to know the marketing rates and information about the products that we send. You go to bizworldweb.com, it's called Global Biz, where you can catch up on the details and you will find an option called Oriented Job Sectors, click that and fill the form along with your résumé. I'm sure it's a bit hard but you have some chance. Try it in Japan, Korea because they prefer Indian accent, all the best.' Prashanth's father explained in detail regarding the callers' attending job.

'Thanks a lot, uncle,' he said and ended the call.

'Idiot, he ended the call, maybe he wants the job right now,' Prashanth said in harsh way.

Vishaal saw the Wanted column and the countries who were offering the jobs. He started filling his résumé and sent it to the listed countries through the fax as well as through the Internet. Later, he got the message as he was dreamily looking at Deepthi's beautiful clippings on the screen. Meanwhile, his brother came, rubbing his eyes.

'Vishaal what are you doing at late night?' said a sleepy voice.

'Anna, please can you connect the Internet to my computer, I need it, please don't ask me for what,' Vishaal said and went back to his room without waiting for his brother's reply. Looking at the screen, his brother became suspicious and he went back to sleep. Vishaal didn't sleep; the thought 'Will I get it today itself?' was swirling in his mind and he went near the computer again. He checked the inbox and there was no reply. At late night, 'Vishaal . . . Vishaal,' his mother woke him up. 'What is this?' she asked, pointing out the computer as it was switched on. He gave a sudden jerk and switched off the computer. He didn't speak to his mother and fell asleep.

Next day, Vishaal went to the college. 'I must not think about the job now and I shall fix my mind towards the studies,' he said to himself. Opening the book, he started studying but it was not entering his mind. He was constantly yawning and suddenly hid his face behind the book as he looked at Deepthi. His heart was bouncing but he tried to control it.

After the classes got over, Vishaal reached home and immediately opened the computer. He checked the inbox. 'Not satisfied with your qualification.' He got all negative results and became very disappointed. Only four countries were left and he felt very nervous. Deepthi's photo fell from the book as he was pressing his fingers hard and stared at it constantly after he took, keeping it close to his chest, 'I hope now at least I shall succeed,' he said with a smile and gradually fell asleep.

The clock struck 2 a.m. Vishaal woke up with a sudden jerk and rubbed his eyes. Turning towards the computer screen, he opened the inbox with shivering hands. He broke as the negative result appeared on the screen, and pushed all the sheets and the books aside. He sat on the floor tiredly and saw a letter fallen a yard ahead from him. As it was Anu's letter, he took it for reading again. Suddenly, the screen became empty as he started reading. After reading, he looked at the screen; there was one country left and the words came bouncing on the screen: 'You have been selected for the interview, for details please contact through fax, the number is 524-866-8578 or email to swedencocoa@ rediffmail.com.'

After looking at it, he screamed, 'Thanks a lot, Anushika,' and all of them came near him in shock. 'Oops! Sorry,' he said and ran into his room. He could not stop thinking, and after an hour, he went near the computer. He collected all the information about the interview and, with relief, went to sleep.

Next day, Vishaal reached the college early to see his love. After the classes were over, he went to a vacant place in a corner of the college grounds. 'Hello, welcome to India, sir, it's a pleasure speaking to you, I have found out about the stockholding company's details that were given for . . .' He was practicing in his own accent and deeply involved with his presentation. He didn't see Deepthi and her friends while they were passing by him and her friends gave a confused look at him.

A little later, Chandana said, 'I think he must have gone completely mad.' Deepthi threw a sharp look towards him from the top floor as he was speaking to himself. Prashanth came near him,

'Dude, tomorrow we have a chemistry test,' Prashanth said.

'Oh, thanks, you reminded me but how can I manage? Today I have an interview.' Vishaal sounded worried.

'Great, dude, all the best!' Prashanth sounded excited and went to the library for collecting some question papers but it was closed. He called Arun quickly, 'Do you need the papers tomorrow?' Prashanth asked him but Sandhya had received the call.

'Yeah, we need them right tomorrow itself,' she replied.

'Oh no, Sandhya, I gave it to Vishaal,' Prashanth said, and continuing, 'I'll try my best to get the question paper with notes,' he said and ran towards Deepthi.

'Deepthi, one sec please, can you give me your papers and notes?' he asked, and her eyes half closed. 'Take it,' she said removing sheets from her bag. Receiving it, he asked, 'For you?'

'No, I have another copy of it,' she replied and left the place after wishing him goodbye.

Prashanth immediately started his bike and reached Anu's college. As he came near them, she said, 'Hey, have you got her photo?' Anu sounded very eager.

'Oh, sorry, I forgot in the tension of the class test tomorrow,' he replied, and turning towards Arun, he said, 'Take these notes, be careful with these.'

'Why?' Arun asked with a perplexed look.

'These are the notes of Deepthi, our Vishaal's Juliet,' he replied. Hearing this, Arun gave surprised look and started thinking, 'I think is it not that Deepthi, right? Forget it.'

After Prashanth left, he opened her notes and started studying. He found some physics problems were wrong in those notes and tried to work. He could not, and after getting Nirmala's help later, he solved the problem finally.

Meantime, 'Sick, can't it be like this?' Deepthi was trying hard to solve the problem for the past hour, and with frustration, she threw the book aside.

Later, Arun gave a call to Prashanth 'Hello, dude, did you get the fifth problem right from the last year's physics paper?' he asked.

'No, I . . .' he stammered.

'OK, fine, I'll explain, you add first and expand the formulae of the temperature then calculate the scaling . . .' Arun started with a hint and taught him to solve the problem.

Widening his eyes, Prashanth said, 'Wow, you're brainy.'

'OK, tell your friend that she's done it wrong, I think even she might be struggling to solve it,' Arun said.

'Dude, she's torturing Vishaal a lot, so let her suffer,' Prashanth said in a grudging tone.

'No, dude, ha, got an idea: you explain the problem and then pass the credit to Vishaal. At least she'll have a good impression of him.' Arun sounded a bit excited.

'Yeah, sounds great,' Prashanth said and ended the call.

Later, Prashanth gave a call to Deepthi and asked whether she solved the problem. 'No.' She sounded tired and he explained how to solve the problem.

'Oh, thanks a lot, see, you have become so brainy.' Deepthi sounded very relieved.

'No, I don't want any of your thanks. This problem was being solved by the person whom you thought dead,' he sounded in a sharp tone and continued, 'Hello . . . Hello, sick, I knew you would end the call,' he angrily murmured to himself and threw the mobile aside. Deepthi had not ended the call; she was actually speechless.

That day was Vishaal's interview date; he woke up around 3 a.m. and sat in front of the computer. He contacted the company through Internet for appearing in an online interview, and a lady appeared on the screen. Vishaal's throat was dry because he was getting tense, and he greeted her. He answered the questions and spoke well for almost an hour, and she gave him complete details about the company. Later, the lady said, 'Congratulations, Vishaal, you're appointed as customer care for Sweden Cocoa. Working hours is six hours, from 5 p.m. to 11 p.m. IST. Six working days and Sunday is holiday. We will pay you $250 per month, all the best. The stock and the rates shall be running live on your screen within five minutes. I hope you have got the job process.'

'Yes, madam, it's a pleasure to work for your company. Thank you,' Vishaal replied.

'I'll join you tomorrow,' the lady said and disappeared from the screen. He fell on the bed, with relief.

Vishaal, becoming energetic, rode his bike to reach his college. 'I must surprise Anushika, I won't tell her right now,' he thought in his mind.

After reaching his College, he dreamily said, 'Hi, your shadow has made me feel nice,' as Deepthi passed by him with her friend.

'He's gone mad, he's looking at the ground and speaking,' Chandana said. Deepthi didn't react and continued to walk as her friend was whispering in her ear.

He took his chemistry book to read and a little later, Prashanth came and explained some lessons, as they had a test.

In the college, during lunchtime, 'Vishaal, Vishaal, hey, see Kirthi Bhabi . . .' Prashanth said as he saw her coming in a Scooty.

'OK, bye, dude,' Vishaal said, walking towards Kirthi and sitting on the bike behind her. She stopped in front of a restaurant and both went inside. Vishaal becoming curious,

'Oh, how come you got me here, have you got an increment?' he asked and Kirthi dully nodded her head.

'No, for knowing what's in your mind and your brother has given Internet connection to your computer. I'm really very sorry that I checked your files. What's the need to work? Your father and brother can afford everything for you. What's the problem that's troubling you? Tell me, I can't wait anymore.' She sounded upset.

'Bhabi, you're my special friend, you will be the first person to know, but now I can't tell the reason. Sorry, please,' Vishaal said with a pleading look. Both left the restaurant after having coffee.

Kirthi gave some useful suggestions to him, as she was well experienced in her job. He was trying to grasp her idea; he spoke very well with the customers and did his job well. Vishaal was very exhausted, as he had to balance the job as well as his studies.

Anu wondered, as she had not received any calls ever since she gave him the letter, thinking what he might have thought about her suggestion.

'She's upset as there were no calls,' Arun thought and saw Anu and Sandhya enter the gate. As the mobile beeped, Arun stood up. 'He gave me a missed call,' he said in a screaming voice towards Anu. She came hurriedly and grabbed the mobile immediately.

'I can't hold back anymore, I have to share this information with her,' Vishaal said to himself and started dialling the number.

As the mobile rang, Anu was very excited. Looking at her excitement, Sandhya said, 'Remember you're just helping him but you're not his loved one,' and left the place. Suddenly her heart, which was popping with excitement, pushed her into depression, and tears filled her eyes. Feeling sad, Arun could not say anything. Anu swallowed her words, and controlling herself, she greeted him, 'Hi.'

'Hi, Anushika, I don't know how to thank you, I got the job and you know how I'm feeling, it is just great and all this is just because of you . . .' Vishaal spoke at length and she could not control her feeling. 'Congrats,' she said and ended the call, crying.

'Oh, I wanted to say something else,' Vishaal thought and gave a call again but Anu moved away from the place as soon as she heard the mobile ringing and Arun received the call. 'Anushika, I want to share this wonderful moment directly, shall I come to your college, if you don't mind? Please?' He sounded very energetic.

'Hmm . . . sorry, dude, she already left, bye,' Arun said.

'Fine,' Vishaal replied and ended the call.

Later, Vishaal started scribbling emotionally on a sheet.

Looking at it, Prashanth said, 'Dude, Deepthi will blast me, she will never trust me then,' becoming tense as Vishaal was writing something on her test papers. Chandana came near them for collecting Deepthi's notes from Prashanth.

'Stop it!' Chandana shouted as she saw Vishaal writing on the notes.

'How dare you?' she said and pulled the papers. Later passing those notes to Deepthi, Chandana said in an irritated voice, 'You know, that rascal has scribbled something on your papers.' Deepthi searched all the papers and finally found the paper on which Vishaal wrote. She squeezed that paper into a ball shape without glancing at it and threw it away. A little later, she saw the paper ball rolling on the ground and slowly turned back. She ran towards it as the college maintenance staff was sweeping the ground. She quickly picked up the paper and unrolled it. Her face became darker after reading it and she read it again and again. 'Oh, I never thought,' she murmured to herself and some change happened in her mind. She looked around and immediately kept it in her purse. She dully walked back towards her scooter.

Later, Vishaal called up Anu and informed her about Deepthi's birthday. 'Will I be able to wish her a happy birthday, hardly fifteen days left.' He sounded restless.

'Whether you greet her or not, that's not the point, you have to plan something which makes her feel happy. That's more important than you greeting her, wait—' Anu gave a pause, thinking. After a while, she said, 'Yeah, I got an idea, you indirectly gift her something, otherwise, is it possible for you to drive her to something like a play park or nature world?' Anu sounded doubtful and hearing that, he said excitedly after a pause, 'Yeah, great idea, but yeah, got it, my friend owns the Dress World franchise and I'll consult him. She regularly visits there. There are so many gift schemes, and I shall see that she gets the gift hamper through my friend with his help indirectly.'

'What if she won't turn up to the shop?' Vishaal sounded dull, losing some hope.

'Let's hope for the best to happen. Beyond that, what else can we do?' Anu also sounded a bit disappointed and ended the call.

'Oh, I made you upset,' he said to himself, looking towards the mobile.

It was Sunday evening, Vishaal visited his friend's shop and informed him about the plan. His friend laughed at him. 'How come such an imagination came into your mind? I'm cent per cent sure this must have not emerged from your mind,' his friend said. He knew Deepthi as she was a regular customer.

'Yeah, your guess is right, this idea is my friend's,' Vishaal said with a smile. He selected her favourite colour dress, which was displayed on a doll. His friend enquired details regarding the Nature Play Park tariffs for special arrangements through a call and asked Vishaal about the arrangements to be made on that day. His friend's eyes widened at the list as he explained about the arrangements and continued to speak to the manager of the play park.

'Hey, I need to know the total billing. How much it would cost, including this dress?' Vishaal said softly, and his friend enquired about the billing amount. After enquiring, his friend started writing on a pad.

'I have booked for five guys including you, they won't postpone it if three days are left from the date of booking and your total amount is . . .' And Vishaal's cheeks started heating up as he was tense that the bill would extend more than his budget.

'It comes to 16, 500 rupees,' his friend said.

'Thanks, dude . . .' Vishaal said in great relief. 'Now I'll pay ten thousand, the remaining I'll cover next weekend,' he said with a smile and gave a packet containing money.

'Great, friend, let this venture succeed, your love shall soon reach its peak,' his friend said in a breathy voice.

'Yeah, sure, but only if she comes to the shop,' he said and left the shop after wishing him goodbye.

Deepthi and her friends sat in a circle in the college, discussing. Deepthi's mood was looking dark.

'Oh, Deepthi, this Saturday is your birthday, why are you looking so dull? Come on, cheer up. Why can't we hang out for shopping?' One of her friends came up with an exciting idea.

'No, Subbu, not interested,' Deepthi replied in a tired voice.

'No, we have to go; you have to show that rogue that you are very happy without him,' Subbu said, dumping a burger into his vast mouth.

Her face fell, and she didn't speak a word.

'Birthday comes once in a year. Don't take silly things into your mind and keep being bothered about that, throw them all aside,' Chandana insisted.

'OK,' Deepthi replied with a slight unwillingness in her heart. She was back at her home. 'Mom, I'm going out tomorrow for shopping,' she said while having dinner.

It was Tuesday morning, and Deepthi got ready for the shopping. Vishaal gave a call to the Dress World courtesy wardrobe to enquire whether Deepthi visited the shop.

'No, dude, she hasn't come yet. Relax, there's lots of time, don't lose your hope,' his friend consoled him, but Vishaal was tense.

Later, Deepthi entered the mall with her friends, and all of them entered the Archies world to buy some greetings for the birthday girl. The wording and surroundings in the gift gallery gradually brought a smile to her lips.

'OK, almost over and last thing left is a dress for the birthday girl.' Chandana sounded bubbly.

'No, I don't need a new dress, there are so many of them lying in my wardrobe. I have hardly worn them, and besides, my dad is also gifting me a dress,' she said dully.

'Deepthi, I don't like when you talk like this. OK, if you won't, I'll buy one for you, let's go to Dress World,' Chandana said in a sharp tone.

'No, no, I'll buy it, but casual wear,' she replied.

Deepthi and her friends entered Dress World. Vishaal's mobile beeped. 'Your love has entered my shop, be ready to open your heart for her entry.' He smiled at his friend's message and looking up, he said in a breathy voice, 'Thanks a lot,' and leaned against the wall of his terrace garden. His friend quickly went near Deepthi to greet her and even she greeted him back.

'Show me some of the latest cool dresses in medium range,' Chandana asked.

'Please come to that counter,' he said and showed varieties of dresses. Chandana and Subbu were busy nearly thirty minutes with the casuals, but Deepthi was looking at the display of dresses, and her eyes slowly turned towards a dress which was displayed on a doll. After the selection of her dress was over, she enquired about the displayed dress.

'Sorry, miss, it's newly designed and has been reserved for the gift scheme, after a fortnight, you'll get the same if you want,' Vishaal's friend replied politely, and Deepthi collected the dress paying, RS 780.

As they were leaving, Vishaal's friend called them. 'Excuse me, I forgot to inform you that there's a gift hamper inside the dress cover, sponsored by the dress company. The lucky numbers are displayed there, if the scratched card number matches that displayed number, that particular gift will be yours,' he explained.

After hearing him, Subbu said, 'That's all bogus. Just to boost their sales, they will plan. I have never seen someone getting scheme prizes in my life. Even if they get one, it will be a small gift. Take that card yourself.' He hogged the popcorn.

'It's your wish to try it or not. What will you all lose if it is tried? It's my opinion,' Vishaal's friend sounded calm, and after a pause, Chandana said, 'OK, he's right, let's try,' and removed the card from the dress. She started scratching using her nail, and they glanced at the board as the number appeared in the gift card. Everyone's eyes were focused on the card except Deepthi, who was dully looking at the display doll.

'Woohoo!' Everyone shouted as the numbers came, identical to the number displayed on the board. His friend was pretending to attend to other customers; the number was 464512. Chandana sounded excited and passed the card to Vishaal's friend.

He took out sealed gift envelopes and searched for the envelope bearing the card number. After finding it, he gave it to Deepthi.

'Miss, congrats, yours is a lucky hand. Please let me know the gift that you got, I shall inform the company to arrange for giving it to you, please open it,' he said with a dignified manner, and Chandana opened the envelope with an excited look.

Seeing her excitement, Subbu said, 'No need to get so excited about the gift. You might get a steel bowl or a tray—that's all,' hogging another popcorn packet.

Looking at him, Chandana said angrily, 'Shut up,' and there was a letterhead on the envelope, printed as '**Zoom Dress Manufacturing Company**'.

> Congratulations! You are a lucky winner to have won four gift coupons to visit the nature park plus a gift, including free pick–up from and drop to your place. Kindly enter your names and details below:
>
> Name of the winner ....
> Address ....
> Date of your visit to Nature Par ....

(Conditions apply; dates cannot be changed when only four days are left as per the date mentioned by you. Gift is not transferable.)

Deepthi's friends became excited as they read the details in the envelope, of the gift hamper. Chandana passed the letter to Vishaal's friend.

Looking at Deepthi, he said, 'Wow, excellent,' and asked the details, but Chandana gave the details as Deepthi remained silent. After filling the form, he asked her to sign. 'No, no, please,' Deepthi hesitated.

'It's your birthday, come on, shut up, idiot,' Chandana said in an angry tone, and Deepthi signed it unwillingly.

'Happy birthday in advance, miss, hope all of you have a great day. Thank you for visiting,' Vishaal's friend said and wished them goodbye with a bow.

All of them left after wishing him goodbye.

'Oh, it's already getting late, come on, let's keep all these in the house,' Deepthi said.

'Almost two classes must be over,' Subbu said with hiccups.

Later, Vishaal's friend sent a message to Vishaal.

'The work is done; everything went according to the plan.'

Meantime, Vishaal was on the college grounds, and he smiled after looking at the message. 'With God's grace, I shall see her birthday celebration in the nature park,' he said to himself dreamily, looking towards the flying birds.

Later, Deepthi walked into the classroom with not much energy.

'What are you thinking?' Chandana, Chaitra, and Subbu were buzzing around her almost the whole day, for convincing her to come along to the nature park. Deepthi finally rescued her from their requests after the classes, but they didn't leave her and they were sending messages and called her constantly.

Later, in Deepthi's house, 'What is this?' her mother asked when they heard a tango tune. It was really joyful, and Deepthi ran outside the veranda to hear the music. Her friends were holding a banner: 'Please let's go'. Deepthi gave a tired look and kneeled right at the place with a dull look. She got up as they stopped playing music and went inside, closing the door. She recalled her past birthday with Vishaal and the gift he gave. She began to feel restless. 'More than staying here with past thoughts, let me move, I shall not disappoint them,' she thought and saw them all walking sulkily as she opened the door. She clapped, and they all turned to her. She showed her thumbs up with a smile; as they saw her, everyone jumped with joy.

Vishaal, leaning against a pillow, said in a pained voice, 'Deepthi, please come, I'll be waiting for you.'

In Deepthi's house, there was a loud scream on Deepthi's birthday. Rubbing her eyes, Deepthi opened the door. All her friends came to her house with colourful gifts, but her heart did not have colourful hopes. Wishing her a happy birthday, they all hugged.

As Vishaal got a call from Prashanth, he said, 'I'm the most unlucky guy in the whole world.'

'Why are you talking like this?' Prashanth asked worriedly.

'I'm not able to wish my loved one a happy birthday. If she won't come, I just can't think of that,' Vishaal said with a heavy heart.

'Don't worry, dude, she'll definitely come, your effort won't go to waste since you have really strived hard,' Prashanth said, consoling him, and ended the call.

Later, riding on his bike, Vishaal reached the outskirts of Bengaluru with little hope in his heart.

Deepthi dully looked towards the phone as though she was expecting a call from Vishaal and got a call.

'Hello, good morning, madam, this is from Nature Park. We have sent a car right to your residence, madam.' One of the clerks gave a call to Deepthi.

'Yeah,' she said with disappointment and slowly walked down the street. She entered the car as she heard the car's horn and sat beside the window. Her friends Chaitra, Chandana, and Subbu were already seated.

The car started, and the journey began with boring songs and some jokes.

'Join us,' Subbu said as Deepthi did not show any interest, nor participate with them.

'Subbu, please, I'll hear the songs, you guys please carry on,' she said and connected the earphone to her mobile. The car went on smoothly like a plane as it was moving on a highway road, and later some of her friends fell asleep. She jerked as the car driver had applied brakes suddenly, and Subbu opened his eyes wide but later continued to sleep. Chandana didn't wake up as she was drowned in sleep, busy snoring. Combing her hair, Chaitra was admiring her face in the mirror.

'Twenty kilometres to Mekedatu falls,' Deepthi saw a board as the car was moving fast.

'Are there any waterfalls?' Deepthi sounded curious asking the driver.

'Yes, ma'am' there is a big waterfall,' the driver replied and Deepthi smiled.

Later, Chaitra, peeping out of the car's window, put her head out completely, 'Hey, two kilometres more, we are almost near,' she said, exclaiming. Hearing her, Subbu and Chandana woke up suddenly, and to feel fresh, Deepthi asked for some mints from Subbu. 'This is Vishaal's favourite,' she thought and peeped out. Meanwhile, in the nature park, Vishaal was sitting on a swing alone and waiting eagerly for Deepthi's arrival. Wetting his lips, he said dreamily, 'I hope you shall feel very special, my love.'

All of them got down excitedly, and their faces were blossoming like spring, except Deepthi, who was looking dull.

A caretaker of the nature park, receiving them, said, 'A warm welcome to all of you,' and after checking the gift coupon, 'Who is the birthday girl Deepthi?' the caretaker asked.

Meanwhile, Vishaal, leaning against a glass frame, tensely looked at her to see her response. As everyone was looking at her, she slowly raised her hand like a small kid. A curve on his lips slowly appeared, and his heart expanded, urging him to hug her, but he controlled himself. All of them were very curious to go inside the nature park.

'Wow!' Deepthi and her friends shouted as the guard opened the gate, and the surroundings had changed their dull faces into glowing flowers. Using mud lamps, they had formed 'Happy Birthday Deepthi.' Vishaal's heart was popping out to see her being surprised. After looking at it, she was stunned.

A little later, the caretaker said, 'Please let's move.' Unnoticed, Vishaal followed them. A little later, they saw two ladies who had dressed in bright violet saris were holding a bouquet and a gift cover. They presented it to Deepthi, and she looked perplexed. Looking at the gift, Subbu asked, 'Gift for us?'

'It's only for the birthday girl,' the lady gently replied with a smile, and they served some snacks and fruit juice. Later, the ladies took Deepthi into a room to dress her up, and they asked her to open the gift packet. Deepthi was completely shocked as it was the red dress which she had seen in Dress World. After they dressed her up, with a little touch of make-up, she looked like a beautiful doll. The minute Vishaal saw her, he kneeled on the ground right at the place he was standing. He couldn't see anything other than her, as his eyes were blocked by her beautiful image. 'You look so beautiful,' all of them together said. Chips dropped from Subbu's mouth, as he saw her.

All of them jumped to enjoy thrilling rides, and Deepthi didn't stop laughing. As Deepthi was screaming joyfully, Vishaal, becoming happy, felt more thrilled than her. She enjoyed each and every second of all the rides which were giving different thrills. Vishaal's heart was popping with joy, and he was feeling like joining her.

After the rides, the caretaker took them to an open field. The words 'Happy Birthday Deepthi' were written on a huge hot-air balloon. Everyone screamed 'Wow!' and clapped their hands as she entered the hot-air balloon's basket. It slowly rose into the sky, and she was stunned by the atmosphere around. She could see the view beyond the park. 'Please turn back,' she heard the caretaker's voice and slowly turned back. Looking at a huge waterfall, she felt like jumping. She also felt as though her worries were moving out of her mind and she was floating in the pleasant clouds. Facing the sky, Vishaal stretched his hands sideward, and Deepthi also did the same. After a few minutes, the balloon slowly landed down and she came out. All of them came near her.

'How was the ride'? Subbu asked.

'No words can express it, we must go there,' she replied in a dreamy voice.

Becoming curious, Chandana asked, 'Where?'

'For seeing a waterfall,' Deepthi replied excitedly.

'We can't go by vehicle, madam, we should go by walking,' the caretaker said.

'No problem, it will be like trekking.' Chaitra sounded excited and turned back to see Deepthi, but she had already trotted some distance ahead. They all walked about ten minutes and looking at the muddy slope, Subbu asked tiredly, 'How many kilometres?'

'Only three kilometres to reach the place, sir,' the caretaker replied. Hearing that, Subbu sat on the ground.

Pulling his shoulders, Chandana said in a dragged voice, 'Come on, Subbu.'

'I can't, you all move.' Subbu sounded exhausted.

Tapping his shoulders, Chaitra said with a smile, 'Subbu, come on, you can burn your calories, and you will grow slim.'

'Shanthi will start liking you by admiring your figure,' Chandana said, giggling.

'OK, for Shanthi's sake, I'll come,' he said and got up. Through the bushes, they all started walking slowly on the slippery mud path.

Deepthi was enjoying nature around them and saw many villagers doing pottery works. All of them went near them to look at their work of making pots. Chandana fell in the muddy water while walking, and all of them burst out laughing. She winked her eye at Subbu and Chaitra, and they pushed Deepthi into the muddy water. Deepthi stared at Subbu with a grudge and met Chandana's eyes. They slowly stretched their hands pretending to get up, but instead they pulled Chaitra and Subbu as well into the muddy water. The pot maker started singing a song and all of them danced. Vishaal had disguised himself as a villager to see Deepthi's excitement. Seeing her dance, he had forgotten himself completely.

Deepthi saw the waterfalls from some distance; leaving the group, she ran towards the waterfalls to reach them early and smelt the fragrance of flowers and the wet mud around. The weather started drizzling, reaching there; she blindly jumped into the water and she splashed the cold water on herself. She soaked in the richness of nature and felt as though all her stress and worries had flowed away along with the flowing water. Later, all her friends joined her to play in the water. Near the waterfalls, Vishaal was hiding behind a tree to peep at her; while she was splashing the water with complete force, a few drops fell on Vishaal's cheeks and he felt very happy. Having lightened their stress, they all returned to the nature park later.

Deepthi cut the birthday cake and her friends stuffed the cake into her mouth. As Deepthi gave the cake to the caretaker, he went and gave a piece of it to Vishaal since he knew that Deepthi did not know that Vishaal had arranged all this. He enjoyed biting into the delectable cake as it had a touch of Deepthi. They all had a great feast later. All of them relaxed on the swings, which were fixed alongside the path after every couple of trees. Vishaal sat on a swing, as Deepthi left the place.

Looking at her from some distance, he spoke to himself. 'When will you give a place in your heart?' A little later, the caretaker came near them and gave a bunch of blue bellflowers and a gift box to Deepthi. Offering a handshake, she said excitedly, 'Oh, thank you, I really enjoyed, it was a great pleasure coming to this place.'

The day was almost over and it was around half past 7 p.m. Vishaal looked towards the sun, which was hiding behind the clouds.

Standing on a huge rock, looking towards the sunset, he spoke dully. 'Oh, it's time, even my loved one will hide in her house. You should have stayed for some more time.' They all waved their hands at the caretaker, as they were leaving the nature park. The security guard bowed at them but Deepthi was looking at the gate and didn't feel like leaving the place. They all got inside the car later.

'Hello, hello.' Chandana snapped her fingers near Deepthi's pointed nose, and said, 'Open the gift quickly,' and Deepthi gave the gift to them. They all didn't have patience and opened the wrapper in a hurry. It was a toy of twin baby polar bears sitting back to back.

'Wow, how cute,' all of them said loudly, but meantime, Deepthi was dully looking outside. Hearing them, she looked towards the polar bears with a jerk. Surprisingly, she took it from them and with tears filling her eyes, thinking deeply, she hugged it. Seeing Deepthi in tears, Chaitra sounded upset. 'What's your problem?'

'You know, I think that all these were not a bumper lottery, whatever you all have thought,' Deepthi said in a sharp voice.

'What do you mean?' Chandana asked. Subbu stopped chewing the cookie and gave a puzzled look at her.

'I am telling you this because tell me something, how can they know that the bluebells and polar bear are my favourites, they had also prepared all my favourite dishes. It is just unbelievable,' Deepthi said in a thoughtful voice. Contrary to her guess, Chaitra said casually, 'Maybe it is a miracle.'

'Such miracles do happen in life, there is nothing to get so worried about.' Subbu aired his view and continued to hog the food.

'No . . . Subbu, no,' Deepthi said firmly, nodding her head, and continued, 'Only my dad and Vishaal know my favourites,' she said, and there was a long pause in the car. Everyone remained tired and Chaitra yawned.

'I know!' Deepthi sounded high-pitched; all of them jerked with a serious stare at her, and she continued, 'I think it's my father who has done all this, never in my life have I come across such a wild happiness. Father was telling me on the phone that he's giving a surprise for me,' Deepthi said excitedly but they didn't respond much to her excitement and they all reached their houses around 9 p.m.

Deepthi, entering her house, called, 'Daddy . . . Daddy!' without responding to her mother. Realizing that he was not in the house, she looked at her mother.

'Deepthi, Daddy called up and said that he'll come tomorrow. By the way, how was your day?' her mother asked.

'Yeah, fine,' she sounded a bit disappointed and went to her room.

Next morning, Deepthi, waiting for her father, was biting her nails tensely. She became happy, throwing her arms around her father as he arrived after a long period. 'Belated happy birthday, sweetie,' her father greeted her and kissed her on her forehead.

'This is my surprise gift,' her father said and gave her a huge gift box. She was perplexed and said thanks with not much energy. Looking at her reaction, tapping her cheeks, her father asked, 'Why do you look so tired?'

Her mother, intervening, said, 'She has been to Nature Park.'

Deepthi, looking at her father, said, 'See, Dad, what they have gifted me,' showing him the polar bear, and continued, 'I didn't like them much.' Saying so, she gave a sudden look to catch his reaction.

'Oh, you shouldn't have gone there for straining yourself. I sent 5,000 rupees, why didn't you celebrate by having a party with your friends? Anyway, see my gift.' Her father sounded a bit excited.

Deepthi, having some clash in her mind, opened the gift box. It was a laptop and a beautiful dress, her father becoming rather excited. 'See, this is my surprise,' he said. To have some better feeling, she pushed away all her confusion for a while and hugged her father.

'You have to stay the whole day with me,' she said in a warning tone.

'Yes, sweetie, I promise you,' her father said.

The confusion had taken Deepthi's depression over. Next day, she reached her college.

Chandana, meeting her, said, 'Hi, Deepthi, see, he's ignoring your birthday, he's happily playing throw ball,' Chandana said in a grudging tone as both passed by Vishaal.

'Stop it . . .' she said and walked away fast, trying not to look at him. He slowly turned back to see her as soon as Deepthi left the place and called up Arun's mobile later. He got the reply 'This line is busy, please try later.'

'Oh, shit . . .' Vishaal said and went inside his classroom later.

In the Presidency College grounds at evening, Arun was looking at his mobile. 'Oh God, eight missed calls,' Arun said, and all of them stared at him.

'OK, let's give him a missed call,' Anu said eagerly.

'Wait, Anu, even we are curious to know, turn on the speaker,' Sandhya said. Arun smiled and gave a missed call.

Vishaal saw his mobile. 'Hey, it's Anushika.' He sounded very energetic and called her. 'Hello, Anushika, yesterday's events have brought me the most wonderful and the happiest moments in my life ever. I'm getting the feeling of true love and many wonderful things have happened . . .' Tears dropped from his eyes, and after a pause, he told each and every thing that happened in the nature park and finally, he said in a very emotional way, 'Deepthi didn't get any doubt, and I forgot everything looking at her smile. It was you who opened the door of my happiness. You're the reason for all these feelings to emanate in my heart. I want to see you right now. Please don't give any excuses, I'm coming.'

'Wait, Vishaal, I can understand how excited you are, but please, I promise you will see me the day when your love succeeds,' Anu convinced him.

'OK,' he replied in an unsatisfied manner but he decided to meet her directly and rode his bike towards Presidency College.

Later, all of them left the college except Anu and Arun, who were left alone.

'I'm so happy, Arun, thanks a lot, I'm not feeling like going home,' Anu said and gradually closed her eyes. She opened her eyes immediately.

'Arun, the way he expressed himself, you heard, right? I don't think he will keep his words this time, there are chances he might come, it's better to leave,' Anu said in a doubtful way.

'Oh yeah, as you wish, let's go,' Arun said.

'Bye, Arun,' she said and went quickly walking towards the bus stand.

The very next moment, Vishaal zoomed in full speed and he saw the college gate was closed.

'Hello, uncle, I need to meet . . .' he enquired of the security guard disappointedly.

'No, all the students have gone.' The security guard gave a sharp reply. Ignoring that, making his hands into a loudspeaker, he called her loudly, 'Anushika . . . Anushika.'

'Can't you understand? Just go,' the security guard said angrily. Vishaal, becoming impatient, gave a call to Arun.

Throwing a wide-eyed look at his mobile, Arun received the call.

'Why you all didn't stay for a while?' he sounded very impatient.

'No, sorry, she had already left since she had lots of assignments to do,' Arun said in a sharp voice and ended the call immediately. Arun was in the restaurant right opposite to the college and was actually looking at him. Disappointedly, Vishaal left the place later.

'My goodness, how exactly did Anu get to know about his visit?' Arun said in a surprised voice and left the place to reach his home.

College students had begun showing seriousness as their final exams were approaching and only about four months were left for preparation. All the students were attempting trial exams themselves in order to prepare for their final exams. One day in the college, giving a fed-up look at her physics textbook and then looking at her friends, Anu said, 'These lessons, I'm finding them hard.'

Looking at her sharply, Sandhya said in an angry tone, 'All these days you were very busy speaking with Vishaal, which one do you hope that you will find it easy ha?' Becoming dull, Anu didn't say anything and Sandhya continued, 'Better you avoid contacting him for a month, you will automatically get closer to the books,' Sandhya suggested. Arun, who was working out the problems of chemical reactions in the book, stopped and started thinking for a while.

Anu started studying for the exams seriously, and she was feeling some of the problems were complicated in physics and mathematics. Arun expounded some of the lessons to her, which she was finding it difficult.

One day, while Arun was explaining some problems to Anu, he got a call.

Giving a sharp look, Arun said, 'It's Vishaal . . .' and she took the mobile from him. 'Anu, but . . .' He hesitated.

'Hi, Anushika,' Vishaal said in his usual voice.

'Hi, how is she?' Anu asked.

'Yeah, before she was looking frustrated but now she's confused,' he replied.

'Yeah, don't worry, one day or the other, definitely she will understand you,' she said and Vishaal smiled. 'Your exams, sorry, our exams are nearing,' Vishaal said.

'Yeah . . . this month I'm preparing for the practicals, so if you don't mind, can you call me up after this month?' she said in an uneasy manner.

'Oh sure, but at least can I contact you with one line of message a week?' Vishaal asked, and hearing that, Arun gave an irritated look and turned towards the other side.

'Yeah, sure,' Anu said in a breathy voice and ended the call.

Later at night, Anu on the terrace looked at the gibbous moon. 'Oh no, I will not be able to speak with him for thirty long days, my goodness, it's all just because of these books. Fine you're helping me always, by sending my messages to him. Good night and sweet dreams, Vishaal,' Anu said to herself and blew on her palm pointing towards the moon. 'I have to go and study physics, bye, my friend,' she said, waving, and left the terrace.

All the college students were stressed a lot by their studies, especially Anu, who was feeling it quite hard since she had to study all at once. All three of her close friends were helping her out to make her understand clearly, especially Arun. Almost a month was over.

One day in the college, looking at Anu, Sandhya advised, 'OK, you finally finished physics, you keep on revising it and regularly work out mathematics in college itself,' and after a pause, 'OK, bye, everybody,' she said, pulling Anu's hands.

'No, Sandhya, you move, I'll come later.' Anu sounded uneasy, and everyone had a question mark; they left looking towards her, except Arun. While Arun was solving mathematics problems, Anu was walking up and down impatiently.

Looking at her, he said, 'Why are you so restlessly walking? Instead, you can work out mathematics,'

With her face pale, she sat beside him. 'OK . . .' A little later, she said softly, 'Thirty-two days are over but still Vishaal hasn't given a call,' and Arun threw a sudden look at her.

'Maybe he's busy preparing for his exams,' he said convincingly with a bit of a smile.

After a few minutes, 'OK, bye,' she said dully and walked to reach her home.

Constantly looking towards her, Arun said to himself dully, 'Stupid Vishaal, he's troubling my love a lot,' as she was slowly walking towards the gate.

It was Sunday; Anu got a call from Sandhya right early in the morning. 'Hey, Anu, read the *Times of India*'s Bangalore supplementary on the third page.' Sandhya sounded excited.

'Sorry, I can't, tell me in the college about that whatever you want to show or say, we have not subscribed for that newspaper,' she replied restlessly.

'OK, at least go to your neighbour's house and look for that information, you're useless, bye.' Sandhya put down the receiver with a little anger.

'What is this for?' Anu thought and went to the house of her neighbour who had that newspaper, to see what Sandhya was saying. She opened the newspaper and glanced at the third page.

'Attention, readers, on the eve of Valentine's Day, February 14th, at the palace grounds, a special singing competition will be conducted for the male singers, sponsored by PepupCo Company. They will declare the true lovers of the year and the prize amount will be five lakhs. Those who are selected must bring their loved one along. For details, contact 944 . . . 6633 . . .'

After reading, she said, 'Thanks, aunty,' she said with a confused look and went dreamily thinking of it. 'Oh, right, maybe Prashanth wants to participate and take her or wants to . . .' Anu continued to think. 'Oh, got it, I forgot, wow.' Her mind flashed an idea, and she decided to inform Arun the next day.

Next day in the Presidency College, when Anu and her friends had gathered, she put forth her idea about persuading Vishaal to participate in the Valentine's Day singing competition. 'Yeah, your idea is good but . . . does he have the talent to sing nicely?' Madan asked.

'I know he's a good singer and has won in many singing competitions in his schooldays,' Anu said.

'But, but what . . .' Arun stammered.

'Yeah, I know what your doubt is. It is about Deepthi, right? That's not a problem at all, today is the last day for submitting the names, call up this number for giving their names immediately,' Anu said and gave a piece of newspaper to Arun; instead he stared at his mobile.

'What?' Anu asked.

'But it's better having a word with Vishaal before,' Arun said.

'Yeah, but it will be too late, let's give their names first,' Anu said in a hurried voice.

'OK . . .' he said and called up that number.

'Hello, sir, we wish to participate in the Valentine's Day competition,' Arun said.

'Yeah, may I know the couple's names?' the organizer of the programme asked.

Lifting his eyebrows, he gave a sharp look at Anu and she closed her eyes with a nod. 'It's Vishaal and . . .' Arun stammered as he didn't mention Deepthi's name and gave a pause.

'No issue, since only males are participating, but if they are selected, we need the couple's signature as a proof,' the organizer said.

'OK, sir,' Arun replied.

'Your identity number will be VC- 460, please come on the 5th of February for filling the form and the participation fee will be 500 rupees,' the organizer informed him.

After the classes were over, Arun reached home tiredly. Initially he was tired of Anu's interest and concern on Vishaal. He saw a model of a building. Opening his eyes wider, he said, 'Wow, stupendous, gigantic,' and Nirmala explained to him about the hospital construction.

A little later, pulling his hands, Nirmala said, 'You're coming with me right now.'

'Where do we go?' Arun asked but she didn't respond. He started his bike, she sat behind him, and she told him to go near the BDA complex road. Arun stopped the bike as she told him to stop near a gate; Arun saw a board with 'under construction' written on it.

'Wow,' Arun said, looking at the twin gigantic blocks with two ramps adjoining those blocks in semicircular shape. Arun, without saying anything, ran upstairs until the last floor.

Nirmala called him but he did not respond. He climbed up to the terrace top floor, and becoming thrilled, he screamed loudly. Seeing him sitting on the edge of the top floor with legs hanging in air, Nirmala waved at him tensely to go back.

'Hey, you, have you gone mad? Why have you come up here? Don't you care about your life? Don't put our boss in trouble, just go,' the workers warned.

'Sorry,' Arun said looking at the view of the whole city, which was like a miniature. Meanwhile, using the lift, Nirmala came near him tensely. Looking at Nirmala, he said, 'You know how I'm feeling like the whole world is at the tip of my toe, it looks as though I'm flying in a magical chariot,' and was mesmerized. Nirmala hit him on his head and pulled him back. A little later, they left the place. Arun could not come out from that feeling and was riding his bike in a slow zigzag motion.

'Come on, you'll come across many in your life that will make you feel more thrilled,' Nirmala said, rubbing on his head.

Next morning, as Arun got a voicemail from Vishaal, he reached the college early. Dressed up in a wine-coloured dress with exclusively designed silver anklet around her heels, Anu was looking very attractive. Arun was looking at her admiringly, not noticing she was tapping her delicate feet on the ground. 'Hey,' she said in an excited voice as she looked at Arun and he jerked. As he came near her, she took the mobile from him.

'Voicemail,' he said and Anu pressed the buttons in a hurry.

'Oh, my friend, I missed you all these days. Can I call you?' As Anu heard Vishaal's voice, she immediately gave him a missed call. Soon she received a call from Vishaal.

'Hi, Anushika, I missed you a lot, so how is your preparation for the exam going on?' Vishaal asked.

'Yeah, that's going on, forget mine, are you ready to prepare for a special exam?' she said in a bubbly voice.

'Special?' Vishaal was puzzled.

'Yeah, special, I have given your name for the Valentine's Day singing competition since Prashanth had told me once that you're a good singer. Firstly you must try to be selected and you shall persuade her to come along if you are selected,' Anu sounded very energetic and there was a pause. He was surprised and could not say anything but he was not very cheerful about her idea.

'Anushika, do you think this will change her?' he asked in a doubtful voice.

'Yeah, this will work, trust me . . .' Anu gave him details about the event and ended the call.

'Exam,' Vishaal asked to himself with a smile, and as a ball came rolling near him, he kicked it across the field.

Meantime, in the college, Deepthi was with her friends. 'Next week is Valentine's Day,' Chandana said.

'So what?' Deepthi asked. Subbu, looking at her, said, 'At the palace grounds, there is some programme. My brother is going with his girlfriend,' and he took a bite of a burger.

'Oh, then who else can he go with? Aha, can he with a boyfriend?' Deepthi said, combining her laugh with frustration.

A little later, as they were discussing, Chandana said, 'Hey, Deepthi, see, he's our college captain,' and showed her a tall handsome guy who was wearing spectacles and was looking innocent. Deepthi looked once and ignored him. She took out a practical record to write but Chandana was tapping her back.

'His name is Sandesh,' she said.

'So why are you telling me all this?' Deepthi asked, and after writing some notes, she left the place.

Next day, Vishaal went to the organizer's office to pay the participation fees and enrolled his name for the selection. He got tense, as he saw nearly 200 participants were there for selection. Only 15 participants for the final event were to be selected, and almost all the participants had given the famous songs for singing. Vishaal straightaway went near the music band and gave his own lyrics to the music tune setter.

'Sir, please set the music for this song,' he pleaded, and one of the musicians, after reading the song, asked, 'Who's the great lyricist?' and laughed teasingly.

'I've written it, your encouragement will bring my love back, I'll definitely be able to win her love if I get selected. Please don't disappoint me, sir,' Vishaal replied with a heavy feeling.

One of the senior musicians tapped him and said, 'For true love, we are always ready to help. Don't worry, we will set the music for this song. OK, fine, we want to hear the song first.'

Vishaal sang emotionally and the whole music band clapped after hearing the song.

Showing thumbs up, the senior musician said, 'Fine, your work is done,' and Vishaal's name was put as the last for singing since the musicians had to set the music for his song.

The selectors had started hearing the songs to select the finalists. The time was around 11.30 p.m. when Vishaal's name was announced and one of the selectors, yawning, asked sleepily, 'How many more left?'

'He's the last participant, sir,' one of the organizers replied.

'OK start,' another selector said yawningly.

Holding the mike, Vishaal said, 'Thank you.' Many participants who were about to leave the place turned to the stage and stood silent as he started singing. The whole atmosphere had turned into a silent zone except for his song, and the music band also gave astounding music for his song. One of the selectors stood up slowly and clapped his hands.

Later, the organizers contacted Vishaal through the phone to inform that he had been selected for the final event. As soon as he learnt that he was selected, he sent a message to Anu.

Next day, Vishaal called up Anu and she congratulated him for being selected. 'Do you think she will come?' he asked her doubtfully.

'I think you can ask her,' Anu said in a casual way.

'What? Oh my God, no way,' he replied in a firm voice.

'The time has come for you to reveal your feelings, invite her to come along, let's see how she responds. If she won't, then keep asking her again and again until she's fed up and warn her not to go with somebody else, all the best, bye,' Anu said and gave back the mobile to Arun.

Hearing that, Arun asked, 'What are you saying?' and was confused with her intentions but she smiled.

Later, Vishaal saw Deepthi was walking in the field alone.

Bracing himself, Vishaal called her in a low tone, 'Deepthi. . . Deepthi . . .' but she walked a few yards. He made himself strong again and called her loudly. She stopped but didn't turn back.

'Deepthi, I'm selected for the Valentine's Day singing competition, please come with me, please . . .' he said in true-hearted persuasion, but she walked some distance away. Following her from behind, he said, 'Deepthi, wait,' and she didn't wait.

'OK, fine, but I can't bear you going with others,' he said loudly in a warning tone but she didn't react and walked quickly. He screamed, 'All right . . .'

'Still he hasn't changed his mentality,' Deepthi thought with frustration.

'Oh, Anushika, what is running in your mind? It is so unpredictable,' Vishaal thought and left the college.

Next day, Deepthi reached the college to attend special classes but the classroom was empty and she could not find any of her friends. Wondering, she went down the stairs and enquired of her classmate on the college field about the chemistry class.

'Maybe he's busy with his household chemistry,' he replied and went to play football. Giggling, she sat on the college grounds' steps. As she took her mobile to hear the FM radio, a tall and handsome guy came near her.

'Excuse me, I'm Sandesh, studying in BSc second year, nice to meet you,' he introduced himself, and Deepthi just smiled at him. After a pause, Sandesh asked with a short smile, 'If you don't mind, can you come along with me for an outing on Valentine's

Day? Chandana had agreed to come along with me but she couldn't as she has to attend some function.'

'Sorry, I am not interested,' she replied, giving a short smile, and there was a pause. He made his spectacles proper and sat a little far away from her.

'I'm not even interested in all this stuff, you can ask Chandana about me and she only suggested to me to ask you. All my friends are making fun of me being gentle. Many have proposed me with evil minds. I won't care about them, but these days they all are teasing me so much that I can shut their mouths if you come with me. I'm alien to these love matters. It will be a great help for me,' Sandesh said in a gentle way.

Deepthi thought deeply without giving a reply; she walked into the classroom and couldn't concentrate. 'OK, fine, Vishaal, I'll teach you a lesson and also it helps Sandesh,' Deepthi thought and met him after her classes were over.

'Excuse me, Sandesh, I'm coming,' she said as he was with his classmates.

'Thanks a lot,' Sandesh replied and she went to her home later.

Next day, in the college, Vishaal's friend Disha came hurriedly.

'Vishaal, you know Deepthi is going to the Valentine's programme with Sandesh, BSc student. I came to know from Chandana,' she said, breathing hard. Vishaal, thinking deeply, asked her doubtfully, 'Disha, can you please come with me on that day?' but she nodded with a supportive smile.

'Thanks, your name on that day . . .' Vishaal hesitated.

'My name will be Deepthi, only for that day, all right?' Disha said, and after wishing him goodbye, she went away hurriedly.

A day before Valentine's Day, Vishaal was completely depressed. Knocking on the partly opened door, Kirthi entered Vishaal's room.

'Hey, what made you come inside without having your dinner? And you didn't remove your shoes also,' she said and came near him with some snacks and curry rice.

'No, Bhabi, I'm not feeling hungry,' he said and later fell asleep.

On Valentine's Day, Vishaal got ready with a dull expression, and feeling the same, Deepthi also got ready. Staring at her birthday dress, she wore a simple dress. Disha also got ready. Vishaal started his bike to go and reached the palace grounds. He stood outside waiting for Disha. Deepthi got a call from Chandana after she reached the palace grounds.

'Hello, Deepthi, are you at the venue? I'm happy that you agreed for accompanying Sandesh to see the Valentine's programme, it'll do him really good. You know Vishaal is going with Disha bearing your name,' Chandana said at a stretch.

'I just reached the venue, OK? Enough of your information . . .' Deepthi ended the call calmly. She turned back and saw Vishaal was standing. Even he saw her and she turned towards the other side.

A little later, Sandesh saw Deepthi. 'Hi, friend, oh, I forgot your name,' he said as he came near her.

'Deepthi,' she said dully.

Disha came hurriedly.   'Hi, Vishaal,' she greeted him.

'Hi,' he replied with not much energy. They all entered inside later.

The whole palace grounds looked like a carnival, and many couples were roaming around cheering their friends; some were hugging and some others were waving their hands. Most of them dressed in their best attire with beautiful hairstyles for the Valentine's Day occasion. A huge open stage was erected. The organizers had marked a big heart shape measuring about ten feet in the centre of the stage, for placing firewood on the marked line. They had put up a huge tent covered with beautiful cloth and illuminated the stage using red lights in the front and the side portions of the stage. The palace ground was looking very exotic with attractive varieties of roses and hanging frames along with love thoughts.

Deepthi and Sandesh sat on the chairs as the competition was about to begin. Sandesh, looking at Deepthi, said, 'You should have seen those girls, they looked as though they were fuming at you,' and he giggled. Deepthi didn't take his words seriously and thought about Vishaal; her eyes were fixed on the stage. All stood up as the finalists entered the stage and they received a huge ovation. They all bowed towards the audience and took their seats meant for the participants. The participants wore glittering dress with a heart design and they looked very enthusiastic except Vishaal.

The organizers had placed firewood according to the heart-shaped markings and they had left some vacant space for the participants to enter into the heart shape. They poured kerosene oil on the wood, lit it, and it started burning. The flames raised two to three feet, and it was forming into heart-shaped burning flames. Everyone whistled and some were shouting. The organizers had arranged doctors, ambulance, and firefighters as safety measures in case of an emergency.

Holding a mike, the programme anchor stepped onto the stage, and the whole audience cheered as he walked on the stage.

Looking at the audience, he said, 'A hearty welcome to all the lovebirds present here.' Cheers arose from the audience and he continued, 'The competition will begin very soon. I welcome Ms Lily, the managing director of Dove solutions. Mr Kishore, a great choreographer. Mr Charles, a famous playback singer, and Mr Dev, chairman of PepupCo. All you loving hearts, please give them a big round of applause.' And as the clapping receded, he continued, 'They have agreed to be the judges to decide the winner of this Valentine Day's competition, and it has been a great privilege and honour for all of us. I request them to take their seats,' the anchor said. Waving at the audience with broad smiles, they took their seats. After that, looking at the audience, the anchor said, 'Dear loving birds, love is all about pain and tolerance. A true love doesn't care about anything. The competition will begin to find the true lover. Give a big round of applause to fifteen finalists, they are . . .' The anchor announced the names of the finalists. He then continued, 'Each participant has to stand in the middle of the heart-shaped flames to sing and tolerate the heat. Whoever among the finalists complete the song, those will be eligible for selection as true lover of the year. The award will be announced in accordance with the judges' view, enjoy the most memorable evening, thank you, one and all.'

'The first participant is . . .' The anchor called the first participant's name. He entered inside the heart-shaped burning flames and sang very beautifully. As he completed the song, his face turned red with sweat pouring all over his face due to high temperature. The organizer immediately took him for first aid and they poured cold water on him.

After testing his pulse rate, the doctor said, 'He's OK. Give him some cold juice.'

The anchor called out the next participant and he could not complete the song. He ran out of the stage and all of them burst out laughing.

A couple of hours later, Sandesh said to Deepthi, 'OK, let's go to eat something,' and they both left the place to eat something hot as it was very cold.

A little later, Deepthi said, 'OK then, I'll go, it will be late.'

'OK, bye, thanks a lot, Deepthi,' Sandesh replied.

'It's all right . . .' she said with a smile and walked a few yards.

'Wait, I'll leave you near the gate,' Sandesh said and went with her up to the gate. He turned to go back into the audience gallery.

'The last participant is Vishaal . . .' He walked onto the stage and looked around at the audience. There was a pause.

'To whom are you going to dedicate this?' The anchor broke the silence.

'To my loved one Deepthi.' As Deepthi heard this, she stopped walking. Disha stood up and waved her hands at Vishaal. He entered inside the heart-shaped burning flames. All his thoughts had begun to rush into his mind as he closed his eyes, and when he started singing, Deepthi ran inside the gallery, with teardrops falling from her eyes.

Oh, love . . . just reach my love . . .
Shine in my gloomy life, oh my love . . .
Ohooho, love, just love me forever

Least I wanna be is a bird in your cage
May I feel your breath near . . .
Splash your tears, oh babe . . .
Heart's burning . . .

Least you can show is some feeling on my love
Ohooho, feel at least on my heart's ash . . .
My love Ohooho my love . . . oh my love . . .

The grounds had become wholly silent as he began singing, and the background music also gave an excellent temper for his song. Emotions ran high in the hearts of everyone who listened. Nearly ten minutes had passed, and kneeling down, he sang completely but nobody knew that he had fallen unconscious on the ground, until later. As they realized that he was unconscious, one of the organizers and two other persons lifted him from the heart-shaped burning flames and took him out.

'He's amazing, whoever his girl is, she's damn lucky,' Sandesh said and turned towards Deepthi. Teardrops falling from her eyes, she ran towards Vishaal. She opened a water bottle's lid quickly and made him drink. As he felt her touch, he opened his eyes and smiled at her. Deepthi pretended to act normal and left the place immediately without any expression.

Only six participants were able to complete the song, including Vishaal. The judges were busy in calculating the points, and one of the judges pointed out some mistakes in Vishaal's singing but the other judge argued in favour of him. Finally, all the three judges left it to the senior judge, Mr Charles, to decide who the winner was going to be. The senior judge stood on the stage, and holding a mike, he started speaking.

'Hello, everyone, happy Valentine's Day to you all, I am thankful to the organizers for inviting me as a judge for this extravagant Valentine's Day competition. All the participants tried their best; we have finally selected Manish and Vishaal.'

Excitedly clapping their hands, the whole audience cheered after hearing the names. After the cheering settled, he continued, 'Both have spent almost the same time in the circle and they have completed the song. Manish sang well without any technical mistakes and secured high points.' The judge's view wrapped the audience with silence and very few cheered with tension. 'But Manish has sung a famous movie song, whereas Vishaal, in such a short period, having a true feeling in his heart, sang a song of his own lyrics. He also has sung it beautifully with some pardonable mistakes, now I'll announce that the runner-up is Manish.' And hearing this, standing up, the whole audience cheered. Heart-shaped shiny paper pieces fell on Vishaal. The sponsors presented the prize money and a bouquet to Vishaal. Offering a handshake,

Manish hugged Vishaal later. A little later, after hugging his college friends, Vishaal looked around to see Deepthi but she had already left the place.

Deepthi, reaching home, blindly fell on the bed, and tears were rolling down her face. Pressing her face on a pillow, she thought, 'Oh, it's an unbelievable change in your behaviour and you're bearing the pain for my sake. You made me understand what true love is and showed the world as well. Oh, now I understood why you warned me not to come with another guy, purposely drove me to come with another guy so that I can watch you sing,' and she wept until late night.

The doctor had advised Vishaal to take three days' rest, and his face had blisters due to high temperature. His parents came to know about his participation in the Valentine's Day competition and warned him not to get into all such risky activities. Vishaal innocently nodded his head. As his father left the room, his grandpa entered.

'Grandpa, I did it.' He sounded very energetic.

Winking his eyes, his grandpa said, 'You are born to win.'

Next day in the college, as soon as Arun came near Anu, he got a call from Prashanth, who informed Arun about Vishaal's condition. Hearing this, she took Arun's mobile and called up Vishaal tensely. 'Yes, Anushika, it's surprising that for the first time without waiting, you called me up by yourself.' He sounded excited.

'Yeah, tell me, how are you?' Anu sounded worried.

'Yeah, nothing serious, just slight rashes, I'm fine. No words to praise you, Anushika, your guidance has enabled me to build my character, and you know, Deepthi looked very worried and made me drink water but she went away by the time I could speak to her.' And he told her what happened at the programme in detail.

'Don't worry, she will definitely come back to you, take care,' Anu said confidently.

'Hope so, OK, bye. Oh, I forgot that I'm sending her photo snaps through Prashanth,' he said and ended the call.

Turning towards Arun, Anu said to him, 'Oh, Arun, the pains that caused wounds in her heart by Vishaal in the past are almost healed, she's beginning to feel good about him now.' Imagining Vishaal and Deepthi together, she left the place with rich hopes.

Seeing her going, Arun murmured to himself, 'You're striving so hard for your loved one to be happy by sacrificing your own love, for another girl. Is this what is meant by real love? I am so unlucky that I'm not able to find a place in your heart as your partner,' and feeling heavy in his heart, he hit the ground.

That day in Stephen's College, Chandana said, 'Hi, Deepthi,' and Deepthi, without replying, walked away. Her eyes moved around where Vishaal used to sit; since he wasn't there, she disappointedly climbed up the stairs. She kept her bag in the classroom and came back near the corridor to have another look towards the college grounds' steps. Later, she entered the library room.

'See, Vishaal has donated the complete prize money to Ramanashree blind school, I saw his photo in the newspaper.' Deepthi was shocked as she heard and immediately took the newspaper to see his photo. After looking at it, she said, hugging the paper, 'Oh, Vishaal, your presence earlier troubled me, but your absence is hurting me now.' Deepthi sounded very pained; she recalled each and every word of Vishaal and the pleasant days she had spent with him.

Vishaal's newspaper photo clipping was displayed on the college bulletin board. Including the principal, everyone felt very proud of him. Prashanth couldn't believe his eyes, seeing Vishaal's transformation in his attitude; he thought dreamily, looking at the bulletin board, 'No, it's not you, Anu shaped our character in the right way, we both owe her a lot, I know very well that we can't repay.'

Next day, Prashanth drove his bike straightaway towards Presidency College; he came near Arun, giving him the cover. 'Hi, Arun, Vishaal has given Deepthi's snaps, I think he will attend his classes today, it's already late, OK, bye,' Prashanth said and hurried to start his bike. Arun sat on the playground steps and fell into thoughts, holding Deepthi's photo cover. From Arun's hand, the photo cover came sliding down; some photos fell on the ground. He picked up the photos and looked at them. 'Oh my goodness, my guess was right, now let her find the true love in Vishaal,' Arun said to himself and saw Anu coming at him hurriedly, and Anu was looking at Deepthi's snaps.

'Oh, I want to see them both together. OK, let's get Prashanth's help to see them, unnoticed. Please call him,' Anu pleaded with him.

Arun was thinking, 'Ha, she's very much excited about Vishaal and Deepthi now, after seeing them. Once and for all, she loses interest in him definitely, instead keeping her anxious throughout, let's do some plan today itself for showing them to Anu.' And she restlessly looked at Arun as he was thinking deeply. 'OK, let's both go and see them. I'll call Prashanth to ask about where we could see them both,' he said and called Prashanth immediately.

'Yeah, tell me Arun,' Prashanth asked.

'Anu wants to see Vishaal and Deepthi, unnoticed. Have they come to college today?' Arun asked.

'Dude, only Deepthi came but he rang me and asked to arrange a meeting with Deepthi. Probably even she's desperate to meet him since she asked me yesterday about his health. I'll try to convince her. The classes will end at 4 p.m. and both of you come near our college around 4 p.m., then I'll call you for any matter, OK, bye.' Prashanth ended the call.

Anu, hearing that, sounded very bubbly: 'Oh, I immediately want to wish Vishaal well and send him a flower bouquet.' She asked Arun to call Prashanth and take note of Vishaal's address and as he took note, Anu took Arun to the nearby florist shop. She selected a violet-and-white combination bouquet and wrote on a small greeting card, 'My best wishes to your love, may it succeed and reach its peak, from Anushika with love.' Arun's face fell as he saw the wording.

Giving Vishaal's address to the florist, Anu said to the owner, 'Please deliver it to this address,' and paid the amount.

An hour later, Vishaal received the flower bouquet and read the message written on the greeting card.

'Oh, Anushika, thanks for your wishes,' he said and rested the flower bouquet closer to his chest.

That day, Deepthi, with a dull look, entered the college gate, hoping that he would turn up today at least. After she came to know that he didn't come, she was dragging her legs and restlessly entered the classroom. The clock struck 4 p.m. and the classes came to an end for the day. Meanwhile, Vishaal was standing on the flyover, which was in the final phase of construction.

A little later, seeing her alone in the classroom, one of the peons reminded her, 'Hello, the classes are over. What are you waiting for?' and she stood up to leave the classroom. With tears in her eyes, she went to the college field and, kneeling, rested her head on a bench. As she saw someone's feet near her, she ignored them.

Tapping her back, Prashanth asked, 'Why are you crying?'

Sobbing, she looked at Prashanth, 'You know that the love now he's showing to me, I'm not able to take it, and I feel like killing myself. I need strength to carry on his love, my heart wants him but I'm not able to . . .'

On a flyover which was under construction, with tears rippling in his eyes, resting the flower bouquet close to his chest, Vishaal kneeled, as he could hear Deepthi speaking to Prashanth, since Prashanth had called Vishaal unnoticed and Vishaal was listening to their conversation.

'All these will get solved within no time if you come along with me,' Prashanth said, consoling her. In the meantime, Vishaal became alert to hear her reply. Deepthi slowly lifted her head and Prashanth offered his hand to help her get up but Deepthi stood up with a bench's support. 'Yes, I'll come' she said and went near the stand for taking her Scooty. Meanwhile, Prashanth immediately called Arun to inform him of the spot where Deepthi and Vishaal would meet.

A little later, as she came near him on her Scooty, 'Follow me,' Prashanth said and started his bike.

Meanwhile, Vishaal jumped with joy as he heard her voice that she was coming. Later, Prashanth, riding his bike, looked behind to see Deepthi, who was riding her Scooty and then, pointing her towards the flyover, he said, 'You will find your love there,' and went. Deepthi rode near the flyover and parked it. She went running, and all the construction workers curiously looked at her. Vishaal completely leaned on the grille and his thirst for love was becoming more. Deepthi's eyes in tears made her see him blurry. As she approached very close, he smiled and gave her the flower bouquet which was given by Anu. Deepthi opened her mouth to say something but he kept his finger on her lips, and looking up at the sky, he hugged her tightly. Deepthi couldn't control the emotions that were flooding in her heart and she hugged him tightly.

'Wow, never in my life have I seen this kind of a . . .' a female voice emerged.

'Great, you made it possible,' a male voice replied. They both were none other than Arun and Anu, who were peeping at them behind a huge machine. Vishaal and Deepthi were slowly walking and had completely immersed their hearts in their own world.

On the flyover, looking at those lovebirds walking, Arun said in a loud voice, 'Anu, they're gone.'

'No, I can still see them,' Anu said dreamily. Becoming jovial, throwing her dupatta up, she shouted, 'Bye . . . bye, both of you, I'm so happy. Woohoo!' Offering a handshake, she said, 'Arun, thanks a lot,' and took his wrist closer to her face. Arun was almost paralyzed, as she had never been so close. 'OK, bye, Arun,' she said later and left the place with lightened heart.

Later, Anu reached home. Anu's mother opened the door. With a happy face, she went inside her room, and her mother followed her, posing her questions. 'Mom, I'm happy because all my doubts got cleared, no confusion forever, especially practicals. That's why I was late,' Anu lied. After reading some notes, she went to the terrace and kneeled down facing the sky.

'Oh moon, they have finally won and will float in the ocean called love. Though I could not get my Vishaal, at least you shall remain as my friend until my last breath. I'm feeling like hugging you but . . .' Anu hugged the moon in her imagination and blew on her palm pointing towards the moon.

Next day, Vishaal and Deepthi entered the college together. All of them shouted and clapped their hands. Everyone shouted as all his friends lifted him, threw him up high above, and caught him. Sandesh, the college captain, wished congrats to Deepthi and offered a handshake to Vishaal.

ANU AND ARUN

*A*run gave a small treat in the college canteen to his friends and they were enjoying it.

Sandhya, chewing a burger like a cow, pointing at Anu, said, 'Tomorrow another treat . . .'

'It's her birthday, right?' Madan said.

'Whose birthday?' Arun asked in a breathy voice, and Anu smiled at them.

'Tomorrow is your victory day,' Madan murmured into Arun's ear. Anu went to the staffroom, for submitting her practical record book. Meanwhile, they all discussed about celebrating Anu's birthday. A little later, Anu came near them, and Sandhya, looking at her, said in a sharp voice, 'Anu, all three of us are going to give you a great surprise and you need to come at seven sharp.'

'At 7 a.m., right? No problem,' Anu replied.

'No, 7 p.m.,' Madan said.

Anu opened her mouth wide. 'Why can't we celebrate here,' she said in a tired voice.

All of them nodded their heads and said 'No' in chorus.

'OK, tell me where to come,' she asked in a grudging voice.

'You know Sri Ganesha temple near BDA complex?' Madan asked.

'OK, my celebration is in the temple?' Anu asked in surprise.

'No, nearby there's an under-construction skyscraper,' Madan replied.

'Shall I tell my parents about this?' Anu asked a bit nervously.

'That's your headache,' Sandhya replied with frustration.

A little later, 'OK, fine, bye,' Anu said dully.

As soon as Anu turned to go, 'Yesss,' Arun jumped high with happiness and he pretended to be normal as Anu turned back.

On the way back home, Anu was planning how to convince her mother and passed her house gate, as she didn't realize. 'Oops,' she was exclaiming and tapped her head as her sister called her, and she came back towards the gate. As the day passed, all went to sleep.

'I hope he shall be happy forever,' Anu whispered to herself as Shwetha was sleeping next to her. Anu gradually fell asleep.

Arun was waiting impatiently and felt happy as he saw Anu dressed in white, as it was his favourite colour. She looked very gorgeous and he greeted her. 'You're looking very beautiful,' he said and she smiled.

'Oh, OK, where are the others?' Anu asked and she started counting the floors. 'Oh my God! Twenty-two floors!' she said in a breathy voice.

'Anu, once you told me that you wanted to yell out standing on top of a mountain and I think you can get that kind of feeling today, come on,' Arun said.

Holding his hand, Anu said, 'Yeah take me,' and he took her onto the terrace of the building. Arun was holding her hand. 'OK, ready, one, two, three, start . . .' and she ran up to the edge and shouted 'Woohoo!' Anu was thrilled, and looking at Arun, she said, 'I'll do it myself alone,' and as she ran up to the edge, her long dress caught her feet and she slipped. Arun ran near the edge. 'Anuuu!' He screamed and saw her falling down.

Arun suddenly got up from his sleep, sweat was running all over his face. Hearing him scream, Nirmala came rushing into his room. Breathing hard, he murmured, 'Oh! It shouldn't happen to Anu.' When Nirmala asked why he screamed, he replied that he had a bad dream in which his friend met with an accident.

'Nowadays your thoughts are going deep about your friends. Better stop it, or else every day you will experience regular nightmares like this,' Nirmala said impatiently and left.

Next day, Anu's parents and Shwetha wished Anu a happy birthday and they hugged her. She got a call from Sandhya.

'Happy birthday, keep smiling every minute of your life and give me a chance to celebrate every hour with you,' Sandhya read out Arun's message.

'Thank you but this is sounding a bit romantic, it must sound friendly. If Prashanth comes to know, he will kill me.' Anu sounded happy. 'OK, bye, my mom is calling me,' Anu was about to end the call.

'No, wait, it's Arun's message—' Before Sandhya could complete these sentence, Anu had disconnected the call.

'She always keeps running even I didn't wish,' Sandhya said and gave a frustrated look towards the receiver.

Anu got ready in a very simple way and her father presented her with a new dress. 'Thanks, Pa,' she said.

'Wear it, we all shall go to temple,' her mother said. Anu wore the cloudy-blue dress which her father gifted for her birthday and was looking like a doll. All of them went to a nearby temple later. As it was a government holiday, there was no college. After having lunch, she slept, along with her mother.

After a couple of hours, getting up 'Maa, please, can I go to double road?' Anu requested of her mother.

'Why?' Shwetha, who was lying next to her mother, enquired.

'I didn't ask you, shut up. Maa, please, can I go?' Anu asked and stared at Shwetha.

'Maa, please say something.'

'Why?' Shwetha questioned again.

'Oh God, you both, stop arguing. You are not letting me speak. Fine, why do you want to go to double road?'

'There is a temple and a famous restaurant. After visiting the temple, we will eat something and come back soon.'

Giving a keen look at Anu, Shwetha asked, '*You* means?'

'Of course you and me,' Anu replied.

'Wow! Maa, please.' This time Shwetha jumped on Anu's track and both of them pleaded.

Looking at her husband, she said, 'They want to go for an outing, take them.'

Their father made up his mind. 'Fine, get ready,' he said to them and continued to have a conversation on the phone.

Anu thought, 'My God, what is this?' and became tense but Shwetha was very cheerful. 'God, God help me . . .' Anu was whispering.

Her father got a call when they were about to leave. 'Sorry, girls, I can't, I have to go somewhere else,' her father said after receiving the call and changed his decision. Anu sat on the steps anxiously and Shwetha was looking at the mother.

'You simply disappointed us, at least you can take us,' Shwetha asked in a crying tone.

'No, I have lots of work to do,' her mother came out with a routine answer and saw Anu's dull face.

'OK, fine, you both go,' her mother said and Anu slowly lifted her head.

'Yes,' Shwetha said as Anu stood up to go.

'OK, now it's five thirty, before seven you must be back here.' Her mother threw a condition on them, but Anu was thinking whether she could hold her mother's condition. They both left and later boarded the bus.

Anu and Shwetha reached the temple. After entering, Anu murmured to herself, 'Oh God, somehow Mom was convinced, now I have to convince this devil,' and looked at Shwetha. She was already standing in the line to receive prasadam (sweets given to devotees after worship).

Looking at the temple's clock, Anu thought about how to leave. 'Oh my goodness, it's getting late, I've . . .'

After weaving a lie, Anu pleaded, 'Shwetha, please can I go to my friend's house to see her? She's not well and I will be back in an hour.'

'No, you can't, and if you go, I will complain to Mom,' she said, giving a suspicious look towards her.

Anu, becoming tense, said in a keen voice, 'That's your job, right? You don't have any better work other than complaining about me. I haven't met with her since three weeks ago. If you really understand friendship, let me go,' but Shwetha was throwing another suspicious look.

'Fine, even I will come along with you, let's go,' she replied.

'How can I make you understand, if she has to share something personal, do you think she will share it in front of you?' Anu said seriously and continued, 'See they all are decorating the idol with flowers, you can help them until then. I'll come back within an hour, trust me.' Anu walked a few yards without waiting for her reply as she had to keep her mother's condition and she had to fulfil her friends' wish at the same time.

'Fine, come back soon, only forty minutes, not more than that,' Shwetha said grudgingly.

'Fine, fine, OK, bye,' Anu said in a hurried voice.

'If you come one minute late, I'll tell Mom,' Shwetha again warned Anu but she had already gone and crossed the main road.

Anu was breathing hard as she walked fast and had to cross another main road. She was not able to cross, as the vehicles were zooming like rockets, and she managed to cross the road finally. She saw a skyscraper which was under construction. As she came near the gate, it was completely dark inside. She was a bit scared to enter the new strange place and gathered courage in herself to enter. As she entered, she heard a huge blow of a whistle. She opened her mouth wide, her eyes brightly opened as decorated lights began to illuminate around two giant cranes. Lifting her long dress and heels a little above the ground, she started biting her nails. Her deer-like eyes were moving here and there.

Arun, watching her movement, thought, 'I wish that you have to call my name,' and coming from behind, covered her eyes.

'Ouch,' Anu said and continued in a hurried voice, 'Please, Sandhya, don't waste your time,' and he removed his hands from her eyes.

'Oh shit, can't you sense the difference between the feel of a female's hand versus a male's?' Arun murmured with disappointment.

Turning towards him, she asked, 'OK, where are the others?' and was looking around. Using her pointed finger, Anu started counting the floors.

Seeing that, Arun thought, 'Oh God, she is exactly doing what I saw in that dreadful dream. I shall not take her to the top floor as planned before,' and become very worried. Holding her hand, Arun said, 'Come on, I'll show you the building,' and both climbed up to the third floor.

Looking around, Anu asked, 'By the way, where are these specimens?'

'I think they are roaming around,' Arun replied.

'I can't stay here for more than twenty minutes, I'm very happy, now that Vishaal's matter is solved,' Anu said in a relaxed way.

'God only knows when mine's getting solved,' Arun said in a disappointed mood.

'What do you mean?' she asked and before she could speak further, he asked firmly, 'Do you trust in love?' There was a pause and he continued, 'OK, tell me, does a true love succeed?'

'Yes of course,' Anu replied casually.

'No, I won't believe and then you should have been in Deepthi's place,' Arun directed his deep intention from his heart.

Anu became serious. 'If I was in her place or not, I was happy or not, helping in love matters especially helping the loved one is more than a happiness. I'm feeling that I have achieved something.' Anu finally brought out her view, and he didn't speak a word. There was a pause as both were thinking.

Becoming angry, he asked, 'Then help me with being happy, will you?' She looked at him in shock and he continued. 'You can turn my love into success, it's in your hands,' Arun said very emotionally.

'What are you saying?' Anu said, ignoring it.

'I love you,' he shouted. Tears rippled in her eyes but a soft smile emanated on her lips suddenly. He then continued, 'OK, let us go according to your intention, helping a loved one is something very thrilling but you sacrificed your love. Looking at your thinking, your attitude, your mentality, and everything that you do is actually increasing my love for you day by day.' Arun was trying to make her understand but she couldn't stop crying as she understood the pain he was going through but she could not help him either, as she had already given her heart to Vishaal.

Finally, he said, 'I have been pretending to act like a friend but I can't pretend to be like this anymore. I'm not able to concentrate on anything. It would be better to end my life rather than live like this.' Arun spoke very angrily with tears flowing from his eyes since he vented out all the suppressed feelings that he had been hiding all these days. With a helpless look and tears filling her eyes, Anu walked backwards.

'Sor—' Anu's voice was cut off. Arun turned back suddenly but she was not there.

'Anuuu!' Arun ran quickly towards the edge of the floor, saw her falling.

'My last wish will be the same as my first wish, I must always be with Vishaal and keep in touch with him, my cool friend,' she thought and had a contented look towards the full moon. Arun stretched his hands towards her. All images disappeared as she closed her eyes tight. Arun hit his wrist against a rod and screaming he quickly ran towards the stairs. Anu didn't feel any pain and slowly opened her eyes.

Meanwhile, Madan saw Anu falling; without any tension, he came near her. 'I think your watch has entered a coma,' Madan said and held her wrist. Sandhya poured water into Anu's mouth and she drank it constantly, as she was shocked.

Looking at Sandhya, Madan praised himself. 'I told you right, I was sure Anu loves Arun, see, I was right, she's accepted his love and she's fallen on his heart. I mean, on this heart airbed. How's this proposing style? You know, it was my idea.' Madan again pointed towards the huge airbed, which was in a heart shape, where Anu landed up after falling.

'Arun . . . Arun!' Madan called, looking up.

Anu slowly opened her eyes and saw Arun running towards her. With sweat running down his face, Arun flung his arms around Anu and said, 'You almost killed me, stupid!'

Hiding her feelings, she got up. 'I'm fine, I have to go, bye, everyone,' Anu said and turned back to leave. She saw many poor children there feasting as Arun had made arrangements for catering food. Anu kissed one of the small girls. To stop her from going, Arun came near her but she held his collar and pushed him back forcibly. Looking at her temper, Madan, who had been feeling very proud, was taken aback, and weeping, she left the place.

Anu quickly reached the temple and looked around for Shwetha but she was not in the temple. Anu frantically searched for her, 'Today is not my eighteenth birthday, it's my first day in hell,' she murmured to herself. Finally, she found Shwetha, as she saw her eating ice cream in the nearby restaurant.

Looking at her watch, Shwetha said, 'Twenty minutes late, that's almost half an hour,' and licked the ice cream. With teardrops falling down, Anu slapped Shwetha.

Becoming silent, both turned their faces in opposite directions. Anu and Shwetha reached home later. Shwetha went angrily and closed the door with a bang.

Seeing that from the kitchen, their mother, who was cutting some green leaves and onion, said, 'What's wrong with you both? Always fighting has become your routine job. Whatever, thank God both reached home before their dad could—that's enough.' Recalling the incident, Anu started sweating and splashed some cold water.

Meantime, looking at Arun's bleeding wrist, Sandhya said, 'What is this? My goodness,' and removed a handkerchief.

Seeing Sandhya tying the handkerchief, Madan said, 'Oh, this is the hurt caused by the metal on which he hit his hand,' and Sandhya gave a worried look towards Arun. Sadly looking at Arun, she sounded very upset. 'What's wrong, what happened?' Without speaking, Arun went walking.

Madan tapping her shoulders, said, 'Sandhya, it's getting late, you go, I'll take him to a clinic, let's see tomorrow, bye.' Madan rode and Arun sat behind like an idol. In the clinic, Arun neither moved nor spoke and was quiet. The doctor dressed the wound and gave a tetvac injection.

Madan dropped him up to the house later and Arun got down.

'It's all right, I can manage myself to go in, please.' He sounded very tired.

'OK, fine then, take care,' Madan said, and after wishing him goodbye, he left the place. Arun could not believe that his day was so dreadful and sat near the doorstep. He didn't open the lock and leaned against a pillar. After recalling the incident that happened an hour ago, he completely lost his strength. He got a call from Nirmala, as she had gone to Jaipur.

'How was Anu's birthday celebration?' Nirmala sounded excited.

Pretending to be normal, Arun replied, 'Oh yeah, it was fine.'

'OK, Arun, sweet dreams, I'll miss you. I'll be back in a couple of days. Take care, bye,' she said and ended the call. He was breathing out with relief. 'Ouch . . .' he yelled and stretched his legs on the ground to relax and closed his eyes later.

At late night, Anu suddenly woke up from her sleep. 'Oh, sorry, Shwetha, I hit you, I'm really very sorry,' Anu murmured.

'I can understand, it's all right, arrogant sis . . .' Shwetha replied in a sleepy mood.

'Shwetha,' Anu called her in a soft voice and threw her arms around Shwetha. Both hugged each other later.

Next day, Anu dully got ready for college.

Meantime, Arun was irritated, as the sunrays were falling on his face since he slept outside unknowingly, and he blocked his eyes using his palm. Realizing what he had done, he immediately went inside and took a cold shower bath.

In the college, Madan and Sandhya while discussing, not noticing that Anu was coming near them. 'Oh, how come my plan went wrong; actually I told him to say, "I'm ending my life if you don't accept my love" and if she didn't accept, then to fall on the air bed, instead she fell on the airbed. He spoilt my plan and ruined his chance, stupid . . .' Madan blindly blabbered.

Sandhya saw Anu. 'Shut up, hold your tongue, something really might have gone wrong. Don't raise this topic, see, Anu is coming,' Sandhya said and pretended everything was fine.

Anu dully walked towards them.

'Happy birthday, Anu,' Sandhya said, hugging her, and meanwhile, Prashanth came near them and he wished Anu a happy birthday.

'Thank you . . .' she said in a very low tone.

'We prepared a study schedule for the final exam, and from tomorrow, we'll study accordingly,' Prashanth informed them.

Putting his hands in his pockets, hopping around them, Madan said, 'Yeah, we have to plan up.'

Looking at Anu, Prashanth said, 'Soon, you will have nice days, OK, bye,' and left the place after wishing them.

Anu didn't understand what he said and ignored it. She knew Arun would not come and managed only with physics. There were hardly two periods for the whole day.

Meantime, Arun reached his favourite park for studying. He climbed to the tree house; he sat on the sliding chair and started reading. After a couple of hours, he closed the book, as he could not study further. He calculated how many days were left for his exams and there were thirty-two days ahead. After writing a study schedule for the final exams, he hurriedly got down using the rope and immediately took his bike to zoom towards the college.

Holding some rolled sheets, Arun entered the college grounds and sat on the steps. While going down the stairs, Sandhya saw Arun, and without hearing Madan's call, she blindly ran towards Arun. As she came near, she asked, 'How's your wound?' and he lifted his head. She had a closer look at the wrist to check whether it was still bleeding.

'Yeah, I'm feeling better,' he said in a very soft voice.

Madan came near Arun. 'Gone crazy, you've come riding alone.' He sounded tense.

'I am fine, OK, take these,' he replied and passed the rolled sheets to them.

'One more thing, half of the class is not attending classes anymore as the exams are nearing,' Sandhya said.

Tapping on a rolled sheet, Arun said, 'Give it to Anu, tell her to study according to this,' and turned to leave the place after giving it to Sandhya.

He turned back as Sandhya caught his hands and said, 'Wait, she's coming.'

Anu, going down the stairs, came running anxiously towards them, and Arun felt some kind of pleasant feeling in his heart.

Touching the bandage, she asked, 'How are you and your hurt?'

'It's just got cured,' Arun said to himself, and looking at her, he said, 'I heard you're not coming from tomorrow, follow this timetable, all the best,' and changed the topic. He was a bit nervous and depressed while talking. Later, he left the place, and after few hours feeling a little better, Arun, closing his heart, opened his mind for studying hard.

Next day, Arun came to the college and straightaway went to the lab. To help some dull students, he explained and did some of the lab experiments. Anu was scratching her head, as she could not solve some of the mathematics problems and tried hard, piercing her mind, and finally got rid of them. She checked all the solved problems again and they were not accurate or close to the answers mentioned. She got frustrated and jumped to the other subject. She hardly studied for three hours and fell on her bed to relax.

Deepthi became a bookworm; her heart and mind was clear to understand and store the books' contents. Sandhya warned Prashanth as he would sometimes while away his time in asking the known subject, just pretending to have doubts, but he would feel relaxed after speaking with Sandhya. Sometimes, Sandhya was going to Anu's house to work out mathematics together. One day, Vishaal sent a message: 'Hi, Anushika, all the best and I won't disturb.' Almost three weeks was over. Anu finished three subjects but she was nervous and confused to some extent.

All of them packed their minds for the finals.

One day, Madan called Arun. 'How's your preparation going on?' he asked.

'Yeah, it was going on well but now it stopped,' Arun replied. 'Why?'

'Because you are speaking with me now.'

'Come on,' Madan said, giggling.

'Fine, bye, I'll see you soon,' Arun said and ended the call.

One day, Sandhya called Anu, after speaking, finally,

'Oh I forgot, what you are wearing day after tomorrow for the graduation,' Sandhya asked Anu with excitement.

'Let me see, not yet decided,' she said with not much energy.

'OK, bye.' Sandhya cut the call.

On the day of graduation in the college, boys in their suits were looking handsome, and in their saris, the girls were looking very pretty. All the students stood in a line uniformly, in a different atmosphere. Arun's eyes slowly moved towards the girls and looked for Anu but couldn't find her. Sandhya and Madan were waiting for Anu; Sandhya was looking beautiful in a blue sari. Madan was looking pale as he wore his father's upsized suit and its tie was dangling. Looking at the tie, Sandhya made it proper. 'Stop it, don't embarrass me by tying it in front of everyone, especially girls around,' Madan murmured, seeing that some girls were giggling at him.

As Anu had not turned up yet, Sandhya said, 'Come, let's go.' Madan went but Arun didn't join them. Humming a favourite tune, Arun was looking dreamily towards the gate. As someone tapped him from behind, he turned back suddenly. Anu stood right in front of him. After seeing Anu with Arun, Madan and Sandhya came near.

'Oh, Anu, you're looking gorgeous,' Madan said.

Arun felt like kissing Anu. Sandhya stood still and then kissed her cheeks. Arun blushed as he saw it.

'How come you dressed differently from others?' Sandhya asked.

'Oh I'm fed up with the sari, so I dressed up in a suit,' she replied. Later, they went to have dinner. Looking at Anu having her dinner, Arun thought, 'You know how beautiful you are and it's tempting me to zoom with you for dancing on the moon.'

'Hello, dude, have your dinner, this is not the time for dreaming. I'm not sure about your dream but my dream will turn out true,' Madan murmured. 'Ouch,' Madan yelled as Arun poked his leg, using a fork.

Later, everyone left the college after having their dinner except these four. They were discussing on the field about their exams, which would start in few days.

Suddenly remembering, Anu said, 'Arun, one more thing,' and she was struggling to pull out something from her pocket. After pulling out a sheet, Anu asked, 'Can you explain this problem?'

Keeping her hands on her head, Sandhya said, 'Oh my God.' Madan captured that scene using his mobile and she chased him.

'Yeah, sure,' Arun said, laughing, and explained.

'Thank you, you became strained in teaching me this problem, hope this will come up in the exam, thanks a lot,' Anu said, and after wishing all of them goodbye, she left the college.

All of them were studying deeply, especially Arun, but on the other side, the minute he closed his eyes, he was seeing only Anu. He used to think of her at that moment.

'Three days left, *huff*,' Anu blew hard and was trying hard to lock all the lessons in her mind. The days finally kicked them into the exam hall and everyone looked very serious.

The examiner distributed the question papers; Anu took her pen and started thinking for a while. Arun started writing and Sandhya was biting her pen. During the mathematics exam, Anu stared with a smile at Arun after glancing at the last question, and that was the one she was taught on the graduation day by Arun. Arun gave his paper and smiled at Anu as he left the exam hall. The days were running with lots of sincerity, burden, strain, confusion, stress, and confidence, and a lot of different feelings were filling the college's atmosphere.

One fine day, it was the last exam, and Anu felt the question paper was very hard. It was biology; she gave the answered papers fast and walked out of the exam hall. Arun gave a tense and a confused look towards her and continued to write. After the exam, all of them sat in a circle.

'How did your paper go?' Sandhya asked.

'Yeah, OK,' Arun replied in a breathy voice.

'I think I might lose six marks, instead of explaining the symptoms of tumour I have explained about the structure, gone,' Sandhya said disappointedly.

'It's all right, calm down, it's useless worrying now,' Arun said.

'He's right,' Madan said with affirmation.

After a long gap, Prashanth called up Sandhya, and speaking, they were in their own world. In Stephen's College, throwing her arms around Vishaal, Deepthi was discussing the question paper with him and they left the place later.

Later, as he got Vishaal's message, Arun showed it to Anu.

Feeling happy, Anu read the message: 'You will definitely succeed.'

'OK, shall we all hang out somewhere,' Arun said with excitement.

'Sorry, I'm going out with Prashanth,' Sandhya said and he looked towards Madan.

'Sorry, dude, today I'm busy in helping with my cousin's marriage function,' he replied, and giving a keen look at Sandhya,

Madan said, 'OK, plan up for tomorrow because all of them are curious to meet their loved one.' She hit Madan's shoulders.

Looking at Anu, Arun asked, 'What about you?'

'Sorry, only a few minutes,' she replied.

'Thank God he's saved,' Sandhya said, and Arun gave a fishy look towards her. Anu smiled and ran towards the edge of the compound.

'I think he will call me today,' Anu whispered, and Arun was left speechless. As Anu was thinking about Vishaal, Arun held her wrist.

'What are you thinking?' Arun asked.

'Nothing,' she replied and took away her hand.

Giving his mobile, he asked, 'Do you want to speak with him?' and she was about to press the buttons but gave it back to him, saying no.

'Fine, bye, Arun,' Anu said.

'Tell me when we are going to meet,' Arun swiftly asked her.

'As soon as possible, my friend,' Anu replied in a keen voice.

'Anu, I wanted to show you a place. I'm sure you will love that place,' he said as she was leaving but Anu went, smiling.

Tapping grilles, Arun murmured angrily, 'Before, I used to love her smile, now it's torturing me.'

Becoming free birds, Vishaal and Deepthi went for a great ride on the bike. Arun, alone, went to his favourite place on the treetop.

During holidays, Anu's parents planned a three-day trip for going to Kerala. On the day of the journey, while packing, 'Anu, you pack all these things. Have you taken that pink dress?' her mother reminded her. Anu was dull, but at the same time, she was very happy to go and they reached the bus stand later. As the bus moved, Anu passed her time with Shwetha until the bus lights were on. It was around eleven o'clock in the night; they were already out of Bengaluru and it was breezy.

A little later, Anu opened the window completely and her dupatta was flying outside the window. She took it inside and wrapped it around her shoulders. Peeping out, she saw the moon travelling along with her. 'Oh, I know you can't stay without me,' Anu said with a feeling. 'Now hmm . . .' Anu was trying to imagine Vishaal and wished, hugging herself, 'Fine, if you're sleeping, have a pleasant warm sleep,' and she blew on her palm pointing towards the moon. At the same time, lying down on the swing, Vishaal was in the terrace and felt the same chilly feeling which he had felt before. He gave a sudden jerk.

'Who is this, is it Deepthi?' He thought for a while. 'My heart is saying no. Forget it, let it be.' And nodding his head, he said, 'Anushika deserves credit, I must meet her. Goodnight, Anushika,' and went down the stairs later.

Anu closed her eyes and fell asleep. Around 6 a.m., the clouds had covered the mountains partially and the sun had already risen. The bus horn had disturbed her and she woke up. As she opened the bus window, she felt a cool breeze. The golden sunrays fell on her face and she felt the warmth of the early morning sunrays. Later, as they reached Kerala, they got down from the bus and walked towards the foot of the mountain. The climate was very pleasant and cool. They had to climb about 2,500 steps and also had to walk further to the hilltop to reach a temple.

Before, several times, Anu had visited the place along with her parents. After reaching the foot of the mountain, they freshened up and began climbing. Seeing them climbing, their parents were very happy, and even they were enjoying the beauty of nature. While climbing, Shwetha was energetic and Anu was dead tired. After half the climb, Anu sat down, and rested her head on her mother's shoulders. As Shwetha pulled her, she continued climbing and both were at the mountaintop later. When Shwetha screamed 'Woohoo . . .' with joy, it was echoing. The surroundings were filled with greenery; Anu felt as though she was sitting on an emerald throne and the world was below it. Looking at the splendid view of the forest and birds of different species, her tiredness vanished. There was a beautiful temple and its steps were made of wood.

While Anu was looking at the view around, her father said, 'Hello, you can see it later, it's already late, temple's closing time,' and she became alert. She removed her footwear and washed her hands and legs. Feeling thirsty, she drank some water; meanwhile, a saint holding a brass pot came near the water tap to collect water and he stared at her smilingly but she gave a forced smile. Anu entered the temple, sat on the ground, and prayed for a while. She was glowing with happiness as she came out of the temple. She sat outside the temple since her parents wanted to show the horoscopes to the saint personally, for knowing future prospects.

Inside the temple, her father asked, 'When will be the right time for Anu's marriage?'

'Oh, her horoscope is wonderful, within three years she will get married,' the saint replied and her parents exchanged happy looks and came out with broad smiles.

Looking at Anu and Shwetha, their father said, 'We're going to meet a saint, you both stay here until we come back,' and left the place. The time was around five o'clock in the evening. There was a narrow lane and a huge park behind the temple. It was covered with a fence all around and both went down the wooden steps. They saw many cuckoo birds were cooing. Anu looked at the beautiful view and felt like singing. She sang her favourite song and heard a flute playing in tune with her song. Following the direction of the flute music, through the broken fence, they entered the park. Anu yelled 'Ouch' as her hair stuck to the fence and she slowly removed it but her ears were pressed to the music.

Shwetha, opening her mouth, said, 'Wow! What a view.' There was a large grass field and huge trees around. Shwetha saw a swing dangling from a tree branch; she didn't notice that it was broken and ran blindly to sit on it. *Dhupp*, she fell on the ground. Seeing her rubbing her hips, Anu laughed, and both somehow managed to play on the swing for some time after setting it right but when the swing broke again, Shwetha with disappointment, said, 'Oh, Didi, let's go back near the temple.' But seeing that Anu's eyes were searching for something else, Shwetha said frustratedly and loudly, 'Oh, Didi, I'm going, I'll call you when Dad comes,' and left the place.

As Anu heard the flute's music again, she walked some distance further and saw a cute girl playing flute behind a tree and went near the girl. The girl, seeing Anu, smiled and, holding Anu's hand, took her near a tree and was trying to explain in order to show something but Anu couldn't understand and the girl gave a helpless look at Anu.

The girl was gesturing and Anu started singing with a curious look towards the girl. The girl showed her thumbs up; looking at the tree, she continued to play the flute but Anu could not understand about the tree.

Giving a surprised look at the girl, Anu said, 'How sweet, how come you know this tune? How talented you are.' Covered in fog, the atmosphere became dark and she pointed towards the foggy street. And from afar, in the middle of the foggy street, a handsome spectacled guy holding a violin was walking slowly. Gradually, as he was approaching, the violin music was penetrating. Anu could not make out who the guy was and realizing later, as though like a dream she was mesmerized with excitement, 'Oh, it's Spandan!' Anu shouted and ran towards him.

'What a pleasant surprise! How come you are here, in this place? Ha, I forgot, you have powers to appear anywhere, right?' Anu said confusingly with some blend of excitement.

Giving a pitying look towards the girl, Spandan said, 'I'll be in touch with some special persons, this girl is one among them.' Holding Anu's hand, the girl took her near a tree; she showed her mother's face which was carved on the tree bark and was trying to explain it.

Spandan, looking at the girl, said dully, 'She's lost her mother in an accident and her father, who is my friend, has become insane after the tragedy, of all the worst is that she lost her voice, she can't speak and the temple's priest is taking care of her now.'

'Oh, she's alone now,' Anu said sadly.

'No, how can that be? I'm with her,' Spandan sounded in a breathy voice. Gesturing at Spandan, the girl started playing the flute and Spandan played the same in violin. Both played funny tunes and the girl giggled. A little later, he walked along with Anu and waved his hands at the girl.

'Spandan, looking at your journey after your life, even I am feeling like accompanying you,' Anu said dreamily.

Holding her wrist, Spandan said, 'Anu, don't ever think of it, not even in dreams. Come on, I'll show you something exciting.'

'One minute,' Anu said and ran towards the girl hurriedly. She gave her a handful of chocolates and kissed her. Towards a sloppy narrow lane, Anu and Spandan went walking later.

Seeing Anu from afar, Shwetha shouted to the heights, 'Idiot, tell me where you are going,' but Anu could not hear and Shwetha saw Anu disappearing. Shwetha sat on a step restlessly and started playing the games on her mobile. Anu walked until the end of the deep narrow lane and entered the forest zone.

Spandan pointing straight ahead, said, 'Anu, if you pass along this stream, you will come across a beautiful view.'

Looking at the stream, she asked, 'Yeah, but how deep is this stream?' and before she looked up, Spandan had disappeared. As Anu moved her legs into the stream, she slipped off and slid into it. As the stream carried her along with it, closing her eyes, she screamed and suddenly stopped. She opened her eyes later, and her elbows were bleeding.

Anu slowly got up later and was stunned as she looked around. As her eyes were completely fixed on the vast range of colourful wild flowers and trees, she didn't move a bit. Through the congested space, the sunlight was trying to peep into the dense forest, and she could hear the loud sound of gushing water. She continued walking and stopped as the huge plants with big leaves blocked her way. She could not go further and she jumped to see beyond those plants but they were too high. She could hardly reach them and she was hissing as her elbows were burning. For seeing the view, she pulled a plant down to the ground. 'Ouch,' she yelled as it had thorns on it. To have a look, she raised her head and saw clouds. Though her hands were bleeding, she bent another plant to have a clear view and didn't realize or feel the pain as she saw a huge waterfall. To form a huge splendid waterfall in that territory of nature, all the streams were being united. Looking at the waterfall, Anu exclaimed, mesmerized, 'Oh, what a creation, amazing, healed my pain.' Lying down near the stream, she splashed the water on her face.

Covered with fog, the atmosphere had completely changed. It was looking as though the fog had covered up the mountains like a blanket. The leaves were dancing as she hummed a beautiful song. Her eyes moved towards a cave which was beside the waterfall; getting scared, she hesitated to go but she gathered courage to have a look inside finally. Walking inside, she exclaimed '*Wow!*' with her eyes wide open as the bright rays were penetrating a small gap and focused on a pond where beautiful flowers and plants had grown. Anu shouted, 'I just love you all,' and it was echoing. The time was six o'clock; it was almost getting dark.

Meantime, 'Didi . . . Anuuu!' Shwetha and her parents were shouting, and her mother was almost about to cry. Two old persons who looked very strong were helping them in searching for Anu. A little later, carrying a big basket on her head and wrapped in an old patched sari, an old woman wearing big earrings, with a shrunken face, was coming out from the dense forest. As she approached them, speaking in their native language, the old persons enquired of the old woman.

Showing the direction, the old lady replied in a sharp voice, 'Ha, while coming, I heard some voice.'

'Can you take us to that place, granny?' Anu's father asked but as she couldn't understand his language. The granny stretched her hand at him and he gave her some money; she smiled and left the place. After guessing where Anu could be found, the two old men, using a rope, were sliding down smoothly; they went down deep since they were used to getting down the depths for plucking the wild fruits as it was their livelihood. Looking at the depth, Anu's mother was scared and Shwetha touched the rope for going down as she was thrilled and curious to get down. As her father gave a stern look, she immediately stepped back. After landing deep down and looking around, the two old men shouted. Looking down the hill, Anu's parents shouted.

Enjoying the richness of nature, Anu was drowned in her own world. As she heard some voices and sensed some danger, she got up quickly for hiding. Hiding behind a tree, she saw two old men shouting and speaking in their native language. 'Your parents are looking for you.'

Anu was not familiar with their language but she could make out with their words. She ran in the direction where they were looking around.

As Anu approached, the old men said, 'Oh, you're here, the goddess has helped you, it's very dangerous here. Come, maa,' and they took her on a different route. Anu didn't feel like leaving the place and entering into the material world, which was full of anxiety and pain. Her heart was pulling back but her mind pushed forward to go with those men. They kept on walking and came out from the forest finally.

Anu saw her parents and they looked very tense. As she came near them, her father was looking at her angrily. 'Whhaatt . . .' He slapped her.

'You think you can wander wherever you want?' her mother blasted.

Turning towards the two old men, her father said, 'Thanks,' and gave them money. It had already become dark. A little later, they left the place and went to a nearby town by car. Her father's slap didn't hurt Anu's feelings, as she thought that of course any father would react like that, and later, her mind journeyed into the world of nature's beauty that she had witnessed. Her father was interested in sharing the tense incident to the driver.

After hearing about it, the driver gave his opinion. 'Oh my God, that place is very dangerous.'

Anu, becoming angry and looking towards the driver, murmured, 'Idiot, you're a fool to say that, sick . . . I think, your thoughts are dangerous.'

After a pause, the driver continued. 'There have been many evil attacks, especially in the caves, oh, your daughter is lucky nothing happened, the goddess Rajarajeshwari helped her,' he said exaggeratedly. Anu, remembering the beauty of that place, said to herself, 'Senseless fellow, such a beautiful place.'

Later, they all got down from the car and her father paid the money to the driver. They entered a boarding place for staying but Anu stayed behind.

'Hello, mister . . .' Anu called the driver.

'Yes, maa.'

'Do you have any proof that evil attacks are going on in that place, have you seen it?'

'No, I have heard people saying.'

'OK, now see it from your own eyes,' Anu said and gave him a scary, dreadful look. He immediately started his car and, in no time, zoomed away from the place. Holding her stomach, she burst out laughing, and when she turned back, her father met her eyes but she immediately kept quiet.

Meantime, when Sandhya called Arun, commenting on Anu, 'She's not fit to be my friend and didn't say a word that she's going out of station,' she said angrily. Arun was very disappointed and didn't speak a word. Sandhya continued, 'Hey, come on, only for two days and she will come back,' she said convincingly but Arun had ended the call.

Later, trying to make his mood a bit better, Arun went out and reached his favourite park. Looking at the flower plants, Arun thought, 'I know, Anu, you're right in my heart,' and raised his head dreamily towards the sky.

Next day, Anu's family visited a temple. Later, they packed everything and left the place to reach Bengaluru. The bus moved around 4 p.m. It was raining heavily; her mother pulled her as she had almost put her head outside the window, and closed its glass. The time was 11 p.m.; the driver stopped the bus to relax. Including Anu, most passengers were out of the bus, and she stood near the edge of the road, where it was on the top of the hill's curve.

Meantime, at the construction site on the top of the terrace, Arun sat thinking about Anu. 'I'm missing you a lot,' he said and looked up at the sky. 'I love you, Anu.' As Arun shouted, Anu felt some kind of shivering in her heart and later, after everyone boarded, the bus started.

At 6.30 a.m., the bus reached Bengaluru. 'Anu, get up,' her father said. Opening the window, Anu sadly looked out. They all stepped tiredly into their house later.

Meantime, Sandhya was snoring and got a call from Arun. Dragging her mobile, she said sleepily, 'Oh no.'

'Hello, please call her up now,' Arun said.

As Sandhya heard him, 'Oh, this fellow,' she said in a crying tone and cut the call. He called her again.

Becoming a bit angry, Sandhya replied, 'What's your problem, won't you leave me to have a pleasant sleep?' and switched off the mobile. She continued to sleep and got up with a jerk as the clock alarmed. A little later, she said, 'Oh God,' looking at the missed calls, and there were nearly ten messages and missed calls. All were from Arun and she immediately dialled Anu's number.

With anger, Sandhya said to herself, 'Even if now you won't pick up the call, I'll kill you.'

'Hello,' Anu said in a very gentle way.

'Hello, lady, were you on this earth or not?' Sandhya asked.

Recalling her experience, Anu replied, 'Maybe not.'

'Why did you leave for the trip without even saying a word?' Sandhya asked.

'Sorry, sorry,' Anu quickly said.

Showing a bit of anger, Sandhya said sharply, 'Come right now, I mean right now to college, we all need to meet you.'

Anu was thinking, 'I think Vishaal might have called up but now should I go. How shall I convince Mom? OK, expressing real reason, I'll try for getting permission.'

'Ma, everyone has planned up to meet in the college, please, can I go?' Anu requested her mother.

'Why?' her mother asked.

'Just like that, Ma, many days are over and today is going to be our last meeting, please, Mom,' Anu pleaded more.

'Fine, come back soon,' her mother finally agreed.

Anu wore a jacket and left immediately. She got the bus right at the bus stand and reached the college. Looking around, she excitedly shouted, 'Hi, everybody!' but could see none of them and sat on the steps; slowly, faces appeared side by side as she was waiting dully, firstly Arun, Madan next, and Sandhya lastly.

Looking at them, Anu said in a hurried tone, 'Idiots, why are you guys so late?'

Madan with gesturing, quickly replied, 'OK, OK, waiting for just about half an hour, you are feeling like this. Imagine us, we were waiting for two days, how would we have felt? Especially Arun?' He continued, 'Why you didn't tell us about your trip?'

'I never thought you guys would react so much just for not informing, sorry,' Anu replied.

Meanwhile Sandhya, becoming restless, said hurriedly, 'OK, there is no time for discussing all these.'

As usual, all were sitting in a circle and had a great time having fun. They discussed about the results and were selecting future courses. While conversing with each other, Arun, looking keenly at Anu, asked, 'So how was your trip to the hill station?'

'Can't express,' Anu stressed the words, closing her eyes. Seeing wounds on her elbow and then pointing at them, he asked, 'What are these?'

'These are my expressions,' she replied with a broad smile. He stood up, giving a confused look at her and walked few steps away from her.

'You know, I felt sick, something was torturing me if you're not with me, please, Anu . . .' Arun said to himself and turned towards her, but . . .

'Had Vishaal given a call,' she eagerly asked and he didn't speak a word but to get back his patience, he looked up the sky.

Meanwhile, Sandhya and Madan went to a nearby Pizza Corner to get pizza and sent a message to Arun that she would be back within ten minutes.

'Arun,' Anu called him in a low tone and he gave a serious look at her.

'Many days have passed, I feel like seeing him,' she said desperately.

'Anu, I'll change my SIM card,' he said to himself but did not reply.

Becoming disappointed, Anu looked up the sky, saying, 'I want to speak with you, Vishaal, please call me,' and blew on her palm pointing towards the sky.

Seeing that, he asked curiously, 'What are you doing?'

'Nothing,' she dully replied and drew him to some other topic.

Meanwhile, Vishaal became frustrated since he didn't have any message from Arun. He called up Arun several times but got no response from him. Vishaal said with frustration, 'OK, let me try again,' and called up again. Arun, thinking that Sandhya had called, received the call without looking at the caller's name, and he was shocked hearing Vishaal's voice.

'What happened?' She grabbed the mobile and spoke.

Vishaal, not realizing that Anu spoke, and hearing the response, said, 'Oh, Arun finally now your mobile felt pity on me.' Vishaal sounded tired.

'No, I didn't feel pity, I felt like talking to you,' Anu replied with a smile.

Becoming relieved, he said, 'Anushika you, I missed you so much,' and started elaborating on his rejuvenated friendship with Deepthi, not letting Anu respond to his talk. Meanwhile, Arun picked up some pebbles from the ground, and focusing on a point, he began throwing them to control his temper.

Finally realizing, Vishaal asked, 'Oh, fine, sorry, by the way, how are you?'

'I'm fine,' Anu replied.

'OK, stop hiding yourself, I want to see you.'

'Don't worry, I'll meet you at a convenient time,' Anu replied.

'OK, Anushika, now I'm feeling quite relieved. So I hope our next meeting will be face to face, not on the phone, bye.'

Feeling better, Anu replied, 'OK, let's see,' and ended the call.

While she passed the mobile to Arun, he asked in surprise, 'But how did he come to know that you're with me?'

'I think it's a coincidence,' Anu replied casually but Arun was perplexed. 'Oh God, it's getting late, OK, bye . . .' Anu said and stood up to go.

'Anu, I want to know how he called up as soon as you wished something and blew on your palm,' Arun asked again and Anu burst out laughing; she said, 'It's black magic.'

'What?'

Looking at him, she replied with a cute smile, 'Oh, it's a love magic,' and walked towards the gate. Again turning, she said, 'Hello!' As she shouted, Arun slowly lifted his head with a smile. 'It won't work for all, only for people where they retain their love in their hearts forever, remember this,' Anu said and waved her hand.

A little later, holding pizza boxes, Sandhya and Madan came hurriedly near Arun, looking around. 'Where is Anu? I got her favourite hot chilli cap,' Madan asked, but Arun, remembering Anu's reasoning, was smiling himself. After having pizza, all of them left for their dwellings.

A few days later, Sandhya rang up Anu. In a gushing voice, Sandhya said, 'Hey, tomorrow, get ready, I have a plan for taking you out.'

'What plan?' Anu asked.

'Leave it to me, it's my job to take you out, get ready by 10 a.m. sharp,' she said and ended the call. Next day, Anu woke up late and got ready in a hurry.

Throwing a suspicious look at her, Shwetha asked, 'How come you have dressed up so well?'

'If I won't dress up well, you also object to me, and if I do, even then you will question me. What's your problem?' Anu replied seriously.

Their mother smiled at their arguments and, looking at Shwetha, said, 'Stop it, I only insisted to her to dress up well, I'm taking her out.' As someone rang the bell, Shwetha went to open the door.

Sandhya, entering, said dully, 'Hi, aunty, hi, both of you.'

'Come, let's go,' she whispered at Anu and pretended innocence as soon as she saw Anu's mother coming near them.

'Where?' Anu asked. Sandhya, looking at Anu's mother, said in a dull voice, 'Aunty, one bad news, our chemistry lecturer has passed away.'

Hearing that, Anu said, 'What?' and was shocked.

'Yes, Anu, that's why I'm going there to see, will you come?' she asked but Anu hesitated, looking at her mother.

'You go, teachers are equal to God,' her mother said.

A little later, Anu and Sandhya dully walked out from the house. After boarding the bus, they stood standing as all the seats were occupied. Anu, seeing Sandhya's smiling face, asked doubtfully, 'Is it true what you said?' .

Tapping Anu's shoulders, she coolly replied, 'Hey, come on, I hate chemistry sir, he's sick of all.'

Becoming a bit angry, Anu said, 'Stupid, how could you come out with such a big lie?'

In a convincing manner, Sandhya said, 'No other way for bringing you out, Prashanth is coming along with Vishaal and Deepthi to introduce me. We have planned to get together in a park, and you can see them, right?' as Anu was buying tickets from the bus conductor.

Hearing that Vishaal was coming, Anu said hesitatingly, 'Oh no, I just told you that I want to see them but not to meet them directly right now.'

Looking through the bus window, Sandhya said, 'OK, you both can see them without their knowledge.'

'Is Arun coming to see them?' Anu asked, giving a keen look at the road.

'Oh, wait,' she replied. They finally got down from the bus and went walking towards the park.

Entering the park, Anu thought tensely that Vishaal shouldn't see her. A little later, Arun, looking cool in a red jacket, came near them and wished them well. Pointing at Arun, Sandhya said, 'See, this guy will take you,' and giving Anu a bow later, she said, 'Go, my bride.' Anu gave a grudging look at her.

A little later, Sandhya saw Prashanth entering the park, riding on his bike. 'Fine, guys, OK, go, Prashanth is coming,' Sandhya said hurriedly. Pointing a direction to Sandhya, Arun said, 'OK, fine, we both will be there,' and turning towards Anu, said, 'Come on, Anu, I'll show you something really wonderful.' Anu slowly stepped forward and went behind him.

Arun took her near the treetop hut. The ladder rolled down, as he pulled the rope. Anu looked at him until he reached the treetop, and looking down, he said, 'Come on.' After removing her footwear, she curiously, slowly climbed up to the treetop. Arun stretched his hand to hold her hand, and as he held hers, he pulled her to get onto the treetop platform. She was surprised as there was a sliding chair, flower vase, and a lovebird cage. Hardly two people could fit on the treetop; looking at the view, Anu was mesmerized and she could almost see the whole park.

'Woohoo!' Anu shouted.

'How is it?' he asked but Anu did not see him, and was excitedly looking around.

'Unbelievable,' Anu replied and sat on the sliding chair.

A little later, Anu saw Prashanth introducing Sandhya to Deepthi and they both hugged. Constantly looking at them, Anu didn't move her eyeballs, and actually her eyes were fixed on Vishaal and Deepthi. She said, 'Shh,' as Arun tried to divert her attention from seeing them, and ignoring him, she showed him her palm to wait. Getting angry, Arun looked at the other side restlessly. 'Oh, Vishaal, comparably you're looking more charming than you did when I saw you at the flyover, she's so lucky to have a guy like you,' Anu thought all this in her mind.

To control his anger, Arun was rotating the bird's cage and saw the four of them laughing and tapping each other's hands. 'How lucky they are, I'm the only one left alone,' Arun thought in his mind.

Later, Prashanth and Sandhya left the park but Vishaal and Deepthi stayed behind. Hugging, they sat near a flower plant bush. Anu saw Deepthi resting on Vishaal's lap, and tears rippled down her face but her smile didn't fade from her lips. Arun turned to Anu, and seeing her, he asked funnily, 'Are these tears of jealousy or happiness?'

Using her fist, she tapped his chest, and holding his hand later, she became emotional. 'Thanks, thanks a lot, you showed me such a beautiful view,' Anu said, and looking constantly towards the couple, she was completely drowned in the world of their love. A little later, turning to the lovebirds, she blew on her palm pointing towards the cage.

Seeing her emotion, Arun, shaking her shoulders, called, 'Anu . . . Anu,' and giving a jerk, she turned towards where Vishaal and Deepthi were seated, but they had left already.

Unknowingly leaning on Arun, Anu asked, 'Where are they?'

'They must have gone into your dreams,' he answered swiftly.

'Oh, sorry,' Anu said as she had leaned against his shoulders.

'That's all right,' Arun replied blushingly.

Anu, pointing at the bird's cage, asked, 'Arun, those lovebirds have got their freedom now, what about these?' Slowly blinking his eyes, he lifted his shoulders with a broad curve on his lips. Realizing his gesture, she opened the birds' cage, and those lovebirds flew away fluttering. As he felt her breathe very near, he became mesmerized. Her hair got stuck to the zip of his jacket. 'Wait, I will help you,' Arun said and slowly removed it.

Feeling uneasy, getting down later, Anu waved, 'OK, bye,' and walked some distance.

He quickly got down from the tree. 'Anuuu!' he shouted and she stopped walking. He ran towards her, blocked her way, and asked her to stay for a while. Anu smiled as she saw him plucking a yellow flower from nearby bushes, and he gave her a bunch of yellow flowers. Receiving it, she said, 'Wow! Yellow indicates friendship—beautiful,' and continued to walk.

'Oh, Anu, when will you have your freedom?' he asked in a high voice, and Anu slowly turned with a smile on her lips, nodding her head. Facing Arun, she moved backwards until she reached the gate. Expecting a positive reaction, Arun desperately looked at her, but Anu walked away.

Anu tensely reached her house; seeing Anu holding the flowers, Shwetha gave a suspicious look.

'It's ridiculous that you had to carry flowers for the funeral pyre and instead you got it from there, don't tell me that you were attracted to these flowers and got these from there,' Shwetha said like a lawyer and continued questioning: 'Did you steal it?' And she burst out laughing. Anu dully put those flowers in front of the idol and walked into her room.

Arun reached home; looking at him, Nirmala said, 'On the 24th it's Mom's birthday, this Sunday we are leaving for Kodai,' and Arun, not reacting much, entered his room.

'Anu, without you, I am leading my life like a machine. When will you accept my love?' Arun thought in his mind and fell on the bed.

Vishaal, in his room, spoke to himself as he couldn't sleep. 'Anushika, I'm desperately looking forward to see you.' From his wardrobe, he took an autograph book of his schooldays that contained his friends' feelings, and he read Arun's message: 'Physically we may be far but your memories shall remain in my heart forever, I'll be missing you, Vishaal,' and he kissed on Arun's signature. While turning some pages, he saw a phrase with no signature on it and that caught his attention. It read, 'Believe your heart's concise, it's always a life indicator and it will help you every second. All the best.'

'You're exactly right, but who wrote this? It must be from a seventh standard friend but I'm not able . . . it's sounding exactly like Anushika,' he thought but couldn't get a clue about the unknown message, and as he slid his hands on the page, Anu felt a feathery touch in her heart. Resting the book on his chest, Vishaal had fallen asleep later.

Next day, Vishaal met Deepthi, showing his desperateness with her: 'I'm not able to meet her, I don't know what's gone wrong with the mobile, nobody picks up, and I suspect something is wrong with them. Even Prashanth is not picking up the call.' Vishaal sounded very upset.

'Relax, soon you will meet her, try out messaging,' Deepthi consoled him.

Pressing the mobile's buttons harshly, Vishaal messaged, 'Anushika, I'm desperate to see you, please. When you will make up your mind?' Vishaal messaged.

Arun, looking at that message, thought, 'I myself am waiting to see her,' and erased it. 'It's better to end this,' Arun said and threw the SIM card. He got a new SIM card with a slight feeling of hope that Anu would also forget Vishaal and soon welcome him in her heart.

Later, Arun called Sandhya, 'Day after tomorrow, I'm going to Kodai,' Arun informed her.

As she received the call from an unknown number, Sandhya asked him, 'But what happened to your mobile?'

'Oh, I changed my SIM card, save this number,' Arun replied in a sharp tone.

'So when will you be back?' she asked.

'After a week.' Arun's voice jumped down.

'Sandhya, can you get Anu to your house at least before I leave? I can meet her there,' he requested.

'I don't think this can be done, let me try,' she replied unwillingly and disconnected. Immediately, Sandhya gave a call to Anu.

'Anu, can you come to my house?' she asked.

'No, Sandhya, my mom won't allow me. Don't worry, I'll meet you at a convenient time,' Anu said and disconnected.

Sandhya was fed up with her reply and messaged, 'Sorry, Arun, she will not be able to meet you.' After reading the message, he became restless and took his skates to go out.

Gliding on skates, Arun entered the park and stretched his arms to feel relaxed. After climbing to the treetop, imagining Anu's smile, Arun lay on the sliding chair and later he got down. Dragging his feet restlessly, he glided on the skates and started humming a tune, which was Anu's favourite.

Meanwhile, riding on his bike, Vishaal saw Arun passing by him, skating, and he stopped his bike, looking back, surprised, at Arun. 'Hello . . . Hello!' he shouted.

Arun stopped and turned back to Vishaal.

'Ar . . . Arun . . .' He swallowed his voice and ran towards him but Arun didn't react much as he was in a disturbed mood. Vishaal hugged him, and Arun gave a broad smile but didn't throw his arms around Vishaal in return. Vishaal was excitedly looking at him.

'My God, I'm very happy to see you back again, is this a dream?' And after a pause, Vishaal continued, 'Oh, I missed you a lot, I have got lots to say,' and his feelings had become stronger and he wanted to share things with Arun, who was smiling forcibly. Vishaal gave a pause and tried to read him, constantly looking. 'You're in love, right?' Vishaal asked him.

'Yeah . . .' Arun said in a low voice. As Vishaal compelled him to reveal about his love, he told him that he was facing problems in his love, and after hearing that, Vishaal said, giving a dreamy look, 'Fine, she likes you as a friend but is not accepting your love.' He then continued, 'Dude, yours is not at all an issue in contrast to what mine was, a girl called Anushika helped me in solving my love matter. I had never even dreamt that my case would succeed, her guidance and talent has enabled me to think positively and made every moment of my life a very special one . . . I got back my love finally, but I haven't seen her so far, except for contacting her through phone. Once I tried seeing her but failed.' He sounded disappointed at the end and continued, 'Oh, sorry, surely with her help, you will succeed. As soon I get her contact, I'll inform her about your problem so she could solve yours,' Vishaal said in a serious tone.

With a blush on his face, hearing the praising of Anu, and feeling nice, Arun said dreamily, 'You're right.'

'Ha, what did you say?'

'I mean your suggestion is right.'

'Fine, who is that lucky girl?' Vishaal sounded very eager.

'It's wrong, I'm very lucky.'

'My goodness, sounds very sincere, surely your love graph has reached its optimum level. Great, Anushika likes such qualities in a person and surely helps such people.'

Unaware of himself, 'I know that,' Arun sounded restlessly.

'Ho, what do you know about her?' Vishaal sounded surprised.

Realizing quickly, Arun said, 'No, no, of course every girl comes forward to help a good person.'

'No, not every girl, rarely like Anushika, OK, what's the name of your love?'

'Anushika,' Arun replied quickly and Vishaal was shocked.

'Hey, come on, it's not that Anushika who helped you, my loved one's name is also Anushika,' Arun lied. Vishaal got Arun's mobile number, tapping his shoulders.

'I hope you shall soon have a great life with her, all the best,' he said, and after hugging Arun, he left the place.

After reaching home, becoming frustrated, he called Sandhya but she didn't receive the call. He came outside, looking up at the sky. 'Anu, I'm going tomorrow, please, can I see you once, just once before I leave,' Arun said and blew on his palm pointing at the sky. Soon he turned back as someone tapped his back, and it was Sandhya.

'I saw you blowing, what, you're acting crazy, you learnt it from that lady, didn't you?' she asked with curved lips, and after taking her mobile from the purse, she said, 'I can't see your face like this, I'll call her, wait,' and dialled Anu's number.

'Hello,' Sandhya said.

'Hello, I'll call her, wait,' Shwetha replied and went to call Anu. Meanwhile, as Nirmala came outside, Sandhya greeted Arun's sister, 'Hi, Didi,' and passed her mobile to Arun for speaking with Anu.

'Hello, Sandhya,' Anu said.

'Hi, Anu, how are you?' Arun replied and Anu felt a bit surprised as he spoke from Sandhya's mobile. Her mother, folding the clothes, was beside her, feeling uneasy.

'Hi, I'm fine,' she stammered a bit.

Hearing her stammering, he said, 'Oh, sorry, only this option left to speak with you.'

'Is everything fine, why are you sounding so dull?'

'No, nothing, tomorrow I'm going to Kodai, so I wanted to inform you and—'

'And?' Anu asked.

'I want to see you before I leave,' he said emotionally.

'Yeah, but why are you feeling so depressed? You are just going for a trip and will not leave us forever, have a nice journey.'

'Anu, I tried out using your magic, truly I wished for you from my heart and blew towards the sky, did you feel something?' Arun sounded very curious, and she disconnected at his question. Laughing, Sandhya accompanied Arun and entered his room.

'I expected this, and by the way, what did she say?' she asked.

Arun hugging a pillow, said, 'Nothing, but Sandhya can you tell me, how will our deepest desire reach our loved one?'

'I have an answer for this question. I had questioned Anu once, she said that love is eternal; if it really comes through the heart, it emits unseen vibration through heartbeat and will reach the loved ones,' Sandhya replied, and giving a dreamy look towards the clock, he smiled.

'OK, bye, I'll be missing you, man. Take care, have a safe journey, bye.' She wished him goodbye and left the place.

Later, Arun helped his sister in packing and he got a call from Vishaal.

'Hi, Arun,' Vishaal said.

'Tomorrow, I'm leaving Bengaluru . . .' Arun informed Vishaal about his journey to Kodai.

'Oh! Well, your mother's birth anniversary, at your Kodai resorts? Don't worry, your mother's blessings shall always shelter you. Have a nice journey, bye, dude.' Vishaal sounded a bit emotional.

'OK, bye dude,' Arun said and thought, 'Oh, he's full of energy with confidence, love brings such a U-turn. He doesn't know it's just because of Anu, and if he comes to know, I don't know how he would feel.'

That night, tapping her fingers on mud pots, Anu was trying to compose some funny beats while Shwetha was whistling in tune with the beats. With frustration later, Shwetha said dully, 'Didi, it's so boring, shall we go out somewhere tomorrow? In case if you get married early, then I'll be left alone.'

'I don't know about my marriage but I have one deep desire that I have to see his, sorry—your marriage,' Anu said dreamily, and hearing that, Shwetha looking suspicious, said frustratedly, 'Stop it, I'm serious. Who knows, you may elope with someone tomorrow. I can make out, I know some guy called you up.'

Opening her mouth and eyes at once, being shocked, Anu said in a sharp voice, 'Yeah, I'm running away, especially I'm fed up with you, all right,' and a windowpane hit with force against the grille. Realizing the lapse she made in her talking, she became breathless and she went near the windowpane, inhaling fresh air. Closing her eyes, inhaling deeply, 'Oh, Vishaal, I love you.' she said to herself and Vishaal felt a chilled feeling in his heart. Shwetha thought that Anu became angry.

'OK, sorry, I was kidding, tell me where to hang out tomorrow,' Shwetha asked, regretting her comments.

'Hmm, let's go to the park . . .' Anu said and was undecided. Meanwhile, they heard their mother's voice from the kitchen.

'Come down, you people, have dinner,' and as both sat, Anu winked at Shwetha.

'Mom, please allow us to go out for playing tomorrow, a shuttlecock tournament for this area's children will be held at the nearby apartment's park. I'm fed up staying in the house for the past month, please, Mom,' Shwetha pleaded with her mother. Giving a fed-up look at them, their mother said, 'Ho, now you have started like your sister.'

'I don't know, I must go,' Shwetha said in a high-pitched tone.

'What time?'

'At ten o'clock in the morning and it will end up at six in the evening.'

'No, before six you must be at home,' her mother said in a warning tone.

Jumping onto her feet, Shwetha said, 'Yes, thanks, Mom.'

Anu, looking at her, asked in a puzzled voice, 'You're bugging me, what tournament?'

'Yeah, really, we have a tournament, for ending up your love into a success, I'm helping you to run away with your boyfriend,' Shwetha replied and as Anu looked calm, winking her eyes, she said encouragingly, 'OK, why are you standing like this? Go pack for tomorrow.'

'Stop it,' Anu said in an angry tone and walked into her room. She was thinking later, 'Why can't I go out?' and some idea was sparkling in her mind. 'Where, yes, to the park, probably they might come, Vishaal, are you coming? No, that won't happen,' she said to herself and stood up thinking, finally, 'Arun, I can't be so selfish, I'm sure you will feel bad, at least as your friend, I must see you off, fine, I'm coming tomorrow,' and she called up Sandhya.

'Yeah, tell me,' Sandhya asked in a rude voice.

'What's wrong with you?'

'Nothing, better you become a stone instead of being a human.'

'Fine, can you come with me tomorrow to see someone?'

'No, I have decided not to encourage your feelings, either your works or services whatever, especially in Vishaal's matter,' she replied in a grudging tone.

'Hello, what are you saying, I called you whether you'll come with me to give a send-off since my best friend is going to Kodai, and at least can I know from where and when the bus will depart?' Anu said in a humble way.

Sandhya, becoming excited, said in a hurried voice, 'Oh! My God, great you finally made up your mind, come to my house, let's go together, he's leaving at 10 a.m. sharp near the Volvo travels.'

'But one thing, don't tell him, let's surprise him.'

'That's your routine job, making him mesmerized and piercing his heart as well, he loves you, friend, he does more than anything your Vishaal does for you. Trust me, the one who will be his life partner, she's the luckiest one,' Sandhya said very emotionally.

'Hello, don't ever think of it, if Prashanth comes to know, then he will kill you and Arun.' Anu said so with a smile.

Ignoring Anu's comment, Sandhya asked seriously, 'Do you think I'm performing some play rehearsal on the stage or what?'

'I don't have answer for this, but surely I'm born for Vishaal, he's a gem,' Anu said in a breathy voice.

'What about Arun?' Sandhya sharply shot the question.

'He's my best friend—that's it. See you tomorrow,' Anu replied with the same sharpness.

'Sick—you're utterly sick. Love virus has attacked her, symptoms seem to be severe. I hope Arun is the medicine to cure her,' Sandhya thought to herself and disconnected the call.

Next day, Shwetha got up and, tapping Anu's cheeks, asked curiously, 'I thought you would have already eloped with your boyfriend, but you're meddling with your blanket. Has your boyfriend cheated on you?'

As Anu was half-asleep, 'Shut up,' she shouted at her, and stretching her arms, she turned her body completely straight. Looking towards the clock, she saw the time was 8.30 a.m. She jumped from the cot, ran into the washroom, and got ready within no time. Looking at Shwetha, Anu asked in a hurried voice, 'Tell me at what time your tournament starts.'

'Ten o'clock.'

'No, Shwetha, I need to go quickly to visit my friend's house,' Anu said seriously. As their mother was inside the kitchen,

Shwetha said in a high voice, 'Fine, Mom, I'm going, bye,' and lifted her eyebrows, looking at Anu.

'OK, wait, even I'm coming, I know your head won't stand in one place,' her mother replied.

'Ma, even I'm going with her,' Anu said.

'No, wait,' her mother said. Shwetha was surprised and Anu was disappointed.

Coming near them, their mother sounded a bit excited. 'If you girls have planned up, then of course your mothers also will land up with them, even we have also planned to get together.'

'Wow, then come on, let's hurry,' Shwetha said. Anu felt as though she had become breathless.

'No, wait! I need to get ready, we will leave after half an hour,' their mother said. Shwetha met Anu's eyes.

'No, Mom, we need to go right now for practicing, please,' Shwetha said in a bit of an angry tone.

Looking at them, their mother warned, 'Fine, go but be careful, and Anu, even you, all right? Be careful and take care.' They came out of the house.

'OK, Shwetha, thanks a lot,' Anu said in a hurry. Both took their bicycles and left the place. Anu zoomed towards the sloppy road and applied brakes near Sandhya's house. She was not able to stop the cycle from banging against the gate, and she lost control and fell down. She got up quickly and yelled, 'Sandhya, come quickly.'

After seeing Anu's sweating face, Sandhya was shocked. Anu wiped off the sweat using her hand and breathing hard, said, 'Come on, let's leave.'

'Wait, I'll change my dress,' Sandhya said hurriedly and turned to go.

'There's not much time left,' Anu said, exhausted.

'Fine,' Sandhya said and wore her footwear and spectacles and started her Scooty. Anu threw the cycle aside and sat behind Sandhya.

Meantime, Arun dully got down from the car. He looked around and slowly was unloading the luggage from the car. Nirmala went and enquired at the travel desk about the departure. Walking restlessly, he took his mobile to call up Sandhya but put it back in his pocket. He sat on the suitcase and started meddling with his fingers. He had lost the charm on his face and looked like a grey cloud.

While passing by, Anu saw a florist shop. 'Stop, stop,' Anu said and Sandhya stopped her Scooty. Coming near the flower stand, ignoring the shopkeeper's reaction, she took a golden yellow flower; she kept a ten-rupee note on the stand and sat on the vehicle quickly.

Looking at her behaviour, Sandhya said, 'You're really funny sometimes, you know. If you show your face, that's more than a golden flower for him,' and giggled. Anu couldn't hear her speaking.

Tensely looking at her watch, Anu said, 'Sandhya, please hurry up, it's nine fifty already.'

Sandhya was going at full speed, but as the clock was running, Anu could not remain calm. They heard some bursting sound and Sandhya stopped the vehicle. They saw that the tyre had punctured. Anu thought, 'What to do now?' and sat on the footpath.

Sandhya looking around, said, 'Come on, the bus stand is just one furlong,' and together went trotting. After reaching the bus stand, they saw a row of buses parked on both the sides. Meanwhile, Arun put all the luggage in the luggage cabin and got down from the bus.

Anu was thinking, 'In which bus will he be?' and looked around worriedly.

Sandhya said a bit funnily, 'Come on, why don't you try out your magic?'

'This is not the time to tease or blabber.' Anu sounded frustrated.

'Oh, I forgot to bring my mobile also,' Sandhya said worryingly.

'Got it, let us go and stand right at the front row of the bus, I'm sure we will find him,' Anu said and they hurriedly walked towards the front row of the buses. Sandhya stood at the opposite row.

Arun was thinking, 'I know she won't come, dreaming about her is like a fairy tale,' and his eyes were filled with tears.

Nirmala peeped out of the window and said, 'Arun, I think the bus will move, get inside.'

'Yes, Didi,' Arun's words were almost swallowed by his weak heart. He turned towards the other side and jerked. Becoming excited, he shouted, 'Anu!'

Seeing Arun, Sandhya said, 'Yess . . .' Sharing their smiles, both ran towards him.

Arun blindly threw his arms around Anu, and she pushed him a bit. She offered a handshake and giving the yellow flower, she said, 'Happy journey,' and he was almost frozen.

Holding Anu's hand, Arun said in a dreamy voice, 'I'll be missing you.'

'No, true friends will never feel like that. Try having a feeling that I'm always with you, it's my promise I'm always with you,' Anu consoled him.

Seeing them, Nirmala got down from the bus and hugged Anu and Sandhya. Arun waved at Anu while stepping into the bus and waved at them until he could not see them anymore. His face had brightened and he got back his charm. Nirmala smiled, looking at his smiling face, which was pale earlier.

'Thank God, at least now I can see your eyes twinkling,' Nirmala said with a broad smile.

'Oh yeah, I'm very much fine now,' Arun sounded very energetic recalling Anu's saying that she would always be with him. Completely leaning back, he closed his eyes. Nirmala gave a sigh and continued to type something on her laptop.

They quickly hired a taxi and Anu finally reached the playground. She got down, and Sandhya, sitting in the taxi, said, 'Don't worry, come on, go.'

Anu innocently walked onto the grounds and saw her mother along with the group of ladies. She saw all the kids were playing. Suspiciously, her mother was staring at her. 'Where had you gone?'

'I . . . I . . .' Anu stammered.

Winking her eye at Anu, Shwetha said, 'You need so much time to get a shuttlecock,' and after a pause, Shwetha asked, 'OK, fine, give.'

'No, it wasn't there, and I tried in all the shops. That's why it took so much time,' Anu lied without hesitation. Hearing their conversation, their mother ignored Anu and continued to chat with her neighbour about some dishes.

As the tournament was progressing, there were people shouting and applauding loudly but not all this excited Anu. Later, she saw Sandhya waving at her after parking the cycle, signalling her that she got her cycle. After getting a response from Anu, Sandhya left before Anu's mother could see her.

'Ma, I'm feeling bugged, shall I go home?' Anu asked her mother.

Trying to read her mind, her mother gave a strange look and said, 'OK fine, go.'

Pushing the cycle restlessly, Anu reached home. She got the keys from her neighbours and opened the door. As her boredom increased, she couldn't even sleep, and her mind was tempting her to go outside. Anu had become worried about Sandhya and gave her a call.

Meanwhile, Sandhya was drinking hot soup, stuffing herself with crispy chips.

'Hello, Sandhya, is everything OK?' Anu asked tensely.

Drinking the soup, Sandhya replied, 'Yeah, fine.'

'Did your father shout at you?' Anu asked.

'No, no, I managed.'

'How?'

'I managed by telling him, "Dad, I got news that the results have been released on the Net, so I went in a hurry but later got to know that it was just a rumour. On the way, I fell, the vehicle needed some work, so I have given it for servicing." He blasted at me later, saying that I'm irresponsible, the same old things I'm bugged with his scolding.'

'You expect him to approach you in a different way daily?' Anu asked, giggling.

'Think so . . . Hey, I forgot to tell you, I'm going to my native place tomorrow and will be back after three days,' Sandhya sounded a bit dull.

'Oh, then you will be missing Prashanth. Is that the reason you are sounding like this?' Anu asked.

'Yeah, Pa, and also my relatives there, they feel that I am a burden. It is just for Dad's sake I'm going,' Sandhya reasoned.

'Fine, happy journey,' Anu said and ended the call.

Looking at the clock, Anu thought to herself, 'Oh, it's three thirty. How come the time is running so slow today? I'm going mad,' and decided to go out. She wore a white dress and decided to leave. She wanted to go without being noticed by her neighbours, so she walked towards the back balcony instead of going out from the main gate. To go down the stairs, she jumped on the back house terrace, as the stairs there were outside the building. After getting down the stairs, she walked towards the bus stand and later reached Arun's favourite place at the treetop hut. She felt like climbing up the ladder, but hesitated, thinking, 'No, I must not; it's not good to climb up to the treetop hut in Arun's absence.' She suddenly heard some music. Realizing this, she said, 'Hey, this is my favourite.' She gave a pause and tried to hear it more clearly, she turned back in surprise, following the direction of the music, and looking around, she saw a group of music band students playing guitar.

In the meantime, Vishaal and Deepthi were also walking in the park. They were completely soaked in the romantic world. They had come to this park because it was far from their residence and they didn't want to be noticed together by people whom they knew. Looking at them, Anu's face blossomed; she absent-mindedly hummed a tune and the students who were playing the music stopped. Realizing this, she suddenly stopped humming and hid behind a tree. As she was watching Vishaal and Deepthi, she saw that Deepthi's high-heeled shoes made her slip on the ground. Vishaal immediately caught her from falling on the ground and massaged the affected heel smoothly as she couldn't stand because of pain. He lifted and carried her up to the gate. They went riding on the bike later. Anu felt great in her heart, as though all happiness in the world was flowing into her heart. She wept leaning against a tree, but the smile on her face didn't fade. Looking towards the sky, she whispered to herself, 'I will not have any sorrow. If my life ends right at this moment, since their love has become so strong and is unbreakable forever, oh God, thanks a lot, I am so satisfied.'

In the park, holding a stick, the security guard shouted at the kids, 'Hey, get out, all of you,' to send them out of the park. Dreaming about Vishaal, Anu sat and could hear the voices of the kids. Looking at the kids and clapping her hands, Anu signalled them to jump over the fence. Four boys and two girls got down, helping each other, and Anu helped a small boy to get down, holding his hands. They all thanked her and she asked their names. They introduced themselves and later played some games together. Tapping hands and then turning around, she taught them some games. Behaving like a kid, she had forgotten the world for a moment. As the weather became breezy, a girl among the group was clenching her teeth and started shivering. Anu removed her jacket and offered it to the girl, saying politely, 'Wear it.' The girl smiled and wore it.

Looking at the kids, she said, 'Come on let's play hide and seek.' Anu sounded very bubbly. They started to play the game. Anu's turn came to search for the kids but it started raining heavily and hailstones started falling along with rain. Looking at the heavy rain, becoming disappointed, Anu gave a sad gesture and slowly all the kids came out.

Pointing out all the kids, Anu sounded a bit louder than her usual voice. 'OK, out, out, everyone,' and nodding their heads left and right, 'No,' they said.

'See the rain has helped me to pull you all out,' Anu happily said.

'No, Didi, it made us stop playing,' one of the boy said in a grudging tone. Though the rain stopped, it was drizzling

Shaking a tree's branch, she said, 'Oh, see, we can still play,' and the droplets fell on their heads. The kids started enjoying, shaking tree branches, and had great fun.

Again, bringing huge thunder along, it started raining heavily. Sensing the situation, Anu said in a serious tone, 'All of you, it's enough now, go home.'

'No, we will play,' everyone shouted, and meanwhile, unnoticed, a girl who wore Anu's jacket hid behind a tree.

Convincing the kids, Anu said, 'No, we all will meet tomorrow surely.'

'Promise,' a girl asked.

Smiling at them, Anu said in a sharp tone, 'I promise that I'll meet you here in the same place again.' Agreeing one by one, everyone jumped over the fence. Helping them, Anu jumped at the end. The rain started pouring heavier than before, and the whole park was looking like a lake. The city had never witnessed such a rain ever since, from the past thirty years.

'Where's Rani?' one of the boys shouted as Anu jumped over the fence to reach her home, and the other kids looked at each other.

Becoming tense, Anu said in a hurried voice, 'Oh, I think she must be in the park, wait here only,' and quickly jumped back. Looking for the girl, she walked down the lane of the park.

Meantime, Arun was right at the top of the mountain, trying to imagine his true feelings from his heart. He stood on an edge, looking down the mountain. 'Oh, Anu, what's life without you? Maybe it's better to end my life rather than living with depression,' Arun thought, and then looking up, he yelled, 'Anu, I love you,' at the heights, and the whole atmosphere suddenly turned foggy. The strong breeze started blowing and the breeze pushed him backwards forcibly. Surprisingly, he felt as though someone pushed him and stopped thinking about ending his life. Turning all around the directions continuously, he yelled, 'Anu, I love you.' And standing quiet later, after a pause, Arun thought, 'You're treating me as your friend but I will love you until my last breath,' and left the place.

In Kodai, seeing him depressed, Nirmala decided to end their stay earlier and to go back to Bengaluru. Her decision made him a bit relaxed. With enthusiasm, he soon packed everything and got into the car. Nirmala wished the manager and the resort staff goodbye. They reached the bus station later.

As the bus started moving, Arun asked the driver, 'At what time will we reach?'

With a restless look, the driver replied, 'By morning—six.'

The dark sky was scattered with stars; looking up the sky, through the bus window, he said, 'Oh, I'm waiting for the sunrise.' After a few hours, the bus stopped. Some passengers got down and the rest were snoring.

Arun, in the washroom, looking at the driver, shot him a question again. 'When will the bus move, sir? Is it possible to reach on time?'

Hurriedly closing his pants' zip, looking angrily at Arun, the driver replied in a high tone, 'Oh, this is the fifth time you asked me, don't you know where to ask?' While coming out from the washroom, Arun requested the driver to start the bus early.

'All right,' the driver said and started the engine. The bus moved, Arun couldn't sleep, and as the bus was nearing Bengaluru, Arun's eyes were brightening more.

Peeping out from the window, Arun said in a heavy voice, 'I'm very much desperate to see you, my girl.'

Though it was cloudy in Bengaluru, the cyclonic effect almost ended with slight drizzle, and on the sides of the road, Arun saw many uprooted trees. 'I think it might have rained heavily,' he thought to himself. Arun, tapping Nirmala's shoulders, he said, 'Didi, Didi, we have reached home.' Yawning, she woke up and looked outside the window. Hurriedly, she pulled the luggage from the shelves; Arun was getting ready to get down, though the bus was moving. The moment the bus stopped, he pulled Nirmala and, getting down, caught an auto before she could say something. 'But, Ar—'

They reached their house. As soon they reached home, nodding her head, she said, 'Hey, just now, oh God . . .' Before she could finish saying, he started his bike and zoomed away. He gave a call to Sandhya and there was no response. He went to Sandhya's house and it was locked. He enquired of her neighbours and came to know that they were not in the city. Becoming frustrated, he said, 'Oh, shit, no, how I can meet Anu?' and later reached his house to sleep, as he didn't have proper sleep for the past three days.

Arun saw Anu climbing the ladder of the treetop hut to reach him but she slipped off. 'Be careful,' Arun shouted and suddenly woke up. Pressing his forehead, he looked at the clock and it was showing five thirty. After freshening up, he started his bike to reach his favourite resting place. Fragrance of the plants and the wet mud was emanating; he smelt it as he entered the park, and the climate was cloudy. Leaning against a tree, inhaling the passing cool breeze, he felt quite relaxed and saw a silver earring embedded with pearls. Picking it up, he was thinking, 'Hey, it looks like Anu's,' and he looked at it constantly. 'Hey that means Anu must have come here,' he thought and kept it in his pocket. He walked towards the treetop and, on the way, saw a big uprooted tree's trunk cut into pieces. He came near the treetop hut; it had completely vanished, and the tree's branches were scattered all over the ground. His heart feeling chill, he thought, 'Something wrong must have happened,' and panicking with a frantic look, he called the security guard's name loudly.

Anu's humming voice began coming from behind as he was looking tensely, turning back in surprise. 'What? Anu . . .' he shouted, and unbelievingly, he followed the direction from where he felt that he could hear her voice, crazily. As the voice become damp and suddenly stopped, he stood looking around.

After a pause, 'Arun,' he heard Anu calling pleasantly, and she was hiding behind a tree. The place was almost becoming dark and he wasn't sure as he felt everything was like a dream. Arun called, 'Anu . . .' and went closer and he saw her dressed in white umbrella-like long skirt and buff petal-sleeved top. In the dark atmosphere, she was looking bright like an angel. Coming closer, sliding his fingers along her cheek, he said with tears fill in his eyes, 'You're looking so beautiful, it's like you have wound up with all the light from the stars in you.'

Pleasantly smiling at him, she said, sounding very emotional, 'Arun, I like you so much, you're my true friend, you helped me so much in fulfilling my wishes, thank you, my sweet friend,' and kissed his forehead. Arun felt as though he was floating in air. 'Arun, you . . .' Before Anu could continue, he hugged her tight, hard, and tears rolled on his cheeks.

'Anu, I love you, I love you,' he repeated, and after releasing his hug, he stood with a keen look. 'Your company is enough, I can breathe.' Arun shot out his inner feelings, and feeling relaxed, he looked up the sky. After a while, stretching his arms, he said, 'OK, promise me that you'll meet me regularly,' and Anu nodded her head. She turned towards the other side and could not control her emotions.

After a pause, turning towards him, stretching her hand, Anu said, 'Wait, you must promise me first,' and she continued, 'If some irretrievable loss happens to you which results in depression in your life, it is OK, not a big issue, but that depression must not lead you to the extent of harming your life, I mean killing yourself,' Anu said with emotion and stress running all over her mind.

'What do you mean by that?' he asked in a confused voice.

Anu, giving a serious stare, said, 'I think very recently such an intention had entered your mind.'

With a surprised look, Arun asked, 'That is surprising, how come you can read my mind so absolutely?'

'I can read your depression easily,' Anu replied calmly.

Holding her hand with both his hands, he said, 'OK, I promise you that I shall never think of it,' and felt some vibration.

Staring seriously at him, Anu again shot her intense view, as she could not trust his reply. 'Let it be for any reason, you must not.'

Covering her shoulders, he said, 'Yeah, I promise.'

'OK then . . .' Anu was about to say something.

Arun, looking at his watch, asked, widening his eyes, 'How come, Anu, it's really surprising, isn't the time running for you?'

Becoming a bit disappointed, Anu said, 'OK then, bye.'

Heartbroken, Arun asked, 'Really? Are you going?' As she walked a little distance away from him, something began poking his heart.

Slowly, she turned back. 'Arun, can you drop me to my house, please,' Anu's voice was sunk in the sweetness of melody and he was shocked. Jumping high, he caught a tree branch.

'Yesss,' he exclaimed happily. Seeing him swinging Anu giggled.

Arun and Anu walked towards the bike later. As Anu sat behind him on his bike, he felt as though he was on a red magical carpet and floating in clouds. While riding, her hair was dancing with a cool breeze on his cheeks and that made him mesmerized. Riding slowly, with a blush on his face, he said, 'It's my special ride with you,' and nodding her head, she smiled. As her house became nearer, shaking his shoulders, Anu said, 'OK, OK, stop, stop,' but he couldn't hear her.

'My house is located behind this road,' she said loudly, and becoming disappointed, he stopped his bike.

'Anu, can we have some hot food together?' he asked pleadingly.

'Oh no.' Saying this, she gave a pause, and looking around, she said, pointing in the opposite direction, 'Fine, let's have some chats over there,' as there was some food stalls on the footpath.

They crossed the road and reached the food stall; he got a plate of a hot spicy dish and offered it to her. Instead of eating, she fed him but he couldn't swallow it as happiness had filled his stomach.

'Yummy, right?' she asked and Arun was stunned.

Becoming surprised, he asked, 'Is it really that you are doing all this?'

Caressing his hair, she said, 'Yes, fine, I have to move soon, bye.'

Kissing on her wrist, Arun said, 'Anu, you made this day very special to me,' and she tapped on his wrist smilingly.

As she was about to move, he asked, 'Anu, where exactly do you reside?'

Turning back at him, she replied, 'Just behind the parallel street and the left side dead end, it is the third one, the green building,' pointing back with her thumb. 'Bye,' Anu said and slowly walked away.

Looking at her blankly, not realizing that she was not on the street anymore, he stood like a statue until the chat seller, closing his stall and becoming curious, came near him. Removing keys, Arun started his bike, as the chat seller was observing him, and looked at the earring that had fallen on the ground from his pocket; he took it and put it back in his pocket. 'Why can't I take this as a reason to visit her house, yeah?' he thought and went riding to the back street. He stopped his bike a few yards away from the green building. Looking at the green building, he thought, 'What is this?' so many people near Anu's building,' and thinking further, 'I hope it must not be something related to her marriage proposal, let me call up Sandhya.' He called her up but no response and gave a frustrated look. Looking at the building, Arun decided, 'Fine, who cares, let me go directly to her house. If anybody asks, let me pretend to ask some address.' Arun planned and made up his mind to go inside.

Arun came near the house, and his heart started beating faster as he saw people who were very dull and depressed. Near the gate, Arun stammering, asked, 'Excuse me, uncle, what happened?' and that man pointed inside, with no expression, dully. He made up his mind to go inside and removed his shoes.

Hearing cries inside, his heart felt frightened, and as he entered, looking at a frame, becoming frenetic.

'Hey, no . . . no . . no.' He went backwards, banged against the wall, closing his fists tightly. 'How come Anu . . . Anuuu!' he shouted loudly and all of them looked at him.

Taking out the flowers from Anu's photo frame, he said, 'All of you have gone mad, stop this, stop all this nonsense, for God's sake,' and throwing flowers aside, he hugged the frame.

Angrily, seeing that, Anu's father slapped him and pushed him hard on the ground. 'You, brainless, give it to me, have you gone crazy or what? She's no more. Who are you, by the way? Don't create a scene here, just get lost,' Anu's father said, crying, and pointing at Arun, he said, 'Send him away, please, throw him out.'

While they were pushing him towards the gate, Arun said in a high voice, 'Now that's not the matter, she is alive, trust me.'

Someone from the crowd murmured, 'Oh, I got it, he must have fallen madly in love, and becoming heartbroken, he does not believe that she is dead.' Ignoring the people around, with tears rippling, Arun rushing inside went near Anu's mother, who sat like a statue, almost paralyzed.

Looking at her, he said, 'No, aunty, all that is going on here is a lie, don't take it to your heart, trust me, Anu is alive, I . . . I'll tell you, just now, sorry, half an hour back, I dropped her, she even said bye,' and continued, 'Really, aunty, I swear, believe me,' in a shivering voice.

An elderly person looking at him asked, 'OK, where did you drop her?'

'At the end of the street, maybe she didn't come here, wait, she must have gone somewhere. I'll bring her,' Arun said and searched the area around.

Becoming disappointed, Arun went to Sandhya's house and saw her father lay down on a sliding chair alone. Coming near, he asked, almost crying, 'Uncle, did Anu come here?'

'Arun, sorry to say, but Anu is no more,' Sandhya's father replied worriedly.

'Even you're with this answer, I think all of them have gone mad,' he thought and felt frustrated. Pulling his hair, he sat on the ground, and he asked, 'OK, where is Sandhya?' and stood up to move.

'She, I don't know, maybe she's gone to Anu's house. An hour before, we came to know about the tragedy.' As Sandhya's father said this, he went back to Anu's house with a slight hope but he saw the same atmosphere and saw Sandhya coming out from Anu's house. As soon as she saw Arun, she came near him, and holding his cheeks, she cried uncontrollably, which she had suppressed before.

Banging his fist hard, crying, Arun said, 'Oh, Sandhya, don't believe them. Two hours ago, I dropped her at the back street, she was with me since evening, nobody believes it.' Sensing his mind's disturbance, Sandhya immediately called up Nirmala and she tensely came to Anu's house.

Nirmala entered the house and prayed so that Anu's soul would rest in peace. After consoling Anu's parents, coming out with tears in her eyes, and not seeing Arun, she reached her car.

'Didi, Didi . . .' Sandhya called Nirmala but she didn't respond. Arun stood like a rock.

Meanwhile, Madan came and as he saw Arun, saying, 'Arun . . . Arun . . .' shook his shoulders. Seeing him not responding, he went near Nirmala to inform her of Arun's condition.

After a pause, 'Oh, at least will you believe me?' Arun asked and was almost tired.

'Oh, come on, let's go away from here,' Sandhya sounded very depressed.

'Shut up! Let these people come to know that I went to the park . . . I saw Anu.' His words were shivering. Madan came along with Nirmala near Arun and pulled his hands to take him along up to the car.

Seeing that Arun was resisting and not willing to come, Sandhya said in a high pitch, 'Arun, stop it, why you are behaving like this, huh?'

Nirmala seeing them pulling, gesturing at Sandhya, 'OK, trust him, Anu is alive, she's alive, let's search . . .' Stressed the sentence twice. Hearing that, Arun sat in the car, and meanwhile, Madan took Arun's bike.

Arun recalled each and every scene from the park until her house with Anu. After reaching the house, they forcibly took him inside. Helplessly, Sandhya and Madan shared concerned looks and stood looking at Arun.

With a consoling look, Sandhya said in a sharp tone, 'Arun, if she is alive, why should you cry and feel so depressed? You don't have to prove it to anyone. If you think Anu's alive, let's look for her tomorrow.'

Turning towards the other side, Arun said, 'Yeah, you're right. I don't have to prove it to anyone,' and Madan, giving him a hug, caressed his hair. They then went to their homes. Nirmala was controlling her tears and was trying to be normal.

Fixing Anu's image in his eyes, he didn't move until the next morning. Next day, Sandhya and Madan came to Arun's house and Nirmala opened the door. As Arun wasn't there, 'Where's Arun?' Sandhya asked.

'He left in the morning itself, I think he must be . . .' Nirmala also could not speak further and went inside weeping. Madan and Sandhya sadly left from there and reached Arun's favourite park. Leaning against a tree, they saw him sitting. Coming near him, Sandhya called in a very low tone, 'Arun.' He pretended to be fine and with his red soaked eyes, he smiled.

'Even if you don't speak, your eyes are speaking, man,' Madan said slowly. Arun didn't move and was blankly looking towards the ground. Sandhya, looking at Arun, said, 'OK, fine, let's believe that you met Anu and dropped her to her house but you have to know what actually happened on the day you left for Kodai—that was around four o'clock, heavy rain poured with huge hailstones, uprooting several trees all over Bengaluru . . .' Arun felt a bit poky in his heart, as she was coming closer to the conclusion of Anu's disaster. Sandhya, turning back and calling the security guard, requested, 'Uncle, please come here, tell us what happened on that day.'

Looking very disturbed, the security guard said tiredly, 'Yes, pa,' and continued, 'That girl had come, I had gone to my quarters, and before that, I had sent out few slum kids from the front gate, because if they enter, they pluck the flowers and leaves. By the time I returned, I saw them playing with the girl. I thought she might have pulled them from the compound grille, even my daughter was playing with those kids and I went to have tea. It started raining heavily later and your friend helped those children to jump over the compound grille to go outside, but one child was left behind . . .' Arun's heart was drowning uneasily in a pool of pain but his face remained still. 'Your friend jumped inside from the compound to find the girl, to send her outside the park with other children. My daughter saw your friend searching for the girl, and your friend finally found the girl under a tree. She quickly went to reach her; a powerful lightning with big thunder had struck the tree where the girl stood. She quickly ran and pushed the girl aside, the tree fell on your friend.' The security guard's words were gradually receding. He then continued. 'Sacrificing her life, she saved the girl, great, the one who got saved is the only witness to all this and the park was closed for two days, yesterday I got orders from the corporation to open it,' the security guard said and walked towards the gate.

Seeing his ignoring reaction, Sandhya kneeled down helplessly. 'OK, you still don't believe. I am really sorry; your heart is not ready to accept this, right? OK, fine.' Sandhya angrily stood up and pulled a small girl towards him. 'See, she's the proof, children never lie to anyone, this was told by your loved one,' she said, raising her voice emotionally, and the child stood with a frightened look.

Arun, not facing them, yelled, 'Stop this nonsense, please leave me alone, I bet she's going to come, Anu is going to come.'

Hearing that, patting him on the back, the girl said in a frightened voice, 'Yes, uncle, you're right, Anu Didi will come, she promised me also.' Arun, who was facing towards the other side, slowly turned towards the girl, and he immediately threw his arms around the girl. Constantly staring at the girl's jacket, with excitement, he said, 'This is Anu's,' and the girl nodded her head up and down.

With a relieved look, 'See, I told you guys she's fine,' he said.

Looking sharply at the girl, Sandhya asked, 'Come on, tell me what happened on that day.'

'Didi helped us to get inside the park; we all enjoyed in the rain and played so many games. It again started raining heavily and I was standing under a tree. She pushed me and that tree fell on her,' the girl replied. Her parents came, and the girl went along with them to light candles near the uprooted tree, paying their respects to Anu's soul.

Arun was suppressing all his depression and was left only with tears. After lighting candles, as the girl passed near, Arun was looking towards the girl; he showed his arms, trying to imagine Anu, and the girl came running near him.

'Can you give me this jacket?' he asked in a pleased manner. The girl smiled, removed the jacket, and gave it to him. He took the jacket and hugged it. He removed his jacket later and gave it to the girl. The girl met Sandhya's eyes.

'Take it,' she said in a low voice with a smile. Arun became frightened as he saw many people lighting candles near the uprooted tree.

Holding his collar, Sandhya said, crying, 'She is dead, man! I don't have any more strength to prove that Anu is dead, nobody expected this disaster would happen, open your mind to realize the truth.' Becoming depressed, facing the other side of the tree, Madan wept, hiding his face. Controlling himself later, he threw his arms around Arun, and meanwhile, Sandhya slapped Arun hard and Madan was shocked. Arun closed his eyes tightly and hard, Sandhya shaking his shoulders.

'I applied this therapy to you since you only said once that if anyone is paralyzed or very emotional, give them a tight slap and they will become conscious. You are not accepting the tragedy since your heart doesn't have enough strength for it. "This life is full of joyous moments and tragedies. The one who faces all this is an achiever," you told me this once, and how could you behave yourself like this? OK, let me get on to your track that Anu is alive but only for loved ones. If you have seen her, that means she's fine, but according to this world, she is dead,' she said emotionally and, pulling Madan's hand, left the place.

Often turning his face towards Arun, Madan said worriedly, 'Do you think it's good to leave him alone?' while they were leaving the park.

'Let him relieve all his feelings himself, I think that will make him feel better,' Sandhya said firmly and they both left.

Hugging Anu's jacket, looking up the sky, Arun screamed high above, 'Anu, you ruined my wishes, how could you leave me and go?' with pain squeezing his heart.

Prashanth messaged Sandhya, saying, 'Hello, Sandhya, I want to see you right now. Not bothering to see me even after four days, what's wrong?'

After reading the message, Madan said, 'It's not good to hide this from Prashanth.'

'Yeah, I will call Prashanth to inform him about Anu's tragedy, and I'll tell him not to inform Vishaal of this. If he comes to know, it won't be good,' Sandhya said.

'Oh, how could we leave him just like that, if he—' Before Madan could end the sentence, she covered his mouth.

'Arun is not a coward, our best friend and moreover, Anu's best friend.' Sandhya sounded very confident.

Leaving her near her home, he said, 'Sandhya, call Nirmala right now and tell her to go near Arun, bye,' and left the place.

Calling Arun continuously, Nirmala became tense and frustrated as he didn't respond. At 9.30 p.m., the security guard thought of telling Arun to leave the park but he understood his feelings, and after locking the main gate, he left the place without a word. 'I can't leave him alone like that, I think I must go before bad decisions capture his mind,' Nirmala thought and could not sleep the whole night as many thoughts were swirling in her mind. She was waiting for the next morning.

Early morning, Nirmala left the house and reached the park. Closed eyes with wet eyelashes, Arun lay down on the ground. Nirmala, seeing him in that condition, felt very sad. Taking his head on her lap, she gently tapped on his cheeks. Her tears dropping on his face woke him up but he felt it was hard to open his eyes as the sunrays were falling on his face. As he slowly opened his eyes, Nirmala smiled at him with a helpless look; saying 'Didi,' he immediately got up. Making his funky hair proper, he leaned against the tree. 'Sorry . . . I . . .' he said.

Looking at him with pity, 'I know that it is really unfair to lose Anu, especially because she was your loved one. I can understand the pain that is flooding in your heart. Oh, this disaster is unbelievable, but she has sacrificed her life to save someone. You should take her as an example to help others,' Nirmala consoled him but he turned to the other side, pulled his hair hard.

Noticing his frenetic behaviour, catching his collar, she said, 'Surely you'll bring me to this place like you.' She then continued, 'I mean even I have to face the same fate. Your love was given birth a few years back, but my love, affection, and dreams about you were given birth the minute you were born. If you are not happy, then even my life is utter waste, understand?' Nirmala said spontaneously and Arun immediately hugged her.

He wiped his tears and as his throat was getting dry, he made himself strong to speak and said, 'You have mistaken me, Didi, even you're my life and actually more than my life.' Arun was hugging her, and Nirmala cried. Throwing their arms around each other, both went walking slowly later.

After Anu's death, a few days passed by; looking at Arun's depression, Nirmala became anxious although he started behaving normally. Later, Nirmala was discussing with Sandhya and Madan: 'He's speaking to himself in his room, sometimes he smiles and again cries but from yesterday, he's looking calm. I think I need to consult a psychiatrist.' Nirmala sounded very tense.

'Yes, Didi, even we can't see him like this, it's better to go for this option rather than convincing him. Don't worry, we will not let him lose himself in life,' Sandhya said and Nirmala tapped her shoulders. After having a word with Arun, Sandhya and Madan left his room later.

Later, Nirmala met Dr Siddharth; she explained everything about Arun and the incidents of his life. She asked his opinion.

'Nirmala, of course I'm a psychiatrist and surgeon but I'm not an expert to give my opinion for these instances. I believe there's something beyond science. One of the world's most renowned psychiatrists and my senior, Dr John Muller, can clear your doubts. He lives in Germany and often visits India. I'll inform him to meet me when he comes to India. Arun's problem can be solved through his suggestions.' Later, wishing the doctor goodbye, Nirmala left the place.

A few days later, Nirmala got a call from Dr Siddharth. 'Hi, Nirmala, I enquired about Dr John Muller visiting India. He will reach India tonight. I have fixed an appointment with him and he's coming to our nursing home tomorrow evening around five o'clock.'

'Shall I bring Arun along with me?'

'No need, he must not know that he's being treated for his mental condition, OK, bye.'

Next day, Nirmala reached the nursing home and entered the doctors' cabin. Inviting her, the doctor offered her a seat. A few minutes later, dressed in orange clothes, a person entered the cabin and looked like an Indian saint with long white beard. Looking at him, Dr Siddharth got up quickly as he entered and hugged him. Looking at his appearance, Nirmala was surprised. As he sat, Dr Siddharth introduced Nirmala to Dr John Muller.

A little later, Nirmala said everything in detail about Arun's love and his behaviour. After hearing her, Dr John Muller said, 'Ha, I remembered as you were telling this incident, even I had an experience during my childhood when I was about thirteen years old. I was so passionate about cops and I was trying to act like them. I was pretending to shoot the criminals in my imagination. One day, I saw my neighbour friend shooting with an airgun and I asked my mother to buy an airgun. She couldn't get me the gun since we lived in a very small village where the shops didn't sell airguns. My father was working in a city as labourer in a factory and my mother had told me that she would get it when my dad came, in the meantime I became so passive about airguns and began to think about them so much that my thought was penetrating all over my body and all around my surroundings. One night, I got up and began to search for an airgun all over the places in my house, thinking that I had kept the gun somewhere in the house. I understood that it was my illusion only after I got the airgun from my dad. There is nothing to be surprised in Arun's behaviour.'

There was a pause. 'I'm very curious to know but I'm thinking whether to ask,' Nirmala said in a doubtful voice.

'Don't worry, child, I'm here to clear your doubts, you can put forward any question,' Dr Muller said humbly.

'Do ghosts really exist on the earth, and after death, what happens to our life?' Hearing Nirmala's question, Dr Muller laughed and was tapping his kneecap.

'This question is not only haunting you, but most of the individuals on this earth. Everyone wants to know about the life after death. Scientists, scholars, psychologists, parapsychiatrists are trying to find out. Throughout my career, even I was haunted by the same question in my mind and I read all the holy books of all religions to find an answer. Doing extensive research on this topic, searching for the answer, even I travelled and visited many saints in the Himalayan region.

'Finally, I concluded that there's a natural mechanism by which the entire universe functions, I'm terming the whole universe as single body, including all the galaxies and whatever exists beyond our perception or know-how, wherein our earth may be equivalent to a single tiny live particle which exists in our body. And that tiny particle affects or reacts by several known and unknown factors with various chain of a mechanism which exists in our body. In the same way, even birth and death of living bodies are a result of known and unknown process which is happening on the earth. People of ancient civilizations might have had more knowledge or ability to know about the universe, those learned people might have written it in the form of stories mentioning nature's power as God, and that one is the creator and conductor of the universe as the lord in many mythologies to make the common people understand about the universe. The people gradually began to pray to please those powers, later they went on with many rituals, including sacrificing lives, etc.

'Modern science only believes in what it can see, it won't accept by hearing the experiences. Scientists never believed in ghosts or unnatural events happening around. They believe that those are fictions and are fit to be seen only on big screens. Scientists termed ghosts' existence as superstitious and bogus, it's meant to frighten and cheat people. Now visual technology has improved rapidly. Using sophisticated infrared cameras and unidentified voice detectors, many enthusiastic paranormal researchers are venturing out to research the existence of ghosts and they are airing it on the Discovery Channel. Now giving it a scientific term, scientists are terming the existence of ghosts as negative vibration, but at the same time, they deny the existence of ghosts.

'Coming to the subject of life after death, what happens to our life or soul, many people had begun to say that the one who does good deeds on the earth will reside in heaven and the one who does bad resides in hell. This theory was spread by ancestors to prevent sins or crime and to create fear among the people not to get into bad deeds. High above the sky, there's no separate place called hell or heaven. After the death of any living body, its soul or life's elements or atoms remain around us in the earth's atmosphere and are untraceable. Take an illustration of a plant, it has a life, it breathes, feels, and grows. A plant takes its birth from a seed that has come from the earth's properties; the seed is an immovable and lifeless property. Other elements present in nature, such as water, air, light, and heat, help in bringing life to a lifeless seed by converting it into a plant. It means life's elements or soul are definitely present in the earth's atmosphere, and that elements entered in or activated a lifeless seed to convert it into a plant. In the same way, it applies to other living creatures present on the earth.' Meantime, one of the nursing home staff entered the chamber and served coffee to them.

After drinking coffee, Nirmala asked, 'Why are some humans said to have become ghosts after their death?'

'There are two kinds of death, natural and accidental. Natural death means the life in the body stays until the body stops functioning by natural wear and tear of the body, the life in the body feels desire or acceptance for leaving the body voluntarily and begins disintegration of its life or soul from the body mould. Life or soul disconnects its memories of the past life later and that soul or life may take rebirth by natural process, forgetting about the past life. Whereas, in an accidental death caused to the deceased by murder, accident, suicide, etc., if that deceased's life or soul had any passionate desire for its loved one, or unfulfilled wishes or wishes to take revenge against enemies, the deceased's soul or life won't disconnect its memories of the past life and that soul remains as a separate entity in nature since it had left its body mould unexpectedly. It tries to take refuge with another living body or it interacts with the loved ones by creating an illusion in their minds since they also have been thinking about the deceased person. The soul, which has past memories, may drive its loved one or enemy to end their life, some souls might help the loved ones, it all depends in what circumstances a person dies. There's no end discussing about life after death, I have told you very precisely, honestly my views and interpretation may be not cent percent correct,' the psychiatrist said.

'What treatment will be required to end my brother's depression?' Nirmala asked restlessly.

'When she was alive, did she love your brother?' the psychiatrist asked.

'No, I don't think so. She was actually treating my brother as a best friend although he loved her.'

'Then it is OK, I think her wishes still remained, since she saved another life. I don't think you all will have a trouble with the soul, instead her soul might help your brother. His depression will reduce as the time passes. Follow my instructions; I'll let you know what to do through Siddharth,' Dr Muller said and Nirmala nodded her head with relief. After an hour, Dr John Muller left the nursing home.

After reaching home, later, holding a bowl of food, Nirmala entered Arun's room. 'Yeah, I know, Anu, don't worry, both will be fine. I think you're worrying a lot about him, think about yourself also,' Arun was murmuring in his sleep and Nirmala heard his murmur. She sat near him and caressed his cheek. Opening wet eyelashes, Arun woke up and sat on the bed. Nirmala helped him in leaning against the pillow and stretched her hand towards his mouth to feed him dhal rice, but pushing her hand, he refused.

Seriously staring at him, she said firmly, 'Arun, if you don't eat, even I won't eat.'

'Oh please, I'm not able to swallow it. Anu came in my dreams and she's not with me really. I'm almost going mad,' he said, crying, and pressed his face on the pillow. Nirmala put the rice bowl aside and, holding his shoulders, she said emotionally, 'You have got to achieve so much in your life and you shall know your achievement will be her achievement. I mean, why you can't fulfil Anu's wishes and her dreams.'

Listening, Arun said in a dreamy voice, 'What's Anu's dream?'

'Who else knows better than you?' Nirmala replied.

Blankly looking at the ceiling, Arun said, 'Yeah, I must fulfil her dreams,' and Nirmala fed him a bit forcibly.

Later, Arun stood up and walked out from his house. He went to the bus stand where Anu used to wait for her bus. He recalled Anu going in the bus and slowly peeping out towards him. While dreamily looking at the vehicle, a lady stood beside him. She called, 'Anu come fast . . .' As Arun heard, he gave a jerky look and a cute small girl came jumping back of her mother. 'Don't jump like that, Anu,' her mother shouted at the girl. Waving at her, he smiled, and waving her hand, the girl smiled back at him.

Arun reached the construction place where he had celebrated Anu's birthday. Looking up at the sky, Arun said in a loud voice, 'Anu, I'll not cry anymore, I will love you forever.' Looking towards the bright full moon, he continued, 'Oh, you're very happily glowing without any feeling,' he said and closing his eyes, he lay down.

Later, Nirmala called Arun on his mobile; the ringing mobile hadn't alerted him as his mind was blocked by Anu's memories. Seeing Arun lying down on the terrace, the security guard of the construction site rang up to Nirmala, informing her about Arun. Along with the driver, she came rushing near the construction site. Using the lift, she went up to the terrace; she came near him and shook his shoulders but he didn't wake up. She sprinkled water on him and he could see blurry faces.

Nirmala, breathing hard, said, 'Oh, Arun, why don't you let me stay peacefully? The minute you go out, I get so tense.' Giving her the water bottle to drink from, with a restless smile and stammering, Arun said, 'Didi, you're thinking I'm a roadside Romeo, right?'

'No . . . I . . .' Nirmala stammered.

'No, I'm not feeling like drinking liquor. If in case I feel that, then I'm not fit to be your brother and Anu's friend either,' he said in a breathy voice; he got up, holding her arm. 'Come, let's go,' he said and they reached home.

Arun got an email, which read, 'All the best,' when a day was left for the results to be announced, and it was from Sandhya.

'Thanks and wish you the same. Tomorrow, I need to meet you at the earliest possible time,' he replied and he was desperately waiting for the next day. On the results day, he rushed like a rocket to the college early but the gate had not opened. 'Hey, come, what are you waiting for, stupid? Bye, hey, you know . . .' Often all these words were pronounced by Anu and her voice was echoing in his ears. Gripping the college gate, he closed his eyes.

As Sandhya threw her arms around Arun's shoulders, he said in a jerky voice, 'Oops, sorry . . .'

'How are you?' she sounded very concerned.

'Fine,' Arun said with a short smile on his lips but he looked pale.

'Promise me,' she asked.

Giving a confused look at her, he replied, 'For what? OK, fine, I promise.'

'Promise me that you won't cry if in case you see anything related to Anu, I mean, her results,' Sandhya stammered. Arun dully nodded his head and Madan came near them. All the students entered the college and they prayed for Anu's soul.

A little later, the result boards were put up and everyone gathered near it, except Arun. After looking at the result sheet, coming near Arun, 'Wow Arun, congrats, yours is 96 per cent,' one of his classmates said and left the place. Sandhya didn't feel like moving forward to see her result, Madan pulled her and took her towards the board.

Madan, pointing at her result, said, 'Why are you so nervous? You have got 85 per cent,' and Sandhya's shivering finger slowly slid from top to bottom of the result list. Looking at 'Anushika 62%' on the result board, she sat on the floor and started weeping. Consoling her, Madan took her to a nearby bench to sit and said, 'Come on, friend, if you cry like this, then how will we console Arun?'

Wiping her tears, Sandhya said, 'Oh yeah, I am sorry,' making her mind strong, and both came near him.

'Congrats, Arun,' Madan said.

'Yeah . . . thanks,' he smiled with not much excitement and sat on the steps where he used to sit with Anu. 'I didn't see her again except in dreams, I don't know why I'm not able to see her,' he said in a low voice; hearing this, Sandhya suddenly turned towards Arun with an excitement on her face.

'Oh, Arun, did you remember that Anu was saying something, and we thought that she was crazy?'

'What?' Arun asked and jumped on the next step where Sandhya was sitting and caught her shoulders. 'She told us that she was meeting a guy above in the arts section, later she came to know he was already dead . . .'

'Wait . . . wait . . .' He was trying to get her view as well as the clue and immediately ran up the stairs towards the last floor. Madan also went behind Arun but Sandhya, gesturing, caught his wrist and stopped him.

Arun entered the classroom and there was pin-drop silence in there. Looking around, he asked in a loud voice, 'Is anybody here?' and it was echoing. He gave a curious look towards the bench, which had the carved words 'I love Kirthi'.

'Arun, it's a secret, anybody who has true love in their heart, they can see their loved ones who are dead. I know you won't believe it, you always think practically, it's true,' Anu words were wandering in his mind, 'Anu . . . Anuuu,' he yelled but he could hear only his echo.

'You still doubt my love? You are still thinking that there is no true love in my heart—fine, I'll prove myself,' he sounded in a challenging way although he was feeling disappointed, 'I will fulfil your wishes,' Arun said in a loud voice and left the classroom later.

Arun didn't feel like leaving the college. Thinking something, he stood near the bike, looking at the steps where Anu used to sit usually.

Touching his shoulders, Sandhya asked 'Arun, shall we go?'

'Yeah, sure,' he said with a jerked voice and started his bike to reach home.

After hearing Arun's percentage, Nirmala felt very happy, giving him a gift. 'Arun, you'll have some surprise,' Nirmala said and kissed his forehead but he was not so excited. Tapping his shoulders, she said, 'Well done, you got a good percentage, keep it up.' He slowly opened the ribbon and it was a laptop. Arun, throwing his hands around Nirmala, said, 'Thanks, Didi.' .

A few days passed, Arun appeared for the CET exams, and as the results were to be announced in a week or so, Nirmala, patting him on the back, said, 'Next month, there will be counselling, so better be ready with the final decision about the course.' The days were going as usual.

One day, Sandhya called Arun and said, 'Hey, Arun, it's becoming hectic, Prashanth called me up and told me that Vishaal had come to our college yesterday,' she said tensely.

'What?' Arun asked shockingly.

'You don't worry, Prashanth will manage something. Vishaal went to the office and he tried to collect Anu's address, thank God that before he approached the office staff, I informed the office staff not to give any details about Anu.'

Giving a sigh, Arun said, 'Thanks, you helped me breathe back normally.'

The days were going very slowly and Arun was getting bugged. He was getting calls every day from his friends, especially from Vishaal.

'Dude, I'm going mad without hearing her voice,' Vishaal said in a depressed way.

'You're going mad, but me, I'm feeling like as though I'm living in a desert, with nothing left,' Arun also said in the same tone.

'Why, what happened, you broke up with her?'

'Almost,' Arun sounded in a breathy voice.

'Oh sorry, you know it's common to happen in such matters, almost a tsunami had occurred between me and Deepthi but that sweet angel helped us in bringing us together. Now a beautiful relationship has formed, we are ready to move anywhere in the world but I can't see my mentor. I want to meet her. I'll find her definitely and she will cure what is hurting in your heart, that's for sure,' Vishaal consoled him, and as there was no response, he said, 'Hello . . . hello . . . Arun.' Meanwhile, Arun threw the mobile on the bed and went onto the veranda. He bit his lips to control his cry, and Vishaal was thinking, 'Ho, he must have felt bad. Don't worry, you will soon be fine,' said, looking at the blue sky.

The CET results were announced and Arun was the one amongst the top hundred rank holders in science courses. While having their dinner, Nirmala said, 'I won't force you to enter any particular course, I have left it to your wish but choose something related to biology.'

Later, Arun opened his laptop and started browsing the Net to check out what courses he could consider for his future but couldn't decide on any one. He was feeling somewhat stressed and left the laptop switched on. He fell on the cot and, as it was night, gradually fell asleep. He woke up early in the morning and felt like drinking something warm. He prepared coffee for himself and his sister. He went to Nirmala's room but she was not there and he came to know from the driver that she had gone for a morning walk.

Arun took his coffee cup and went to his room. Slowly sipping the coffee, he looked at the street, thinking seriously about the course he should be choosing. Snapping his fingers, he jumped next to his laptop, saying, 'Oh shit, I left it on,' and to his surprise, there was a message in his inbox from an unknown sender whose email ID was trustme@google.com. With a confused look, he thought, 'I haven't given any e-mail ID to anyone, how is it possible that someone . . .' and he opened the inbox and read, 'Why can't you try out the neurosurgeon + psychiatrist as your career?

If you choose this, you can read people's mind to solve their problems.

It's good for your future . . .

Trust me . . .

Your friend.'

Arun was almost frozen.

Arun was soaked in confusion as to who it might be who sent him this message.

Biting nails, he said in a breathy voice, 'Got it, this is amazing, these words sound exactly like Anu's,' and as he slid his finger on the screen, Anu's face appeared. With a smile, he said in a low voice, 'It's become your habit to surprise me,' and he was thinking, 'Let me keep this as surprise.' Filling the counselling form, he said to himself, 'As you wish, Anu, to make your wishes come true, I will always stand by, I love you,' as the windowpanes started banging as a result of a strong breeze. And looking towards the window, he said, 'I know you didn't like my last words, I am sorry, all right,' and went down to the living room later.

The counselling date was nearing and Arun was looking calm but Nirmala seem to look very tense.

On the counselling day, Nirmala asked in a rising voice, 'Still haven't decided your course?'

'Fine, come on, let's go, I'll let you know there,' Arun replied coolly.

'You're disgusting,' she said and sat inside the car restlessly. He sat beside Nirmala and pressed the touchpad. Anu's photo appeared on the screen, the letters came rolling on the screen, 'Neurosurgeon.'

Seeing it, Nirmala said, 'Wow!' and threw her hands around him. The driver looked with a smile at them through the mirror. Becoming a bit tense, Nirmala said, 'But I hope everything goes fine.'

'Don't worry, everything will go on well,' Arun replied coolly. As they entered the CET cell, he sat in a row in the counselling section. Later, the message 'All the best' came and he smiled at the message as it was from Sandhya. Madan had already wished him well early in the morning.

Later, a counselling member called his name; after the counselling, he was selected. He got a seat in the Trinity Medical College and it was the best college in the city but it was quite far from his residence. Nirmala hugged him excitingly. Arun checked email the next day; 'All the best' was the message sent by Anu.

After a couple of weeks, Arun's college started and all his friends had landed in different colleges as they all had taken up different courses. Sandhya took BE in electronics and Madan had taken BSc in physics. Arun became very energetic and Nirmala was very happy seeing that he was back to normal. He entered the college and it was well equipped with good facilities. He didn't interact much with others.

When Arun tiredly came back home, Anu's image on the laptop's screen was making him feel relieved. Like before, he went into his study world, collecting necessary information from the library and the Net about the internal structure of nerves. Studying hard, he went deep into the topic but he was sparing some time for meeting Sandhya and Madan regularly. He finished his first year and got holidays.

Vishaal had taken BE in electronics. One day, he met Arun in the park and they discussed about their subjects. 'You know, Deepthi is going mad by choosing the medical course,' Vishaal commented on Deepthi but Arun was getting bored with her topic. Vishaal continued, 'I have made up my mind to search for Anushika during holidays. I discussed it with Deepthi, she told me that her cousin works in the media, I will get his help,' Vishaal said.

Arun was a bit tense as he was speaking about Anu, and after a pause, Vishaal said, 'Hey, by the way, what about your love?' Vishaal sounded very eager.

'I broke up with her, it is almost one year now,' Arun replied.

'Oh my God, this is really serious,' he said in surprise and continued, 'Then Anushika would feel this is hard to deal with. OK, no problem, she will solve it just like that but I doubt that your loved one hasn't reacted a bit also after you being on her for two long years,' Vishaal angrily said in a high-pitched voice.

'It's wrong to count the days for love. Love always stays in my heart until the world ends or maybe forever.' Arun sounded very emotional.

'I . . . I actually didn't mean it in that way, I meant to say that she's heartless without any feeling,' he said, and hearing his words, Arun pressed his fist hard as he commented on Anu.

'Stop it, enough!' he said in a loud voice and left the park. 'Arun . . . Arun . . .' Vishaal called him but he went away. Frustrated, Vishaal said to himself, 'Sorry dude, I thought you would get better than her.

Later, Arun went to Sandhya's house, and hearing about Vishaal's comments, Sandhya consoled him, 'Relax, why are you so tense? He doesn't know that Anushika is your Anu. If he knew, he would have never commented anything like that,' and he left her home after a while.

Next day, holding the *Times of India* newspaper, Nirmala came near Arun. 'Have a look at this, open to page number 18, see the ad . . .' Nirmala said in a hurried voice and he turned the page to read.

'You were with me in each and every footstep of my difficult and painful life but you disappeared when I stepped into a wonderful life. I need you, my friend. I want to see you, Anushika. I want to . . .

Your loving friend

Contact - 299.................
Address - .... Koramangala'

'What the hell is this? He's gone crazy, and this is not good to keep these matters in silence, it's better to speak out,' Arun said in a very angry tone.

A little later, Arun got a message from Vishaal: 'Tomorrow is Valentine's Day, can you come tomorrow at —? Sorry for . . . if I have hurt you, I hope even you shall be soon with your sweetheart.'

Arun read the message and ignored it.

Later, looking at Anu's image in his laptop, Arun said to himself, 'You have done so much for him, because of you he's living happily. I cannot bear his negative talks about you. God only knows when I'll reveal everything about you.' He then continued, 'Anu, your loved one has called me for the Valentine's Day treat, I swear I'm feeling so sick of him. Please advise,' and he forwarded Vishaal's message to trustme@google.com and later fell asleep.

Next day, Arun woke up around 7 a.m. He was surprised as he saw a message on his laptop: 'Can you do me a favour? Please send lavender and bluebell flowers with lots of love to my Vishaal.

Happy Valentine's Day to all of you.' Arun shivered and felt as though worms were moving in his stomach. Later, after buying a bunch of flowers, he went to the graveyard and placed the flowers on Anu's grave. Tears rippled in his eyes as he kissed the granite of her grave. Later, Arun sent a message that he would come to meet him.

In the Coffee Day restaurant, turning pages of the menu, Deepthi asked restlessly, 'Hey, when is he going to come?' They both were looking quite pretty, with Deepthi being dressed up traditionally and Vishaal, looking handsome like he always did, wearing a bright-colour T-shirt. Wearing a blue jacket, Arun entered the restaurant, as Vishaal ran towards him. Throwing his arms around him and offering a handshake, Vishaal said in a low tone, 'Happy Valentine's Day,' as Arun gave him a flower bouquet, and turning towards Deepthi, Vishaal introduced Arun, 'Deepthi, he's my friend Arun.'

She was frozen looking at Arun, she replied swallowing, 'Hi, yeah, hello, sorry, hi,' and after a pause, she was pretending to call someone. 'One second, excuse me,' she said and left the place. Ignoring Deepthi leaving the place, Vishaal started to speak with Arun, but while replying, he was looking around to see Deepthi, and as he saw her, she immediately pretended to speak with someone on the phone. Looking at the bunch of flowers, Vishaal thought, 'Hey, this is Anushika's favourite,' and as he kissed the flowers, the surroundings became breezy.

A little later, Arun stood up. asking, 'Excuse me, can I . . .' He moved.

Looking at the flowers, Vishaal replied dreamily, 'Sure . . .' and Arun went near Deepthi.

'Hi, Deepthi,' Arun said in a casual voice and she shivered, giving a jerk, feeling guilty, and he continued, 'Come on, relax, this is your new life like a new track and you're very lucky to have such a guy, surely he makes your journey wonderful, come get in,' Arun said. They both went inside and sat beside Vishaal.

Looking at her, Vishaal said emotionally, 'Deepthi, this is unbelievable, these are Anushika's favourite flowers and she insisted to me to present you such flowers once. "These flowers are lucky to present for loved ones," she used to tell me.'

Arun wanted to speak about the newspaper ad, hence he changed the topic and said, 'Why don't you understand, Vishaal? I saw the advertisement in the newspaper. That will not work. You were saying that the girl's, I mean, your friend's family is orthodox, so how can she come forward to see you? Better forget it, your life is going on well, then why do you want to meet her?'

Becoming a bit angry, Vishaal said, 'What do you know about her? I am waiting with rich hopes and looking forward to meeting her. I thought you would support and help me in finding her. Don't try to disappoint me, I'll never lose hope, I'll definitely find her.' Vishaal became depressed and continued to speak 'The day you fell in love with that heartless Anushika, I mean, your Anushika, even you became heartless,' he said, giving a serious stare.

Angrily banging the table, Arun said, 'No, you're wrong, I think you're heartless, more than you, I know about Anushika, alright,' and went away.

'Arun!' Deepthi called him and ran towards the exit door hurriedly. Meanwhile, Vishaal rested his forehead on the table. A little later, looking towards the lavender flowers, he recalled Anushika's each and every word, and as he kissed the flowers, his tears fell on the petals.

Deepthi, coming near him, said in a convincing manner, 'Vishaal, relax, you have no right whatsoever to rate his love. It's not fair, they will have their own liking.'

Giving a jerky look at her, Vishaal asked, 'One minute, what did he say?' and continued, 'Ha, he said, more than you, I know about Anushika.' Who's Anushika and why did he say something like that?' he wondered.

Saying, 'Anushika,' Deepthi was more flummoxed. Looking at the flowers, Vishaal said, 'Hey, he's hiding something, Anushika likes such flowers but how come Arun and the way he sounded was like that? He knows her well, one second . . .'

'Why have you become so hypothetical to his words? Sure, he just blabbered something in anger,' Deepthi said.

A little later, Vishaal gave a call to Arun and the line was busy. 'Oh shit! He hasn't given me his address also, what do I do now?' he said and became very disturbed.

Saying, 'Vishaal,' Deepthi caught his shoulders.

Becoming frustrated, he said in a high voice, 'Please leave me alone, I'm going mad.' Both left the place later.

Later, without having his dinner, Arun dully walked inside the room. Looking at him,

Nirmala said, 'What's wrong with this fellow? Sometimes he will be fine, sometimes he looks as though someone has pan-fried him,' and continued to draw the structural designs.

Arun opened his email and as there was no message from Anu, he said, 'I had expected this,' and with anger looked up at the ceiling. 'I'll tell him about you, I can't bear his talk anymore.' Arun sounded very upset.

Next day, Arun received a message from Anu, 'I think telling him everything would be better. I would like to see how he would react I mean how he feels.'

Vishaal was trying to call Arun and it finally rang. 'Hello,' Arun angrily received his call.

'Arun, please don't confuse me, reveal her identity, I think you know my friend Anushika as well,' Vishaal said and continued, 'Hiding that, you're troubling my heart, is this my destiny?'

Meanwhile, Arun was looking at Anu's image on his laptop's screen as Vishaal spoke and he cut the call unknowingly.

'He is sick . . .' Vishaal hit his wrist against the pillar and Arun realizing immediately dialled Vishaal's number and he quickly responded to the call.

'You know, the heartless Anushika is none other than your childhood friend Anu and my friend as well. Every second, she was thinking good about you and your future. How did you forget your classmate Anu, I mean, Anushika?'

Hearing this, Vishaal became stunned, dropped his mobile and sat on the ground. He recalled each and every moment of Anushika's help. 'I'm sorry . . . I'm extremely sorry . . .' Vishaal murmured with regret.

Vishaal blankly drove his bike back to home and entered his room. He fell off to sleep thinking about Anu. As he saw beautiful eyes, he suddenly woke up, 'Oh, these eyes, it's Anu . . . Anu . . . Anu came in my dream, it was she who used to come in my dreams like an angel many times.' Thinking all this, Vishaal didn't sleep the whole night.

Next day, walking restlessly in tension, Vishaal gave a call to Arun but Arun didn't receive the call, though he called repeatedly and stopped calling.

After a while, Sandhya gave a call to Arun. Looking Anu on the screen, 'Let him feel as much pain as he gave Anu,' Arun said in a grudging tone.

'No, Arun that's wrong, you should not do that. Even Anu had not accepted your love—that means even you're suffering, right? Then why don't you curse her?' Sandhya said. 'I bet you he's now feeling a lot, Prashanth told me that he didn't return home until late night, it's better to tell him everything,' Sandhya requested.

Later, Vishaal called him up and Arun picked up the phone.

'Yeah, Vishaal' Arun said dully.

'Please don't frustrate me, I'm feeling like killing myself. Tell me, where is Anu?' Vishaal pleaded.

'Tomorrow morning, come to the park near St John's Road, you can meet her there, I promise,' Arun replied and disconnected the call.

Wiping his tears, Vishaal said happily, 'Thank you, thanks a lot!' and he ran to the terrace. He remembered once his mother was saying about the Lord Krishna's love story where his childhood friend Radha sacrificed her love, although she loved him. Looking at the full moon, he felt some kind of chillness in his heart and lay down on the swing. Deepthi had called up several times but Vishaal had not responded to her call. She was almost angry so she stopped calling him disappointedly.

Later, a pleasant breeze made Vishaal fall asleep on the swing. Early morning, as the birds began chirping, he gave a sudden jerk, got up, and ran down the stairs. Quickly getting ready, he wore a red jacket and, riding his bike at full speed, went to a florist shop. He bought Anu's favourite flowers and reached St John's Road.

Arun, in blue tracksuit, said 'Hi,' after seeing Vishaal, and both coming near shook their hands. Vishaal was looking around desperately to see Anu, and thinking suddenly, Vishaal said, 'Wait . . . wait, before meeting her, I need to listen to your love venture so that I can make her realize about the commitment of your love, so she could help you succeed,' Vishaal said in a bubbly way and Arun, smiling restlessly at him, said, 'You can't, not even in dreams.' There was a huge lake and they were walking on the bridge.

Becoming surprised, doing back walk facing Arun, Vishaal asked, 'Why, why can't I, don't I have that much right?'

'Fine, I'll tell you, you wanted to know about us, right?' He said everything that had happened from the beginning and finally said that her looks made flowers dance, her smile made petals smile, her presence was the fragrance of flowers. 'I don't know how to express when I fell in love with her but this is how I felt.'

Saying, 'Amazing,' Vishaal felt very inspired and Arun continued, 'I thought she was born for me but when I came to know that her love was dedicated to you, from that minute, I started hating you.' He sounded very depressed. Hearing this, Vishaal realized why Arun had lied about his loved one and was shocked that Anu still loved him, and the flowers glided down from his hand.

Arun caught them before they could fall; giving him the flowers, he said, 'You could not read her love, but at least hold her wishes,' and left the place to jog around the park. The sun was looking dull, as the clouds had partially covered it.

Vishaal, looking at the morning sun, was thinking blankly. 'Oh, Anu, what a sacrifice, for my happiness, you helped me in getting back my loved one although you loved me,' Vishaal said with a smile and tears filling his eyes. Desperately, he jogged around in the park to look for Arun. As Arun came near, he asked, 'I want to see her right now, please, and my heart is bouncing for her. When will Anu come here?' and he was very excited to meet her.

Pointing at the back gate, 'Anu is there,' Arun said.

'She's there,' Vishaal repeated unbelievingly.

'Yeah,' Arun said.

Looking in the bike's rear-view mirror, Vishaal combed his hair, made his jacket collar right, and both went walking towards the back road later. Giggling himself, he recalled Anu in his schooldays and every scene of her. Both crossed the road, as there was not much traffic.

Looking around, breathing hard, 'Where is she?' Vishaal asked and Arun pointed towards the huge rusted gate. Vishaal gave a suspicious look at him and walked behind him. Strong breeze was making the trees branches zoom and it was very pleasant inside.

As they entered the graveyard, looking around, Vishaal said in a suspicious way, 'Is Anu here?' and his heart felt heavier as he was getting closer by and plenty of petals had fallen on the graves. Converting his hands like a hand loudspeaker, turning all around, he shouted, 'Anu . . . Anu!'

Holding his hands, Arun said, 'Come, I will take you,' and took him through a narrow space. Vishaal's heart started beating faster. The weather had become breezier, and an old man came limping with a stick and wished Arun well. He took out fifty rupees and gave it to the old man. The old man smiled and left the place. Vishaal couldn't understand what was going on.

Arun, pointing ahead, said, 'See your Anu there.' Vishaal ran like a mad person and turned back to Arun. With a confused look, he stood and waited for Arun to come.

'See, she's behind you,' Arun said.

Hearing this, Vishaal was frozen and slowly turning back as he saw 'In memory of our sweet Anushika.' He dropped the flowers, and the grave was decorated with flowers. Tapping his shoulders, Arun said, 'You're too late.'

'You're lying,' Vishaal said and pulled Arun's collar hard. He said the whole incident about Anu's tragedy. Becoming depressed, Vishaal slid his hands on the stone and banged his head against the stone. It started raining heavily. Leaving Vishaal alone, Arun dully went to his favourite place and sat where Anu took her last breath.

Later, Arun got a call from Prashanth. 'Hello, Arun, Vishaal met with an accident while driving his bike, sustaining head injuries. He's been admitted in a nursing home and he's completely unconscious.' Arun immediately reached the nursing home and saw Vishaal's parents were waiting outside the ICU room. Vishaal's mother was crying very badly and told him that Vishaal had been kept under observation with the help of a mechanical ventilator (respirator). After checking Vishaal, the doctors came out from the ICU room.

'Sir, how is he now?' Arun asked the doctor.

'Arun, as a medical student, you need to know. Come,' the doctor said and both entered the ICU. Vishaal was lying down, with life support systems. The doctor was none other than Arun's professor.

Later, Arun said, 'Don't worry, uncle, he will be fine.' Coming out and seeing Deepthi crying, he called, 'Deepthi.'

Consoling her, Arun said, 'Trust me, he will be fine.'

'Sorry for Anu,' Deepthi said, crying.

Later, many specialist doctors checked Vishaal. Arun become busy collecting the reports and information. They finally operated, a critical operation that took nearly four hours, and everyone looked tense. After a day had passed, coming out from the ICU room, the doctor said in a low voice, 'He's out of danger, but he's still in coma. He will take some time to come out of it,' and none of them were satisfied with his answer.

Arun went inside the doctor's room to clear some doubts. 'Sir, I don't think it's so easy to cure him, right?' Arun asked doubtfully.

Removing his spectacles, the doctor said, 'Yeah, it's in his parents' hands how well they look after him, if he gets back to normal, it will be a miracle.'

Arun left the room and informed Vishaal's family what the doctor said. He met Deepthi in the hospital canteen later and told her about Vishaal's condition. Deepthi went out with tears. 'Sorry, Anu, seeing him in this condition, I know even you would be feeling the pain,' Arun said to himself and could not control his feelings as he felt very heavy in his heart. He left the hospital and reached his home. He told Nirmala everything as she enquired about Vishaal's condition and finally said, 'Didi, I have to do something so that he becomes normal again.'

'Arun, I wish you succeed, our project is getting closer, so we shall keenly work for it also,' Nirmala said firmly.

'Yeah,' Arun replied and went to his room.

As usual, Arun started going to his college and reached final year. Giving a patient's record to each student, the professor said, 'This is the main turning point in your career, and if you achieve it, then you shall be the masters in the field of neurosurgery,' and he told them to start the treatment. Everyone curiously took it, and a few of them were tense. Day and night, Arun started working on it, putting lots of effort, and reading more and more books had made his eyes stuffed. He was often visiting Vishaal, and one day while talking to Deepthi, Arun consoled her, 'Come on, Deepthi, it's your career, don't play with it. I can understand your situation but you are at the final stage. Work hard and for time being, please come out from your depression, there is no other way.'

Deepthi gradually went back to her studies.

Arun didn't move his book from his eyes. The days went on and he got a great result. There was a campus interview and the probationary selection as well. Arun finally achieved his goal and delighted Nirmala's heart. Her wishes and dreams had become true. But it was to Arun's disappointment he got an appointment in Mumbai, as he didn't want to leave his sister.

Later, Arun got a message from Nirmala's office to come immediately. He dully went to the office and she gave him a letter. He threw his arms around Nirmala as he read the letter that he was selected for a probationary training. It was a neurological research medical centre in Bengaluru. It was the hospital where Nirmala was a partner and also the in-charge of its construction. Dr Siddharth had become the head of the institution.

Becoming happy, Arun said excitedly, 'You know why I'm feeling so happy?'

'Why?' Nirmala asked, giving a broad smile with a confused look.

'Because my Anu had stepped into this hospital,' Arun said.

'Oh, all the best,' Nirmala said and hugged him.

Arun went to the neurological research medical centre. Arun had completed two years of probationary period and profoundly completed the course. The days were going faster, and Arun was treating a lot of patients successfully. He spent most of his time in treating the patients. But Arun was feeling the days were going slower as his loved one was no more and his friend Vishaal had not shown any improvement as well.

Deepthi was doing her medical practice in Chennai. One day, Deepthi called him up from Chennai. 'Hi, Arun,' And she asked, 'How is Vishaal?'

Meanwhile, Arun was near Vishaal and replied, 'Yeah, still he's in the same condition, I'm speaking in front of him,' and he slid his palm on Vishaal's forehead. Hearing this, Deepthi said, 'On the speaker, Arun, let Vishaal hear my voice.'

Arun kept the mobile near Vishaal's ears; Deepthi spoke. 'Tomorrow I'm coming, Vishaal. I've missed you all these days, I'm frustrated without you. I love you,' she said and kissed her mobile. His face was dim with shrunk forehead and his eyes were still open. After a pause, Arun said, 'One more thing, I have to attend a campaign in some village so I won't be here for a week, OK, bye,' and ended the call. Arun successfully completed the campaign in the village and returned.

In the neurological medical centre, the senior surgeon as well the dean of the college was addressing the junior doctors. 'Each of you must take up a patient's case separately and should analyze the health and mental condition for treating the patient. Everyone should submit the patient's treatment report once in a week without fail. All of you will get the patient's details tomorrow. This will be a final test to prove themselves as specialists. In future, of course you all will have to face challenging tests but this one will be a first test for moving to the next level in your profession and thereafter your journey starts as a specialist doctor,' Later, the day's classes were over.

Arun removed his spectacles and lay down on the cot. He felt nice and smiled, closing his eyes as Nirmala was massaging his forehead.

'Hello, doctor, you have to look after the patients. If you're tired like this, then how will you handle the patients?' said Nirmala, who made fun of him, and he sat leaning against the pillow later.

'For the first time, I'm taking a patient's case individually, I'm feeling somewhat—' Arun sounded surprised.

'Are you becoming tense?' Nirmala questioned.

Taking out the patient's report, he replied, 'No, not at all, but it's unbelievable,' and he opened the file. The report was about the weakness of nerves of the patient called Rohit Sharma. 'This case looks like it's simple, we can make cure him with medicines and it's not a serious one,' Arun murmured to himself and put the file aside. Nirmala went down the stairs to bring him coffee later.

Next day, Arun opened his laptop to download the patient's condition and looked at Anu's image on the screen. Looking at an email, his eyes turned wide with astonishment as there was a long email from her. 'Oh, it seems something serious,' Arun said in a low tone to himself, and he read, 'Arun, why can't you take up our sir Subhas Karuna's case? He was one of our college's beloved sirs. He's done so much for the society and fought against criminals. Why can't you be a helping hand to him? I mean, you know he's lost his memory for the past eight years. You can bring him back to normal, I hope you have that capability, all the best.' And becoming stunned, he began sweating. Removing his spectacles, he said in a breathy voice, 'Great.'

Later, Arun reached the neurological centre. 'Good morning, sir, a small request.' Arun spoke with his senior doctor.

'Yeah, tell me, Arun,' the senior doctor asked.

'Can I take up another patient's case?' he asked slowly.

'Why, are you feeling that this case is difficult?' the doctor asked.

'Not at all, I have another option if you can accept it, sir, he's lost his memory for the past eight years, sir,' Arun said.

'Oh, you need to get on to the critical case directly. I don't mind, go for it, but on one condition: firstly I want to see the patient's history and you will be reporting all the details as and when you check,' the senior doctor said. After wishing him goodbye, Arun went for wards' round-ups.

Next day, Arun went to the Presidency College to meet the principal and wished him well.

'Yeah, tell me, have you studied here before?' The principal sounded perplexed and was trying to set his spectacles right on his bony nose.

Offering a handshake, he said, 'Yes, sir, I'm Arun.'

'Now what are you doing?'

'I finished my medical, sir.'

'Oh well, it's nice to hear.'

'Sir, can you tell me about Prof. Subhas Karuna? I mean, about his past life before joining this college.' He sounded very desperate.

'I know but not much in detail. He often spoke about his best friend Ram Desai; you can ask him if you want to know the complete details. I will give you the address,' the principal said and gave him the address.

'Thanks a lot, sir,' Arun said and came out from the principal's room.

Arun walked towards the field, turning back to his past memories. With a blank look, imagining Anu, he sat on the stairs blindly.

Later, tapping his shoulders, the security guard said, 'Hello, sir, it's time up, we are closing the gate.'

With a sudden jerk, Arun enquired, 'Oh, do you know an old man called Srinivas Gowda?'

'I don't know, sir, I joined here recently,' the security guard replied. Arun didn't feel like leaving, but with heavy heart, he left the place. He dreamily leaned against the gate and he looked at the spot where his friends were usually grouping, including Anu.

'Hey, don't think so deep, I'm always with you, right? You're often speaking with me and I can know every feeling that arises in your heart.' He felt as though Anu was speaking but he could see no one in the field, and he left the college.

Later, Arun reached Ram Desai's residence, pressing the call bell several times. 'Excuse me, anybody here?' As there was no response, he was fed up, and a little later, he went to the neighbouring house and said, 'Hello, I'm Doctor Arun, where's Ram Desai?' he asked the neighbour.

'He's gone to his village long ago,' the neighbour replied.

'Can you tell me where exactly he's gone?' Arun enquired in detail.

'He's gone to Kurubana Halli near Mandya.' The neighbour patiently gave details.

'Thank you, sir, can you give his contact number?' Arun asked and the neighbour obliged. Later, he gave a call to Ram Desai.

'Hello, this is Ram Desai, tell me.' He sounded polite.

'Hello, sir, I'm Dr Arun, can I come to your village tomorrow? I need to speak to you about Prof Subhas Karuna, I was his stud—' Before he could finish, Ram Desai replied, 'No, I don't know any Subhas Karuna,' and disconnected. With frustration, Arun gave him a call again.

'Sir, please trust me, the principal himself has given your address. I know Karthik and about the foundation,' Arun said, pleading.

Accepting finally, Ram Desai said, 'Fine, you come by 8 a.m.'s train and stay at the Mandya station, I'll receive you.'

'Yeah, sure, thank you, sir,' Arun said and ended the call.

Ram Desai immediately called up Karthik.

'Yes, sir, how is Subhas, sir?' Karthik asked.

'He's as usual, no change and no reaction either. A guy called me and said that he's Dr Arun. He took out your name and enquired about your professor. Do you know him well?' Ram Desai asked, and Karthik, becoming curious, said firmly, 'Ha, Arun, ha, I knew him well, he mentioned doctor. I think he's completed his medical. OK, no problem, you can meet him.'

'OK then, bye,' Ram Desai said and cut the call.

Next day, Arun boarded the train. Later, through the train's window, he saw women going in a line, holding paddy grass in a paddy field. As he saw a girl catching a pot, he suddenly stood up and he pulled the chain quickly. As the train stopped, he quickly jumped out from the train and ran between the paddy field to reach her but he fell on the ground and couldn't find her. Looking around, he screamed, 'Anuu . . .' and his head was right below the hot fuming sun. He could see Anu covering her face to protect herself from the bright sunrays, and everything vanished in no time.

A little later, the train in-charge shouted, 'Hey, who pulled the chain?' and got down from the train. Coming near Arun, he gave an angry fuming look at him.

'Sorry, sir,' Arun said.

'Do you know that you have to pay 1,000 rupees as fine?' he said and Arun gave him the money. As Arun was looking around, the train in-charge asked, 'Why did you pull?'

'I saw a girl . . . my girl—' he stammered.

'No, don't fall in such love, you're looking very innocent, don't pull the chain again like this,' the train in-charge warned before he could finish. Arun slowly nodded his head. He saw the passengers were murmuring and they were giving grudging looks at him.

'Sorry I went to search for my love but she wasn't there,' Arun said in a high-pitched tone but everyone ignored him.

Looking towards the paddy field, Arun sat restlessly and later moved to the next coach as Mandya station was nearing. He stood near the door and got down at the Mandya station. He enquired about Kurubana Halli and gave a call to Ram Desai later. Ram Desai asked Arun the clothes he was wearing; as he said, 'Sky blue with grey jacket and cream jeans,' someone touched his back later and Arun turned suddenly.

'I'm Ram Desai, and you?' he asked.

Offering a handshake, he replied, 'I'm Dr Arun, pleased to meet you, sir.' Ram Desai boarded a local bus, accompanying Arun. Later, after alighting from the bus, both went in a bullock cart, as the village was about three kilometres ahead.

Later, getting down from the bullock cart, Ram Desai walked towards the large wooden gate, and there were many goats wandering around the place. Looking around, Ram Desai opened the gate and entered the house. It was an old building and was supported by wooden pillars. Arun saw a family group photo frame and thirty-two members in it.

Pointing at a person in the frame, Desai said, 'See, I'm here, this is my family photo.' He showed Arun and continued, 'This is my ancestor's house, our childhood life was wonderful. Subhas and I used to run around the fields, plucking green vegetables and leaves to give them to our mothers and they were so delicious, do you know why?'

Arun stood blank and Ram Desai laughing at him, said, 'Because we had stolen them,' and further continued, 'In every stage of our life, we both stayed together in happiness and thorny moments. Oh, why did you want to know about him?'

Stammering, Arun said, 'Because I was his old student so . . .' and continued, 'I want to know . . . to treat . . .'

'Fine, I'll tell you in detail, we were both together and were brought up here in this village. Subhas's father was arrested during the Quit India movement. Boycotting the studies, we both participated along with other students though we were studying in high school. Subhas headed the students to protest and the police officers started beating us. Rescuing us, in turn he beat the police very badly. He was arrested, and you know, his mindset was like his father. After independence, we all moved to Bengaluru and shifted our family to stay there permanently. Later, he got his job in the Presidency College as a lecturer, after twelve years he got married and got a girl child later. Feeling proud, he named her Prajwala. Our deep friendship had enforced us to stay in houses opposite to each other. I had a son serving in the army and I lost him in the Indo-Pak war. After a few years, my wife also expired in depression.

'Subhas didn't allow me to go back to the village. I stayed with him and used to play with his daughter. I had great time with her, and several times it made me feel that if my son was alive even he would be having a daughter like this. The days were going happily and they celebrated her daughter's seventh birthday. Meanwhile, his wife, who was pregnant, had a miscarriage and that resulted in her death. The girl was left lonely and he had lost himself. Giving advice, I said, "Subhas, if you're like this, who will look after your child? Don't be distressed, think of your daughter's bright future ahead, your wife's soul will feel happy," and he started his routine life. He had to go to Mumbai since his mother had died in his younger brother's house. Forwarding her responsibility on me and with an aged woman who was looking after her, he went, leaving his daughter alone. I stayed in his house and he used to call up every day to speak with his daughter. One day, while I was going for a morning walk, I saw some young guys watching at the gate who were looking drunk. As I gave them a serious stare, they went back and I told the maid to be careful and I went to market later.

'Meanwhile, on the terrace, Prajwala was playing with a ball. As the ball fell on the ground, the girl called the maid but she didn't respond as she was busy preparing breakfast. To take the ball, the girl went down the stairs. Meantime, one of the guys in the gang, who was hiding, entered the house. As he tried to catch the girl, she screamed at the maid but she was far from her and could not hear. The maid finally heard the girl's scream, she tried to rescue the girl but as she saw weapons, she fainted and was on the ground. Those guys pulled Prajwala into the room and tried to molest her. Trying to escape, she ran and went to the terrace frantically. As they chased her on the terrace, the girl jumped from the terrace to escape from them and died on the spot. The police investigated and arrested those guys later. One of the guys was a minister's son who tried to molest the girl and he had been charge-sheeted on several rape cases before. Though the court had pronounced life imprisonment, his father's influence had facilitated him to escape while on the way to the prison.' After hearing this, Arun's blood began boiling and closed his fist tightly and hard.

'Even I was the reason for the girl's death,' Ram Desai said with depression.

'No, sir, please calm down, it is not your mistake, it's our society's fault and others should have come forward for rescuing the girl.' Arun sounded upset.

Further continuing, Ram Desai said, 'After the incident, Subhas Karuna didn't even speak a word, he was immediately taken to the hospital and there he neither cried nor moved. The very next day, he disappeared from the hospital. After a few years, I saw him with some gang and came to know that he had begun to punish criminals.'

Arun worriedly said, 'After sir was injured, Karthik had given me an address to escort him. Thereafter I don't know whereabouts of sir. I couldn't even find Karthik, I want to see them.'

A little later, through a narrow passage, Ram Desai took him from the back door. They entered a small room and Arun couldn't believe his eyes. He saw Subhas Karuna lying down on the bed. He slowly opened his eyes later. Checking his injured head, Arun smiled at him. 'Those goons tried to track his whereabouts and they finally traced him. As they had planned to attack, Karthik rescued your sir from them and he was brought here later. I've been looking after him since then,' Ram Desai said.

'Sir, now already eight years are over. I will take care of sir now; I mean I'll take him to the hospital for the medical treatment. It's a very safe place. Please send him with me,' Arun requested, and meantime, Ram Desai got a call from Karthik. He informed Karthik about Arun's view and gave the phone to Arun.

'Hi, Karthik, I'm taking sir from here.'

Before Arun could continue, Karthik said, 'Hi, Arun, you can take him for the treatment but be careful. I have completed my police training. Now I'm in Bengaluru as SI in Banashankari police station. You take note of my number, call me in any emergency, take care, OK bye,' and he ended the call. Later, Arun gave a call to Nirmala for sending the driver to Ram Desai's house and informed her of the address and the exact location.

Later, Ram Desai served lunch to Arun; he asked about Subhas Karuna's past medical records later, and thinking slowly,

Arun questioned, 'Sir, do you have any things that belonged to his child? I mean Prajwala's belongings.'

Recalling, Ram Desai said, 'No, I don't know what happened to all those things but he had given me a video camera with a couple of tapes, to keep it safely.'

'Can I have it, sir?' Arun sounded doubtful. Throwing a serious look at Arun, without speaking, Ram Desai walked inside the room and he came out with the medical records and the videotapes.

Giving the medical records and videotapes, Ram Desai said worriedly, 'If my friend gets well soon with these, that will be more than enough for me.' Inserting the tape into the video player, he played the tape and he could see blurry figures. After setting it right, he saw Subhas Karuna feeling very happy looking at the just-born baby, and from the day she was born, he had taken her video until her seventh birthday. He saw Subhas Karuna's excitement and happiness seeing his daughter's first walk. Later, rubbing his nose, Arun turned off the video player and silently walked out to see whether the car had arrived.

After an hour, the driver Lokaiah entered Ram Desai's house. Arun and the driver carefully carried Subhas Karuna and laid him comfortably inside the car. Offering a handshake to Ram Desai, Arun said, 'OK, sir, bye, you shall see your friend soon in a normal state hopefully,' and the car moved.

Later, bearing a fictitious name in the hospital records, Subhas Karuna was admitted in Arun's hospital and he was kept separately. In order that his identity remained unrecognizable, his head and face were shaven neatly.

A few days later, after reading all the medical records of Subhas Karuna in detail, Arun rang up Karthik and he asked about the details of Subhas Karuna's daughter's molester.

'Yes, Arun, I was enquiring but I think we need to give some gap for the enquiring process because his father has become an ex-minister now. If I start enquiring openly about the case, some informers in our department will alert him to be careful and he might vanish. As far as I know, he's secretly roaming, bearing other person's identity. I have already put up my guys near the ex-minister's residence for surveillance.'

'Do you have his photo?' Arun asked anxiously.

'No, the police have destroyed all his records and evidence when his father was a minister. I'm still trying to find his photo through the old newspaper photo clippings. By chance I may find it in the bureau office, I mean, if sir has kept it secretly. Today I'm going to look for it,' Karthik said and disconnected the call.

Karthik immediately went to the Presidency College, taking the bureau room door's key from the office, opening it, he entered the room and the place was almost empty, with an old cupboard. The room was filled with dust and he stood for a while with disappointment. Looking around, he saw some newspaper rolls which were stuck to his footwear; taking it, he looked at those paper sheets and it was dated back to twenty-five years. Becoming curious while looking at the news contents of that paper, he saw a photo with news report below. The news pertained to Subhas Karuna's daughter, and he read the news report. He was relieved as he got the culprit's identity and the photo as well. The culprit was charged for several rapes and murders, and his name was Afzal.

Later, checking all other criminals' photos in the criminals' data records, Karthik found that Afzal almost matched a guy named Acid Rafiq, who was aged about forty-eight years and he was convicted for raping nearly twenty women and killed twelve of them. He was in the absconding list, and Karthik sent both the photocopies to his guys for the identification. Day and night, his guys watched the ex-minister's house, and one late night, disguising as a fakir, Acid Rafiq finally entered the minister's house and Karthik's men followed him up to his secret hiding spot. The court had already passed an order to catch him dead or alive, and he was in the encounter list as well. Karthik rang up to Arun and informed him about his findings.

'Soon he will be encountered, we have made up final plans to end him with utmost secrecy,' Karthik said grudgingly.

'To make sir's treatment a bit easier, and a help from you, is it possible to take . . .' Arun spoke in detail.

'Yeah, sure, I'll make it,' Karthik said and ended the call.

The time was around 11 p.m. and a narrow street almost looked deserted. Failing to start their scooter, two ladies stood helplessly near the scooter, looking around. Since they wore shorts, both looked very attractive and sexy. After some time, seeing them from a nearby building, a guy came out enquiring and pretended to help them. Inside the building, peeping through a window, another guy was looking at the ladies; his mouth watered since for a long time he had not had sex and he was none other than Acid Rafiq alias Afzal. Gesturing at the other guy, he came rushing outside to catch the ladies. As they were trying to catch them, one of the ladies kicked hard on one of the guys' sensitive spot. Holding it, screaming loudly, he was on the ground and he was Afzal. The other guy received a severe blow on his stomach; meanwhile Karthik and his men soon covered both the guys. Filming them, they broke their arms and limbs with severe blows on their body. One of Karthik's men poured acid on Afzal's face and his loud outcry reached the sky. A lady pierced an injection coated with Mruthyu moolika on both the guys. Later, they left the place, and in the early morning, both criminals lost their breath with dreadful pain.

Next day, the incident had become a main headline in the newspapers and TV channels. Hearing of the death of Rafiq and the other guy, everyone in the city was relieved. Giving an interview to the news reporters, Karthik said, 'The investigation is on and our guess is that someone close to them might have done this due to some personal rivalry. Anyway, the most wanted criminal is no more. We will investigate further, thank you,' and left the place.

After a few days, Karthik came to the hospital and gave the videocassette to Arun. Later, Arun in his house was training a small girl. 'Hey, Latha, come on, scream, yes, scream, yeah, exactly like this, OK, remember.'

A little later, curiously looking at them, Nirmala said, 'What! Arun don't say that you have got bugged of the medical profession and want to get into some film direction,' as Arun was training the neighbour's daughter to say a sentence.

'No . . . I just . . . just like that, I was bored,' Arun stammered.

'Hey, what, you guys are hiding something.' Nirmala sounded suspicious and the girl ran away. Nirmala felt peculiar, seeing him working out with some sound systems and speakers. 'Actually what are you up to?' she asked him curiously.

'Oh, I'll let you know soon,' Arun replied with frustration. He prayed to his mother and left for the hospital after having a light breakfast along with the small girl.

In the neurological medical centre, Mr Ram Desai was waiting desperately to see his friend.

After reaching the hospital, Arun called Karthik.

As he was driving, Karthik replied, 'Yes, Arun, I'm on the way.'

Later, Subhas Karuna was taken to the soundproof room, and Ram Desai went running behind the stretcher. He caught his arm and kissed his wrist.

Tapping Ram Desai's shoulders, Karthik said, 'Don't worry, sir, he will be fine.'

Arun took Karthik and the small girl into the soundproof room. Becoming anxious, the girl was looking all around. Arun connected his heartbeat to the cardiac reader. The pulse rate was going normal and it was constant. The nurse gave an injection and Arun told the nurses to move out later. Arun fixed the earphones to the girl and Karthik. Standing next to the sound equipment to adjust the volume, Arun asked with a keen look, 'Are you both ready?' and raised his thumbs up at Karthik to turn on the tape recorder.

'Daddy . . . Daddy . . . Daddyyyyy!' It was Subhas Karuna's daughter Prajwala's voice and they had recorded it from the old videocassette.

'Help me, Daddy, please get up, they're going to kill me,' the girl screamed in Subhas Karuna's ears. Arun was observing the cardiac reader and Subhas Karuna simultaneously, and the pulse rate was normal.

'Sweetie, go on with the same way, good, keep continuing it,' Arun said in a low voice, and the girl gestured as she had the voice contact with Arun through the earphone. Arun again raised his thumbs up, and Karthik played the cassette again. The cardiac reader started increasing as soon as his daughter's voice came out, and the pulse scale started increasing.

'Come on,' Arun said and the girl screamed more loudly. 'Yeah, yeah, come on . . .' Arun gestured continuously and raised his hand upwards to scream more loudly. A little later, Subhas Karuna breathed out very hard and pushed the girl. 'No!' he shouted and became unconscious later.

'Nurse,' Arun yelled and ran towards Subhas Karuna. He pumped his heart quickly, and Subhas Karuna opened his eyes slowly. He closed his eyes as the nurse injected.

Seeing Subhas Karuna pushing the girl, Karthik felt very happy. He quickly went outside and threw his arms around Ram Desai.

Later, tapping Arun's shoulders, the senior doctor praised him. 'Great job, his pulse rate is running normal, you have done a very difficult task.'

'Will he be fine?' Arun asked.

'Yeah, but you have to keep him under an intense observation since you have recalled him into the past incidents and still he's in the past. There are chances that he might again lose his memory,' the senior doctor gave his opinion and Arun was not happy at what the doctor said.

Arun immediately spoke to the nurse about his condition and the treatment to be given. Later, Subhas Karuna opened his eyes slowly and suddenly turning around, he screamed, 'No, don't kill her . . . I'll kill you all!' and Arun immediately pushed Karthik in front.

Meeting his eyes directly, Karthik said firmly, 'Relax, sir, I killed them, your daughter is safe with us, see,' and he pushed the girl towards the professor.

Arun gestured to the girl, and she, realizing, said, 'Daddy, I'm fine now,' and threw her arms around him. Arun observed the cardiac reader and the pulse rate was becoming normal. Though Arun was sweating, he felt very relaxed and came out to have some water.

Turning towards Karthik, Arun said, 'Now slowly sir is remembering all the incidents back in his mind, I think you know his past very well, so you need to stay here with him,' and Karthik hugged him with tears in his eyes. Later, Arun went home.

Around midnight, Arun got an emergency call from the hospital. He immediately woke up and reached the hospital.

The professor frantically shouted in a high tone, 'I want to kill him! I want to finish him, move out of my way all of you,' and sounded very pained as well. He was losing his balance, he had fallen on the ground. He saw a medicine bottle come rolling near his feet, and taking it, he hit hard on the ground to break it. He showed the sharp broken glass pointing towards Arun and the nurses standing around.

Arun, coming near the Professor in a prompt way, said sharply, 'Sir, whom do you want to kill? Tell me, I will bring them here.'

The Professor tried getting up but he couldn't. Looking at Arun later, the professor said, 'No, I don't want anybody's help, leave me,' and went he sliding on the ground using his palms and weak knees.

Arun, turning back, called loudly, 'Karthik come inside,' and the professor gave a jerky look. Ram Desai and Karthik came running inside, and the professor showed the broken glass even to them. Seeing his behaviour, they were shocked.

Becoming heartbroken, Ram Desai said, crying, 'Kill me, man, instead of dying every second with pain, it's better to die at once. I have remained calm all these days just because of you. If you're acting wild like this, not even recognizing me, then for whose sake shall I lead my life?' As Arun gestured at the nurse, she took Ram Desai out.

Looking at the professor, Arun said firmly, 'Professor, please trust us, firstly watch this video and then decide to go, we will let you kill whomever you want to,' and meanwhile, Karthik played the cassette. Afzal appeared on the screen and the professor's eyes slowly moved towards the screen. Though he looked aged with change in hair colour, nevertheless, Afzal's face resembled almost as before. Recognizing him, clutching the glass hard, Subhas Karuna screamed angrily and his hand started bleeding. Karthik went forward with a tense look, but Arun gestured at him not to go. The professor was so angry that he felt like smashing the screen and his eyes turned red.

Looking at the screen, 'He's dead,' he said in a hard grudging voice.

'Yes, sir, he's no more,' Karthik said proudly and stood in front of the professor. As Subhas Karuna felt dizzy, all of them lifted him and they put him on the bed. While Arun was injecting medicine, the nurse, using a probe, was removing the glass pieces carefully and dressed the wound later. Later, she gave him glucose drips and injection. Arun watched the cardiac reader and saw the heartbeat becoming normal.

Arun breathing hard, said with a short smile, 'Thank God, your friend is back to normal.' With happy tears in his eyes, Ram Desai took his wrist closer to his chest. Arun tapped Ram Desai's shoulders and Karthik greeted him.

As morning was approaching, Arun and Karthik went to the terrace, to inhale cool air. Karthik took out the filmed cassette of Afzal's encounter from his pocket and set it afire. Looking at Arun, Karthik said, 'All these days, I had the tension since we had left only this proof behind his death, now it's over,' and the cassette was burning right in front of them. As smoke began rising, 'Atishoo hey, I'm allergic to this plastic burning smell,' Karthik said, sneezing.

Arun smiled and said, 'Of course, but you're more allergic to criminals,' and Karthik giggled. Later, the birds started chirping and the sun rose by spreading its golden rays.

Pointing towards the sun, Arun said, 'This world shall be filled with brightness and shall spark like that.' Arun kept his calls unanswered as he tiredly got back to home later.

In a park, while Nirmala was jogging along with Dr Siddharth, she was excitedly sharing her happiest feeling. 'Yes, now all my responsibilities are over, I am left with only one responsibility—that is to see a life partner for him, thereafter I'll relax.' And after a pause, Nirmala said with a smile, 'Today is his birthday. Through email, I have sent him the brides' details along with their photos.'

'All the best to you and the bridegroom,' the doctor said and they continued to jog towards the car.

Nirmala got into the car and reached home later. She entered Arun's room and saw him sleeping. Entering the washroom, she took a jug of water and she splashed it on his face. Giving a big jerk with shock, seeing that he was wet, he chased her. Snatching the jug, he splashed the remaining water on her face. Looking at them, one of the maids was murmuring to the driver, 'Many years were over seeing something like this. After such a long time, they are playing again.' Splashing water on each other, they both were running all over the garden.

Later, offering a handshake, she said smilingly, 'Fine, happy birthday, there's a surprise gift for you, see your email.' At breakfast, swallowing hot lemon rice, he gave a puzzled look at his sister. He walked into his room later and checked his email; he saw many girls' snaps with their details, all lined up on the screen. Angrily murmuring, he left the house and headed towards the hospital.

Reaching the hospital, Arun straightaway entered Subhas Karuna's ward. 'How is he now?' he asked the nurse.

'Sir, he's still unconscious,' the nurse replied.

Looking at the cardiac reader, Arun said, 'No, there is time, almost half a day left,' and left the room. Arun got a call from Nirmala as he entered his cabin and ignored it.

Hurriedly coming near Arun, a nurse said, 'Sir, an emergency case,' and he quickly went to the fourth floor. Near the emergency ward, he saw many were crying, including a small girl who was knocking on the door.

Arun went inside and saw a woman aged about thirty-five years. Her head was bleeding very badly. Looking at the previous reports, Arun enquired about the case, and it was an accident which had happened about a week ago. Her head was bleeding but other wounds on her body were in the process of healing. They took her to the diagnosis room immediately.

Pulling Arun's coat, the girl asked, 'Will my mom be OK? Tell me,' while Arun moved along the stretcher.

Caressing the girl's cheek, Arun said, 'Don't worry, your mom will soon be all right and she will play with you,' but the girl followed up to the diagnosis room.

After doing the diagnosis, the senior doctor said, 'Arun, that's not so critical, one of the nerves has deeply got hurt and if we operate she will be all right.'

Arun sat in his cabin thinking about Anu and saw Nirmala entering the cabin. He gave a sudden jerk. Looking at him, she said warningly, 'See, Arun, you can tell me your final decision by tomorrow. I don't want our family's generation to end because you are not marrying. I want you to start a new life. This is my last wish,' and she went hurriedly. His head started prickling with pain and dully he walked towards the corridor. He saw the girl sitting on the chair sadly.

'Why didn't you go home?' Arun asked her and she didn't speak a word.

As the girl was sitting alone, looking around, Arun asked, 'Where are the others, your father and your uncle?'

'Will my mom be fine?' the girl asked again, and he smiled.

Later, Arun went to the dining hall to have his lunch. He recalled what Nirmala had told him. 'This is sick,' Arun said and pushed the plate away. He hardly took four to five spoons of rice and came restlessly walking back to his cabin after checking Subhas Karuna's condition. He rested his head on the table and was worried about Nirmala's warning. The time was around 11 p.m. and he was feeling very sleepy, as he had not slept properly for the past four days. He heard someone knocking on the door. 'Yes, come in,' he said in a tired voice, and the door slowly opened. He looked up and it was the small girl. 'Hey, come on, get in,' he said.

'Somebody is waiting for you on the top floor, aunty told me to inform you,' the girl said.

'Who is it?' Arun asked curiously.

'I don't know,' she replied and left the room.

Using the lift, Arun went to the top floor and entered the terrace. The moon was shining more brightly than usual. He looked around to see the lady but there was none. He looked at the sky, thinking about Anu wishing him well, many years back. As Arun said, 'Anu, today is my birthday,' suddenly spreading light across the terrace, a bright transparent flower bouquet in blue and white approached and it zoomed up in the sky. Opening his mouth wide, 'Anu . . .' he called in a loud voice and soon a bright transparent cake with candles lit on it, circling around him, went up in the sky. As he sensed the sound of a birthday song, 'Anuuu!' he went calling loudly all around the terrace and kneeled down tiredly.

'I want to see you or else I don't know what will happen to me. Speak, Anu,' he said loudly with distress. Anu had appeared and looked like a blossomed flower. Arun could not speak as he felt as though something blocked his vocal cord.

'Arun, happy birthday, please cure my Vishaal and get him back to normal. It's my last wish. Bye,' Anu said and kissed Arun's wrist. She vanished suddenly.

Becoming half-conscious, Arun lay down for a while and everything looked like a dream. He slowly opened his eyes and everything was looking blank. As he felt some kind of chillness, he went near the water tap, which was at the terrace corner. He splashed some water on his face and he could make out things around, except Anu. Looking up at the sky, he said, 'Anu, what a surprise, your appearance has made me feel so good, bye,' and blew on his palm pointing towards the moon. He recalled everything that happened an hour before on the terrace, and the girl. He rushed towards the fourth floor later.

Seeing Arun approaching, one of the nurses informed him tensely, 'Sir, I was looking around for you. Only last hour left to regain his consciousness.'

'I'll come soon,' he said and hurriedly looked around for the girl. He went to see the patient who had a daughter who requested Arun to cure her mother. He enquired from the nurse about the patient's condition and came out. Near the emergency ward, on a bench, a person was sitting sadly. Looking at the person, Arun asked, 'Just before sometime, I saw . . . there was a girl here.'

'Girl? No, sir, I don't know. Will my wife be OK, sir? Destiny leaving us alive, it took my six–year-old daughter's life in an accident recently to hurt our feelings forever,' the man said, crying. After hearing this, Arun was shocked and went to Subhas Karuna's ward thinking, 'Why does it happen like this? The most loved ones will leave us and go away.' And reaching the ward, he sat on the chair. Closing his eyes, Arun said excitedly, 'You were right, Anu, whoever keeps true love in their heart can see the good-hearted lives of those who are no more.'

After fifteen minutes, Subhas Karuna slowly opened his eyes. 'Hello, sir,' Arun wished him well with a smile and the professor gave a forced smile. 'How are you, sir?' Arun asked.

'You Arun . . .' he stammered.

After checking, Arun said, 'You will be fine, sir,' and he told the nurse to shift him to another ward. Ram Desai hugged him and cried. Later, he fed some food to Subhas Karuna and helped him to drink water. The professor recovered very soon and was able to walk without any support. The lady who had lost her daughter got operated and she recovered.

Subhas Karuna, looking at his friend, asked, 'When can I be discharged, Ram?'

'Soon, I think tomorrow or day after tomorrow,' Ram Desai replied.

'I mean I need to discharge not only from here, I have to be discharged from this world itself,' Subhas Karuna said blankly.

'Stop it, man, have you gone crazy? Even I was left with nothing and even I could have died. If I had died, who would have looked after you? Tell me,' Ram Desai raised his voice with emotion.

'No, I don't want to live on this earth anymore without my family, my job is over,' the professor said calmly.

Next day, Arun sat leisurely near his laptop and opened the mailbox. He saw a long message addressed to Subhas Karuna from Anu and he curiously read it. Anu had instructed Arun to forward a copy of it to Subhas Karuna. Later, with a copy, he reached the hospital to meet Subhas Karuna. 'Sir, excuse me, please,' Arun asked Ram Desai, and realizing, he left the room.

Giving the message copy, Arun said, 'Sir, this is a message from Anu, Anushika.'

The Professor read, 'To my sweet professor, being strong-hearted, you shall not be distressed; your daughter hasn't left you and gone, and she's with you in your heart. There are so many people like you leading their life alone, especially children in the orphanage. Why can't you treat them and adopt them as your children? You can see your daughter in their happiness, in their achievements, and in every stage of their life. Sir, trust me, you will feel like living a long life, you're not alone anymore and the world is with you, sir. All the best, get well soon and take care. From Anu.'

And the professor wept with a smile, he folded the sheet and rested it on his chest. The nurse injected medicine and he lay down.

As Arun came out from the ward, Ram Desai said with frustration, 'See, Arun, what rubbish he's speaking . . .'

Consoling him, Arun said, 'No, sir, don't worry, he will be fine, tomorrow he will be discharged, bye,' and left the corridor.

Having a week's leave, Arun reached home and saw Nirmala was watering the plants in his room's balcony. As he came near, she asked him in an angry tone, 'Arun, have you decided or not?'

'Please, Didi, stop it, give me some time, one day is not enough,' Arun pleaded.

'Fine, I'll give you a week's time, it's final,' Nirmala said and left the place.

'Oh, Anu, I can't even dream of seeing another girl in your place,' Arun said frustratedly and threw his coat aside.

Next day, he opened the mailbox with little hope that Anu might suggest something, and he saw Anu's email.

'Arun, listen to me. Day by day, you're becoming depressed as none of your wishes come true, the same feeling even your sister is feeling. At least let her succeed in all her wishes. Trust me, I have seen a girl for you and the clue is 46. I hope you will fulfil Nirmala's wish. Yours, Anu.' Arun was surprised as he read.

'What's this number 46, oh, sick,' he murmured to himself.

Nirmala, coming near Arun, said, 'Arun, there's some function in the Ram Krishna orphanage, they have invited me, I'm going, bye,' Nirmala said.

For feeling some change, he asked, 'Didi, may I join you to see the programme?'

'Sure.' Nirmala sounded happy. Arun sat in the driving seat and Nirmala sat next to him. Nirmala wore the seat belt, and staring, she gestured at him to wear the seat belt. He wore the belt, drove the car, and they reached the orphanage. He saw blind girls dancing folk dance very beautifully. One of the organizers started reading the names of the donors later. 'The amount donated by Raja Shekar is 46,000 rupees,' and after hearing the number, Arun become a bit alert. Nobody came on the stage and the announcer repeated. A little later, a beautiful lady came walking onto the stage, and meanwhile thinking of Anu's message, Arun was looking at the ground.

'Sorry, my father couldn't attend, so on behalf of him, I'm Monika and I want to give this but please don't expose the donors' identity for becoming popular yourself. This is not an award function. Helping such helpless children is not enough but must be done true-heartedly,' she said. As she left the stage, Arun looked at her. Later, the function was over.

Arun was coming out; his eyes couldn't escape from seeing her. 'She sounds like Anu,' he thought spontaneously, and as she was entering a car, his eyes caught the car's number, 4646. 'My goodness, stop it,' Arun said to himself with frustration.

'Why? Is something wrong?' Nirmala asked.

'No,' he replied and hurriedly checked his email as he reached home. There was a number 46 in Anu's message and his head almost burst. He didn't feel like seeing the email.

After an hour, Arun restlessly sent a message to Anu. 'Oh, Anu, in life, we feel true love only once, there's no alternative.'

'No, have a look at it once, please. She's meant for you and you're holding a grudge because I had not accepted your proposal,' Arun got a quick reply.

'No, don't ever think like that.' He sent the message.

Arun received the message, 'Then why don't you prove it?' There were many snaps and Arun angrily entered the bride number 46. The screen slowly came rolling, and he was surprised as it was the lady who spoke on the stage.

'Oh, I got it, just because I said she sounds like you. She can't become Anu, all right?' Arun messaged angrily.

'Please watch her eyes once, just once.' He received the reply. Arun watched her eyes with frustration.

After a pause, he received the message again, 'Calm down, relax your mind. Every human being needs a life partner to share and she's the best for you.' Arun closed the email. As he came out of his room, Sandhya was speaking with Nirmala.

'Hey, Sandhya, you surprised me. Why didn't you call me up and tell that you're coming?' he asked.

'I wanted to surprise you. I called up Didi whether you're here and she said yes, that's all . . . I landed up here just like that,'

Sandhya replied with the same naughtiness and enthusiasm that she had in college. Nirmala giggled at their conversation and served some hot snacks and coffee.

Arun became surprised, checking emails from his laptop daily, as there wasn't any message from Anu. Looking at the lady, he felt some positive feeling in his heart. 'OK, if me marrying her makes you feel happy, then I will marry her.' Arun sent the message to Anu and there was no reply from her. Seeing him agreeing to marry, Nirmala felt very happy.

Later, recalling Anu's wish to treat Vishaal after getting the consent from his parents, Arun went to the hospital where he was being treated. 'Sir, I'll take up Vishaal's case, sir,' Arun said to the senior doctor who was handling Vishaal's case, and he agreed. Arun took all the details about Vishaal's condition. He shifted him to his hospital later and started treating him.

'One day, you will be healed completely. My friend has started treating you, and you will be back to normal. I love you, Vishaal,' Anu said to herself and blew on her palm pointing towards Vishaal.

Seeing her, Arun said in a loud voice, 'Anu . . . Anuuu! Listen to me.' She turned back smiling but vanished.

Hearing Arun yelling, the senior doctor asked, 'Oh, what is this, Arun? I think you're involving a lot in this case, why did you yell, being a doctor? I didn't see anyone here. Don't fall into such emotion being a doctor, relax. Are you OK?' and the senior doctor left the corridor.

Becoming excited, Arun said dreamily, 'Oh, Anu, often you're visiting him. Fine, then at least I can see you in this manner,' looking towards the glass, and he went back to his cabin. Arun was very excited, as he saw a letter posted to him, and it stated that he had been selected for the neurosurgery practice in United States. Though Nirmala felt happy, she was unwilling to send him as the training period was to last for six months, but finding no other way, she agreed to send him.

Later, Nirmala felt deserted as she was lonely, and Arun's childhood memories made her feel better. Fixing the dates for Arun's marriage, Nirmala was waiting for Arun to step onto India. Arun successfully completed the training and was back to India. Reaching home, he went to the park immediately and felt very nice taking the fresh air around.

Finally, the marriage took place. 'Don't worry, Deepthi, next is yours. Dr Arun is handling the case, he will get well soon,' Sandhya said in the marriage hall to Deepthi. Thinking about Vishaal, she smiled with a blush.

Expecting that Anu might turn up to see him, Arun was looking all around but he could not see her. Sandhya and Prashanth had already married a year ago, and they were welcoming the guests. Madan was standing with his life partner.

'Arun weds Monika, both are looking lovely and are made for each other,' Nirmala said. Nirmala was very happy and Arun had never seen her so happy ever before.

'Thanks a lot, Anu, because of you, she's so happy,' Arun said to himself, and finally the marriage was complete.

Everyone went home, and Arun was looking a bit dull as he didn't see Anu. Having taken responsibility of handling the marriage event, and to make it happen smoothly, Sandhya and Madan had helped Nirmala a lot and they went back home tiredly. The days were running but Arun was not so romantic with Monika though he treated her in a friendly manner. He was helpful to her and seeing their understanding, Nirmala felt very happy.

One day, Nirmala opened the laptop and selected the Europe tour package for sending Arun to honeymoon with his wife.

As Nirmala insisted, Arun said dully, 'No, please, I'm not in a mood to go.' Nirmala and Monika exchanged looks.

Monika, intervening, said, 'Fine, let's go to Kodai since you said that place is very heart-touching, right?' and Nirmala felt happy with her decision.

Looking at Arun, she asked, 'Yeah why can't you go?'

'Oh, stop it, please leave me alone for a moment,' Arun replied restlessly.

Seeing Monika sitting sadly, he said to himself, 'Oh I can't see her like that.'

'Monika, you want to see that place, fine, we will go,' Arun said unwillingly but Monika, not noticing him, jumped happily. She went to inform Nirmala about his acceptance and Arun, coming near Nirmala, requested, 'But a condition, I want my friends to come along, please.'

'Yeah, I'll arrange for it,' Nirmala said.

'Yeah, he's right,' Monika said with affirmation.

'I have to come back soon after three days since I can't leave Vishaal alone,' Arun said. Two days later, the journey began.

The birds started chirping and the slight drizzling woke up Arun suddenly. To him, everything looked calm; looking around, he recalled last night's incident and felt everything like a dream. For the first time in his mind, he had begun to think about the *future journey*. 'Good morning, sir,' one of the resort staff greeted him. Monika saw Arun speaking with a waiter and tensely ran towards him down the stairs.

'Oh, Monika will be very worried, I spent the whole night here in the garden,' Arun said to himself and ran upstairs; both met each other.

'Sorry, Monika, I—' She had already hugged him.

'Happy birthday,' she greeted him with happy tears and gifted him. His heart began emanating a bit of love for her.

'Oh, it's nice,' Arun said.

Hurriedly climbing the stairs, he said, 'Monika, we must leave Kodai immediately, I have an important case to attend to.'

'Relax, we will move,' Monika consoled him and he was happy with her reaction.

Later, Monika hurriedly packed everything.

'Yeah, packing is done,' she said. Patting her on the back, Arun smiled. All of them came holding a big cake and wished Arun happy birthday.

Hogging the cake, Arun said, 'Sorry, guys, I'm too late, I have to check out,' and pulled Monika's hands.

'Why?' Sandhya asked disappointedly.

'Sorry, I must move, I have to attend to a case immediately,' he replied. They both quickly moved towards the car, and the weather was very cold and breezy. He removed his jacket and covered her shoulders. She smiled and continued to watch the view around. His friends had previously decided to stay for few more days. The resort's car dropped them at the bus station. They finally reached Bengaluru.

Quickly getting into a taxi, Arun said, 'Please go to Neuro Research Centre.' Later, 'Yeah, stop here,' he said and got down near the hospital.

'Sorry, Monika, take care, bye,' Arun said.

'It's OK, all the best,' Monika said and directed the car driver towards the residence.

Looking at Vishaal, Arun felt sorry and guilty.

'Oh no, the excitement of Anu appearing near Vishaal had taken out the interest in treating him with seriousness. She's my loved one. I can't disappoint her,' Arun said to himself and started diagnosing Vishaal again. His life was supported by mechanical ventilator (respirator). Arun again studied Vishaal's medical reports carefully. Later, glancing at previous treatment chart, he instructed the nurse to inject fluids according to new prescription. After observing his progress for about six months, his facial appearance had begun to change a bit; though he lay down like a statue, his body began to react positively to the new medicines. Arun began to feel a small ray of hope.

As days went on frustratingly, one day, Arun asked the nurse to leave Vishaal's room and closed the door. The time was around 6.30 p.m. 'Anu, you have to come. You promised him that you're going to meet him directly,' Arun spoke loudly but there was no response, and after a pause, Arun said loudly with distress, 'Come on, Anu, speak with him,' and switched on the audio player in which he had recorded Anu's favourite tunes. He sat on the chair, desperately looking at Vishaal and thinking something; he fixed earphones in Vishaal's ears. Looking around, Arun angrily murmured, 'You are really sick, Anu, you promised him that you would meet him directly, are you feeling shy or what?' He was surprised as he sensed that Anu's favourite song was coming from the other direction and that Vishaal's cheeks were shaking a bit. He quickly went to inform the other senior doctors, and soon the door closed itself as soon as he left the room.

Looking like an angel with glowing shadow, Anu came near, caressing his cheeks smoothly. 'Vishaal, get up,' she said in a soft voice. Keeping her soft petal-like palm on his chest, she kissed his cheeks and her glowing shadow immersed into his body later. His feet began to move slowly, his lungs started functioning and his sense organs began to react. Anu's glowing shadow came out from Vishaal's body later, and becoming conscious, he got up slowly. Smiling, she gave him a beautiful transparent bunch of flowers and he felt as though he was holding air pressure. Hearing the music around, looking at her, he said softly, 'Anu . . .' and lifting his hands slowly, he slid his pointed finger on her forehead until her crescent-like chin. Anu saw a smile on his lips as his finger went inside her face, sliding her hand on his cheeks. 'See, I kept my promise, I met you,' Anu said, and Vishaal felt a feather-like touch.

Throwing his hands around her, he said dreamily, 'I love you, Anu,' closing his eyes, and she felt as though all her happiness was arousing in her heart.

Realizing what he just said, she immediately went back and said, 'Oh no, Vishaal, you love Deepthi and shall keep your promise.' Vishaal was shocked and was stunned, and she continued, 'She's been waiting to see you become normal for the past seven years, she loves you so much.'

'But you've been waiting for fifteen years,' Vishaal said, and his eyes were filled with tears.

'No, you're wrong, surely I know you love her, now you're loving me but feeling differently just because I helped you. Your heart is showing me gratitude but actually your heart is filled with Deepthi's love.'

Anu gave a keen look at him. 'The desire of my heart shall be your future and your happiness. You shall remain happy forever with her and I hope you will understand. Mine has become an eternal life, and just because of you, I am held back. Please release me from your heart,' Anu said emotionally. Weeping, Vishaal hugged her and Anu kissed his cheeks.

Holding the door's key, a person came running to open the door.

Meanwhile, waving her hand, Anu said, 'Your love is waiting for you, goodbye,' and as he gestured, she vanished.

As the door opened, everyone was surprised and Arun looked very tense. Vishaal became conscious and felt like a dream. All of them were very eager to see Vishaal, but Arun stopped them from entering and checked his condition. Insisting for them not to disturb him much, he allowed Vishaal's family members to see him later.

After a few days, hitting Arun's ribs slowly with his fist, Vishaal said, 'Idiot, you were the reason for this.' Arun, tapping his shoulders, said, 'You're a big idiot,' and they both hugged each other. Vishaal's eyes slowly moved towards the glass door and saw Deepthi. Arun understood and left the place. Deepthi was crying as Vishaal stretched his arms and she was unable to control herself. A little later, she went running towards him and hugged him tightly. After a few days, Vishaal was completely fine and was discharged from the hospital. His family members were very thankful to Arun. Later, Vishaal and Deepthi's marriage was fixed and they got married.

Turn overleaf

WHAT HAPPENED NEXT?

Arun and Monika understood each other. Carrying, she had completed seven months. One day, Nirmala invited Prashanth, Sandhya, and Dr Siddharth to her house for a treat. Cracking jokes at each other, everyone sat leisurely. As Monika was feeling uneasy, Nirmala gestured at her to take rest and she went to her room later.

A little later, Arun, looking at everyone, said seriously, 'Please listen, everybody, I wanted to tell you all some unbelievable instances that happened with me. I am sorry for hiding all this from you guys until now, but I know you all wouldn't have believed it and instead would have thought that I have gone mad. Really, whatever I am going to say is true and what I'm going to say is all about Anu,' and everyone's ears strained waiting, further thinking what he would say. Further continuing, 'I was secretly receiving emails from Anu, if you all want to know, check my laptop. She even selected the course for me; I directly saw her several times and spoke to her. You all will say it's superstitious.'

Meanwhile, Nirmala and Siddharth's eyes met, and Arun looked at everyone to read their expression.

Nirmala, looking at Arun, 'Even we are very sorry for hiding something from you and I was thinking when to reveal all this to you. You deciding to reveal all this have given me a way to reveal. Are you receiving any emails from Anu now?' she asked.

'No,' Arun surprisingly came out with quick reply.

'I think there are no more e-mails to you from Anu,' Nirmala said.

Becoming astonished, he said, 'How do you know that she's not sending me emails? I kept her email ID and mine very confidential, even from you.' He sounded surprised.

Sandhya, intervening and looking at Arun, said, giggling, 'Trustme@google.com—that was Anu's e-mail ID right?'

Shockingly getting up from the chair, Arun said in an unbelieving voice, 'Stupid! How do you know that ID? You fooled me by taking Anu's name.'

Nirmala, tapping his shoulders, said, 'Arun calm down, I'll tell you everything that happened. Actually, the day you said that you saw Anu even after her death, I became tense and curious. I consulted the most famous psychiatrist, Dr John Muller, without your knowledge and he gave us some suggestions. It's very real that Anu only had sent messages to you, and you know why, one day, worrying about you, I went to my room. When I was half asleep, as some light disturbed me, my eyes opened slowly and the room looked blurry. In a blurry vision, I saw you sitting in front of my laptop. I was about to call you but, feeling paralyzed, I couldn't. I watched you operating my laptop with my eyes half-closed and your appearance looked very strange. After half an hour, you left my room.

'Later, I met Dr Siddharth and explained to him what had happened in the room. We again discussed with Dr Muller. "Oh it's not him; Anu's soul is using him to operate the laptop. I think you must deal with this very carefully. You must keep watching your brother's every movement especially at night, otherwise there are chances . . . you understood what I said," Dr Muller suggested to me. So I fixed CCTV cameras secretly at various points in both the rooms and it was mainly focused towards your laptop. I purposely kept my laptop in the room at nights. Once in a week, we were gathering to review the CCTV recordings, and through the phone, I was in touch with Dr Muller to inform him of how you were behaving. Later, studying your behaviour, Dr Muller instructed us, "I think she's not troubling Arun, my guess is some of her wishes remained in her soul unfulfilled, she mingles in nature as her wishes turns true, try to find your brother's secret e-mail ID to which she's sending, then only we can know her wishes." Without knowing yourself, actually you were operating my laptop at late nights. Later, Dr Muller came to a firm conclusion that she was guiding you as a friend and helping you. One day, while you were operating my laptop, as you were disturbed by a sound, you left in a hurry. I mean, Anu left and we finally were able to trace the secret e-mail ID. Through the zoomed lens, we found your secret ID as well as Anu's e-mail ID with password from the CCTV recordings. We all went through Anu's messages later. Oh, she's great. Sorry, Arun, I was forced to do all this for your well-being,' Nirmala said on a sharp note.

There was a pause, and Arun was deeply thinking as he felt that it was unbelievable. Keeping his pointed finger on his lips, 'But still I don't understand how you fixed up me and Monika,' Arun asked.

Sandhya pulled his sleeves. 'Stupid fellow, you refused Didi's suggestion to get married. We surely knew that you would never marry, and Nirmala Didi told us to search for a suitable bride for you. Monika is a far relative to my dad. Seeing her, Didi was quite satisfied. Her father also agreed happily and gave her photo. I only sent messages through Anu's e-mail ID, hoping that you would agree to Anu's suggestion,' she replied.

'Oh, you guys trapped me in such a tricky way,' Arun said in surprise and chased Sandhya as he tapped hard on her back; everyone laughed.

A little later, breathing hard, looking at Sandhya, 'OK then but giving clue about Monika is your idea,' Arun asked.

Prashanth intervening, 'No, no, it's mine, dude, one day, we all met Monika's father in his house. He was very addicted to numerology and started telling about the fortunes based on it. "What's your numerology lucky number, uncle?" I asked him out of curiosity. Revealing his lucky number, he continued saying that his house number is 46 and his car number is also 4646 and so on. "OK, uncle, even we will make use of it," I said. "What?" he asked confusingly. "Nothing, uncle," I replied. Later, thinking that his lucky number might prove to be lucky to his daughter as well, I suggested Sandhya to use that number for giving a clue to you. It worked out so well, now 46 is your lucky number, am I right?' Prashanth said, and everyone burst out laughing.

Punching on his stomach, Arun said, 'You liar, even you made a fool out of me.' Nirmala called them to have lunch and everyone had a great feast later.

Later, Sandhya gesturing at Nirmala, she said winking her eyes, 'It's been a long time since we have gone outside together, let all of us go for a ride,' she said winking her eyes. A little later, they all sat in a car. Looking through the window, Arun saw the car was heading near the Presidency College.

Pulling his collar, Nirmala said, 'Arun, so far you saw Anu in illusion, but now I'll show you her directly.'

'Oh, you're confusing me, fine, let's see, come on, show me my Anu,' he said in a breathy voice and a little later, the car stopped.

After everyone got down from the car, pointing towards some far distance, Nirmala said, 'See there.'

Arun looked at the direction shown and saw a huge gathering. Lining up through the barricades, the people were moving slowly, and five to six thousand people had gathered.

Looking at the crowd unbelievingly, Arun exclaimed, 'Oh my goodness, today is Anu's birthday,' and it was the place where Anu took her last breath. All of them stood in a queue, and he saw the people carrying flowers to pay their respects to Anu. From afar, Arun saw Anu's photo frame, and chanting prayers, a large number of children sat.

While moving in the lane, Nirmala looked at Arun, 'I'll tell you more about Anu that you are unaware of. You know, she's the inspiration behind our projects. I was appointed as an adviser for the town planning committee; they had given me the task of clearing the slum areas and to rehabilitate the slum people. I had visited the Kannan slum area also, and I saw Anu with some elder volunteers running the study centre and the training programmes for the slum children. I was very much impressed seeing their service to the poor. I gave my opinion to shift the slum people elsewhere and convert the area into a garden. Everyone strongly opposed there, but you know what her opinion was? "Didi, it's not a good idea, nearly ten thousand people's livelihood will be at stake. In case it is converted into a park here, who will enjoy it? Only the rich will experience the joy, everyone had become the member of our welfare organization, the government shall give a chance to improve their living and our slum welfare organization has collected 5,000 rupees from each family as savings. Is it not possible to build low-cost houses for these people and leave some space for a park as well? They are ready to give their saved amount if the government agrees and helps them construct houses for them." Even an MLA named Kanda swami also intervened and requested, "Sister, we won't allow this place to be converted into a park, Anu's suggestion is good, I'll try my level best to convince the government. Please do something good for these people." Then I asked Anu, "Arun always speaks excitedly about you. I think he loves you. Don't you think he's too early to fall in such things, do you love him? I'll be happy if he thinks about such matters after completion of his studies. Frankly, what's your opinion?" You know what she replied?'

Arun's eyes widened, and Nirmala continued, 'She looked at me seriously and said, "I love him so much, love does not come with an appointment or at a pre-fixed time to start loving, it can come at any time, any moment, and anywhere, I won't leave him until my last breath," and she winked her eyes. Becoming restless, I turned my face restlessly, laughing. "But I love him as a true friend forever, I want his company in my happiness and at difficult times. I shall remain in his heart as a true friend," she said smilingly, and tapping her shoulders, I invited her to come to my house. "No, Didi, let him not know about our meeting. If he comes to know, then he will think that it is easy to convince you about his love towards me and then he will often try to call me to your house," she said. From the beginning, I knew she looked at you as a friend. Later, I inspected the whole area and gave my recommendation to the town planning committee.' A little later, they reached near Anu's frame and lit candles. Arun saw Anu's parents with tears in their eyes. All of them sat later, Arun saw Subhas Karuna, Ram Desai, and Karthik coming near him, and they wished all of them well. Subhas Karuna looked very energetic and sat beside Arun. Wearing new clothes were many handicapped children with smiling faces.

Looking at Subhas Karuna, Arun asked, 'How are you, sir?'
'Oh, I'm very much fine, Anu has changed my life and even my character. Using weapons, I fought violently against the criminals, I tried to smash them completely, but I couldn't, instead criminals' strength had risen manifold. She converted the criminals' heart silently and stopped the cropping up of future criminals by showing the right path to these helpless children. She has converted the miserable lives into happy lives, and we can see their happiness. She has shown us the right way,' the professor replied emotionally, and meanwhile, many children came near Subhas Karuna and sat beside him, calling 'Grandpa . . . grandpa.'

'I have joined as a volunteer in a children's welfare organization,' Subhas Karuna said.

Turning towards Nirmala, Arun said in a breathy voice, 'Didi, you're right. I thought Anu belonged only to me and drowned in an illusion. I can see Anu in every child's face,' and she watched whether he become emotional again but she saw his smiling face and his eyes were fixed on the crowd. The programme ended with prayers, and everyone started moving.

As Arun was watching the people around, Nirmala said, 'Arun, come on, let's go.' All of them stood up and walked further instead of going near the car. Becoming curious, Arun questioned Sandhya through gesture, 'Where?' and she also gestured at him to move. Looking at them, Nirmala smiled. After walking nearly half a kilometre, Arun was surprised and could not believe his eyes as he saw a huge gathering, lanes of small buildings, and a beautiful park in front. They came near a beautifully crafted arch later. Giving a flower bouquet to Nirmala, MLA Kanda swami invited them and gave them scissors to cut the ribbon. As Nirmala cut the ribbon, everyone clapped, and happily the children shouted, 'Woohoo!' With their belongings, going through the arch, Arun saw people entering into the houses. Spreading its golden rays, passing through the arch, falling on Arun's face, the sun was going down. Lifting his head up, he saw beautifully molded letters, 'ANU COLONY', on the arch's top.

****

Author's note to the readers

The readers are at liberty to assume whether or not some souls of the deceased characters in this novel created illusions in the minds of some living characters and also drove them to do some tasks for fulfilling their wishes *or* conclude it was purely fiction.

Printed in the United States
By Bookmasters